Girotondo

Also by Tanya Jones

Ophelia O. and the Mortgage Bandits
Ophelia O. and the Antenatal Mysteries
Trotter's bottom
Survival Guide for Chess Parents

Tanya Jones

Girotondo

The Crystal Bard Press

Girotondo is first published in 2006 in Ireland by
The Crystal Bard Press, Ennis, County Clare.

www.crystalbard.com

ISBN 1-905733-00-3

Copyright © Tanya Jones 2006

The author has asserted her moral rights.

This book is sold subject to the condition that it shall not, by way of trade or otherwise, be lent, resold, hired out or otherwise circulated without the publisher's prior consent in any form of binding or cover other than that in which it is published and without a similar condition being imposed on any subsequent publisher.
No part of this publication may be reproduced or transmitted in any form or by any means, electronic or mechanical, including photocopying, recording or using any information or retrieval system without the prior permission of the publisher.
All the characters in this book are fictitious, and any resemblance to actual persons, living or dead, is purely coincidental.

Cover design by Jet the Dog.

Printed in Ireland by Colour Books Ltd, Dublin.

For Martin

I

There was nothing remotely scary about the bearded man. Really, his face was rather pleasant, in a bland, rich tea biscuit sort of way. Pippa noticed him first at the airport gate, when the queue began to form and he lifted a small child over the rope to reach its mother. His beard had a new look about it, his pink-brown cheeks not yet shifted into its contours, but when the little girl grabbed it, the pain seemed real enough.

He was there again at the baggage reclaim, craning across the chugging conveyor belt to pick up his backpack. Pippa's case was almost the last to arrive; huge, unmistakably nylon, and corsetted in yellow security tape. It reached the top of the upward slope and paused, teetering drunkenly, before falling flat on its face, a disreputable granny at an upmarket wedding. Pippa, emerging from the loo, ran forward to claim it, but the handle had fallen inwards, and she could get no grip on the corners. It had been a cumbersome brute even when it was new, lugged to college for the first time, full of trust law and brave intentions. After seven years the itch was getting unbearable. She must have given a small squeak of annoyance, because the bearded man, ambling away towards Passport Control, turned back and in a single fluid gesture, reached over and rescued it.

'*Grazie tante.*' she said, her first Italian on Italian *pavimento*, but he smiled and replied with a gutteral accent.

'No problem.'

He was youngish, about thirty, rather heavily built and very blond. But to someone he was an object of terror.

There is an arrivals barrier at Pisa airport, behind which friends, relatives and colleagues are supposed to wait. Some do, of course. The English do, and the Germans and the Dutch, welcoming their house guests to Chiantishire or the Garfagnana. The taxi drivers do, and the more aloof businessmen, distancing themselves from the somersaulting toddlers and the mammas who brave the one-way doors to enfold their returning *ragazzi*, famished after a week of *schifoso* English food. And the young man in spectacles did, dapper enough to be Italian in his polo shirt and pressed chinos, but far too pale and uncertain. He held a neatly written cardboard sign, unobtrusively, as though its two words might cause offence.

Pippa pushed her trolley down the corridor behind the man with the beard. He carried only his backpack, a sensible, twenty-first century construction, waterproof, breathable and festooned with velcroed pockets. Into one of these he was stowing his passport, so carefully that he didn't look up as he passed through the doors, didn't hear the bespectacled man's indrawn breath, see his fingernails turn white against the card or his grey eyes, enlarged by the thick lenses, blink and blink again. The bearded man passed straight ahead, through the outer doors and into the Tuscan night.

Pippa stopped in front of the second man. He was three or four inches shorter than her and he was still trembling.

'Hi, I'm here.'

He shook his head, a baby gerbil bereft of its nest. 'No no. You've made a mistake. I'm....' He gazed down at the cardboard sign as though wondering how on earth it could have got into his hands. Then, with a rush of relief. 'I'm waiting for someone.'

'You're waiting for me.' said Pippa gently. 'I'm Philippa Laud.' She pointed at her name on the card.

'Jeez, I'm sorry. I'm a poet, you see.'

Pippa's heart plummeted, taking her face, all too visibly, with it. He watched them fall.

'It wasn't meant to be an excuse. Just – in the early stages of a thing, I go a bit cookie. It isn't genius, just bad manners.' He smiled suddenly, a rather large smile for his face. He still looked like a small rodent, but a more robust one. A hamster, maybe. 'On the way to the airport, at the edges of the fields, there were these girls.'

'Girls?'

'*Girls*. Waiting.'

'You mean you thought I...?' She looked down at her travelling clothes, the soft baggy layers that had seen her through from the dawn chill of Scunthorpe coach station. The figure underneath wasn't completely hopeless; she still got the 'not of many of those in a pound' gag from the odd workman, but the last time she heard it, she'd been walking away, and it wasn't a delayed reaction. As for her face, it did all right in an English courtroom, but so did most that were topped with their own hair and bore no immediate signs of apoplexy. She had freckles and eyes just on the green side of hazel, but had missed the red hair to go with them, and had to make do with dark mouse, streaked with chestnut after a good summer. Her nose was cheerful but inelegant and she had the kind of mouth that had to keep smiling, otherwise the workman would call out that it might never happen.

'Sorry again. I'm still basically a hoser, I guess. We didn't get many hookers back home, least not that I ever came across. And then I had a bit of a shock just now.'

'Do you want to tell me about it?'

For a moment she was back in the office, bracing herself for the story: the stockpile of marital grudges, the neighbours' festering feud or the chaotic mêlée of a building dispute. But she had left that life, those loquacious miseries. She wouldn't have clients any more, only students, colleagues, bosses and friends. Which category the poet fell into, she wasn't yet sure.

'No, it's nothing. Thought I saw a ghost, that's all. Very Henry James.' He gave an abrupt shake like a small dog emerging from a pond, and put out his hand. 'Could we start over, do you think? I'm Gray Garrett. Well - Graham.' 'Gray' was an innovation, and he still felt like an impostor whenever he used it.

'Pippa. It was you, then, who sent the email? Gray at pick-a-sadding?' It sounded even more implausible than it had at the time.

'Picca-casa-ding. *La Piccola Casa d'Inglese.* The language school.'

'Of course. And you're the, what, Director of Studies?' The slim paperback concealed in her hand luggage, *How to Teach English Abroad with No Qualifications Whatsoever*, was already coming in handy. But Gray laughed.

'Nothing so grand, I'm afraid. I'm just a teacher, too, trying to keep body and soul in some kind of equilibrium until the world recognizes my contribution to lidderature.' He grimaced. 'So, only another three hundred years to go.'

'And you're American, right?'

'Canadian.'

From the smouldering sensation in Pippa's cheeks, she guessed that they were as beetroot-coloured as the British passport she still clutched. She only knew one thing about Canadians; that they detested being taken for their brash neighbours.

But this one didn't seem to mind so much; just stood gazing at the concrete staircase, presumably contemplating an ode to *Donky Rock Hair*, the unisex salon on the first floor.

'Gray?'

'Mmm?' He twisted his mouth into a tight rosette and sucked it into one cheek, looking more than ever as though he were doing something technical with a sunflower seed.

'How do we get to Lucca? Do you have a car or something?'

He thought it over for a moment. 'Probably a something.'

The something was straddling two parking spaces, as if unsure whether one would be enough, although it could probably have fitted inside a largish litter bin. It was white; very battered, very old, and very Italian.

'*Cinquecento* - the classic model.' explained Gray, opening the unlocked right-hand door with a chivalrous gesture. '*Prego.*'

'I can't.'

'What is it, claustrophobia? It feels bigger once you're in, Mounties' honour.'

'No I mean I haven't passed my t.... Oh of course, it's left hand drive. My turn to go - what was it you said?'

'Cookie?'

'I knew it was something close to my heart. I got through seven extra-large Millies on the flight.'

Whether the cookies were to blame or not, it took some serious negotiation between Pippa's elbows and knees before she managed to wedge herself inside the car. She hunched her head, tortoise-style, between her shoulders, trying not to imagine how many other scalps had been crammed against the roof and which of them were responsible for the oily green smears. With a Schrödingen disregard for the conventions of spatial physics, her suitcase was upended in the tiny boot, removing any hope of either rear visibility or anything approaching equilibrium.

'Is this your car?' Pippa asked, as the engine sneezed into life and they shot forward into the kerb. Gray shook his head distractedly, searching for reverse gear.

'Eenie's.'

'Ian?'

'E and E.' He had found it now, and the car spurted backwards before stalling inches from a large Mercedes. 'Sorry. Never used a stick-shift back home. Elsa and Elisa. Owners of the school.'

'Elsa and Elisa. I'll try to remember. Who else is there I need to know?'

'That's it, really. Just the old ladies and us two teachers. I've only been here since last August myself. E & E do all the admin but they're not exactly webwise, so when Zena shogged off, and they needed someone fast, I fixed it for them. I want to set up a proper interactive site for the school, but the old dears don't go a bundle on the idea. They keep explaining how they're scared of spiders. It's a fascinating glimpse into the operation of metaphor, but it doesn't get us much further forward.'

'Hang on a moment.'

Gray's foot stamped on the brake and the suitcase made a bid for freedom. Pippa unglued her forehead from the tiny sun visor.

'I meant the conversation, actually. Who's Zena, and where did she go?'

'Sorry, didn't I say? Your predecessor. Now she really is a Yank. She left on Monday night, without a single word. Not as reliable as us Colonials, you see.'

'You don't mean this last Monday night, do you? The day before yesterday? Wow. The advert was up yesterday lunchtime. I thought I was quick getting here.'

'No point in letting the grass grow.'

He illustrated the principle by cutting across a decorative verge into a stream of oncoming traffic, executing a U-turn across a raised concrete island and following signs for some disturbingly major roads. The suitcase leapt in the air a few times, surveyed its surroundings, considered the folk wisdom about the frying pan and the fire, and jammed itself back into the Cinquecento's boot.

Gray now appeared to be driving in the cycle lane, or maybe it was just the gutter; although to judge by the speed of the traffic overtaking them, it was probably the safest place to be. Unless, of course, you happened to be a cyclist.

'Do you believe in God, Philippa?'

Oh no. She'd known there had to be a catch. It had all been much too easy; the advert on the TEFL website, the flurry of emails, the ludicrously cheap last-minute flight. And this was why. They didn't want her mind at all, didn't care about her complete absence of finely-honed teaching skills or meticulous analysis of English grammar. No, it was her soul they were after, and the souls of all those poor benighted Italians whom she was to lure into the trap. No wonder they felt uneasy about spiders. She dared a sidelong glance at Gray's serious profile. Yes, he was just the type. If she was really lucky they would only be rabid evangelicals. If not....Images from every cult scare story jostled into her mind: enforced multiple marriages, mass suicides, a complete embargo on the latest Red Hot Chili Peppers album. Perhaps she should throw herself out of the car here and now, on the slip road to the Strada Statale Aurelia. Only judging from the contortions required to get into the car, they would be past Livorno by the time she worked out how to extricate herself. Honesty was unlikely to be the best policy, but it was all she could think of for the moment.

'I'm not sure. I think so.'

'Well, could you give Him the benefit and PRAY!!'

They had reached the end of the slip road and were presented with a stark choice between the S.S. Aurelia and the crash barrier. Judging from the mangled state of the steel, many before them had chosen the second option. Gray closed his eyes, muttered some tribal Canadian incantation - Pippa thought she caught the word 'Frontenac' - and jerked the steering wheel to the left. There was a violent rattling, a cacophony of horns, like the brass section of the LSO warming up and a screeching scrape of metal down the left hand side of the car. Seconds later it was balanced by a glancing impact on Pippa's door, as they were overtaken on the right by a tiny three wheeled Ape truck.

'There.' said Gray with satisfaction. 'Not too bad this time.' He glared at the dusty Ape trundling in front of them at a steady seven miles an hour. 'He had a nerve, that guy. What d'ye think, Pippa? Reckon we can pass him?'

But the power of speech had left her. Gray might not be the most macho of men, but the bravura of snatched survival clearly coursed through his genes like the rest. Or maybe it was just the effect of six months' driving in Italy.

'I think....' she began, when her vocal chords disentangled themselves, but the rest of her sentence was swallowed by another shriek from the left wing; the sound of fingernails on a blackboard amplified by a googolplex or two.

'Maybe not.' said Gray, waving a hand in apology to a

disappearing Alfa Romeo, its bumper festooned with small pieces of Fiat. 'I guess we'll just hunker down here, then. Was there something else you wanted to ask?'

One or two queries sprang to mind, such as the nature of the celestial vacuum that replaced the Italian Highway Code, but with the exhaust clanking behind them, the ambiance was ill-suited to cosmological debate.

'About Zena,' she bawled, simply for something to say, resigned to her inclusion in next morning's auto-fatality statistics, 'Where's she gone, exactly?'

As she spoke, the rest of the exhaust fell off and the noise diminished slightly.

'Greece, I think. She'd been talking about it for months, how she was going to take the railroad across to Ancona then pick up a ferry to Patras. It's a pity she didn't give E&E any notice, though. Things were pretty chaotic on Tuesday morning.'

'She really took off without telling anyone?'

'Not a word. Zena wasn't exactly the type for a tearful farewell scene but even a note might have helped. The first we knew of it was when she didn't turn up for her nine o'clock lesson. She didn't answer her cellphone either, so I called round at her flat. It's only a couple of minutes walk from the school.'

'And she'd gone?'

'So far as I could tell. She didn't have much in the way of personal possessions, at least not here in Italy, no books or CDs or photographs, and not many clothes, either. I don't think I ever saw her in anything but jeans and a couple of T-shirts. But her passport had gone, and her driving licence. I knew where she always kept them, and she never took them out, unless she needed ID for something. It's such a hassle if you lose things like that, especially in Italy. Oh, her cellphone was there, but it was only a cheap one, and out of credit, so I guess there'd be no point in taking it to Greece. Anyway, E&E didn't have anyone else, and my schedule's packed, so they asked me to see about finding someone.'

'But what if she comes back?'

Gray shrugged, glancing lightly off the crash barrier. 'Have to fight it out, I reckon. She's in breach of contract, so there shouldn't be a problem.'

Pippa thought about trying a hollow laugh, but decided she had probably had too many cookies. 'You haven't had much to do with the law, have you?'

'Torts and moots? No, nothing. Oh yeah - you were an advocate, weren't you, back in England? You'll be able to fix it, if we run into any problems. Anyway, she won't be coming back, you can bet your bottom dollar on that one. Whoa!'

Gray wrenched the steering-wheel to the right, flinging his body after it, and manhandled the Fiat off the Aurelia and onto a deserted side road.

'I thought we'd take the scenic route.' he explained, apparently unaware that darkness had now fallen completely, and that the only light, apart from the moon and stars, came from the Fiat's own single functioning headlamp. 'Kind of like a literary trail. Over there, for example,' He waved a nonchalant arm towards a looming hillside, its base scattered with orange pinpricks, 'is San Guiliano Terme. The Shelleys moved there when Pisa got too jam-packed for them . The main piazza's still named after Percy Bysshe. Cool, huh?'

'Cool.' agreed Pippa, gazing out into the night. A stanza of poetry, dormant for years, rose from the dusty cellars of her memory.

> 'When the lamp is shattered,
> The light in the dust lies dead -
> When the cloud is scattered,
> The rainbow's glory is shed.'

'Hey! You're a fan, too!'

'I was once. Before I went to - ' what would they call it in Canada? '- law school.'

'Yeah, it's heavy, that stuff. I knew a guy from high school who went in for it and he worked like seventeen hours a day I guess it doesn't leave a lot of time for poetry.'

Pippa gave a murmur of agreement, feeling faintly dishonest. It hadn't really been restrictive covenants or the Unfair Contract Terms Act that had nudged Shelley out of her life, only Jonathan's vociferous disapproval.

'There's nothing in poetry.' he had pronounced, with the certainty of a man who'd just laid a large bet on his own forthcoming partnership prospects . 'No useful contacts, no money, no causes of action, even, except for a few squalid wrangles. It's fine to have a cultural hinterland, especially for a woman, but you'd be better sticking to opera and fine art.'

'You'd be better', from Jonathan, had always been more in the nature of a command than a suggestion, and so poor Shelley had been sidelined, along with her tartan tights and slipper socks. But now that that she had been formally designated a Rather Unsatisfactory Girlfriend (the final email had used lower-case, but the words were always capitalized in Pippa's mind) there was no reason why she shouldn't read poetry. And wear slipper socks, come to that, if it got cold enough in Tuscany. The tartan tights, she decided, could remain in exile.

Gray had been thinking along the same lines.

'You ought to start again. Italy's a great place for new beginnings. And for English literature. It's the main reason I came here. Now Byron...'

A long and complicated story of the mad bad Lord, the firebrand Shelley, an impetuous servant and a Pisan soldier occupied the rest of the journey, so that Pippa only needed to give occasional grunts of interest or outrage. Intent on making her grunts as intelligent and gratified as possible, and on trying not to flinch whenever Gray overtook a scooter, she hardly noticed that the countryside had given way to strung-out suburbs before they passed through a gate in the great ramparts and were at last in the ancient city of Lucca. Inside the walls there was almost no traffic, and only a few stray cyclists and pedestrians. 'Lucca shuts down early.' explained Gray, turning down a cobbled street only inches wider than the Fiat. 'All the nightlife's over on the coast at Versilia. I could drive you over one evening if you like.'

Pippa snatched at the first excuse to hand.

'I think I'm getting a bit old for discos, actually.'

'Old? Are you?' He turned to peer at her in the near-darkness, searching for signs of a face-lift or two.

'Well, twenty-five.'

'Huh.' He turned his attention back to the street, just in time to avoid a thirteenth century chapel and a couple of plump poodles. 'Zena used to go and she was forty-three. Mind you, it's not really my scene, either. I prefer - oh, here we are.'

He stopped the car suddenly and the engine stalled, dying away with a disturbing finality.

'We'll get your bags out and I'll move it later.' said Gray, without conviction. 'At least - I know a guy with a breakdown truck.'

II

Glancing nervously back at the Cinquecento, as though expecting it to explode at any moment, Gray approached one of the tall dark buildings that lined both sides of the street. He rang a bell beside a dim doorway and was answered by a burst of crackling, then a guttural buzz as the heavy door released. Pippa, feeling like a small hobbit entering the Mines of Moria, slipped in behind him, just making it before the ancient locks snapped shut.

The hall, lit by wall lamps, was large and bare, the pale stone relieved only by a few ancient bicycles, a litter of supermarket circulars and two huge black motorbikes. A staircase disappeared into the gloom.

'How many floors up?'

'Only five.'

'There's no lift, I suppose?'

'Lift? You mean elevator? No chance. This is an ancient and illustrious city, not a downtown shopping mall. You've only got the one bag, haven't you?'

In the end they lost count of how long it took, but that might have been the limoncello. They lugged the case up the first flight of steps, Pippa heaving from above while Gray crawled beneath. It should, she thought, have been a relatively simple operation, despite the treacherously uneven wear on the stone steps and the handle's woeful lack of commitment to its case. But the brief ebullience that had propelled Gray from the airport had apparently expired with the Cinquecento, so that now he seemed barely able to support his own weight, never mind the 14.9 kilos (a hard stare from the check-in Gorgon for that one) of Pippa's baggage. Whatever it was that had scared him so much at the airport (surely it couldn't really have been the innocuous Teuton?) had obviously had a longer-term effect than he'd liked to admit. What was it he'd said – seen a ghost?

'Ooorrrhh'

'What?'

But this whimper was all too evidently mortal. He made a heroic effort, Narcissan if not quite Herculean. 'Poets in Italy. Never a good move. Take Shelley.'

'I've got my hands pretty full already, thanks.'

'Pyre,' he panted, wincing. 'Beach – Via – reggio.'

He lapsed into a gasping reverie. That pattering sound must be his heart, giving up at last, like so many before it. He thought of Keats dying in Rome, with only the faithful Severn at his side. Could Canadians get consumption? At least Gray - or would it be Graham at the last? - was dying in the company of an Englishwoman. He would need some suitable words of farewell; 'Watch out for the knobbly bit' didn't quite strike the right valedictory note. Then they reached the landing and he saw the slippered feet coming down before him.

Pippa, still shuffling backwards and trying, by sheer willpower, to maintain the suitcase/handle nexis, hadn't noticed the pattering sound, or that it had ceased. She had, perhaps, a second's warning, a sudden engulfing scent of eau-de-cologne and then there she was, reversed into a squashy embrace of angora, lavender and face powder. It was like being cuddled by a giant perfumed koala, except that this marsupial, unless she was really losing it, had at least seven limbs, two rounded pouches and two breathy nuzzling snouts.

'*Ciao, cara.*' came a voice in her hair. '*Benvenuto in Italia.*'

'Do stop smothering the girl, Lisa. I can hardly reach her.'

Finally, just as Pippa had resigned herself to a fatal ingestion of toxic fuzz, she was released, turned around and held at arm's length for inspection. There was nothing for it but to do a bit of inspecting back again.

Almost everything about them was soft, from their candyfloss clouds of white hair, one tinged with a touch of periwinkle, the other with rose, down through the woollen layers of grey-blue and heather to their silvery support tights. Only the tips of their noses were sharp, and the darting mischief of their blue eyes. One noticed Pippa looking down at the low pumps, like ballet slippers, which they wore on their tiny feet.

'We wore heels in the past,' she explained, gesturing over her shoulder to emphasize the tense, 'but it is too dangerous for Helsa in these days.'

'Speak for yourself.' said the other. 'It wasn't me who went arse over tip yesterday morning.'

'Is it my fault that you spindle my breakfast milk with the whisky? I tell you many times, Helsa, it is too strong before lunchtime on this stairs.'

'*These* stairs.' said Gray, in automatic teacher mode. 'Plural noun, countable. Or you can say "staircase".'

'Your English is very good.' said Pippa, to soften the criticism.

The purple haired matron laughed gently. 'But I *am* English. *Sono inglese, infatti.*'

'Oh Elisa!' called an indulgent voice from the stairs above. A small man came into view, smiling widely. With his scrubbed pink skin, plump torso and single tuft of fluffy white hair, he looked exactly like a newly bathed baby. 'How forgetful you are.'

Only the slight stress in the middle of 'forgetful' indicated that English was not his native language. 'It is Elsa who is English.'

'Of course she is, I mean I am. Sometimes I wonder exactly what it was you were smoking with those Hell's Angels, Lisa. You've never been the same since.'

'It was thirty years since, and you were there also!'

'Ah, but I didn't inhale. I should explain. Poor Philippa must be thinking she's arrived at a madhouse. This is our school - *La Piccola Casa d'Inglese* - The Little House of English, obviously. Ridiculous name but we seem to be stuck with it,'

'Only because you can't agree on an alternative.' put in the bald man.

'*The Lingo Lounge* is ludicrous and vulgar. I've been reading Nancy Mitford to Lisa for the past fifty-five years, and she still hasn't grasped that only a hotel can have a lounge. And possibly the cheaper sort of cruise liner. You might as well call the place *The Teaching Toilet* and be done with it.'

'What is so much the better about *The Linguistic Academy*?'

'Everything. Taste, refinement, intellectual pretension. That reminds me, didn't we put out a bottle of limoncello? And a buccellato? Bring them down, won't you, Otto dear, and little Graham? We'll have the welcome party here before we tackle Philippa's monster. May we sit on it, by the way? Lisa's knees aren't what they used to be.'

'They will last longer than your eeps, Helsa.'

'I'll bet you fifty thousand lire they don't.' They settled themselves on the suitcase, plump legs stuck out in front, with little heaving sounds coming from beneath their tweed covered rumps.

'Where was I? Oh yes, the school. It was founded by Elisa's father, Signor Rossi, at the end of the war. He thought that if we in Europe could all speak the same language, there would be less chance of our fighting each other again. His original plan was to teach French, wasn't it Lisa?, but a nasty experience with an *escargot* changed his mind. Lisa and I were only girls then, of course, and I was still at home in Camberwell with Mummy and Daddy.'

Pippa, guessing that this would be a long story, settled down on one of the stone steps, then, as the chill penetrated the last M&S layer, hastily stood up again. Elsa continued.

'Then in 1951 I got married, and we came to Lucca for our honeymoon. It wasn't well-known in those days, none of the tourist hordes we get now, but Rupert was frightfully sophisticated and said that Florence and Rome were quite *passé*, while Venice was just a giant puddle. So Lucca it was, for the shortest *luna di miele* on record. On the third night Rupert ran away with one of the chambermaids and the contents of my jewellery case. I was determined not to go home - Mummy had never liked him and I couldn't bear to hear her voice. "I did *warn* you, darling." So I stayed in Lucca, sold my wedding ring and went to work for Lisa's *babbo*. Oh, the limoncello, lovely. Give Philippa the first glass and make sure you fill it up.'

It looked like neat Jif, smelled like Grandma's boiled sweets and kicked like a kangaroo on speed. The buccellato, not to be outdone, masqueraded as an quiet fruit loaf until the moment Pippa bit into her thick slice, when it exploded concentrated aniseed across her paralysed taste buds. The only way to cope with either, she soon decided, was by generous application of the other. Fortunately that seemed to be everyone's opinion, so that none was totally sober by the time Elsa rejoined her story.

'So Lisa and I started going around together. Safety in numbers, you know. Plus the men used to take us for sisters. They got quite excited when they found out we didn't even speak the same language.'

'*Very* excited.' added Elisa. 'Especially when we were telling them ...'

'Never mind all that.' said Elsa quickly, taking a swig of limoncello to cool her flushed cheeks. 'Rock and roll had just arrived; it was bound to go to our heads.'

'Heads is not what I am thinking of.'

'Elisa! *Non davanti ai bambini*. Anyway, the chambermaid, who was a simple country maiden, or had been until Roop caught her bending down to scrub our bridal bidet, didn't enjoy his favours any longer than I had. Within weeks she'd been dumped for a Florentine countess. Actually she turned out to be neither Florentine nor a countess, but the widow of a Neapolitan jam jar manufacturer. But she was genuinely both rich and pious, so Roop found himself with a life-long meal ticket, while I, as the wronged wife, got bucketsful of lire in conscience money.'

'Which she shared with the *cameriera.*' added Elisa confidentially.

'Well, the poor darling, it was really her not me that the Contessa pinched him from. And she had a rather more tangible memento of Roop's gymnastics than I did. Two, in fact. They're over fifty now, the twins, with their own canning factory in Torino. What goes around comes around, as the dear hippies used to say. Anyway, I stashed my bit away for a rainy day – and when it rains in Lucca, be assured, you'll know about it.'

The others, mouths still stuffed with sodden buccellato, rumbled their agreement. 'This time it came ten years later when Signor Rossi decided to retire. I bought half shares in the school and the other half went to Lisa. We've been running the place together ever since.'

'But no men now.' said Elisa mournfully. 'Only Otto. And so,' her blue eyes shimmered, 'we must find a younger man when we need a really good hoaver'aul.'

The relish in her voice was blood-curdling. A piece of Pippa's buccellato decided to take the scenic route down her windpipe and it took another glass of limoncello to shift it. Was this stuff really supposed to be drunk in half-pint tumblers?

'Elisa,' chided Otto gently, 'you are a little naughty, shocking your English guest.' He turned to Pippa, at least she assumed he did; the moonlike blur seemed to swivel in her direction. 'She is talking of their *Motorrader.* You saw them in the hall?' He gestured down the stairs towards the two massive Harley-Davidsons, rearing black out of the gloom.

'I am sorry, Feeleeppa.' said Elisa, without noticeable contrition.

'Not Fee Lee Pa.' corrected Elsa. 'Philippa. All one word, quickly. Philippa.'

'Fffflipper?'

'It'll do.'

'Oh Lord!' cried Gray, staring down the stairwell. 'The car! Elsa, Elisa, *mi dispiace...*'

'*Cosa?*'

'*La macchina. É rotta. Tutta rotta.*'

'*Bravo!*' said Elisa. '*Parli italiano bene, ora.* What are you saying, my dear? The car? That old thing. *Non importa.* Helsa will take you tomorrow on the back of her *moto.*' A small, strangled noise came from the back of Gray's throat. 'You prefer not? *Va bene* - Helsa?'

Elsa thrust her hands deep in her cardigan pockets and took out a packet of Post-It notes and a felt-tipped pen. She wrote '*macchina - riparata*' on one, and stuck it on Elisa's back. 'It's the only way to remember.' she explained. '*Guarda.*' She turned her back to Pippa, displaying a sticker on her own shoulderblade. '*Filippa.*' it read. 'Teacher new.'

'Oh, Elisa.' said Gray. 'How many times? Adjective *before* the noun.'

'*Si, professore.*' laughed Otto. 'But now we must think about this case - shall we take it up? No, let me. You have had a tiring trip, and it is always chaos at the airport. Did you meet anyone else there, Gray?'

Gray, who was bending to help Elisa up, stiffened. Even his eyes were still.

'What do you mean? Who did you expect me to see?'

'No one special, Gray.' Otto's voice was soothing. 'It is just that one does, often, see a friend, leaving or arriving. I did not mean to disturb you.'

'Oh, I see.' Gray smiled, maybe a little too widely. 'I was just afraid there might have been an errand I'd forgotten about.'

The case was, as Otto had said, heavy, too heavy for anyone to face carrying any further, and so Pippa, feeling reckless, opened it there on the landing, and they all trudged up with teetering armfuls of underwear, tights, paperbacks and CDs. The school itself was small and neat, just two classrooms and a reception area, and smelled as such places always do, of furniture polish, disinfectant and something else, sweetish with decay. The drains, no doubt.

'Shall I take Pippa to bed?' asked Gray, when the last layer of luggage detritus had been dredged, full of damp cough sweets and unwrapped tampons.

Elsa answered first. 'What a good idea. An erotic initiation into the life of the tribe. Very Margaret Mead. She ought to be a virgin, really, but I suppose that's too much to hope for. Do we all stand round and applaud your technique?'

'I meant show her the apartment.'

'I know you did, treasure. We're not quite such wicked old women as that, not even Lisa. Go on, children, run along. I hope the flat's all right for you. Most of our teachers use it for a few weeks until they get themselves sorted out with something more permanent. Zena did, didn't she, and you, Graham and...'

'It's over here.' interrupted Gray, opening a door beside the photocopier. Three photocopiers, Pippa noted with detached interest. Limoncello didn't wear off all that quickly.

III

The bearded man found a seat at the back of the bus, sat down and unzipped his rucksack. Yes, the passport was still there, still new, despite the foldings and refoldings, the rubbings with sand and soil, even the dregs of coffee he had dared to spill on its persistent purity. He opened the back cover and stared at the photograph, as intently as the immigration *poliziotto* had done. It had passed. One blond German was much like another. His eye caught the name beneath and he winced. *Helmut Lebens*. He'd been given no choice, of course; Helmut Lebens had been available and so Helmut Lebens he was. The Gamesmaster had made that quite clear.

'The hard part is over, my friend. From now on there are only two rules. The first you know; you cannot break it by accident. If you should deliberately disobey it,' his soft voice hung in the morning air, ' - you know the consequences. The second needs your vigilance. You must be Helmut every moment of the day and night: wake as Helmut, eat as Helmut, speak as Helmut, make love as Helmut, sleep in Helmut's dreams. You can do this?'

'Yes, yes.' he had said, impatient to be away on the adventure, not knowing then how great a part of himself would be left behind, how much could never be Helmut. There had been a Neoplatonist once, he remembered, who had claimed to be Dionysius the disciple, seeking credibility for the wilder visions of his mystic philosophy. The deception had worked for centuries, but finally he had been found out, and was known ever after as Pseudo-Dionysius. Perhaps that was the answer. Yes, until it was over, if, indeed, it could ever be over, he would remain, in his own mind at least, merely Pseudo-Helmut.

Alone in the tiny flat, someone inside Pippa's head was testing out roller-coaster rides, a nasty portent of what tomorrow might feel like. The contents of her suitcase were still heaped in the foyer outside but she had fished out her toothbrush, a packet of aspirin, a large carrier bag and a random selection of clothes. It was the old, pre-Jonathan, hangover routine.

'Teaching tomorrow, yeah?' had been Gray's parting words as he backed towards the door.

'What time?'

'In the morning.' The mere phrase struck an ominous knell. She felt like crashing out straightaway, but she needed to be prepared for an early start. Leaving the heap of clothes on the floor would be asking for trouble, with an unfamiliar loo to be reached, probably in a hurry, and no visible bedside lamp.

If there was no lamp, there was at least a bedside table, with a sensibly sized drawer. She eased it open, ready to dump her things inside, only to find it already full, crammed with jeans, a couple of T-shirts, underwear and socks. One of the previous teachers must have left them behind, probably after a limoncello-imbued night like this one. Unless Elsa and Elisa, sated with the cultural superiority of Lucca, were in the habit of dressing up as teenagers and biking to the coast for a brief bop. A tempting thought, but the jeans couldn't be more than an English size eight, and even Elsa would be a generous sixteen. At least the clothes were clean. She would put them in the carrier bag and ask someone about them in the morning.

Sliding her hands under the pile, she almost missed the short hard edge. It could have been one of many things, most of them distastefully intimate: pills, tampons, Durex... Perhaps she ought to check, just in case it was one of those shrieking rape alarms or a clock set to go off at half past four. She drew the object out carefully, between finger and thumb.

Nothing too bad: neither medical nor electronic, only a transparent plastic packet crammed with small documents. The first, with only its back showing, was slightly smaller than a savings book, with a navy blue cover. She slid it out and turned it over. The embossed eagle glared sideways, contemptuous.

PASSPORT
United States of America

The limoncello ebbed away, a sober chill rushing into the vacuum. She opened the cover, fumbling the blank pages. Zena Margaret Carson. Date of birth 3rd January 1959. There couldn't be two Zenas, not both American and the same age. The rest of the documents were hers too: a driving licence, travel insurance and U.S. bank statements. At the back was an envelope with notes inside, two hundred dollars and six hundred euro.

With a quick pulse throbbing through her temples, Pippa pushed the papers back into the packet and shoved it into the carrier bag with the clothes. She remembered what Gray had said: 'Her passport and driving licence had gone. I knew where she always kept them.' So why were they here? Could it mean that Zena was here, too?

It was a ridiculous idea. But ridiculous ideas, especially those fortified by midnight *digestivi*, can be difficult to shift. She tried to ignore it, washing with the cold water and apple-scented soap, pulling on a long T-shirt, clambering between the cool, old-fashioned sheets. No chance. Until she knew, she would lie awake till morning.

She got out of bed again, wincing at the chilled tiles under her bare feet. The return of the slipper socks felt more enticing by the moment. But for now there was more to worry about than a few prospective chilblains. A compulsive disorder, she supposed it would be called, the neurotic conviction that a professional predecessor was concealed in your crannies. Or just plain paranoia. Either way, she would need to search methodically to have a hope of outwitting it. Under the bed, then. Nothing, not even dustballs. Cupboard under the sink? Zena would have to be an anorexic dwarf contortionist, but Pippa wasn't ruling anything out. There was washing-up liquid, bleach and a pink bottle labelled *100% Alcool* which might come in handy later on, but no teacher. She padded around the rest of the room, tapping the walls in search of hidden compartments, until even the whispering voice was satisfied that nothing larger than a basil leaf could possibly be concealed.

Now the shower room, long and narrow, no wider than a corridor. The usual offices stood in line, to porcelain attention: basin, bidet, loo. At the end was a frosted glass door into the shower. Pippa stood in front of it for a moment, feeling the tension build in the joints of her fingers. This was the only possible place and that was why she had left it until the end.

A proper heroine would have paused for longer, cranking up the Hitchcockian suspense; but then a proper heroine wouldn't still be yearning after slipper socks. The floor was even colder in here. She opened the door indifferently, as though searching for hidden Americans were a normal part of her bedtime routine. And of course there was no one there. No one, that was, unless she counted the small spider whose complex web spanned the ceiling, or the glossy black bug scuttling down the drainhole. But one thing was strange. The wall of the shower opposite the open door, which would normally hold nothing more mysterious than a soap dish, was set in its own frame, with a handle and a key in a rusty lock. Reminding herself briefly that this second door, by some quirk of Italian architecture, might lead into another apartment altogether, and bracing herself to be propelled into a showering Lucchese, she turned the key. Despite the rust, it rotated easily, suggesting regular use. Or at least recent use.

The chill on her face and neck told her immediately that she was outside. As her eyes grew accustomed to the light, a little from the moon, some from the streetlamps below, she saw that she stood on a tiny balcony, just large enough for its two peeling wrought iron chairs, a pentangle of overhead washing lines bearing a row of crusty dishcloths, and a rusty ladder leading upwards. There was no point in stopping now. The crusting metal of the rungs was odd, but not unpleasant, on the soles of her feet, and the climb was easy, only twenty steps until she clambered out through a small hatchway.

She stood on a cracked stone slab, still warm from the day's sun, gazed about her and sighed. All around, shimmering in the silvered light, was a roof garden, overgrown, studded with chimneys and open on four sides to the city below. The view, as she bent gingerly over the creeper covered railing, wasn't that of the guidebooks, Lucca set out in mathematical harmony, quartered by the Roman roads and encircled by the perimeter walls. She would need another hundred feet to see that one. Instead, she leaned out over a crazy juxtaposition of roofs, shutters, and towers, punctuated by more terraces like this, a secret city halfway to the sky.

She stood still for a few moments, breathing deeply, feeling the tension and the fear ebb away. The air smelled of herbs and tobacco and the lingering flavours of someone's late supper. These were the only mysteries left, she told herself. Gray's stories of Lucchese intrigue, the trangressions of Castruccani, the baroque city rivalries, had simply gone to her head, assisted, no doubt, by the treacherous limoncello. But those days were long gone. Even

Shelley and Byron had probably been too late. And as she relaxed, the solution came easily, laid out before her like the rooftops. So simple, so obvious. She scrambled down the ladder and turned, sleepy at last, towards the shower door. It was then that she felt the touch on her shoulder.

Charles looked out at the soft blue light, and the words repeated themselves in his mind. *Charles looked out at the soft blue light.* Now he knew that he was worried. He pushed his left fist secretly into his right palm, the nearest he ever came to violence. No, not worried. Concerned. Worry was for the players, not for him. Something had been bound to go wrong sometime, he had known that from the beginning. All he had to do was wait, and find out what it was. Where she was. He had plans for every eventuality, as long as no one said anything foolish. He thought of the boy, of his pale, nervous hands. It had been a mistake to involve them; the size of the fee had rocked his judgment. He would stick to Europeans in the future; you knew where you were with them, even when where you were was in the shit. He shuddered fastidiously. Charles didn't like that kind of language, even inside his own mind. It was true, though; the gentlemen of the South were far from amused. So where the hell was she?

IV

Pippa didn't scream. Over the next few days she hung on to this, the fact of her not having screamed, as a talisman, a medal bearing witness to her courage. Except that it wasn't really courage, just a plodding English cowardice that would prefer to be garrotted under a line of foreign dishcloths than risk the embarrassment of making a fuss. In any case, she did everything else connected with a scream; clenched her shoulders in a square grip, curled her fingers tightly, even opened her mouth. Only the sound was missing.

The cat on the washing-line, mildly offended, withdrew its tentative paw from Pippa's shoulder, and reconsidered its plan of leaping down to her. Instead it sprang onto one of the chairs and looked up questioningly. Its black body was almost invisible in the moonlight but its legs and face glimmered white.

'Sorry.' Pippa whispered, putting out a couple of fingers, against which the cat rubbed its head in absolution. 'Listen. I've worked out what happened. Zena must have brought that stuff with her when she first arrived. Elsa said she used the flat for the first few weeks. She probably got the same kind of reception party as I did, heavy on the limoncello, and stuffed her things into the drawer as I was going to. Then in the morning she'd have forgotten all about them, put different clothes on, taken some money out of the cash machine - there weren't any cards in the bundle, you know, and never thought about them again. After all, those T-shirts were a bit brash for Lucca, and the jeans looked pretty agricultural.'

The cat raised a questioning paw.

'Her passport? Yes, I suppose she'd need it again, and the driving licence. But she probably thought she'd lost them at the airport. She'd have applied for new ones then, you see, and it'll be those, the replacements, that she's taken to Greece with her. That'll be why she was so careful not to lose them again. Anyway, I'll give them to Elsa tomorrow and let her worry about it. I expect they'll be able to trace Zena eventually and give her the money back.'

The cat listened indulgently, with an air of mild boredom, as though it could have told Pippa all about it from the beginning. And neither of them noticed the flaw.

His name, she discovered in the morning, was Pierrotino, and he was strictly forbidden to sleep inside.

'He's usually so good.' Elsa mused, standing in the dusty sunlight with a tray of coffee and croissants. 'Lisa must have let him in by accident. Odd; she's usually the ruthless one.'

'I think it was me, actually. I had a bit of a midnight ramble and came across him on the washing-line.'

'How very English of you. *Sei fortunato, Pierrotino.* You have *un'amica.*'

Amica, Pippa thought, watching the pink tongue lapping her cappuccino foam, was going a bit far. But *che si ne frega?* as the cheerful Ape driver had called out, as his number plate fell off on to the slip road. On the first day of her new career she needed all the friends she could get.

Half an hour later, in the empty classroom, things were getting critical. *How to Teach English Abroad with No Qualifications Whatsoever* had told her only that Italians had difficulty in distinguishing between the words Tuesday and Thursday (with chaotic consequences for timetables) and that parents liked you to stick to the textbook. Textbook. There was something reassuring about the word. It was a pity that she hadn't had time to provide herself with one to leaf through on the flight. But *How to Teach...* assured its readers that every language school had a well stocked teachers' resource library. Every language school, that was, except the *Piccola Casa.* Elisa had looked mystified at first, before eventually dredging up a hardback book covered with brown paper. If it wouldn't do, she had continued, her floury face creased with concern, there might be others in the classroom cupboard. Only it was so very long since anyone had asked her, and the cupboard hadn't been sorted out for years, it was Helsa's job, and she was afraid there might be mice... Pippa had finally managed to staunch the flow with an assurance that this, patting the brown paper affectionately, was certain to be perfect.

She patted it again now, as if by doing so she might transform it into a modern multimedia syllabus, complete with teacher's book, photocopiable activity sheets and interactive CD-ROM for individual evaluation.

It didn't work.

The King's English for our Little Brown Brethren, read the title page. *For Use in the Colonies and Missions. Particularly Intended for the Instruction of Servants, Native Officials and Local Women of an Accommodating Disposition.*

Hoping that this might merely be an ironic, post-modernist preface, Pippa flicked through the pages.

Exercise LVII:
Select the correct sentence.
> *i.   Lordy, sir, here be your brandy-soda.*
> *ii. Sodthebrandy, oh my Lord.*
> *iii. Here is your brandy and soda, my Lord; I trust that it is satisfactory.*

'Oh God.' It was the second heartfelt prayer in less than twelve hours. She hoped Italy wasn't going to have too pious an effect on her. But there was nothing else for it; the cupboard would have to be braved, mice or none. Where was Pierrotino when she needed him? Judging from the size of the cupboard door, at the opposite end of the room, it was a fair sized space, although probably it contained nothing but brooms and cobwebs.

She was advancing towards it, *King's English* in her hand, and noticing again the odd sweetish smell, when the classroom door opened. Elisa ushered in a boy, or what appeared to be a boy, of about seventeen, slouching slightly, with a large dark eyes and hair in shiny black spikes. He wore Levis, Nike trainers, an Adidas sweatshirt and a badge reading **NO GLOBALIZATION**.

'*Eccolo*! Nicola Columbini, your number one student.' She nodded and shuffled backwards through the doorway like the weather-house woman when rain is on its way.

Nicola? Pippa looked again, more sharply. The figure was slim enough to be a girl's, if a little broad across the shoulders, and distinctly flat-chested. The face? The face was beautiful, there was no other word for it, desert-skinned and delicately chiselled, with those huge espresso eyes. Her gaze flickered lower, to the wispy undergrowth on the chin that might one day become a goatee beard, the trendy, free-floating variety. No, Italian girls didn't grow beards, not until they'd seen off a husband or two.

The boy held out a hand. 'Nic' he said, the baritone dispelling any doubt. "Ow do you do?'

' How do you do?' It was like entertaining the stuffier of Jonathan's corporate clients. She gestured towards the chair she had prepared earlier, half way down the other side of the table, drawn out at what she hoped was an inviting angle. But instead he took the seat nearest to the door, right-angling it for a quick retreat. Pippa groaned silently. It was nice to know when people had confidence in you. Mr Stipple of the Residents' Association used to perch in just the same way, only with his left hand trailing by the spider plant, in case the coffee should be as appalling as he feared. 'Do sit down.' she added, too late and gabbling imbecilically. 'I just have to get another book from the cupb...'

'No!' The brown fingers were tight around her wrist before she even saw his arm move. 'No, please. I like that book.'

'*This*?' She couldn't even bring herself to say the name, flapping the book helplessly with her free hand. 'This *King's English* thing? Are you sure?'

'*King's English*, yes. Very ... interesting.'

'Oh.' Dawn was beginning to break. 'You mean from a post-colonial, anti-imperialist point of view?' This wasn't so bad after all. If all the students were capable of neo-Marxist analysis of their textbooks then she could probably cope. She'd always been better at deconstruction than grammar.

'*Certo*.' He released her wrist to reach towards the book. 'My preferred part .....'

'The Ladies of an Accommodating Disposition?'

He looked blank for a moment, then a smile splintered across his face. It was an amazing smile, the kind that would stop Neopolitan traffic, persuade hardened fascists to buy the *Big Issue* and set any heterosexual woman between fourteen and the mortuary slab wondering which pants she'd put on that morning and whether she'd waxed above her knees. 'The Ladies, yes. Where is the Ladies, please? My mother has need to make *pipi*. Is right?'

'Is - near. Was this the kind of work you were doing with Zena? Exercises from the book and, er, general conversation?'

His smile drooped. 'No. With Zena I am doing the *compiti*.'

'Sorry, I don't understand. *Compiti*?'

'Housework.'

'With Zena you were doing *housework*? She surveyed the room, the scabs of dried Sellotape on the walls and the cobwebs in the high corners. It could explain the strong smell of furniture polish and disinfectant, if not the lurking stench that lay beneath. Had Elsa and Elisa found a cunning wheeze to dispense with the cost of a cleaning lady?'

Nic slammed the heel of his hand against his forehead. '*Buonanotte* Nicola! *Sempre confuso*. Not house. I mean home. *Compiti* is homework, yes? Here it is.'

From his backpack he drew out a folder containing several sheets of paper. The top ones were printed in Italian, some kind of technical instructions, while those underneath were closely written by hand in uncertain English.

'There's a lot here.' said Pippa stalling for time. The Italian was completely incomprehensible to her and the English not much better. There was no way that she could hazard the vaguest guess at the accuracy of his translations. 'Have you done it all this week?'

'Oh yes. Zena is very 'ungry... No.' He stopped himself with a raised hand and a flash of the smile. ''Ungry is *affamato*. Zena is very *angry* if I do not finish. Is okay?'

'I'm sure it must be, yes. It isn't exactly my area. But do you really enjoy this kind of thing?'

'Enjoy?'

'Like it. Do you like doing this type of homework?'

'*Mi gaba?*' He blushed at the plummet into Lucchese. 'No, no, I don't like at all this type of work. But Zena say - says it is the best for me. I must improve my English very fast.'

Pippa leafed through the sheets again, a suspicion rising in her mind.

'Do your parents know that you're doing this work?'

The shadow of the smile retreated even further.

'I am a delusion.' he announced solemnly.

She put down the papers and gripped the edge of the table. There was a constant low level thudding in the back of her head, but other than that she had thought that the hangover was under control. The limoncello must have been even stronger than she thought, if she was still having recognizable hallucinations at half-past ten next morning. Nic was staring at her, his Michelangelo features shadowed with concern.

'It is a false friend, perhaps? *Delusione* is not delusion? When something - some person - is not good as you hope?'

'Disappointment.' The boy's shoulders hunched miserably. 'But

I'm sure you're not.'

Compared to the few English seventeen year olds she had met in the course of their parents' divorces or their own criminal misdemeanours, he was a radiant vision of courtesy, virtue and personal hygiene.

'It's true. All my family; my parents, my grandparents, my uncles, even my sister, they all frequented the *liceo classico*,' He made it sound like a sleazy bar, 'to study the Latin and Greek. From seven generations, I am the only Columbini to choose the *tecnico*.'

'I'm sure it's a very good school.'

'It is,' he said simply, 'for me. I like to work with the machines. But for my family it is a - a disappointment, yes? My father even wanted to call me Niccolo.'

There was evidently something here that she was supposed to understand. 'I'm sorry, I...'

'After Niccolo Machiavelli. The *liceo classico* in Lucca is also named for him. A great man of Tuscany.'

'Machiavelli? It's a Machiavellian school?' With Machiavellian caretakers, she added to herself, and Machiavellian timetabling and a Machiavellian netball team? But to Nic there was nothing odd about the idea.

An awkward pause followed, while Pippa stumbled towards a stimulating question. Nic's parents were presumably paying by the minute, and not for significant silences. 'What kind of machines do you like best?'

'Wind turbines, solar generators, hydroelectric dams. Anything that can change the way we are..' He made a swift squeezing gesture with both hands.

'Strangling?'

'*Si*. We are strangling the earth. Do you know about trees?'

Before she had time to work out whether it was a trick question, he had begun to speak again, words slapping and sliding over each other in his enthusiasm. 'In fifteen years, to *millenovecento*...never mind the date, fifteen years, two hundred hectares of forest is lost, the size of Mexico, and still it happens, one hundred and twenty football pitches every minute. And in Europe too, you know how much of our forest is a virgin? *Uno per cento*. It is shame, yes? And one-half the oak trees is damaged.'

'That's terrible.'

'Very terrible, yes. How much paper do you use in one year?'

'I've no idea. I used to dictate thirty letters a day, and there's the loo, and *Cosmopolitan*...'

'Two hundred and seven kilos, when you are in the United Kingdom. In Italy we are not quite so bad, one hundred and fifty-eight. In the USA,' He pronounced it as a single word, *Ooza*, 'three hundred and thirty-four. And India - what do you think?'

'I...'

'Three point eight. It shows us, yes? I think we are...'

The next half-hour was the easiest four euro thirty Pippa was ever likely to make, as she nodded and gasped and sighed until the *Torre dell'Ore* began its elaborate eleven o'clock chimes.

As Nic packed the papers back in his rucksack, he drew out another sheet.

'I forget this. It's more difficult for me than the *instruzioni*. Is okay?'

It was a menu in Italian, with an English translation of each dish in his own looped handwriting. But Pippa's glance stalled at the pencilled note at the top.

Z. - Please translate asap. Usual rates.

There could be no doubt now.

'What's wrong? Is my English so very bad?'

She told him, before she had time to consider.

'So,' he said carefully at the end. 'I have worked for Zena all this time. I have worked, and she has taken the money.'

'I'm afraid so.'

He glanced down the room, towards the far end. 'The poor lady.'

'What?'

'She was, I think, very unhappy to do this thing. And only for the money. Almost - almost I am sorry.'

'Sorry?'

He hesitated for a moment. 'Sorry she is gone.'

Elisa was waiting for them in the reception area.

'I must pay for my lesson.' explained Niccolo.

'Oh yes!' Elisa sounded surprised; she had evidently had some other motive for hovering. But fees were, after all, fees. 'In lire?' she added hopefully.

Nic shook his head, grinning. This was obviously a regular exchange. 'We have to use the new money now, Signora. It is the law, you remember? The euro.' He pronounced it like the English chocolate bar, thought Pippa, with a sudden rumble.

'*Ma, c'e cosi difficile*! I have used the lira for seventy-two years, the euro for only four months. Four months and we must change completely. *É impossibile!* Of course, for Helsa it is even more terrible. She makes the accounts with shillinks and farthery-bits. *Dimmi, cara*, what *is* a half-crown? '

'Outmoded imperialism, like your textbook. Don't worry about it. But listen, did you say four months? You've only had the euro for four months?'

An uneasy chill was snaking through her bowels; the flaw that even Pierrotino had missed.

'*Si, quattro mesi.*' agreed Elisa. 'But dear Signor Berlusconi, he gave us a *regalo*, a present of Christmas.'

She reached into her cardigan pocket and took out a small plastic calculator.

'*Cosi gentile.*' she cooed, while Nicola restricted himself to a low snort. 'We need only to enter the price in lire.....'

As they pored over the gadget, the main door opened a few inches revealing a narrow band of grey and one small lace-up shoe.

'*Mio Dio, le sorelle!*' Elisa abandoned the euro conversion and reached over her shoulder to retrieve the latest Post-It note. 'Your next class, *bambolina*. Twenty-three nuns for an hour and a half. Have you got enough chairs?'

'I think so.' Pippa wasn't listening, was simply staring at the small dark hand which stole around the edge of the door. 'What kind of nuns?'

'*Sorelle del Santo Mare.* From Madagascar. The sea, to them is a symbol...'

But Pippa had already disappeared, sliding precariously on the polished floor as she skidded through the classroom door. The *King's English* lay on the table, open at the title page. She had to get rid of it quickly, replace it with something innocuous, however inappropriate. She didn't particularly want to spend her first morning in Italy under arrest for inciting racial hatred. Not to mention the danger posed to the nuns' chastity by the Accommodating Ladies' dialogues. Anything would do: E*lementary Horticultural English, English for Trainee Chiropodists, Pre-School Poppets' First Nursery Rhymes...* She wrenched at the handle of the cupboard, feeling the weight behind it.

But what fell to the floor was not *Elementary Horticultural English, Cool English for Backpackers* or even more copies of the *Little Brown Brethren*. What fell to the floor was cold, greenish white and, Pippa strongly suspected, American. It was also undoubtedly dead.

V

Again Pippa didn't scream. It was getting to be something of a habit. No doubt in later life the repression would manifest itself in all kinds of psychological complexes, but she hadn't the leisure to think about that now. There was no point in screaming and so, as long as her vocal chords behaved themselves, she simply wouldn't scream.

Being sick was another matter. At first she thought it was inevitable but as she stood, inches from the body, the wave of nausea drew back and faded. The tightness in her stomach moved up to her chest and she felt only pity and the beginnings of anger. Whoever this thing had been, stiff and contorted at her feet, the humanity had passed from it, and tears pricked Pippa's eyes as she looked down at the waste.

She became aware of sound and movement in the room behind her, a low-level buzz of excited occupation. Twenty-three nuns, all dark-skinned and nearly all under thirty, were gathered around the far end of the table, jostling affectionately, like a litter of well-fed puppies. They had noticed neither the cupboard nor the corpse, but were leaning over something in the middle of the table, craning wildly to turn its pages.

'Don't read that!' squeaked Pippa, feeling like the Keeper of the Vatican Index and sounding like a harassed fieldmouse. Forty-six dark eyes turned to her in calm merriment.

'My grandfather learned English from this book.' said one. 'It was the great delight of our childhood to hear him read from it.'

'My father knew it all by heart.' said another. 'He would recite the best parts after Christmas dinner.'

'My aunt once ran away from home with it.' said a third. 'It was the only way for her to read about the Ladies...'

'...of Accommodating Disposition!' they chorused together, collapsing into giggles.

'Oh!' said the first to recover, looking at Pippa's face. 'Were you trying to hide it from us?' There was a general murmur of consternation. 'How thoughtful of you. But you see, you didn't have to worry. We all know this book as well as you know - *Winnie the Pooh*. It is a part of our childhood.'

'But isn't it...?'

'Racist?' It was the eldest who spoke, a slim woman of about fifty. 'Yes, of course. But if we had waited for the invention of multiculturalism, for anti-imperialism, for inclusive texts, before we learned to read, then we would all be illiterate. Would that be better?' The question was evidently rhetorical, for she didn't pause for Pippa to reply. '*I* think,' she began, and then she blinked twice and her tone changed. 'I think there is a dead body beside you on the floor. Would you like me to inform the school administrators?'

'If you would.' said Pippa, only a little shakily, trying to match the general tone of serenity. But when the sensible black shoes had clicked out of the door, she felt suddenly dizzy and groped for a chair. The other sisters gathered around her, patting her shoulders and hair and making soothing inconsequential little noises.

'Poor girl.' said one. 'What a terrible thing for you to find. And when you were getting ready to teach us, too.'

Pippa blew her nose on one of the twenty-two offered handkerchiefs and managed a smile.

'Don't know what I'd teach you anyway.' she sniffed. 'You all speak perfect English.'

'Not perfect', said a small neat girl with a pretty snub nose, 'but we are Upper Intermediate Level. We still get confused about the Third Conditional. Is it the same as the Subjunctive?'

'*Mamma mia!*' The double-voiced cry penetrated three hundred years of stonework, traumatizing a pair of doves at a critical juncture in their windowsill courtship. Elsa and Elisa had been told.

'Thank you', breathed Pippa, wondering whether that counted as another prayer and promising that, whatever else the next twenty-four hours offered, she would use ten minutes of them to find out the difference between the conditional and subjunctive. One was a mood, she remembered, and the other a tense. Rather like being a teenager.

The older nun came back into the classroom.

'They're calling the police.'

This proved to be an understatement. Unsure which of the

myriad agencies of Italian law enforcement had jurisdiction over a dead body found in a classroom cupboard, Elsa and Elisa had summoned them all: the *Carabinieri*, the *Polizia Stradale,* the *Guardia di Finanzia*, the *Polizia Municipale*, the *Vigili Urbani* and even one or two of the private security firms whose armed representatives patrolled the more cautious of Lucca's many banks. And, Lucca being socially more of a village than a city, and both Elsa and Elisa being universally liked and respected, no one wanted to turn them down.

Within moments the sounds began: the keening sirens, the yelping brakes and the final thudding reminder that the Cinquecento was still blocking the street. In they burst, doggishly enthusiastic, taking the stairs three or four at a time. Since the call was, as far as most were concerned, one of courtesy only, most of the agencies had sent a pair of their youngest, most innocent recruits, those whose presence would least be missed but who could be relied upon to be deferential and sympathetic. Even the Carabinieri were young, too young even to have begun upon the luxuriant moustaches ubiquitous among their middle-aged colleagues.

They crowded into the classroom, following the buzz of conversation, elbowing one another good naturedly and whispering of the previous night's football. One or two gave a surreptitious flick to the shiny buttons of a schoolfriend who had entered a rival service. But once across the threshold they were silent and still. Their work; inspecting shoppers' till receipts, waving plastic lollipops at motorists or giving hard stares, hand on holster, to passing dogs, had scarcely prepared them even for the sight of a dead body, much less its investigation.

Their eyes, drawn back from the huddled thing in the corner, fell gratefully upon the twenty-three calm and comely faces before them. The same idea slid into the mind of each polizzotto. They could interview the nuns. Interviewing a witness was, undoubtedly, the sort of thing that a responsible police officer ought to do at the scene of a crime and, recorded verbatim with painstaking annotation, would produce a report heavy enough to satisfy the most pompous superior. For an Italian institution to take even the most trivial or short-lived action without first lagging itself with layers of paperwork, would be as unthinkable as for an Italian mamma to send her child to school in March, however high the temperature, without a scarf and woolly hat. The fact of the witness being a nun could only be an advantage. The report would not only involve a vast multiplication of names and titles, together with references to the Lateran Treaty, but would, inevitably, bestow some spiritual benefit upon the interviewer. It was probably as good as going to Confession. And if the nun happened to be young and pretty, he could hardly be blamed for that, not even by the most suspicious of wives or *fidanzate*.

There were plenty of sisters to go around, and so no one seemed interested in talking to Pippa, who was neither calm nor sacred, even if moderately comely in the right light. It occurred to her suddenly that someone would have to identify the body, presumably Elsa or Elisa, unless Gray could be summoned from Lucca's eastern hinterlands, where he was engaged all day teaching business English to toilet-roll salesmen. Perhaps she had better find out.

The reception area was empty, but gentle snuffling sounds were coming from the tiny office behind the espresso machine. Pippa was about to try a diplomatic cough when the main door opened and a man came in. He was tall and broad-shouldered, with floppy hair, the colour that Pippa's mother called 'dirty blond'. He wore jeans and a heavy cream fishing jersey with visible stains of coffee and strawberry jam. A flake of the croissant that had completed his breakfast clung to his otherwise rather impressive jawline.

Obviously a tourist, thought Pippa, German or possibly Dutch, in search of Italian lessons. There were language schools, she knew, which offered them, but not, so far as she knew, the Piccola Casa. Especially not at the outset of a murder investigation. She had better get rid of this scruffy specimen as quickly as possible, before he contaminated the scene of the crime.

He smiled and held out a large and grubby hand.

'*Buongiorno.*' His accent was at least as good as hers. Perhaps he was only in search of a launderette.

'*Buongiorno.*' She delved back thirteen years to her brief encounter with middle-school German. '*Hier ist nein Italienklasse.*'

'What?' His eyebrows shot up, disappearing beneath his fringe.

'We don't do Italian classes here.'

'Why would I need Italian classes? I *am* Italian.' He grinned suddenly and wiped the flake from his chin. 'Although a very messy Italian. What do you say - the dog's dinner? My mother is in despair.'

'Yes.' said Pippa, not quite sure whether she was agreeing that he was messy, approving his choice of idiom or simply noting that the woman charged with the duty of tidying him up was still his mother. Hardly surprising; Italian girls were known to be fastidious. 'But what..?'

'Am I doing here? A moment.' He dug in the back pocket of his jeans and extracted, together with a few sweet wrappers and a couple of used bus tickets, an official identity card.

Guinizelli, Pietro
Commissario di Polizia

Pippa glanced up at him suspiciously. If there was one thing he looked like less than an Italian, it was a policeman. He caught her look but misinterpreted the doubt.

'You think I'm too young to be a Commissario?'

'No, not at all.' Pippa's only idea of a Commissario was an elderly man in uniform, adding character to London's West End. Presumably in Italy it was a highish rank in the police force, but she supposed that they had some sort of graduate fast track scheme. He certainly didn't look as though he'd been promoted from the ranks. Anyway, he must have been thirty; hardly a fresh-faced boy. Hardly a fresh-faced man, either, that stubble was a good two days old.

'Too old, then? Or just too *sciatto*? Scruffy.'

His pronunciation of the last word was so fascinating, with the 'r' rolled and each 'f' sounded separately, that she forgot to be embarrassed.

'Anyway, you have a body for me?'

Pippa nodded, a little overcome by the ambiguity, which she hoped was unintentional, and led him through to the classroom.

The scene within was a pleasant one, if you ignored, as everyone else did, the corpse at the back, cutting a *brutta figura* with its twisted limbs and chilly stare. Like a gathering of birds they chattered, the females soft and grey, the males gaudier with their red or white stripes, their flashes of gold and their high black leather boots. Commissario Guinizelli coughed, a cough of authority, undiminished by the sweater. He said a few sharp words in Italian and the men, rather shamefacedly, got to their feet, shook hands with their pious interviewees and filed out of the door. He spoke again, more gently and expansively, and the sisters too disappeared.

'Will there only be you then?' asked Pippa, who had been rather impressed by the Carabinieri's boots. If she'd been interested in men, which she definitely wasn't, not after Jonathan, those boots could have helped matters on quite pleasantly.

'I'm from the Questura.' This apparently spoke for itself. 'The forensic team will be here soon. For now, could you identify the body, please?'

'No, I'm sorry; I can't. I didn't know her, you see. That is - if it *is* Zena Carson. And I don't know who it is if it isn't. I only got here yesterday.' She wished she could manage to sound more competent, even in front of this unprepossessing figure. After all, English was supposed to be her forte. But the Commissario was looking at her with a new interest.

'You arrived in Lucca yesterday?'

'Yesterday evening. From Pisa airport.'

'And before this you were in - Scotland?'

'Northern England. I'm English.'

He inclined his head. 'I am so sorry.' he said, with Byzantine layers of ambiguity. 'And have you been here before? For an interview, perhaps?'

'No, never. It was all arranged by email, in the last couple of days. I was supposed to replace Zena because they thought she'd left. I...' She was going to say that, now Zena had been found, she supposed she wouldn't have the job any more and then she remembered that Zena was dead, if this was Zena, and then the smell seemed to rise up again and there was a dark cloud in front of her eyes...

'Here.' he said, taking her by the shoulders. 'Sit down. You are a little - vertigious?'

'Faint.'

'Faint. Thank you. Adjective.' He took one of the bus tickets and made a note on the back with a stub of pencil.

'It's a noun and a verb as well.' said Pippa, thinking that she might as well get into practice with this teaching business. 'The adverb is 'faintly'.'

'Thank you. You were a teacher in England as well?'

'No. Actually I was a solicitor. A kind of lawyer. *Avvocato.*'

He paused for a moment, bus ticket raised, looking at her appraisingly.

'Good.' he said at last, more to himself than to her. 'An English speaker, apparently not a suspect...' He broke off with a sudden formal nod. 'We must of course check your alibi, ...'

Pippa nodded in reply, rather gingerly, the inside of her skull still distinctly liquid.

'And, for the cake's icing, she has legal expertise. Good, very good.' He mused for a few seconds and then gave the same sharp inclination of his head. 'Do you think you could assist me in this case, *signorina*?'

Since Pippa had qualified, her only experience of criminal law had been to draft the senior partner's mitigation plea after he had been caught in his Mercedes, weaving home from the Rotary Club dinner. There was no need to mention that, though. She twisted in her chair, forcing herself to look at the body. As a hard-nosed investigator she would have to steel herself to these things.

'Don't worry, you wouldn't need to do anything unpleasant. Only a little translation if I get confused, maybe making some notes in English, explaining references, that kind of thing. But only if you're happy with the idea. You won't be arrested if you decline.'

Not a Jonathan-type suggestion then? No, he looked quite relaxed. Alarmingly relaxed, really, for someone in such close proximity to a corpse. It was a real choice, she could say no. She considered the alternatives. Obviously she couldn't teach in this room, and probably not anywhere else in the school either. Unless she shared the loo-roll run with Gray, then, that left skulking in the flat with Pierrotino or doing the tourist bit around Lucca. There was certainly plenty to see, judging by the thickness of the guidebooks. The problem was, she didn't feel like a tourist, wasn't in a holiday frame of mind, and without that the churches and museums would just feel like work. And if she was feeling like working, and she wasn't able to teach, then she might as well do something to help this shambling policeman. In any case, she felt a certain responsibility towards poor Zena, having already taken her job, uncoverered her translation scam and disturbed her body from its moderately tranquil resting-place.

'Okay then, I'll try. And you'll have...' quick flashback to *Inspector Morse*. 'some sort of sergeant with you as well?' Her voice carried a trace of hope. After all, the entire detective squad couldn't go about disguised as dyspraxic Scandanavian fishermen.

He smiled. 'Some sort of sergeant, yes. Come and see my sort of sergeant.'

He padded on his soft shoes, like leather Cornish pasties, back through the reception area, stopping outside Elsa and Elisa's office and nudging the door open. The tiny room was almost completely filled by a large man in a dark blue uniform, seated between the two elderly women and holding their hands in his own gigantic paws. He was speaking very low and they were nodding tear-stained faces, their eyes fixed upon him.

'So you see,' he said (in Italian; Pippa only discovered what it was all about much later) a proper understanding of the Book of Revelation proves that there must undoubtedly be motorbikes in heaven. Dear Zena will, at this precise eternal moment, be revving up a brand new Kawasaki 500.'

'A *Japanese* bike?'

'There is such a thing as purgatory, you know, ladies. A couple of masses and she'll be on the real thing. MotoGuzzi 1000.'

'Oh you *are* a comfort to us, Sergeant. Poor Elsa was getting terribly upset.'

'Nonsense, dear, I was only concerned about you.'

At a cough from the doorway the man stood up, involving less of a change than might be expected, as nearly all his bulk was width. He saluted, very slowly and solemnly, as though it were part of a religious ritual. The Commissario nodded in reply, bowed to Elsa and Elisa in turn, and retreated.

'Sergeant Lenzuoli.' he explained when they were back in the corridor. 'He trained to be a priest but at the last - ditch, do you say? - he changed his mind and joined the police. He's wonderful with the bereaved but active investigation tires him a little. I like to let him use his strengths.'

'Very wise.'

'Yes, he is.' He looked at her again with that odd speculative expression and she noticed the peculiar green of his eyes. With anyone else she might have suspected tinted contact lenses, but they did require a certain minimal dexterity. 'I don't know your name.'

'Philippa Laud. Pippa, I'm usually called.'

'Pippa.' He tried it out, the 'i' sounded the Italian way and both 'p's pronounced individually. 'Peep- pa. And I am Pietro.'

'Pietro, yes.' They shook hands again and something seemed to strike him.

'Do you want to call me 'Pete'?' The name sounded ridiculous on his tongue, the consonants crisp and the final 'e' faintly audible.

She couldn't help laughing.

'I'm sorry. Do you *want* me to call you Pete?'

He looked horrified. 'No, please not. I thought it would be polite to offer. You invited me...'

'No, it doesn't work like that in English. You can be called whatever you want to be.'

'Can you really? How very sensible.' He paused outside the door for a moment, contemplating a land where a Prime Minister could be called by a shortened form of his Christian name, where there was no distinction between *tu, Lei* and *voi*, where you could leave a shop and simply say 'Bye' without the complex gradations of *ciao, arrivederci* and *arrivederla*, where... No, it would never do. He opened the classroom door a little. 'Are you sensible and English enough to come back in?'

Pippa had never before thought of herself as a patriot, but the challenge rang out, stirring generations of bulldog spirit and missionary zeal. Her great-great-aunt had rowed up the Amazon; no doubt she had seen bodies in a more advanced state than poor Zena's. If, again, it was Zena's. Comparing that dead face with the hastily glimpsed passport photograph, she could deduce nothing, except that both were white, female and somewhere between eighteen and sixty. There was nothing else for it. She took a deep breath and pushed open the door.

VI

The fat black telephone purred on the empty desk. He waited for three rings before answering, as though he hadn't been staring at it for the past three hours.

'*Cha...*' He broke off in horror. It was months, years probably, since he had even thought the old name, never mind used it in public. He had always hated it. No, that wasn't true. It was important, especially now, to be accurate. He had been proud of it once, for the glorious ten minutes between Mamma's words and finding the encyclopaedia in Father's study. 'Many great kings had your name, Charlie.' Many kings, yes: the Fat, the Foolish, the Bald, the English weakling, mute at five and crawling at seven, the forgotten Swedes. Even the Holy Roman Emperors were failures. '*Ciao.*' There was no point in thinking about that now. 'Ah, *ciao, cara*. What is it? What's wrong?'

Pseudo-Helmut did full justice to the inclusive breakfast, paid his hotel bill and strode, backpack over one shoulder, into the Pisan suburbs in search of a supermarket. He hadn't come back to Italy for the food; it wasn't even a secondary, a tertiary consideration, but being here now, he might as well make the most of it. He found one eventually, a low greyish structure dumped arbitrarily in a pale dusty car park. But the trolleys, that used to take five hundred lire, needed two euro now, and he fingered hopelessly through his little coin purse.

'Can I give you some change, sir?' asked a voice at his elbow, speaking English. A tall, distinguished African was holding out a two euro coin. Beside him on the ground a sheet was spread out, covered in a bright array of watches, sunglasses and bulky bags of towelling socks.

'I don't want to buy anything.'
'Who does?'
'I'm sorry. That was rude of me.'

'Not at all. We have something in common. I don't want to sell this rubbish, you don't want to buy it. But we each have our role to play. This is what Africans do in Tuscany, we make white tourists feel guilty so they will waste sixty cents on a plastic cigarette lighter. While the Germans – I am right - ?'

Pseudo-Helmut nodded.

'- The Germans buy crazy amounts of food at the supermarket as though, in a city of five hundred restaurants, they might find themselves stranded with nothing to eat. I have telescopic umbrellas, as well. It might rain.'

They both looked up at the cloudless sky.

'Perhaps not. And I don't know about the five hundred restaurants, either. I know nothing of Pisa. I am only here to avoid my daughter's school friends in Lucca. If a man must humiliate himself so, it is better on someone else's doorstep.'

But Pseudo-Helmut, normally such a good listener, had heard nothing past the placename.

'Lucca? You're from Lucca?'

'I am living in Lucca, for nine months now, with my family. We are from Senegal originally, probably you guessed. My name is Etienne.'

'Pseu-Helmut. Helmut.' They shook hands, the two euro coin quietly transferred in the process. 'I see you have some vests...'

Etienne began to laugh.

Pippa and Pietro were facing each other across the big classroom table, munching on enormous filled *panini*, from which slices of tomato were in constant danger of becoming disengaged. A wide shaft of afternoon sunlight slanted across the table and there was no sign, other than a faint smell of disinfectant and traces of yellow tape on the floor, that anything more sinister than eating and talking had ever taken place in the room.

'What would an English detective do now?' asked Pietro, rescuing a long piece of *prosciuitto crudo* which lolled out of his roll like the tongue of a thirsty dog. 'What are the vital clues?' He peered at her over his rather large nose.

Pippa peered back, trying to judge his tone and to compose a suitable reply, as far as was possible with her mouth full of salami. She was beginning to suspect him of being a closet Anglophile, the kind of Italian who read Agatha Christie, affected the manner of an absent-minded Oxbridge don and delighted in archaic idioms. On the other hand, his management of the morning's activities by the forensic team had shown him, surprisingly, to be a rather efficient and sharp-witted modern policeman. It would help to know which persona was asking the question.

'The syringes?' she tried. 'The writing on her arms?'

'Precisely.'

A Holmes enthusiast as well, then.

Before the forensic team had arrived, Pietro had made an initial inspection of the body, with Pippa as close behind him as she could coerce herself. His large hands, in surgical gloves, had been surprisingly deft, passing gently under the limbs and through the clothing. He obviously had inner reserves of hand-eye coordination that he'd never thought to try out at mealtimes.

The woman was very small and thin, child-like in size, although her face, even distorted in death, was drawn, almost haggard. She wore narrow jeans, a T-shirt and denim jacket which, with her short greying hair, gave her an androgynous look, like a young boy suddenly shocked into middle-age. There were no signs of violence on the body but her thin face was swollen with purple-red blotches and there was dried blood around her nose and ears. In the pockets of her jacket were some small change, tissues, a set of keys, nothing unexpected.

But as Pietro smoothed the T-shirt down over the flat ribcage and stomach he felt something raised at its edge. It was a style fashionable that spring, a patchwork design, with irregular rectangles of fabric superimposed on one another and lots of raised edges. A nightmare to iron. One of the patches, a narrow vertical strip just beneath the left sleeve, had been left unstitched at the top, forming a small pocket. Something cylindrical had been pushed down into the pocket, but Pietro's fingers were too large to reach it. Pippa watched him for a few seconds, summoning her courage.

'Let me do that.'

'No.' He shook his head but his eyes were assessing the size of her fingers. 'It might be dangerous. The team will be here soon, with *pinzette*.'

'*Pinzette*?' It sounded like a name in a children's story.

He mimed with his free thumb and forefinger.

'Tweezers.' But he was still looking at her hands. 'You don't want to wait for them, though, do you?'

He smiled, oddly, with only half of his mouth, and for a moment a disarming dimple appeared at the base of his cheek.

'No, you're right, I would prefer not to wait. The forensic boys, they examine everything meticulously, make perfect records, preserve the evidence in sterilized *sacchettini* - and I cannot make head and tail of it. I have no imagination, I think. Unless I find the evidence myself, *in situ* – you can use this Latin in English? Good. As I say, unless I find it, I cannot...' His voice trailed off into a melancholy dimuendo.

'You can't grasp its significance?'

'Exactly. But when it's physically impossible...' He looked ruefully at his large spade-like hands.

'Then you'd better get your assistant to assist, hadn't you? And I don't mean Sergeant Lenzuoli; his fingers looked like three pounds of Cumberland sausage. Come on, let me try. You've got a spare pair of gloves, haven't you?'

'*É impossibile*.' he said with another quick grin, digging in another pocket and drawing out a tiny bundle of whitish plastic. 'But if you insist...'

Her fingers were slippery with latex and nervousness, but after one or two fumbles she caught the object between her finger and thumb and drew it out.

'*Dio!*' breathed Pietro, taking it from her hastily. 'I should have known it would be a syringe. *Maledetto idiota.* Thank God the needle was pointing downwards. I should never have let you do it. If my Vice-Questore found out...'

'Well he won't. Or she, or it, whatever a Vice-Questore is. Just hold on a moment, will you? There's another one. I just have to work it upwards, like threading the cord back through an anorak hood. There you are.'

'*Oh Dio! Il tribunale disciplinare...*'

'Well if you don't tell them, I certainly won't. It's probably a deportable offence, isn't it, interfering with a corpse? Anyway, no one would put syringes in their pocket with the needle pointing up. Or even in someone else's pocket.' she added, as he opened his mouth to interrupt. 'What do you think was in them?'

'I've no idea. No, that's not true. I've got at least thirty ideas, in the top of my head...'

'Off, actually. Off the top of your head.' She would end up like

Gray at this rate, on constant grammar alert.

'*Off*? Why would you - ?' He shrugged. 'I'll make a note of that one later. But there's no point in guessing now. This time I've got to wait for the team. All the same...' He balanced the syringe thoughtfully in his palm, 'Was she a *drogata*, do you know? A drug user?'

'I've no idea. Gray might, I suppose.'

'Gray?'

She began to explain, but he wasn't listening. His slight movement of the woman's body to reach her T-shirt pocket had disturbed the denim jacket, hitching the sleeve up by an inch or so to reveal the wrist beneath. On the inside, where the skin was whitest, two words were written in blue ink, mimicking the useless veins beneath: NO GLOBAL. He checked the other wrist, easing back the cuff until the sharp bones were visible. Only one word on this side: GIROTONDO.

'What..?' began Pippa, but at that moment the forensic team arrived, with their tape, their plastic bags and their cameras. After them came Elisa, on the arm of Sergeant Lenzuoli, who encouraged her with low revving noises. She confirmed in a whisper that, yes, the body was Zena's, and made a swift sign of the Cross. Next came the *medico legale*, who verified, as though verification were necessary, that she was dead, and arranged for the body to be taken to the mortuary for the post-mortem.

Now, at last, Pippa could finish her question.

'But what is a Girotondo?'

He considered for a moment, running his hand up from the nape of his neck so that his hair stood out like a dirty straw halo.

'Literally, you would say 'round in a circle'. It's a children's game; they stand in a ring, holding hands...' He mimed the actions, reaching out to invisible playmates.

'Oh, I see. Like Ring-a-ring-a-roses.'

'Ring-a-what?'

'Roses. It's a nursery rhyme, a traditional English thing.'

She explained briefly, 'It's supposed to be about the plague.'

'How unpleasant. Tell me, can the English ever simply enjoy themselves without making it educational, or healthy, or character-forming? No, don't answer. I am only indulging in a little xenophobia to hide my perplexity. Let us think logically. Clearly we must look at the political explanations first.'

'Which are?' An undercover campaign for the purging of reactionary sentiment from nursery rhymes? An revolutionary cell planning the subliminal indoctrination of the under-threes?

'Forgive me. I've only given you one half of the story. You haven't heard of the *girotondo* movement, I expect? No, it doesn't matter. I don't suppose the English press covers much Italian politics beyond the Mafia and *Il Cavaliero*'s antics.'

Pippa tried to look like the sort of person who would know how much Italian political news appeared in the newspapers, rather than like the sort of person who leafed through the foreign pages with a vague sense of guilt before settling down with the cookery features. She made a non-committal, negative sort of noise.

'I thought not. Anyway, it's quite new. The first was only a few months ago.'

'The first?'

'The first *girotondo*. It's a kind of *manifestazione*. I don't know the English..'

'Manifesto? Like Marx?'

'No, no. A *manifestazione* is when people gather in the piazza to protest, to make their opinions known, to carry flags and to sing...' His voice trailed off, considering the inherent unlikelihood of such a thing among the reserved and conservative English.

'A demonstration, you mean. We have demonstrations in England. I used to go on them when I was a student. And,' she added, scrabbling in the dusty corners of her brain marked 'A Level History',' in the past people got killed on them. Peterloo.'

'Peterloo.' he replied, assuming it to be an English rhetorical convention. 'In Italy people still die.' There was a lugubrious silence before he continued. 'But not, at least not yet, on a *girotondo*. The participants join hands - like the children - around a building to protect it.'

'From demolition?' she asked, thinking about Swampy and the prostrate eco-warriors.

'No, no. You English are so literal. There are worse dangers than bulldozers, you know. Protection from the State, from the government, from losing their independence. They join hands around the courts, for example, to protest at the new judicial laws, around the television studios to protest about the new directors who are imposed - you get the idea?'

'I think so. But what could that have to do with Zena's death? Surely she couldn't have been murdered just for being a member? If there's even such a thing as membership. And the girotondo people themselves, they wouldn't kill anybody, would they?'

The question was meant to be rhetorical but Pietro considered it carefully before replying.

'I think not. They aren't the usual type for that kind of thing. The movement's led by professionals, you see; lawyers, film directors, journalists. It wouldn't be good for their credibility to use violence. Even if they knew how. '

'And the other wrist - No-Global? Would that be the same people?'

'Not exactly, I think. Of course, there would be some...' He demonstrated with two of his bus tickets.

'Overlap.'

'Overlap.' He made a quick note in the tiny space left on one ticket. 'But generally the no-global people are younger, poorer, more impulsive.' Pippa suddenly thought of Nic. 'Not violent, though, or not usually violent, whatever the government said after Genova. I wouldn't expect to see their mark on the dead, not like the star of the *Brigate Rosso.*'

He paused, making the half-smile with the other side of his mouth, where it came out as rueful, almost bitter.

'But in Italian politics there's always a danger of violence. Even in this new century, people are still killing and dying for what they believe. In England it's different, I think?'

'On the whole, yes. Except in Northern Ireland. And animals, of course.'

'Animals?' Into Pietro's head came the sudden vision of black-shirted ferrets meeting anarchist badgers for a quick punch-up. He had read *Wind in the Willows* and plenty of George Orwell, but all the same...

'Animal rights people, protestors against vivisection, fox hunting, fur coats, that sort of thing. They plant car bombs sometimes.'

Pietro was reduced to a wondering silence. His world-view had expanded to cope with many English conventions: tea with milk, dinner before eight o'clock, stopping at traffic lights. He was even making some headway at envisaging sausages at breakfast-time. But to reserve the weapons of political violence to the defence of foxes and mink... He thought of his mother's chickens. Given an egg box or two packed with Semtex, he'd make a fair guess as to which side they'd join.

'Perhaps we ought to try a different angle.' he said at last. 'The classic detective's question. Who was the last person to see Zena alive?'

VII

'Francesca.' said Elsa, circumnavigating Sergeant Lenzuoli, teapot in hand. 'It must have been Francesca.'

Elisa, under the strain of the moment, had retired to bed with a bottle of Vin Santo and the latest copy of *Motociclismo*. But upon Elsa, the crisis, after its initial horror, had awakened a dormant Blitz spirit, an indomitably stiff upper lip and a reawakened craving for real Earl Grey.

'Just a moment, darling. It's bound to be in the diary.' Her mother tongue, unused in its pure form for fifty years, was ossified in the plummy syllables of a pre-war debutante. Not even the Queen spoke like that any more. 'Wherever the diary has poodled off to.' After rummaging through the desk drawers, which were stuffed with support stockings, motorbike spares and uncompleted 1960s tax returns, she found it on the windowsill, keeping the flies off a plate of sagging profiteroles.

'Oh scrumptious! Philippa, angel, these were meant for your grand reception yesterday. How frightful of us to have forgotten them. Do please have one now. And you, of course, officer.'

Pippa duly took one and Pietro three, while Elsa leafed through the diary.

'Where are we now? Thursday isn't it, so Monday would be the fourth. Saint Plato – so unlikely, somehow. Yes, Zena's last lesson was at *dicanove* - what's that in English - seven in the evening - with Francesca Columbini. No one else would have been here then. Gray would be on his way back from Capannori, terrific lavatory places, you know, and Elisa and I would be in the flat. We always allow ourselves a martini at seven. Otto joins us if he's here, but he only got back from Milan last night. He has so many clients there. Poor dears; I suppose it's the fog that gets them down. Then Francesca's lesson would have finished at eight, and afterwards Zena would have locked up. I mean, she would normally have locked up.'

Her voice wobbled a little at the end, and she put out a hand out towards Sergeant Lenzuoli's broad arm.

'That's very helpful.' said Pietro hastily, at a fierce glance from his subordinate. 'We'll leave you in peace now. Just one thing - do you have Francesca's mobile number?'

Elsa did, of course, it being unthinkable that anyone could be unreachable by *telefonino* for a moment of the day or night. Pietro produced his own, a tiny silver oblong, from another pocket of his jeans, and made the call. He spoke in Italian, so quickly that Pippa could only catch the words '*una cosa importissima*' before he had rung off.

'*L'Agora.*'

The Agora (the word comes from the Greek *ægora*, an assembly) is now a small, serene library, tucked away on the eastern side of Lucca, near the Porta Elisa.

'Are you sure we're in the right place?' asked Pippa as they strolled along the shaded cloister and stopped to admire the fountain. She thought of the oversized cucumber frame which housed the local library at home. 'It's very peace...'

The breath to finish the word had been knocked out of her by a solid head in her stomach. The owner of the head paused, smiled angelically and called out '*Scusi, signora*', before scampering away, chased by three or four of his contemporaries. A plaintive voice floated down the cloister, '*Bimbi!*'

'The children's library.' explained Pietro. 'All the elementary classes come to wreak their own particular havoc. Are you all right?'

'Fine.' panted Pippa, who was, apart from a rather too vivid reminder of her lunchtime *panino*. 'Is she a teacher, then?'

'*La Columbini*? No, a student, I think.'

He led her past the three rooms of children's books, where the teacher was being beaten into surrender with the complete works of Geronimo Stilton, and around two more corners into a long hall. The vaguely monastic atmosphere was intensified here by the whitewashed walls, the high windows and the faded fresco which covered nearly half of the far wall. It could have been a medieval scriptorium, except that most of the scholars were bent over laptop computers, instead of parchment, and more than half were women. As they hovered in the doorway, a girl stood up, followed by the man who had been sitting opposite her.

Pietro walked across the cool stone floor, his pasty-shoes making no sound.

'Signorina Columbini?'

'*Si.*'

They spoke in Italian throughout, so that Pippa picked up only the most blatant tones of the conversation. She wasn't really sure why she was there at all, in place of Sergeant Lenzuoli. He had certainly expected to come, heaving himself to his feet in slow anticipation, but Pietro and Elsa had agreed that his first experience of genuine Earl Grey should not be hurried on any account, certainly not the trivial one of tracking down a mere murderer.

'It's all in the pot, you see.' Elsa had explained. 'So few Continentals appreciate the importance of a really well-warmed teapot.'

In any case, it was a relief to get away from that classroom, and the air of awkward grief which hung over the school. Unless that was the point; a spot of occupational therapy for the traumatized English witness. She glanced across sharply but Pietro seemed to have forgotten she was there, speaking to Francesca in a low voice. He translated the whole conversation, or what he could remember of it, into English for Pippa later. Meanwhile she contented herself with looking from one speaker to the next, nodding and smiling. The idea was to appear intelligent and perceptive but she suspected that she looked more like one of those humorous dogs people used to stick on to their rear windscreens.

'I'm Commissionario Guinizelli. We spoke on the phone a few moments ago. Thank you for agreeing...'

'A moment, please!'

The man who had stood up when they came in was now leaning across the table, his spare, almost gaunt, face inches from Pietro's. He was dark and clean-shaven, apart from a disconnected goatee beard which jutted forward as he spoke.

'Oh, Luciano.' said Pietro, in slightly exaggerated surprise. 'I didn't see you, there. *Come stai?*'

'I don't engage in small talk with agents of the State. Francesca, you haven't agreed to talk to this man, have you? Even if you have, your consent was obtained by deception or duress. Probably both. You have no obligation to say anything.'

'I know that, Luca.' said the girl, smiling. She really was, thought Pippa, very beautiful. Tall, with cascading dark hair, she had the kind of serene loveliness that Dante must have seen in Beatrice, fifty miles away in the streets of Florence. In England she would long before have been swept away from school on a lucrative modelling contract but here she was scarcely unusual. 'But I don't mind talking.' She turned to the hovering Pippa. 'I'm a real chatterbox.'

Pippa's little shoots of Italian, just about sufficient to buy an ice-cream, had already been flattened by the volley of conversation, but *chiacchierone* was onomatopoeic enough to give her the idea.

'There's nothing wrong with talking *per se*.' said Luciano, raising his voice, so that Pippa looked around nervously at the other library users, expecting a storm of shushing. But none came. Indeed, most of the students had laid down their pens, pencils or mice and were watching the exchange with open interest. At home, thought Pippa, they would at least have pretended to be annoyed. 'Oral discussion is the authentic representation of dialectic reasoning within a genuinely worker-enabled environment. But *not* in front of the police. Haven't you been listening at any of my lectures? Remember what happened to Pinelli.'

('Who was Pinelli?' asked Pippa later.

'An anarchist railway worker, taken in for questioning after the 1969 bomb in Milan. He died in mysterious circumstances, falling out of a fifth floor window of the police station. Several years later the Commissario in charge of the case also died, only he had five bullets in him at the time.'

'I see.' said Pippa, not at all sure that she did, but even less convinced that she wanted to know any more. The idea she had gleaned of Italy, that it was something like Somerset with more sun and less cider, was rapidly fading. Perhaps her mother was right; she should have tried the Algarve.)

'But Luca!' laughed Francesca, 'I don't even go to your lectures. I'm studying medicine, remember?'

'About time you changed courses, then. What's the point of being a doctor, without a proper politico-scientific analysis of the capitalist system? You're simply at the mercy of the multinational pharmaceuticals.'

'I'll cross that bridge when I come to it.' said Francesca, or rather, literally, 'I'll bandage my head when it gets broken.' The difference was rather telling. 'Right now I'm going to talk to

Dottore Guinizelli. And no, I don't need a lawyer, and no, I don't want you to come with me.'

She picked up a large rucksack from the floor, cradled it in her arms, and strode out of the room, Pietro and Pippa following behind.

Out in the courtyard she was more subdued but still smiling.

'What's this all about, please? It isn't really politics, is it? If it is then I won't be much help. I can never remember which is the Organization of Revolutionary Anarchists and which is the Federation of Anarcho-Communists.'

'I don't think that'll be a problem. I wanted to talk to you about Zena Carson. She was your English teacher, wasn't she?'

'Ye-es.' Her arms tightened around the rucksack and she gently jogged it up and down, as though soothing a fractious baby. 'Is this about her papers? They told me at the school she'd gone away, to Greece, they thought. So surely it doesn't matter now... Or is it a European thing?'

'Is what a European thing?'

'Her papers. Not having the right ones. That's what this is about, isn't it? Is it so terrible? I mean, she wasn't claiming benefits or taking jobs away from Italians or anything like that. And as for tax...'

'No, it's not her papers. I'm sorry to have to tell you this.' His voice was losing its character, fading into officialdom.

'You mean ... What, she's *dead*? An accident, was it? I heard that the Greek drivers are even worse than us. But why are you telling me?' She gave the rucksack another little squeeze, as though it reassured her. 'Oh, I suppose you need to trace her family. I'm sorry; I don't know anything about them, except that they weren't Italian at all. Most of the Americans who come here, they've got some family connection, parents or grandparents who emigrated. So they know a bit of the language and they understand the culture. But not Zena. It was all new to her, all a bit overwhelming. I think her background must have been – how can I put it? - rather Puritan. She couldn't really cope with Italian attitudes. I remember her saying once that the only things we took seriously were pleasures. She thought that was dreadful. I don't suppose all this helps you much, though, does it? I mean, once you've eliminated all the Italians, you've still got a lot of America left.'

'That's true, yes, but it isn't a problem that's arisen yet. The fact is, Zena Carson died here, in Lucca. And it looks as though she was murdered.'

'No.' Her clear skin was suddenly opaque. 'No, that can't be right. They told me she'd left. When..?'

'We're not sure yet. Her body was only found this morning. But it seems as though your Monday evening lesson would have been her last. We haven't heard from anybody yet who saw her after that. I was wondering whether you could tell me about that lesson, Signorina. All the details you can remember. Anything might help.'

She stared at them, clutching the rucksack so tightly that Pippa almost heard it squeak. 'Lesson on Monday? But I didn't have... Oh yes, I remember. We were talking about... I don't know.'

Outside, in the Piazza dei Servi, two cars came to a screeching halt in one precious parking space. There was a loud bump, horn blasts and the sound of raised voices.

'Driving.' said Francesca suddenly. 'That was it. We were talking about driving, how different it is in America. Zena gave me an article to read.'

She burrowed into the rucksack, murmuring to herself, and finally emerged with a photocopied page, a little chewed around the edges. It was a copy of an article from *Italy Daily*, a supplement to the American *Herald and Tribune*, published three weeks before. A familiar lament: the lawlessness of the Italian driver, the needless road deaths, the inefficiency of the traffic police, the incomprehensible system of junction priorities...

'Thank you.' said Pietro, handing it back. 'You still have a *zaino*, I see? But wouldn't you be more comfortable putting it down?'

'I suppose so.' Francesca blushed, placing the rucksack gently on the ground where it leaned against her leg. 'I got so used to it all those years at school that I always forget something if I don't use it. And there's loads of stuff I need now; books, medical instruments..'

'Straw?' He pointed to the wisps poking out of the top pocket.

'Straw, yes.' She looked at him defiantly. 'Biology experiments. It's terrible for the back, of course, carrying so much, but in my case most of the damage has already been done. I don't like to see the little ones with them, though.'

They looked across the courtyard at the last departing schoolchildren, each weighed down by a backpack nearly half his own size.

'One day,' prophesied Pietro, 'we'll think of a solution. Meanwhile, is there any more you can tell me about the lesson? Did Signora Carson seem different at all? Agitated, upset, afraid?'

'No, I don't think so, not more than usual. Like I said, she was never exactly a calm person, and she always seemed to be worried about something. I thought it was just the papers, the *permesso*, you know. She told me once that she hadn't got one, she was officially a *clandestina*. I asked her if there was anything I could do to help, go along with her to some office or other. Sometimes the bureaucracy here is very hard for foreigners to cope with and it's helpful to have an Italian to speak for them. But she said it didn't matter, the system was stupid anyway and she'd be leaving soon.'

'She told you that?'

'Oh yes. She didn't get on with the Italians, most of them, anyway. She seemed okay with me but she complained a lot about other people. And she didn't like teaching; correcting mistakes or explaining grammar. To be honest, I don't think she understood it very well herself. I suppose she'd still be a teacher, though, if she'd gone on to Greece, unless she could get a job as a waitress or something.'

'Would she have made a good waitress?'

Francesca paused to think, and in the sudden silence Pippa thought she could hear small noises, rustlings and piping squeals, with no visible cause. Probably some children left behind in the library. 'Efficient, I suppose. She would have brought the right dish to the right table. But not very welcoming. Poor woman. It seemed to me that she came to Europe to find some sort of peace. I'm sorry it didn't work out like that.'

'Maybe it has, now. Rather a drastic method, though. Thank you, Signorina, that's been very helpful. If we could just go back to Monday's lesson for a moment.'

'Oh. Yes.' Some of the animation had gone out of her voice. 'But there isn't really any more to say. It was just an ordinary lesson.'

'Did you talk about driving for the whole hour, or did you discuss anything else?'

'No, nothing else. It's a big subject, especially for foreigners; Americans, that is, and northern Europeans. They can't believe how dangerous our roads are. They hear all about it before they come, but they think it's exaggerated, some kind of myth. Then when they find out it's true, it becomes a kind of obsession and they can't stop talking about it.'

'In Lucca?' Pietro was incredulous. 'There's nothing wrong with our driving in Lucca. They ought to go to Napoli.'

'Let's ask your friend, then. Signorina,' She switched to a careful English, 'The drive in Italia - how is it?'

Pippa shuddered, remembering the Aurelia.

'You see, Commissario?'

He grinned. 'Now you mention it, I have heard one or two complaints. But did Signora Carson drive herself?'

'In America, yes, but not here. She'd brought her American licence to show me. I got mine out too and we compared them. Oh, and we talked a bit about Fiat and General Motors. She's - she was - interested in politics.'

'Like Professore Bianchi?'

She smiled. 'No one could be quite as interested in politics as Luca. But, yes, I think she went to some meetings.'

'What sort of meetings?'

'I don't know exactly. Left-wing, anti-government, Luca's sort of thing. I'm not really interested, myself. I met Luca through... some other friends.'

The squeaking noises were growing more insistent, and Pippa was growing less and less convinced that they were coming from the children's library. The rucksack gave a sudden lurch and Francesca nudged it with her foot, as though it were an old dog blocking a doorway.

'So you wouldn't know whether she had any political enemies?'

'What, here in Italy? No - no, I wouldn't have thought so.'

'We'd have to ask Luciano?'

'I suppose so. But he wouldn't know anything either; I'm sure of it.'

'You and he, you're,' There was a momentary hesitation, 'good friends?'

She flushed a little. 'Friends. Let's just say friends. I - I like him a lot, but he's very busy. Very committed.'

'Of course. Just one more thing. The end of the lesson - was that the same as usual?'

'I think so, yes. I can't remember anything different, so I think it must have been.'

'Did you leave together, or did Signora Carson stay behind?'

'She stayed. She usually stayed, to lock up, I suppose. Sometimes I'd meet her a few minutes later in the street, if I'd stopped to look in a shop window or to get some money from the Bancomat.'

'And on Monday? Did you see her again after that lesson?'

'I can't remember. I don't think I did. But she might have gone past me while I wasn't looking.'

'Of course. Did you go straight home that day, or were you window-shopping? It might help if you think about what you did on Tuesday and work back.'

'Like when you can't find your purse.' She nodded. 'That's it, yes. I had to make a lot of calls on Tuesday, so I put some credit on my mobile phone. You know, you can do it at the Bancomat machines now. I was there, at the bank on the corner and it took me ages. Then I had a look at the shop next door - they'd got some new denim skirts in the window - and I read through the Teatro Gigli poster to see whether there was anything Luca might want to go to. He doesn't like the theatre in general, but sometimes they do a bit of Pirandello.'

'So you were there for quite some time?'

'Oh yes, a good ten or fifteen minutes.'

'Did many people walk past you during that time?'

'Yes, quite a few, I think. It was a nice night for a *passeggiata*. No one was in a hurry.'

'But you didn't see anyone you knew?'

'No. My back would have been turned to them, but any of my friends, or my family's friends, would have stopped to say hello.'

'And Zena?'

'No. If I'd seen her first, and called out, then she would have replied, but she never made the first move to greet anyone. I'd notice her sometimes, scuttling along the edge of the pavement, head down, desperate not to make eye contact. So, yes, it could have been like that on Monday. She could easily have scurried past without my seeing her.'

Pippa had by now completely lost the thread of the conversation and was watching Francesca's rucksack with horrified fascination. The straw stuffed into the top was evidently in an advanced state of infestation, for it heaved and shuddered constantly. Once she seemed to see a sliver of squirming pinkish-white, and once something shiny and black, that appeared for a moment and then was gone.

'Do you live in the city?'

'Yes, just inside the walls near the Piazza San Donato. Look, I'm sorry, but I've got a lot of work to do. There's a test tomorrow. Do you mind if..?'

'Not at all.' Pietro made a graceful gesture of dismissal and spoke the traditional words of good luck. '*In bocca al lupo.*'

'*Crepi.*' she laughed, and reached down to pick up the rucksack.

She was almost in time. With a final lurch the bag toppled sideways and fell to the ground in a confusion of scrabbling grunts and tiny yelping noises.

'*I miei coniglietti! State tranquilli - vengate a mamma!*' Kneeling on the tiles, in an attitude of reverence, Francesca gathered the rucksack to her breast.

'Delicate, those medical instruments?' enquired Pietro.

She gazed up at him in Pre-Raphaelite supplication. 'You're not anything to do with the security here, are you? If they withdraw my permission I've got nowhere to study except at home, with Mamma leaning over my shoulder and asking if she can test me every five minutes. No, of course you're not.'

All the same, it was Pippa she turned to with the top of the backpack open. 'See?' she said in English. 'Is rrrab-bits babies.'

There were five or six of them curled together, their black and pink eyes round and solemn. Pippa reminded herself not to be sentimental. She had browsed through enough Tuscan cookbooks to know that a rabbit was a staple source of protein, not a fluffy baby-substitute.

'Like Mr. McGregor?'

'In the Potter Beatrix? No, no!' She reverted to Italian, fast and fervent. 'The opposite of Signor McGregor! I'm saving my rabbits, not eating them. My uncle Fabio breeds them for dinner - five times a week they have *coniglio con gli olivi* in that house. I have to pretend I like it, love it, that I'm desperate to cook it for my boyfriend, that I keep the rabbits under my bed to fatten them up. *Zio* Fabio believes it all, he is a crazy carnivore and he can't stand my mother, so the thought of rabbit droppings on her cotto floors... Of course, the poor bunnies get nowhere near our house or the casserole. I take them to the walls and let them go free there. Only it's too cold first thing in the morning, when I come from

Uncle Fabio's, and there are too many dogs. I have to wait for the siesta, when only tourists are around. They love rabbits, the *Anglo-Sassoni*, stroke their ears and give them apples. And I have a secret place - it's safe to tell you this?' Pietro nodded gravely, 'a place near the walls where they can come every day for a good meal of oats and lettuce. You won't tell anyone?'

'Vegetarian's honour.'

VIII

'Are you really?' asked Pippa, when Pietro came to the end of his translation. They were still in the Agora, leaning on the wall and watching the fountain.

'Really what?'

'A vegetarian.'

'Well, I don't eat British beef. So, what do you think of the Signorina's story?'

'She's very nice, isn't she? And the little rabbits are sweet.'

'As you know very well, Signorina Avvocato, that goes no way at all to answering my question.'

'Well, I....'

She was saved from having to say any more by the appearance of Luciano on the other side of the glass door. He was evidently under the impression that this, like the one on the other side of the courtyard, was automatic, for he walked straight ahead, making no attempt to open it, until his forehead collided with the reinforced glass.

Illusion intact, he retreated and commenced a kind of solo Morris dance, prancing forwards and backwards in front of the door and waggling his fingers in the air, in a vain effort to confuse the electronic trigger into acknowledging his existence.

Pietro, either subject to the same delusion, or simply trying to signal the true state of affairs, launched into a little folk dance of his own, embellished with the odd shrug as a counterpoint to the principal theme. For what must have been seven or eight seconds, though it seemed to Pippa far longer, the two men faced each other through the glass, gesturing in frantic symmetry as though performing some grotesque mirrored ballet.

Finally Pippa, who had never much liked folk dancing even at school, yanked Pietro out of the way and opened the door. Luciano, who had been preparing a particularly belligerent docido, stumbled through with folded arms and such velocity that only six hundred years of masonry kept him from promenading all the way into the fountain.

'Is it true?' he demanded, steadying himself against the wall. 'Is Zena Carson really dead, or are you just trying to trap us?'

'Signora Carson has, alas, been taken from us.' said Pietro gravely. 'We are investigating the circumstances of her death.'

'Don't use those bloody Christian Democrat euphemisms with me, Guinizelli. Dead is dead, okay? Not disappeared or extinguished or taken to a better place. And what do you mean by 'we'? Who's this?'

'By 'we', I mean the Polizia, the forces of law and order, the guarantors of Italian justice...'

'Pah!' Luciano made a violent noise, accompanied by an even more violent gesture. One of Pietro's eyelids gave a brief tic. Pippa wasn't sure, but she thought it might have been a wink.

'...embodied, in this instance, in my humble and unworthy self. And this lady is Philippa Laud. She's advising me on the particular linguistic aspects of the case.'

Luciano's hand twitched. He glared down at it, willing it to be still, but the legacy of a good mamma was stronger than the ideological crusade. The hand rose and shook Pippa's.

'Another American spy?' he asked, in cumbersome English.

Pippa was about to reply, but Pietro spoke first, still in English.

'Another? Do you mean that Zena Carson was a spy?'

'I refuse to answer questions framed in the language of global imperialism.'

'*Va bene.*' Pietro repeated the question in Italian. 'We know that she went to political meetings. Were they with your group?'

'What do you know about my group? You've got a file on us, I suppose, back at the Questura. How much of that comes from the CIA? God, it makes me sick, the way not even the fascist tools of the State can get along without American help. It's time for Italy to grow up.'

'I quite agree.' said Pietro quietly. 'We could begin by working together to find out how this woman died. We've known each other a long time, you and I. I know we haven't always seen eye to eye...'

'It was my card.' muttered Luciano.

'What?'

'My *Topolino* card. Class Two at the Scuola Materna. I brought it to school but at going-home time the *maestra* put it in your bag. Not that private property is legitimate, of course, and Mickey Mouse, whatever pseudo-Italian name they give him, is nothing but a weapon of rampant globalization. But my dialectic wasn't so clear at the age of four. I cried for a week.'

Pietro looked genuinely stricken.

'*Porco miseria*, I'm sorry, Luca. I never knew it was your card. I thought Papà had bought it as a surprise. Why didn't you ask for it back?'

'You were bigger than me. Anyway, it probably did me good. Taught me the essentially criminal nature of all quasi-economic transactions. But about Zena Carson, I don't know. If I tell you that we were suspicious of her, that gives me a motive, doesn't it? Then you can pin the whole thing on me. I'd be safer saying nothing.'

'You've already said enough, if I was that kind of policeman. But I'm not, just as I don't believe you're the sort of man who puts personal safety before justice. Anyway, assassination isn't your style, is it, Luca?'

'I'm completely committed to non-violence, if that's what you mean. Whilst acknowledging, of course, the fundamentally murderous nature of the international capitalist conspiracy and the legitimate right of the oppressed to respond in whatever mode they consider appropriate. But I didn't kill Zena. And neither did Francesca.'

'You sound very sure of that.'

'I am. I know it as a fact.' There was a short pause. Pippa had the impression that Luciano had meant to stop there, with no rhetorical flourishes, but Pietro was waiting for more.

'Francesca's problem is that she isn't angry enough. She's quite incapable of looking at society in ideological terms, of identifying the forces of repression. The world, for Francesca, is simply a collection of individuals; potential friends and patients. Oh, and cuddly animals, of course. And she takes all that Hippocratic rigmarole terribly seriously; she's got a load of ethical problems about abortion and stuff. She couldn't kill for anything.'

'Or anybody?'

'You mean me? You've noticed that much then? She's a nice girl; it's a pity she's so bourgeois. No, those Catholic scruples go too deep. They get them young, you know - Nativity plays and First Communion dresses. We can't compete, not with a girl like

Francesca. And I won't get tied up in all that world; monogamy and babies and Sunday supper with the parents-in-law. I need to be free, unencumbered, to continue my work.'

'A bit like a priest.' suggested Pietro.

Luciano frowned. 'That's what Francesca said. But it isn't at all the same. Priests are repressed, inhibited, unnatural. I've no objection to sex, not even to a medium-term relationship, provided the woman's committed to radical socialism.'

'Well, it's a relief to know that.' said Pietro drily. 'Now what about Signora Carson?'

'Zena, yeah... We don't really go for all this patronymic stuff. There's this group in Lucca, right, the Committee for Radical Re-engagement. I'm the...'

'Leader? Chairman?'

'Certainly not. That type of hierarchical formulation simply replicates the patriarchal structures we're dedicated to destroy. Abolish, I mean. Or maybe subvert. In any case, I'm merely a facilitator, a co-ordinator, an enabler of individual autonomous activism.'

'And what forms does this activism take?'

'Purely democratic ones, Commissario. You know; marches, demonstrations, *girotondi*.'

'And Signora - Zena - took part in these?'

'She did, yes. At least at the beginning. The group was only founded last summer, after the election of this crypto-fascist government. Zena came to the inaugural meeting and for the first few months she was really keen. We planned a big demonstration for *Ferragosto* and she did a lot of organizing for that. Although on the day,' he added vaguely, 'we didn't get an awfully good turn-out. I wonder..?'

'I don't think you can blame her for that.' said Pietro, trying not to smile. On *Ferrogosto*, the fifteenth of August, every self-respecting Lucchese, revolutionary or otherwise, was in the mountains or on the beach. The city would have been packed, but only with tourists. He could imagine them, training their camcorders on the feeble protest, listening, bemused, to the crackling speeches, searching their guidebooks for an explanation and concluding that, interesting though it no doubt was, it wasn't a patch on the *Palio* in Siena. 'The date...'

'I suppose you're right. These damn Lucchesi, so bloody

conventional.' At Pietro's raised eyebrows he continued hastily. 'Oh, I know I was born and brought up in Lucca, but my family's not really Tuscan, you know. We're actually Southerners, from Palermo. *Terroni*, I suppose you'd call us.'

'I certainly wouldn't.' said Pietro, with vehemence and complete honesty. For one thing, he wouldn't use such an offensive term of anyone, however earthy their Southern roots, particularly not of honourable Sicilian families, who had their own, rather direct, methods of responding to insults. And for another, he knew perfectly well that Luciano's family had lived two hundred metres away from his own for at least five generations. The sole exception had been one of Luca's uncles, who had once been seconded to Taormina by his banking employers. He had returned within three months, complaining of the heat, the food and the women, and now devoted his retirement to plotting independence for Lucca, along the lines of Padania, the virtual republic which haunts the imaginations of the *Lega Nord*. Luciano himself, Pietro suspected, had never been further south than Rome, and that only on a school trip.

'Zena?' he tried again. 'After *Ferragosto*?'

'Oh yes. Well, she was very positive about it, said that Lucca obviously needed help in dealing with the political implications of the Marian myth and that we ought to do something really spectacular for the *Addolorata*. That's exactly a month later, apparently. I can't say I'm terribly well acquainted with these religious feasts.'

'Was Zena a Catholic, then?'

'No, she wasn't, but she'd read something about Our Blessed Lady -' Luciano blushed at this sudden slip, as thought caught sucking his thumb or nuzzling a teddy bear, ' - about the mythic figure of Mary as a proto-feminist. And she'd got an Italian diary full of recipes and saints' days. But the weird thing was, when it came to it, she simply didn't turn up. She didn't come to the last organization meeting four days before, either. Very strange.'

'Not really. The *Addolorata*, that's Our Lady of Sorrows...'

'That's right. We focused on the sorrows of Italian socialism under this oppressive regime...'

'...is on September 15th, right?'

'Yes, I told you, exactly a month after the last one.'

'So the organizational meeting was on..?'

Luciano counted on his fingers, ' Fourteen, thirteen, twelve, eleven. The eleventh of September. We're not deficient in basic arithmetic, Commissario Guinizelli.'

'No, I wasn't suggesting that you were. What's your subject, again, Professor?'

'Political science. You know that.'

'And there's nothing that strikes you, as a political scientist, about the eleventh of September. September the eleventh 2001?'

'Oh *that*.' He sounded mildly disappointed, as though a promising student had given a pedestrian answer. 'America's little local difficulty with its Middle Eastern ambitions? In my view its significance has been vastly overstated. I've written an article on that very point.'

'To an American, though?'

'What?'

'Its significance to an American. Even a formerly left-wing American. Are you sure that's been overstated?'

'Zena? Zena wouldn't... But she did.'

Pietro and Pippa watched in silence as the sun rose over the horizon of Luciano's brain.

'And the dates fit. She came back to the meetings a few weeks later, as though nothing had happened. But it had, something had definitely changed. She seemed as keen as ever, but she didn't propose things any more, just waited for the others to make suggestions. And she listened a lot. I noticed that, how much she listened, because she never did before. At the beginning, right at the beginning, she'd wanted to do something at Camp Darby. Do you know Camp Darby, Commissario?'

'I might have come across it.'

'Like that, eh? The Imperio-fascist bloc in hedgehog formation. Let me refresh your memory. Massive U.S. military base near Pisa, obscene symbol of Italy's subordination? Anyway, Zena suggested we should all go there and stage a kind of demo at Christmas. Well, I say a demo, more of a vigil. Like a *girotondo*, except that of course we couldn't reach right round the place, there only being nineteen of us on a good day, and fewer when there's shopping to be done. You know that thing in the First World War when the English and German soldiers met and sang carols? Well, we thought we would just go there, as many of us as could make it, and sing to them. In English, Christmas stuff they would know. Peace and goodwill to all men. A bit pious, I know, but it's good propaganda. We knew that security would be even tighter than usual, so we didn't advertise it, didn't tell anyone outside the group.'

'And?'

'And the road was closed. Simple as that. They said it was roadworks, but what kind of roadworks get carried out at eight pm on Christmas Eve? No, somebody knew something. I didn't think of Zena at the time, but after the other stuff...'

'Other stuff?'

'I've got the membership list on my laptop. There, you can pull me in under Data Protection if you can't find anything else. One day Zena asked to borrow it, said hers had crashed and she had some urgent translations to do. Well you know me, I'm not tied up on personal property, so I said okay. She only had it for two days, then said hers had been repaired. That was odd, thinking about it now. Two days to get a computer fixed in Italy? Anyway, during the next couple of weeks the members all got little visits from your colleagues in the military sector.'

'The Carabinieri?'

'The very same. Of course, they said they were doing spot checks, the usual thing, making sure people really live where they say they do and aren't fiddling the property tax. But somehow the conversations always got round to politics and they all ended up with warnings. Nothing heavy, just friendly advice that certain activities weren't - what did mine say? - weren't "consonant with the disposition of modern *Italia*". There were other things too; letters that didn't arrive, strange noises on the phone line, web sites crashing. Nothing unusual for Italy, nothing you could prove without sounding paranoid, but together they painted a picture.'

'Did you do anything?'

'Personally, no. But some of the other members were getting pretty annoyed, and Zena's name was being whispered. Then at one meeting a few people started talking. Nothing explicit, just general stuff about security and leaks, but Zena knew they meant her. She didn't say anything but she never turned up again.'

'How long ago was this?'

'Three, four weeks? I didn't see her after that.'

'But Francesca did?'

'Sure. She was Franca's English teacher, wasn't she? But Francesca never comes to meetings and we don't talk about the group. I guess maybe she heard something at home, but the subject never came up between us. As far as the group was concerned, we were just glad to have got rid of her. Zena, I mean, not Franca. Like I said, she had some good ideas at the beginning, but she was never exactly sweetness and light. And once people started to get suspicious....Well, you can imagine. It was pretty uncomfortable all round.'

Somewhere in the city a bell rang and he looked at his watch.

'*Dio*, is that the time? I've got a lecture in half an hour. Is there anything else you need to know?'

'No. No, I don't think so.' Now it was Pietro's turn to struggle. 'You - you've been very helpful. I appreciate it.'

'Always ready to help the *polizotti*. The boys in blue' he added in English. Almost in English. 'And, er,'

'Yes?'

'Kind regards to your mother.'

'And to yours.'

IX

'And now I need to think' said Pietro, back in the Piazzi dei Servi at the end of his translation.

Pippa wasn't surprised. It had been therapeutic, in a mildly boring way, tracing the long tendrils of incomprehensible speech, but she couldn't have been of any help. 'Yes, I'd better be getting back as well.' What there was to get back to, she tried not to imagine. The third conditional, perhaps.

'No!' said Pietro with the urgency she had once dreamed of inspiring in Jonathan. 'No, I can't think *alone*.' Only an Italian could have said the word with such existential despair. 'I have to do a lot of speaking when I think. I need someone to...'

'Bounce your ideas off?'

'Bounce? Like a ball?' He made a basketball dribbling gesture on the head of a passing nun. 'Yes, it's perfect. How do the English find these idioms? A bouncee, then, that is what I need.'

By now they had passed through the Piazza Bernadini onto the Via Santa Croce, the principal eastern street of the city centre. It was four o'clock and the shops were re-opening after the long lunch and siesta break, their heavy blinds rolling up with sharp metallic clankings. They passed the Body Shop and Pippa felt a glimmer of pride. Idioms and green shampoo. At least there were two things to be said for the English.

'Aha!' said Pietro in his Great Detective voice, as they approached the junction with the Via Filungo. Pippa looked around for the vital clue which must be lying before them. But there was nothing, nothing but tall buildings, obscuring the sun, and a pair of blond tourists locking up bikes in front of the Leonardo da Vinci exhibition. Pietro approached them.

'Excuse me,' he said in English, 'but did you hire these bicycles?'

Since the name of the shop was emblazoned on each frame, it wasn't exactly a breathtaking deduction.

'Yaas.' said the man, with suspicious care.

Pietro took out his identity card. 'I am from the Italian police. Tourist Liaison Division. We are carrying out a *controllo a campione*, a..'

'Spot check?' suggested Pippa, as officially as she could manage.

'Spot check, exactly. On the bicycles. We need to be sure that our very greatly welcomed visitors are safe as they ride about our beautiful city.'

'You need not worry.' said the blonde woman. She had pale blue eyes and a sprinkling of freckles. 'The bicycles are perfectly maintained. We are Dutch, and so we know about these things.'

Pietro shook his head sorrowfully. 'I am so sorry. Italian bureaucracy - you have heard of it, perhaps? We are obliged - absolutely obliged - to take these bicycles away for inspection of the most rigorous nature.'

'But our passports.' said the Dutchman. 'We have left our passports at the bicycle shop. If we do not return the bicycles then we cannot retrieve our passports. We will be stranded.' Stranded, his expression added, in this wild, undisciplined country, where crazy policemen can commandeer bicycles at will.

'Fear not.' said Pietro, who had once played the Archangel Gabriel in an English-language nativity play. 'Return to the bicycle shop and give them this.'

He reached into his pocket and drew something out with a flourish. It was one of the old bus tickets, scrawled over with English vocabulary. The Dutch stared.

'Don't give them this.' he added hastily, 'Tell them that Pietro Guinizelli has the bicycles. Tell them, moreover,' He glanced at Pippa, proud of his choice of word, 'that under the authority vested in me by the Italian government, I authorize you to take two more bicycles, free of charge, for the rest of the day.'

The couple looked at one another in mute bewilderment, handed Pietro the keys to the bike locks and walked briskly away down the Via Filungo, the achievements of Leonardo da Vinci forgotten in the urgent imperative to recover their passports and escape this Mediterranean Bedlam. Next year they would stick to Luxembourg.

'Try a tandem this time!' called Pietro after them, and they broke into a trot. He shrugged. 'Rather nervous. Must be all that cheese.'

He unlocked the bikes and inspected them critically. 'Saddle down a bit, I think. She's taller than you are.'

'Pietro,' began Pippa, feeling that she was playing the bumbling sidekick with rather too much verisimilitude, 'are these bikes evidence?'

'Of course not.' His voice was indistinct as he bent over one of the seatposts. 'They're for us to ride.' He straightened up and looked at her, a dreadful apprehension darkening. 'You can ride a bicycle, can't you?'

'Of course I can. I rode my bike to work every day in England. Well, every day that it didn't rain. Or snow. Or hail. And not when it was foggy, of course. Or icy.'

'Ah. The Occasional Cyclist. It sounds like a play by Dario Fo. Sorry, did you say something?'

'Where? Where are we going on these hijacked machines?'

He shrugged. 'Around.'

'Around.' turned out to mean, as do so many things in Lucca, the walls. Pippa's only previous experience of city walls had been on a school visit to York, where they had trudged in single file through the claustrophobic passages, unable to pass even the most diminutive Japanese tourist without a ceremonial waltz to avoid body contact. Lucca's grassy ramparts were on another scale altogether. Broad enough for motor vehicles, private cars were now prohibited, leaving the tree-lined promenade free for walkers, cyclists and rollerskaters.

'You've really never been on the walls before?' asked Pietro in fascinated pity as they negotiated the steep slope to the top.

'No.' Pippa was grimly determined not to get off and push, and had no breath to spare for idle conversation. The fact that she had only been in Lucca for eighteen hours, eight of them asleep and most of the rest in his own company, was evidently no excuse for not having paid her immediate respects to *Le Mura*.

The views, when they reached the top, were worth the rasping throat and the gap where her knees used to be. On one side they looked down at the city; at the burnt earth roofs and ochre walls, peeling discreetly, like an aristocrat in scuffed brogues. On the other they gazed across the Lucchese plain, towards the fuzzy dark green hills and the distant mountains. Pippa wondered which way she should be looking, and for what. Unless it was the walls themselves...

'No, they aren't evidence either.' But the best place to think is on a bicycle, and the best place to ride a bicycle is on the walls. Qed.'

'Qued? Oh, Q.E.D.'

'You don't pronounce it qued?'

'Never.'

He looked mildly disappointed. 'What about 'very important person'?'

'V.I.P.'

'Not a veep?'

'Certainly not a veep. It sounds like something you clean the loo with.'

He sighed. 'Oh dear. For us it's the height of international chic. Never mind. Are you coming or what?'

He had already set off, pedalling with such furious intensity that Pippa had to stand up out of her saddle to keep up with him and toddlers on tricycles were hastily whisked out of his path. 'Etruscan twit.' she muttered, as she caught up with him at the next but one baluardo. He eased up, backpedalling like a schoolboy.

'What's a twit?'

'Sorry?' It was more of a pant than a word.

'You called me an Etruscan twit. Etruscan I understand. Twit?'

'Oh no.' Pippa stopped, jamming on her brakes so hard that she came near to somersaulting over the handlebars. Insulting a police officer was probably one of the more heinous Italian felonies, like eating salad with pasta or not going to the beach for Ferragosto. She remembered Pinelli and peered surreptitiously over the edge of the wall. It looked like a soft landing, at least.

'I won't throw you over, it might damage the bicycle. Anyway, I take 'Etruscan' as a compliment. 'Twit', perhaps, is not. Is it highly obscene and libellous?'

'Probably libellous. Most things are under English law, but certainly not obscene. It's just a rather old-fashioned word for an idiot. My grandfather used to use it.'

'Then so will I.' In the absence of any further bus ticket-space, he fished a paper bag out of a nearby litter-bin and made his note. '*Twit.* Plural *twits*?' He got back into the saddle and continued at a more civilised pace. 'And now, setting aside your English instincts for fair play and the protection of small pieces of meat, please tell me what's wrong with Francesca Columbini's story.'

'It's that obvious, is it?'

'Sticks out like a sore toe. You've got one of those faces, Signorina, the kind that can't hide a single thought However did you survive in court?'

'I didn't, really; that's one reason why I'm here. But Francesca - it was just the driving licence.'

'Zena's licence? The one Francesca said she was shown? Why is that a problem? Did Zena not drive?'

'Yes, she drove, in the States, and she had a licence. Only it's in my bedside table.'

He stopped pedalling altogether and gave a plaintive sigh. 'I do wish people would tell me things. Please, go on.'

She went on, feeling increasingly foolish, to describe her discovery in the drawer, her irrational conviction that Zena was hiding in the flat and the comforting explanation that had allowed her, finally, to sleep. It all seemed much longer ago than the night before. The only part she left out was her case conference with Pierrotino.

'I forgot all about it this morning until one of the students was paying his bill …'

'The euro.' He nodded. 'Yes, the notes couldn't have been put in the drawer before January. It must have been months before that when she used the room.'

'Yes but that doesn't mean that Francesca was lying. Maybe the stuff was only put in the drawer on Monday night, after the lesson.'

'By who – whom?' He looked like a puppy who has just grasped the point of a lamp-post.

Pippa gave a yes-you're-a-big-boy nod. 'By Zena herself, perhaps - or the murderer.'

'Is the flat usually locked?'

'I don't think so. It wasn't last night, and I didn't notice a key. I just closed the door behind me this morning. But the only entrance is through the school, apart from the shower door I told you about.'

'That doesn't help much, even assuming that Elsa and Elisa remember to keep the place secure when no one's there, which is by no means certain. We've still got everyone at the school; teachers, students, cleaners, who could have slipped through,' he pronounced the word 'sleeped', 'and put the documents in the drawer, not to mention anyone who could wander in while the main door's open. And no one knew before Tuesday that you were coming, did they?

They wouldn't expect the flat to be used.'

'No, of course not. I wouldn't have been here at all if Zena hadn't disappeared. They only hired me to replace her.'

'I see.' He bent over the handlebars for a moment, fiddling with the bell. 'But I'm afraid it doesn't let Francesca off the hook.'

'Because she was the last person to see Zena? The last person we know about, I mean.'

'No, not just that. Her story's still - what do you say? - dodgy? It was raining on Monday evening at eight o'clock. I was cycling home so I remember.'

'So?'

'So it wasn't a "nice night" to go window-shopping.'

'Is that all? Come on - what's a bit of drizzle when there's a new Prada handbag out? You don't appreciate the importance of these things.'

'And you don't appreciate the nature of Lucchese rain. It isn't just 'a bit of drizzle'. When it rains in Lucca it really rains. Buckets, teems, peeses it down, pours like pigs and sheep...'

'You mean cats and dogs.'

'No, worse than that. Even with an umbrella, no Italian would hang around the streets in that. And they certainly wouldn't describe it as a "nice night".'

'So why did she say it then? Why tell a deliberate lie about something so obvious as the weather?'

'I've no idea.' He started pedalling again, as though winding some internal clockwork. After five silent minutes he suddenly braked. 'Let's stop here.'

They leaned their bikes against a bench and looked out across the suburbs, at the petrol stations, the bars and the wide blocks of flats with washing suspended from the balconies. It was messier than the city inside the walls and somehow reassuring.

'What's the safest kind of lie to tell?'

Pippa thought back over fifteen years of unfinished homework, non-existent sleepover parties and unfiled affidavits. 'The kind that's nearest to the truth, I suppose.'

'Exactly. And the most successful alibi is the one that is...' His fingertips rubbed together as if crumbling a fine powder. '...full of little details, internally consistent, you understand, and presented with great confidence. Because it is true, you see, every tiny fact and observation. The only flaw is, it happened at a different time.'

'The lesson...?'

'You see, I remember the Monday before last as well. I'm in a cycling team, nothing high-powered, just a group of us who were kids together, but we go out for a training ride together now and again. Just to make sure that we haven't rusted up entirely. The last time was the Monday before last. It was a beautiful evening, warm and still with just a hint of a breeze and the air full of herbs. I think that was the day Francesca was telling us about. As for this week, either she didn't notice it was raining or she's lost all the details from her mind.' He drew the palm of his hand across his forehead. 'Either way, it doesn't look good.'

'But you don't think she did it, do you?'

'The murder? Probably not. She doesn't seem the type to kill, except perhaps for some great principle. But in that case she'd be proud to admit it, would want to suffer the martyrdom of prison. I've known one or two like that, disappointed we don't have the death penalty. But then,' he shrugged, 'It's dangerous to make these speculations, especially so early. I wouldn't have thought she was the type to lie, either. She's in love with Luciano and so who knows?'

'Could she be protecting him, do you think? Has he got a real motive, with that Committee of his?'

'Oh, he's got a motive yes; a very Italian, very political, very Lucianesque motive. When we were nine he was already reading Gramsci. But I think he was telling the truth when he said he didn't kill her. And even when he said Francesca didn't, although I don't know how he could be sure.'

Again there was a long silence as they looked out across the Lucchese plain, at the glinting Serchio winding west towards the sea. The peace was broken by a jaunty rendition, apparently from nowhere, of *What Shall We Do with the Drunken Sailor*. For a few seconds they stared at one another, then Pietro clapped his hand to the pocket of his jeans.

'I change the ring tone every day.' he explained, drawing out his mobile phone. 'in the hope of finding one I can bear. I don't think this is it. *Pronto? Si. Si. Si. Si, subito.*'

'Agostino.' he explained, retrieving his bike. 'My Sergeant Lenzuoli. Apparently your friend Graham has turned up, in great distress and excitement. He wants to speak to me with the utmost urgency.'

X

According to the best of dictionaries, the word *subito* literally means 'immediately' or 'at once'. But even in disciplined Lucca it can be stretched by an afternoon or two before anyone really notices. It was quite impressive, therefore, that Pietro and Pippa arrived back at the *Piccola Casa* within forty minutes of the sergeant's call.

First, of course, they had to return the bikes, freewheeling down from the walls into a wide square sprawled with bicycles, tandems and pedal-powered carriages. They stopped outside one of the cycle hire shops, where an English stockbroker was trying to negotiate a discount, on the basis, apparently, that he was rich enough not to need it. The woman behind the desk was shaking her head and pointing at a price list, but the twitch at the corner of her mouth suggested that she understood not only the broker's excruciating Italian but also the English asides he was making to his wife.

'*Ciao, Pietro!*' she called, interrupting the Englishman's declaration that he was '*molto influenzale*'. Perhaps it was as well, since the phrase didn't mean, as he intended, that he had friends in high places, but rather that he was infected by the flu in a particularly virulent form. She offered him a cough sweet and continued. '*Lorenzo è in fondo.*'

Pietro nodded, and plunged through an open doorway at the back, leading into a shadowy sanctuary festooned with chains and inner tubes. It was clearly a sacred retreat, unsullied for decades by the female foot, and Pippa had no intention of shattering the tradition. A bit of gender segregation never did any harm, she told herself as she wandered about the shop, peering at black and white photographs of cycle races and breathing in the heady mix of oil and rubber. In any case, apart from the decapitation danger posed by the dangling chain-sets, the men were speaking in fast, colloquial Italian, the nearest Lucca gets to a dialect, and she would have understood even less than at the Agora.

'A policeman!' said Lorenzo, placing an oily hand on the portion of his overalls that covered his heart. 'Exactly what we need. Two of our bikes have been reported stolen. Kidnapped, in fact.'

'*Eccole*.' Pietro made a dramatic gesture towards the front of the shop. 'The case is solved. If only they were all so simple. They got back to you then, the Dutch couple?'

'Only just. They looked terrified. What did you do, get your gun out?'

'That'll be the day. I dismantled the bloody thing within ten minutes of being issued with it and it'll stay like that till I get my pension.'

'You won't get any pension at that rate. What if the authorities find out?'

'My three-year-old nephew has a plastic Zorro pistol. He lends it to me for state occasions. That reminds me, I must bring him in for a proper *bici*. His father's got no idea. Bought him an American mountain bike, can you believe? And my sister married this clown. Anyway, we're on an urgent call, so I'd better make tracks. How much do I owe you?'

'Put your money away, Zorro. Spend it on the young lady instead. *Straniera*, isn't she?'

'English, yes, but it's strictly professional.' His eyelid gave the same tic as before, but Lorenzo, unlike Pippa, had no difficulty in recognizing it as a wink.

At the traffic lights Charles practised the breathing exercise, slowly and calmly, as recommended in the pregnancy manual. In through the nose, a pause, out through slightly parted lips. He liked that, the thought of all those pregnant women with their mouths open, while he stole their breathing techniques. It worked, as well; as he reached the outskirts of Lucca he was beginning to feel in control again. The autostrada had been a nightmare; five hours of crawling queues interspersed with crazy dashes through the tunnels. More than once he'd thought he wouldn't make it. The lights changed, and he gave the last breath out. Calm.

It was definitely a Graham day. However often he tugged at his nape, trying to coax his hair out to a decently poetic length, he remained resolutely Graham. The terrible thing sat on his stomach like a bag of wet sand. All he could think about was unloading it, whatever the consequences. It would be a relief to be prosecuted, imprisoned; any external affliction to balance this plodding guilt. He looked across the table at the bland face of Sergeant Lenzuoli. Neither had spoken for the past half hour. As a well-brought up Canadian, Gray inclined towards the English in his conversational style, and since the weather was fine today, had been fine yesterday and showed every sign of being fine tomorrow, there was little scope for discussion.

Sergeant Lenzuoli, on the other hand, from his days at the seminary, had acquired a wide range of opening observations, appropriate to reluctant confessees, blushing *fidanzati* and parishioners who had received an unexpected windfall from the *Lotto* and might be persuaded to share it for the good of their souls. None of these, however, seemed at all appropriate to the present encounter. He contented himself, therefore, with occasionally covering the young man's hand with his own huge paw and patting it in the style recommended in clerical circles ten years before, though now discredited as potentially ambiguous. Gray gave no response to these gestures other than a faint tightening around his knuckles and an intensified stare at the four remaining crumbs from Pietro's *panino*.

The crumbs were the first things that Pippa noticed, as well, and her stomach rumbled in noisy remembrance.

'Sorry.' she said, sitting down by Gray and immediately standing up again.

'What's the matter?' His voice sounded odd, as though during the half hour he had forgotten how to use it. 'You can sit there, it's fine by me.'

'It's just that...' How could she explain it, that she'd automatically taken that seat as though he were her client, and then she'd remembered...

'That you're on the other side? Yes, I heard you were helping the cops. Paying you well, are they?'

'Gray, I...'

' I'm kidding you. Relax.' That really was a joke. Gray didn't think he'd ever relax again in his whole life. Not that his whole life might amount to much. They didn't have the death penalty in Italy, but there was such a thing as extradition.

'You ought to have a proper lawyer, though.'

'Is that the first thing they teach you at bar school, how to keep your colleagues in business? I don't need an advocate, Pippa. I just want to get on with it. The Commissario, he is coming, isn't he?'

'Yes, he's just in the hall talking to Elsa and Elisa. Otto's just arrived as well; they look relieved to see him.'

'Otto?' The first flickers of hope faltered across Gray's face. 'Maybe they'll let us talk afterwards. There'll be a lot to work through.' Pippa's eyebrows must have assumed a questioning shape, for he went on, almost optimistically. 'He's my therapist, didn't I say? I don't know what I'd do without him.'

There was nothing surprising in the revelation of Gray's having a therapist; rather it would have been astonishing if he hadn't. What was unexpected was that it should be Otto. Pippa would have expected someone flakier, an American, perhaps, or one of those nervy Italians who look as though they ought to be French. Otto, on the other hand, had seemed the sort of kindly, practical man who, faced with a torrent of angst, would cough in mild embarrassment and suggest a cup of tea and a third piece of fruit cake. Her ideas of therapy were obviously wildly inaccurate, gathered at random from Woody Allen films and pre-war copies of *Punch*. She would make an effort to look into the subject thoroughly. After all, there was no point in coming to the Continent if you couldn't shed your insular prejudices. And she might need a therapist herself soon, what with all this not screaming.

Pietro apparently shared her impression of Otto.

'Nice man, that.' he said, coming into the room and sitting down next to the sergeant. He spoke a few words in Italian and then turned to Gray. 'Mr Garrett?' They shook hands. 'You wish to make a statement?'

'Yes.' He swallowed hard. 'I want to tell you everything.'

'That sounds sensible, Mr Garrett. Have you thought about whether you want...'

A small blipping noise came from the pocket of Gray's short sleeved shirt. 'You've got a text message, I think. Please, feel free to check it.'

'No, it doesn't matter. It won't be anything important. Probably the ice-hockey results. Dad insisted I sign up for this service before I left home, but really...'

'Go on, please.' Both Pietro and Sergeant Lenzuoli were growing pinker, agitated at the mere thought of disregarding a *telefonino*. 'The Mississauga Icedogs may have defeated the Erie Otters. It is impossible for you to concentrate while matters of such weight are hanging.'

'Eh?' Pietro's familiarity with the Ottowa League startled Gray into compliance. 'Okay, then. But I don't even like hockey.'

Either he was lying or the message had nothing to do with sport. Whichever it was, he sat motionless for a minute or more, staring at the tiny display and occasionally jabbing at the scroll buttons, while the damp patches under his arms spread across the pale blue shirt.

'Bad news?' asked Pietro gently.

'No. No, it's nothing.' He switched the phone off and replaced it in his pocket.

'You're sure?'

'Absolutely. Nothing at all.'

'Good. I was about to ask you whether you wish to have a lawyer present. I advise you - '

'No. No, I've already told Philippa, I don't need anyone.' He paused for a moment and then spoke in a tone that would have worked as casual if it hadn't been so sickeningly flat. 'I haven't got much to say, in any case. I didn't know her very well and I've no idea how she died.'

'But...' Pietro's brow furrowed, as though at a tricky crossword clue. 'I thought you were very anxious to speak to us. You have some important information?'

'No, nothing special.' His voice was firming up, becoming defiant, a little pompous. 'I merely anticipated that you would want to speak to me, as Zena's colleague and near-compatriot. I thought it would be sensible to get the whole thing out of the way as quickly as possible.'

'I see.' Pietro didn't sound convinced. 'We had better do that then, hadn't we? What did you know about Zena Carson?'

'She was American, from Nebraska, I think, or some such redneck backwater. I believe she came here about six months before me, so that would be just over a year ago. I don't know anything about her life in America - she never spoke about it at all, not family, not work, not friends. No one ever came over here to visit her, not that I knew about, anyway.'

'And in Lucca? Did she have friends here?'

'Not exactly friends. She joined some group or other, the usual Berlusconi-bashing, but I guess she got cheesed off with it after a while.'

'After September the eleventh?'

'Yeah, it could have been. We all got pretty nervous then, especially the Yanks.'

'Okay. What about teaching - did you both do the same kind of work here?'

'Roughly speaking, yes, except that I did all the classes at the paper mills and Zena stayed here. She refused point blank to drive in Italy so most of her lessons were here at the school.'

'There weren't any other English teachers?'

'At the Piccola Casa? No, just the two of us.'

'Thank you, Mr. Garrett. If you could just tell me what you were doing on Monday evening...'

'Why?'

'I think that's obvious, isn't it? I will be asking everyone.'

'I guess. There wasn't anything unusual about it, anyway. I was over at the factories, like I always am, until half past six. It takes a good half hour in the traffic at that time, so it would have been at least seven when I got back to Lucca. I went straight to my flat, got changed, and went out for a *passeggiata* round the walls.'

'Alone?'

'Yeah. I like to walk alone; I don't need to be chattering all the time like some people.'

Pietro glanced at Pippa. '*Touché.*'

'Anyway,' continued Gray with better grace, 'I had a tricky rhyme-scheme to work out. I don't know how long it took me but when it was finally sorted I suddenly found I was ravenous so I had a bowl of pasta and a salad at some bar. And before you ask, I've no idea where. I'd come down from the walls a while before that and I was just wandering until I came across something familiar. I still don't know Lucca very well, not once I get off the main streets.'

'Right. I don't suppose you met anyone you knew while you were out walking?'

''Fraid not. People might have seen me, but I'm a bit distant when I'm working on a poem. I got back to the flat at about half nine and I read a bit of E. M. Forster until bedtime. *Where Angels Fear to Tread.*'

'Yes, I know it. The perils of becoming entangled with Italians. So you didn't come here, to the Piccola Casa, at all that evening?'

'No, why should I? The first thing I knew about all this was when Elsa called me in the morning. Zena hadn't turned up for her first lesson and they thought she might have overslept. It had happened before, usually when she'd been out at Viareggio the night before. I said I'd call round and see, since we lived pretty close.'

'And?'

'And there wasn't any answer. I must have spent ten minutes knocking, my knuckles were raw and every old woman in the place was out on the staircase.'

'One of them had let you in, I suppose?'

'What? Oh – the front door of the building. No, Zena gave me a copy of her key. She was terrified of locking herself out.'

'You had a copy of her apartment key as well, then?'

'I'm just coming to that. After this orgy of knocking – pure *Macbeth* the whole thing - the crones began muttering that I ought to go in to check she was all right. I didn't like the idea; she could have had someone with her - even Zena might have had a sex life - but they were pretty insistent and to tell the truth I was feeling a bit uneasy about her myself. So I let myself in, with the *tricoteuses* crowding as close as they could without actually stepping over the threshold. There was stuff everywhere, you know, low-level chaos; half-empty coffee mugs, last month's papers, discarded underwear,' Gray gave a delicate shudder, 'but somehow I knew straightaway that she wasn't there. The place had a kind of abandoned feel about it. To make sure I looked for her passport and driving licence, and they'd both gone. She never usually took them out with her; she was worried they might get lifted, but she showed me where they were in case of some emergency.'

'But what made you assume she'd gone away for good?'

'Oh, she'd talked about it from time to time. Nothing definite, but sometimes she seemed really pissed off with Italy and said she'd check out Greece instead.' He was silent for a moment, building his courage for a burst of bluntness. 'I don't believe in these superstitious taboos about not speaking ill of the dead. Zena wasn't a considerate person; it would have been just like her simply to pack up and go, or not even to pack up, just leave her junk lying around like it was on Tuesday morning. She wouldn't give notice to E & E, or even say goodbye. I feel crappy now, of course, for jumping to conclusions like that, but it doesn't make any difference, does it, not really? She was already dead, wasn't she, whatever I thought?'

'We'll see what the post-mortem says, shall we? Meanwhile, have you ever seen a syringe like this before?'

'What? No, no, nothing like that. I mean, maybe when I had my last tetanus shot ... I don't like to look at needles. Was that..?'

'Again, we'll have to wait for the post-mortem. You can see, from the plastic bag, that it's evidence. Did Zena Carson use drugs, do you know?'

'What, more than a bit of hash, you mean? I don't think so, but I don't know for certain. It might explain her mood swings, I guess, but I don't exactly have any experience... I'm not really from that kind of background.'

'Evidently not. Well, thank you very much, Mr Garrett. You've been very helpful.' He spoke without expression but Gray seemed not to notice the irony.

'I hope so. Like I said, I didn't know her very well.'

'And you're sure there's nothing else you want to tell us?'

'Of course not.'

There was a tap at the door and Elisa came in with a tray of aperitifs; olives and tiny sandwiches.

'It is our *ora di martini* and we thought... Oh!' Her eye had fallen on the syringe and she faltered, the drinks lapping their frosted rims.

Sergeant Lenzuoli stood up and took the tray from her.

'*Dio Madonna*, not again!'

Pippa took the old lady's arm and helped her to sit down.

'What do you mean, 'not again'' asked Pietro, his voice plunging half an octave. 'Have you seen one of these before?'

XI

'For goodness' sake, Lisa,' came a voice from the doorway, 'Otto and I are dying of thirst out here. I told you just to leave the tray and...'

A pair of furry lilac mounds edged into the room, closely followed by the rest of Elsa's curves. She paused, hands on generous hips, and glared at Pietro.

'What have you been doing to her? You can't bully us like that, you know. I'm still a British citizen and I've got the Consul's telephone number.'

'No, Helsa, it is not the Turd Degree. See?'

Elsa followed her trembling finger. 'Oh Lord, not again.'

'I have no particular desire,' said Pietro patiently, 'to play the hard cop, but would one of you ladies please tell me what you're talking about?'

'It's Johann.' said Elsa, glancing nervously at Gray. 'He was a German teacher at the school for a few months last year. He died here in Lucca, staying at his friend's flat. Lisa and I happened to be there at the time, looking at a second-hand Triumph the friend had for sale. It was utter rubbish, as it turned out, cobbled together from half a dozen write-offs. I don't know why you people don't look into these things. But we saw Johann's body - and we took away two needles like that.'

'Why?' Pietro's voice was dangerously low.

'Why did we take them away? I'm not sure now. I suppose we didn't want people to think, to know, that he'd done it himself. S-suicide. Not after he was so brave. It was all bad enough without that. I'm sorry. We will tell you everything we can remember, if you think it's important. Just,' her voice wobbled, 'could we possibly go back to Otto, now?'

At Pietro's nod, Pippa shepherded the old ladies out into the reception area, where Otto took over. Their angora trailings had scarcely brushed the doorway when Pietro turned to Gray.

'What can you tell us about Johann?'

For the first time, thought Pippa, he really sounded like a policeman.

Gray took off his glasses and rubbed his eyes. His voice was resigned.

'Like Elsa said, he was a teacher here when I arrived. He died a few weeks later.'

'Forgive me, Mr Garrett, if I have made a mistake. But I understood you to say that there were no other teachers.'

Gray could do pedantry as well as any European. 'You mentioned English teachers, I believe. Johann only taught German.'

'Okay.' Pietro's long broad fingers were splayed on the table top, taut, as though under instruction not to drum in irritation. 'Let me make myself a little clearer this time. Have there been any other teachers at all, of any language whatsoever: French, Spanish, Serbo-Croat, Lesser Polynesian, working at the school during the time that you've been here?'

'No.'

'Teachers of any other subject: tribal music, higher mathematics, embroidery?'

'No. Just Zena and Johann.'

'Who are now both dead. A coincidence, Mr Garrett?'

Gray flushed. 'If Johann... Yesterday I thought...'

'Yes?'

'It's nothing.'

'You're quite sure? We seem to be having a lot of nothing today. How did Johann die? Was it really suicide? What did the signora mean when she said he was brave?'

'He had AIDS.'

There was a long silence. Gray sat with hands clasped in his lap, his shoulders slightly hunched and his eyelids blinking too often. The low sunlight shone from behind him, lighting his pointed ears with a pink glow. He could have been a mouse or a silent elf. Pietro began picking crumbs out of his sweater and Pippa stared unseeing at the notes in front of her. Only Sergeant Lenzuoli seemed calm. Finally Pietro spoke.

'Was he...?'

'Gay?' Gray flicked the word out as though it were an insect that had landed on his tongue. 'Yes, he was. In both senses - a remarkable person. And yes, I'm gay too, in one sense only, the only sense I guess you're interested in. Next question: did we sleep together? Of course. After all, we're renowned for it, aren't we, promiscuity? Did he tell me beforehand? Yes. Were we careful? Yes. Am I still shit scared? You bet. '

The words hung in the second silence like a flag draped over the battlements.

'I appreciate you telling me this.' said Pietro as though there were no one else in the room. 'It would help even more if you could tell me about Johann's death. What was the actual cause of death, do you know? An infection, perhaps, pneumonia?'

'I don't know.' Gray's surge of candour was spent. He sounded exhausted. 'It didn't seem important at the time. If someone has AIDS, you expect them to die, don't you? How isn't a relevant question.'

'And when?'

'What do you mean?'

'Is 'when' a relevant question? Did you expect him to die so soon?'

'Oh I see. No I didn't, to be honest; it was a shock when it happened. He didn't seem as sick as all that. He was thin, thinner than he should have been, and pale, and he had a cough, but I wouldn't have thought he was so near the end. I guess he must have been worse than he looked. Putting a brave face on it. At least, that's what I thought at the time.'

Pietro nodded. 'And the syringes? You heard what the signora said?'

'Elsa? Of course. But I didn't know anything about it. Johann must have been on a bunch of medication, maybe he injected some of it.' He flinched and a spasm of pain crossed his face. 'I guess I didn't know him all that well, after all.'

'And the other possibility related to the syringes?' Pietro's English was precise and careful now. It made him sound more foreign than when he made mistakes.

'That it was suicide?' Gray chewed on his lower lip. 'I don't know. I would have said not, definitely not, that Johann wasn't the type. But then, like I said, maybe I didn't know him as well as I thought. When he died, it was at this guy's flat, like Elsa said. I knew him to speak to, he was just a friend. But then there's this other guy, this Thomas, that I knew nothing about, who turned out to be Johann's long-term partner. At least, that's what he said, and why would he lie about something like that? He took Johann's body back to Germany.'

'I'm sorry.' said Pippa, meaning all of it.

Gray gave a bleak smile. 'Thanks. It was a shock to my pride, I think, as much as the other stuff. I guess that's why I'm kinda haunted.'

'But it isn't relevant, is it?'

'Is what?'

Gray and the sergeant had both left, and Pietro and Pippa were alone in the classroom.

'All that about Johann and Gray being gay. Being miserable, more like. Poor lad. You don't have to go into it any further, do you?'

'I don't know.' Pietro's official manner had left the room with the sergeant. Without it, he looked ten years younger and very tired. He ran a hand backwards through his hair until it stood on end.

Pippa stared firmly at the edge of the table, determined not to sympathize. She had never before thought much about Canadians, but in the face of Mediterranean chaos, the Commonwealth forces of decorum had to stick together. And Gray had been kind, and funny, and he liked Shelley. Any of these were reasons enough for fighting his corner. 'What do you mean, you don't know? You could see how upset he was.'

'Upset?'

'Sad, distressed, troubled.'

'No, I understand the word. I'm only wondering if it's the right one. Frightened, I would have said.'

'Frightened, then. It's the same thing.'

'No, Pippa, it isn't. Poor Gray - yes, I agree he's poor Gray - he knew something. Something he wanted to tell us. But then he changed his mind. Why?'

'Perhaps he didn't like you.'

'Very likely.' He looked across the table at her. His eyes were shattered with tiny red veins. 'You don't like me at the moment either.'

'I didn't...'

He waved a hand dismissively. 'Don't worry. It's my job to be unpleasant.'

'I...' No, she couldn't go into all that. 'The thing is, he told you in the end, didn't he? About Johann.'

'Yes, he told us about Johann.' The emphasis on the final word was almost imperceptible.

'That's okay then. I know his alibi-thingy isn't very impressive, but isn't that what you'd expect? And anyway, he couldn't...'

'Couldn't what?'

'Couldn't have...' The words were unexpectedly difficult. 'Couldn't have killed her.'

'In what sense do you mean "couldn't"? Psychologically? How do we know? How many people couldn't kill, would be absolutely incapable, if the provocation was great enough? We know, politically speaking, that Signora Carson was less than straightforward. Perhaps in other areas...'

'The translations.'

'I'm sorry?' His voice was formal again. 'You have some work to complete? I am delaying you?'

'No, not me. Zena's translations. She was getting one of the students to do them for her.' She explained what she had discovered during Nicola's lesson.

'But the student, Nicola, he didn't realise this before?'

'No, I'm quite sure he didn't. But if there was one...'

'Exactly. She could have had quite a - what do you say? - a cottage industry going. We may have to speak to the other students. Yes - I know what you want to say- it isn't a good enough motive for murder. You're right, it isn't, but men and women have been killed for less. Also,' he paused, musing, 'to me it suggests the kind of person that she was: greedy, clever manipulative. There is a crime that uses these - these qualities.' He paused again, waiting for her to catch up. 'A crime that's very often punished by its own victims. And punished by death.'

'You mean blackmail?'

He nodded.

'But who would she have been blackmailing? Gray - about Johann? But no one minds about that sort of thing any more, not even Elsa and Elisa. And anyway, what's it got to do with the writing on her arms? It doesn't make sense.'

'No, it doesn't. At this stage nothing makes sense. We are blundering in the dark, following *lucciole*. Fireflies. But it's not impossible, is it? People do still care, especially families.'

'Not impossible.' conceded Pippa grudgingly. 'Not from that point of view. But physically? Gray's very small. Could he really put a body in the cupboard like that? And he'd have to prop her up in there.'

'You're right. And with almost any other victim, that would be enough - almost enough - to exonerate him. But Signora Carson was even smaller, remember, even thinner. I don't think she weighed much more than forty kilos. A child could have carried her.'

Pippa felt the fight ebbing out of her, leaving only a dull, childish stubbornness.

'I still don't think he did it. And I ...' She completed the sentence silently. I want to go home. 'I'm just tired.'

'Of course. It's been a terrible day, you must sleep. Only...'

'What? What's the matter?'

'Your door. You said earlier that it wasn't locked. Do you have a key?'

'No. There might be one somewhere, though. Do you want to have a look?'

'It might be wise. I don't want to alarm you, but...'

'One murder's been committed.'

'Exactly.'

There was a key, hanging up inside the door, and a complicated lock with a series of solid-looking bolts. There was also, on the outside of the door, a little red button. Pietro locked the door, turning the key until all the shafts were home. Then he pressed the button and the door sprang free.

'Always the same. We love the idea of security, of locks and gadgets and electronic gates. But then we lose our keys, or we're late, or we want to let our friends in, and suddenly the only thing that matters is to get inside. What you need is a bolt and chain, the kind you have in England, but it's too late to fit one now. Have you got a phone, at least?'

'A mobile? Not here, no.'

'You need one. Now. And then some more food.'

'Aoo aw eh aya ooe?'

'I'm sorry?'

Pippa swallowed the last mouthful of pizza crust and tried again. 'Have you always been based in Lucca? As a policeman, I mean?'

'I used to be, but I'm not now.' Pietro dealt with the problem of not talking with his mouth full by the simple expedient of dropping ninety per cent of his food before it got anywhere near his mouth. Behind him, the pigeons followed the tomato and mozzarella trail.

'I'm not really based anywhere, although I once heard a rumour of a desk in Pistoia with my name on it. I get sent all over Tuscany, wherever they need someone who can speak a little English. I usually end up in Livorno hauling in tobacco smugglers. Very dull.'

'Why do it, then?'

'I'm trapped in an obsessive love-hate relationship with the English language. I only began thinking about becoming a policeman when I was fourteen, but I knew at the age of three that I wanted to be British. I was at the playground in Lucca and Mamma had bought me an ice-cream. Of course, I got it all over my red T-shirt, and another little boy was commenting loudly on the fact. "Don't tease him" said his mother, "he's probably English." That's when I knew where my destiny lay.'

'But you don't live in England.'

He shuddered. 'I tried to, I really tried. For a year of my degree course I studied in London, and I really intended to stay. But one night there was a thing.'

'A Thing?'

'I'd rather not talk about it if you don't mind. I still get nightmares. It was a sort of spongy thing, damp and quivering. It simply appeared in front of me.'

'What, a jellyfish or something? At the beach, Southend?'

'Oh no. I don't mind jellyfish. I was at home in my lodgings. The landlady said it was a - let me think - sue it pudding? I would have been happy to sue it if I could have got legal aid. It was the prospect of eating of it that filled me with horror. I took the next plane back to Pisa, switched to law, and thanked the Lord for my lucky escape. 'Here.' he added, passing her the extra piece of pizza in its greaseproof wrapping.

'No, you have it. You're obviously in greater need of Italian nourishment.'

He shook his head. 'I've got a bulging fridge to go back to. Mamma worries if I don't have a three-course *spuntino* before bed. Anyway, you know how to use the phone?' They were back outside the *Piccola Casa*, from which the Cinquecento had at last been towed away. 'You remember the numbers I've programmed?'

'One for your mobile, two for the Questura, three for the Carabinieri, four for your mother. Why would I want to call your mother?'

'I don't know really. I always put my mother's number in. You might get hungry again.'

'True.' She pressed the entryphone buzzer and Elisa's voice sang from the little grille. 'Flipper? *Sei tu*?'

'*Si*.' She pushed open the door and ran up the stairs.

'*A domani!*' called Pietro from behind her.

At the top, Elsa and Elisa were waiting, in long flowered nightdresses and soft velvet slippers.

'*Brava!* You've been out with the policeman?'

'Er, sort of.' Pippa wasn't quite sure about the implications. 'Just to get a phone and some pizza.'

'Pizza!' they sighed together. 'So delightful to eat pizza with a beautiful man.'

Pippa, thinking of Pietro's chin, was dubious. 'I'm sure it must be. He isn't my type, though. I prefer real Englishmen.'

'Understandable' said Elsa briskly. 'You must be exhausted now, though. He might look better in the morning.'

'I am a bit tired, yes. Perhaps I'll get to bed now, if that's all right. Is there anything I ought to do here? Lock the front door, switch off the lights?'

'Oh that would be kind. Lisa gets so terribly worried about fire. Italian wiring, you know. We have to turn everything off at night.' Elisa whispered something urgently. 'Yes of course, I'll tell her. Especially the photocopier, Lisa says. She was terribly upset on Tuesday morning when we saw that *povero* Graham' - so even they called him that - 'had left it on standby all night.'

A shaft of light pierced the grey shadows of Pippa's mind.

'Are you sure it was Gray? Someone else might have been the last to use it.'

'Oh no, dear, we'd unplugged it earlier, before our martinis. And it was definitely Graham. He left a sheet of exercises inside that he'd written himself.'

'By 'and.' added Elisa. '*Come coscienzioso!*' They sighed together, '*Com'industrioso!*'

'Er, *si*.' agreed Pippa. 'Of course.'

In the chill of the Tuscan night, long after Pippa had fallen asleep, three men were still gazing at the stars, at one constellation in particular: Orion the Hunter.

For one, it was an unequivocal symbol of hope. Pseudo-Helmut would find what he was searching for, exact whatever justice was needed, recover his name, his dignity, his life. Meanwhile he had to get back to the hotel; the doors were locked at midnight and it wasn't the kind of place to dole out gratuitous latch-keys.

Charles would have preferred another cluster of stars; Casseopia, perhaps, or Libra. He had always been suspicious of machismo. Still, the day hadn't ended so badly, considering its disastrous beginning. The boy would need constant surveillance of course; regular reminders of his precarious position. Again he cursed himself for involving the Americans. (To Charles, they were all Americans.) Science required experimentation, naturally, but he wasn't sure that the southern gentlemen would see it quite like that.

But for the third man, the hunter was nothing but a mockery. He stood out on the tiny balcony, between the tricycle and the clothes airer, and tried to imagine the touch of the African night. Nothing came. Nothing but the creaking of the door behind, a soft step, a voice.

'Was it so bad, Eti?'

'Worse. I sold a three-pack of sleeveless vests.' The pause was like a reproach. 'Only a three-pack of sleeveless vests. A nice German lad bought them, trying not to show that he felt sorry for me. What does a German in Italy need with vests?'

'It isn't always so warm.'

'You're telling me, girl. How are we to heat this place in winter? Look Julie - I think we should talk about...'

'No.'

'But...'

'No. We stay together, and we stay within the law. We haven't come so far as to forget that. Now come inside. Come inside, my love.'

XII

Pippa was woken by the sound of *Amazing Grace* and a soft weight on her heart. Her first thought was that she'd died, and the Sunday school teacher had been right after all, her second that there was fur in her mouth and her third that Gray had been lying. She heaved Pierrotino off her chest, reached out for the new phone and pressed buttons at random until the electronic plinking stopped.

'Hello?'

'You should say *Pronto* now you're in Italy.'

'*Pronto*, then. It's Pietro, I suppose. What does *Pronto* mean?'

'Literally, "ready".'

'Well I'm not saying it then, because I'm not. I was in the middle of a nice dream about heaven. What time is it?' She could hear noises in the background: voices, clinking cups, the hiss of an espresso machine. He was presumably having breakfast in a bar somewhere, sprinkling his fellow customers with flakes of brioche and the foam from his cappuccino.

'A quarter to ten. You slept well, then. Your guardian angel must have been watching over you. And nothing happened in the night? You've nothing to report?'

'Nothing, no.'

'Excellent. *Nessuna nuova, buona nuova*. How do you say that in English?'

'No news is good news?'

'Simple as that.' There was a pause and a rustle as he made a note on his napkin. 'Look, I have to do some paperwork and telephoning this morning. Can I catch up with you this afternoon? About four, at the school?'

'Fine, yes. See you then.'

She switched off the phone and uncrossed her fingers. Anyway, she hadn't exactly lied. The thing about Gray and the photocopier wasn't precisely something that had happened in the night, only something she'd been told about in the late evening. The distinction was crucial. As for whether it was 'anything to report'; that was surely a matter of judgment. And it was far too early to exercise that before breakfast.

Pietro stuffed his own phone back in his jeans pocket, remembering to put the keylock back on. The memory of the time he'd accidentally telephoned the Vice Questore while leaning against the wall in this very bar, still haunted his nightmares. It wasn't so much the fact of the call itself, or even its duration, for the entire second half of the match, that had caused the trouble, so much as the final result, and his 'unseemly' celebrations at Juve's victory. Well, he wasn't to know the man was a lifelong Roma fan. All the same, Pietro hoped he would never again hear such an apocalyptic voice emerging from his own back pocket. There was something disturbing Rabelaisian about it.

He was relieved that Pippa was okay, though not so surprised as he would have been if he hadn't, at two hour intervals throughout the night, phoned her guardian angel in person, stationed in a spare bedroom across the street. He had planned to send one of the junior recruits, Campomeli, perhaps, who was always up for a bit of overtime, but Sergeant Lenzuoli had offered to do it himself.

'Just let me stay. I'm accustomed to vigils. And this way you don't need to bother with the paperwork.'

'But the overtime pay, Ago? If I don't fill in the right forms...'

'What do I need overtime pay for? I can't spend the salary I get at the moment.' He changed the subject quickly to avoid revealing what Pietro already suspected, that the major part of his monthly *stipendio* went directly to a variety of discreet charitable causes. 'Anyway I've got a good book I want to finish. I'd be up all night reading in any case.'

Pietro had agreed, as usual feeling guilty that only he, and one or two of the officers at the Lucca Questore, had any idea of the sergeant's abilities. The trouble was, it was so helpful to introduce him as a sleepy buffoon. Off their guard, people let all sorts of things slip that they would never tell Pietro. And Agostino didn't mind, had laughed when Pietro finally screwed up his courage to mention it.

'Of course I know they think I'm a fat fool - I really would be one not to have noticed. Why should I mind? It's at least half true, in any case. Look, Pietro,' He was supposed to say 'sir' or 'Commissario Guinizelli', 'I didn't join the police to be respected. I joined to do a job. I didn't lose my vocation when I left the seminary, I just found it somewhere else. If I stood on my dignity all the time, I'd not only look ridiculous, I wouldn't be one-tenth of the little use I can be at the moment. So just forget it, okay? There are plenty of people who like getting credit. They can have my *avanzi*.'

Pietro laughed. He thought of his mother and her own *avanzi*, the left-overs from dinner that went to the pig or her beloved chickens. He guessed that there hadn't been many on young Agostino's plate.

Now he smiled at the memory but he still felt uneasy. He wished he could at least tell the English girl the truth. Such a funny little name - Pippa - like the chirping of a small bird. She reminded him of Mary Poppins; all that careful dignity and something quite different underneath. Maybe after this case was sorted out...

Meanwhile he added a couple of bars of chocolate to his *conto* at the bar, paid, and walked out into the morning sun. In the Piazza Grande - its official name, the Piazza Napoleone, used only by tourists and mapmakers - the sergeant was waiting, sitting on a shaded stone bench with the morning's *Il Terreno*. They walked together across the square and out of the walls at the Porta San Pietro. Near the station, when the chocolate had run out, Pietro spoke for the first time.

'I really appreciate what you've done, Ago, but you'd better get home now. Catch up on a few hours' sleep.'

'Thanks, but...'

'You're not assigned to anything else at the moment, are you?'

'No. When the message came through that you'd asked for me, the V-Q here took me off the current job.'

'Which was?'

'Credit card fraud.' Agostino wrinkled his wide nose, making him look even more like a benevolent boxer. 'And I wasn't sorry to leave that behind.'

'Ah, that's what happens when you come from an ancient banking city like Lucca. No real earthy crime, nothing but money. Maybe we should get ourselves transferred to Napoli.'

The Questura was easily visible as soon as they turned the station corner; not so much for the two flags, the Italian tricolour and the EU ring of stars, which hung together over the main doorway, as for the crowd at each entrance: black, yellow, brown and white faces, each bearing the same expression of weary resignation.

'*Stranieri* department still busy then? Poor souls.'

Pietro half-expected to be taken for an itinerant Albanian himself, but the sergeant's presence was imposing enough for two, and the crowd parted without a murmur.

'I've sorted out an office for you, on the first floor at the end of the corridor. Giorgio's old room.'

'Of course.'

'Do you want me to come up with you?'

' I think I can find my way up one flight of stairs, thanks, whatever the English girl might think.'

'You haven't quite convinced her yet, then?'

'Of my devastating charm and forensic acumen? Not quite, no. She's humouring me. The English always think of us as children, but as far as Pippa's concerned, I'm not out of the *asilo* yet. That reminds me…'

'We need to check her flight from Stansted. I'll get on to it straightaway, shall I?'

'If you would. It'll only be a formality, but I ought to be able to say we've checked. Just in case she turns out to be a crazed mass murderer. You can never be sure with the English.'

Walking along the first floor corridor, Pietro always remembered the first time. The details of how he had got there were hazy; he had been fourteen, or maybe fifteen, warned by a passing officer for riding his Piaggio without a helmet, or with a passenger, or without lights. Maybe, even, he had been only thirteen, too young to ride a scooter legally at all. Something more must have happened - he'd been cheeky, perhaps, or asked the rapid-fire questions that were always being mistaken for cheek - for the Polizia didn't usually concern itself with juvenile traffic offences. Whichever it was, he had been escorted up here for a little talk with old Giorgio and had emerged forty minutes later convinced not only of the essential propriety of the *motorino* regulations, but also of his own immutable destiny as an officer of the Polizia. Lucca being Lucca, with a grapevine among the old men in the sleepy bars and piazzas that put any merely female rumour mill to shame, his grandfather had known the story by next morning, and his uncles by lunchtime, but it had been worth it. Giorgio had still been there ten years later, when Pietro had finished the *liceo* and university, at the end of the corridor to listen to the young recruit's uncertainties and minor rebellions. It was he who had recognized Pietro's temperamental unfitness for the routines and hierarchies of the conventional departments, never mind the impossibility of his ever keeping a uniform clean for more than half an hour, and had, by judicious words at the right time and to the right people, helped him first to move into the plainclothes detective division and eventually to create his own English-speaking niche within it.

Giorgio had retired three years ago, but it still felt odd not to knock before going in.

'Who is it?'

Pietro hastily closed the door again. Obviously the room had been double-booked. Unless.... There was something ominously familiar about that voice. He knocked decorously, his heart plummeting.

'Enter!'

He had been right. Behind Giorgio's old desk, his chin on his hand in a Socratic pose, lounged Vice-Questore Umberto Bisbigli. He raised an aristocratic eyebrow over his gold pince-nez and gestured to a chair.

'Be seated, my boy.'

Pseudo-Helmut looked up at the Leaning Tower for the seventeenth time and, for the seventeenth time, decided against buying a ticket. Down on the ground, amidst the other tourists, he was inconspicuous enough, but once on the steps he would lose his anonymity. People liked to look upwards, even in this sun, to watch their foolhardy peers. All the same, he couldn't skulk about in the Campo dei Miracoli forever. To do what he had to do, to do it properly, he had to go to Lucca. If sending a message would have been enough, he could have sent a message from Hamburg in safety. He could, he supposed still do it that way if he lost his nerve, take a bus back to the airport and the next northbound plane, pretend that he'd never disobeyed the injunction. One more look at the Duomo doors and then he would make up his mind.

'This is an awkward case of yours.' said the Vice-Questore in a querulous tone, as though Pietro himself were responsible for the inconvenience of Zena's death. 'Americans are always problematic. They have difficulty in seeing the broader picture.'

In that, at least, Pietro could sympathize. The 'broader picture' was Bisbigli's monomania, a Casaubonesque vision in which every aspect of Italian life; politics, religion, food and culture, was subsumed in a general theory of police practice. No details of the theory had ever been produced and if any unwary underling sought to ask, as Pietro himself once had, how exactly the semiotic works of Umberto Eco related to tax evasion in Pistoia, Bisbigli would close his eyes in patient suffering and whisper, in English, 'Only connect'. He had long ago been promoted out of his home station of Empoli to the safety of a 'roving brief' across Tuscany, supervising a range of inter-force programmes including Pietro's Anglocentric missions. The wide-ranging nature of these initiatives naturally required Bisbigi's presence at all the principal functions of the region, particularly those celebrating the excellence of Tuscan food and wine. It was rare, therefore, for him to be sighted before the late afternoon.

'No sir.'

The Vice-Questore flinched and Pietro hastily amended his agreement.

'No, Professore.'

The source of the title was obscure, but for the past six months Bisbigli had, using his techniques of silent anguish, managed to persuade the entire Tuscan force to address him by it. Only Pietro still forgot.

Bisbigli stretched out an arm to make a minute adjustment to his Armani cuff. He surveyed his perfect fingernails with satisfaction.

'What, Commissario, do you understand by the term "plainclothes"?' He used the English word and Pietro was momentarily disconcerted.

'*In borghese*, sir?'

'If you like, if you like.' He was dangerously genial. 'Personally, I find the London usage more comprehensive. "Plain". After your years of linguistic study, Pietro, what does the adjective "plain" call to mind?'

'Er, ordinary?'

'*Ordinary*, Commissario? *Ordinary?* Dear me. I sometimes wonder what we were thinking of, promoting you to this sensitive position. Maybe you would be happier in some less demanding role. Crowd control at football matches, perhaps? I remember what a keen *tifoso* you are. Would that be - *ordinary* - enough for you?'

'Yes, Professore. That is... No, Professore.'

Bisbigli smiled, a sad smile of infinite patience. '"Plain" to me, Pietro, evokes a range of Platonic concepts. The classic, the timeless, the elegant. Would you describe your own costume in those terms?'

Pietro considered for a few seconds. It was a warm morning and he was wearing one of his Hawaiian shirts, the ones his mother had bought from the supermarket because they didn't show the stains. His jeans, he thought, might be described as classic, had they been Levis or Wranglers. Unfortunately they were neither, but cheap Chinese imports from the market, with fraying seams and pockets in peculiar places. As for his comfortable Cornish pasty shoes...

'No, Professore.'

'No. In fact, to use the Italian form, it isn't even bourgeois, is it?

'No, Professore.'

'The next time we meet, Pietro, I would like to see you dressed in a style which does credit to the traditions of our service, to the achievements of the Italian *stilisti*, to the fusion of society and culture represented in our unique role. Do I make myself clear?'

'I've got to buy a suit?'

The Vice-Questore sighed. 'How reductive you are, my boy. It must be all that time you spend with the English. A *good* suit, yes. Appropriately dressed, it is not out of the question that you might accompany me to one or two of the important functions which my position requires me to attend. This lunchtime, for example, I am obliged to visit Montecarlo to be present at the opening of a new wine festival.'

So that's why he's skulking around Lucca so early, thought Pietro, trying to look enthusiastic. He had no objection whatsoever to drinking the wines of Montecarlo, but preferred to do it at home, with friends, family or a good book, rather than in some stuffy marquee to the accompaniment of pompous speeches by the Vice-Questore and his cronies.

Before he was called upon to say anything, the telephone rang. Bisbigli answered it.

'*Il Professore*. Yes, yes, I have Guinizelli.' By the short and curlies, thought Pietro. 'Certainly, send him up.' He replaced the receiver and looked triumphantly at Pietro. 'The pathologist is here, to deliver an oral report concerning the cadaver of Signora Carson. As you know, my time is precious, but I am prepared to remain here for long enough to receive this information and to discuss its implications. As a scientist myself, it may well be that I can cast some light upon this unfortunate case and assist the *dottore* in formulating his conclusions. The name was unfamiliar to me and I presume therefore that he is a relatively young and inexperienced man.'

But the pathologist, who came into the room a minute later, with only the most perfunctory knock, was not a young man. Even the short, untidy hair, jeans and enveloping white coat provided only a few seconds' ambiguity: the rounded face and figure were undoubtedly feminine.

'Hi.' she beamed, bouncing into the room on the balls of her tennis shoes. 'I'm...'

'Alessandra Binni.' interrupted Pietro, somewhat to his own surprise.

'Pietro! I saw the name Guinizelli, but I didn't know...'

The Vice-Questore cleared his throat reproachfully. Forty-five seconds was far too long for him to be out of the limelight. Alessandra stuck her hand out and he took it, inspecting his palm afterwards.

'Don't worry.' she said, noticing the long reddish streaks. 'It's rust, not blood. Some guy's Ape conked out by the station and I gave him a hand with it.'

'How reassuring. You two are old acquaintances, I understand?'

'That's right. Ali's dad used to...' He broke off. It wasn't always a good idea to give away too much information to Bisbigli. But Alessandra didn't mind.

'...patch up the old Guinizelli Fiat. Kept it on the road for years. We've got a garage in the village. Just general stuff, petrol pumps, bodywork, basic repairs. Pietro's dad's got a posh Japanese four-by-four now, so he goes to the fancy dealers in town.'

'Fascinating' said the Vice-Questore with a yawn. Somehow the automobile culture had been missed out of his encompassing vision. 'You yourself, I assume, play no part in this familial enterprise?'

'I did.' she said cheerfully. 'Left school at fifteen and went straight into it. But after three months I was bored stiff. There's a very limited number of things that can go wrong with a car, and hardly any exciting ways to fix them. It occurred to me that human bodies would be much more interesting than car ones so I went back to school, got my head down and seven years later became a paediatrician.'

'*Complimenti.*' said Pietro, and Bisbigli managed an approving grunt.

'Thanks, but that didn't work out either. The *bimbi* were fine, but I couldn't stand the parents. And they couldn't stand me, either. They wanted me to keep the children off school for three weeks with every little cough and cold when they'd have been far better out in the fresh air. And then I kept forgetting where I was, and referring to the kids as cars. The last straw came when some frightful mamma made a formal complaint. All I'd said was that her son needed a kickstart in the mornings. I switched to pathology after that. Dead patients don't moan so much.'

'This is most interesting,' said the Vice-Questore, consulting his Rolex, 'but perhaps we could get on to the subject of Signora Carson? Unless it would be better for me to telephone your superior?'

'Oh no, that wouldn't do any good. He's off sailing in Capri somewhere. This one's my pigeon.' She pulled a sheaf of handwritten notes from her pocket. 'Let's see. Oh yeah. Cause of death suffocation; I expect you'd worked that out already.'

'The swollen face and bleeding from the nose and ears?' asked Pietro.

'That's right. No serious injuries, but a bit of light bruising, mainly to the skull, shoulders and upper arms. The interesting thing is what's inside the body.'

'Drugs?'

'Of a sort. Methohexitone. That mean anything to you?'

'Zilch, I'm afraid. Professore?'

'What?' Bisbigli had been doodling on a notepad, apparently perfecting some learned wisecracks for his lunchtime speech. 'Oh Pietro, surely you don't expect me to spell out something as elementary as that?'

Alessandra smiled. 'It's a barbiturate, an anaesthetic, used in operating theatres.'

'In hospitals?'

'Of course. We don't tend to cut people up on kitchen tables any more. And they weren't just traces, either. The amount that we found in the body was roughly what you'd expect for someone who died during a major operation. '

'But there wasn't any sign of one? An operation?'

'Oh no. What were you thinking, that some consultant botched the job and hid the evidence? Where was the body, anyway? No one told me that.'

'In a classroom cupboard.'

Mamma mia. Well, they don't generally operate on school desks, either. Anyway, there hadn't been any surgery, and there wasn't anything to suggest the need for it, either. No cancer or even pregnancy. The stomach was empty, though, as if she was being prepared for something.'

'Probably on a diet.' put in Bisbigli. 'I know what you ladies are like.'

'Not me. I eat like a bloody horse. But yeah, she did look a bit anorexic. Oh, and there was morphine as well, in one of the syringes and in the body. A smallish dose that one, though. Methohexitone can be painful to inject, so it's pretty standard to give a bit of morphine first. Well, I say standard, but actually methohexitone isn't generally used in Europe any more, only in the States. It's cheaper than the alternatives, propofol or etomidate, but it's not really so safe. In England, for example, you can't get it commercially at all.'

'Could it have killed her? If she hadn't suffocated, I mean?'

'Not directly, no. The metho dose was large, like I say, but not excessive. It worked out as one point five meg per kilo of body weight, and she didn't have many of those, poor girl. It would have cost a lot more to put me under. It looks as though it was measured out by someone who knew what they were doing. There are side-effects, of course, and potentially lethal ones, heart failure mainly, but if you monitor carefully you're usually all right.'

'And the other syringe? The one without the morphine?'

'Yeah, there were traces of metho, so it looks as though that's how it was administered. There was a fresh puncture hole in her right thigh. That's normal, intravenous admin, with a one per cent solution. You can take the intramuscular route, but that's trickier and you're talking about five per cent.'

'And the other two, that I sent round last night?'

'Syringes? Yes, the same, methohexitone and morphine. They'd been hanging around for a while, though, hadn't they? Several months, I'd have said.'

The Vice-Questore stood up. 'Thank you very much, Signorina. I think your little project has told us all we need to know. It was obviously a case of accidental death. This unfortunate lady, her brain weakened by prolonged dieting, began to experiment with drugs as, regrettably, so many of our young people do these days.'

'But this wasn't a recreational...' Alessandra didn't yet know not to interrupt Bisbigli mid-flow. He glared at her and continued.

'Excuse *me*, signorina. One thing I have discovered, that you obviously have yet to learn, is that, for these poor people, there is no distinction between the medical and the hedonistic. She obviously got hold of these particular substances from one of her contacts...'

'Have to be a hospital, I think, or large-scale pharmacy.'

This time he didn't even trouble to glare. 'And, not knowing their strength, took a massive overdose. It's very sad, of course, but really nothing that we need expend any more time upon. I'm sure the relevant authorities can complete the paperwork. Now, if you'll excuse me, I must be going. I believe that my little speech, *Viniculture and Vice*, will be what is known as a keynote address.'

He glided out, leaving Pietro and Alessandra staring in bemusement at the empty chair.

'So,' said Pietro, 'once more our perspicacious leader has solved the case. Zena injected herself with morphine and unavailable methohexitone, battered herself around the head and arms a bit, climbed into the cupboard, wedging the door firmly behind her, and suffocated herself. Oh, and she made a few notes on her wrists just to give us a bit more to talk about.'

'Simple when you think about it. Time for a coffee?'

XIII

'*Eccola!*'

'Sorry?'

'Here it is. You can open your eyes now.'

Pippa did, and raised her eyebrows in polite bewilderment. Elisa chuckled.

'You don't know it, eh? *Eccellente.* But now I must depart. Your first student is almost upon you.'

Alone, Pippa prowled around the empty classroom, identifying the small changes: the new posters, the crystal vase, even the table rotated through ninety degrees. Elisa was right; it could have been a different room, were it not for the menacing cupboard at the end, its door ineffectually shrouded by a poster for the Uffizi gallery. Whether or not they had cleared it with Pietro first she didn't know; it seemed a little early for such a drastic crime scene makeover but it was certainly too late to start making difficulties. She was relieved, too, that they had lined up a lesson to mop up part of the long morning, although she knew nothing at all about the intended student. Even the barest single fact would have been helpful: gender, age, level of linguistic competency. Although, with the *Little Brown Brethren* still her only teaching material, perhaps it wouldn't really make much difference.

A mild knock came at the door, but it was only Otto.

'Do you like it?' he beamed, waving an arm at the flowers and list of irregular verbs. 'The girls thought it would be better so. With another half hour' - he pronounced the 'l' in 'half' - 'I think they would even have repainted it for you.' He settled himself at the table and took out a slim packet of cigars.

'Do you mind this? Please, do tell me. Zena minded very much.'

'No, but...'

'*Portacenere*? I have.' He drew a small china ashtray from his pocket.

'It isn't that. I ...'

'Would like a cigar, too? Forgive me, I am very discourteous. Please, please, take. One for now, one for later.'

Pippa laughed. 'No, I don't smoke, thanks. But I like the smell. It's just that I'm waiting for a student.'

Otto's smile, were it possible, grew wider still.

'Those girls.' He shook his head in mock despair. 'They are very, very naughty. I *am* your student.'

'Oh. Oh, I didn't realise. I'm sorry.'

'For what?' He laid the unlit cigar on the table. 'This must all be very difficult for you. A strange country, a new job, they are hard enough to begin with. But you, you have to deal with this terrible thing as well, this discovery you have made. You must be kind to yourself, Philippa, you must give yourself time to be sad.'

''S'alright.' she said gruffly. If she had to cry in front of anyone, Otto was probably the least worst option, as Jonathan used to put it. On the other hand, as long as, with Great-great-aunt Henrietta's chromosomes, her upper lip could remain rigid, she wasn't going to encourage it to wobble.

'You prefer not to talk about it?'

'I...' How could she put it, without sounding either rude or impossibly repressed? 'It doesn't seem quite fair.'

'Fair?'

'You're here for an English lesson. I can't just turn the tables and make it into a personal therapy session.'

'Ah. You know my profession, then? But please, don't worry. Often my lesson with Zena would be so, and then, when she came to me, I would learn a little more English. I don't like to have so many boundaries.'

'You were Zena's therapist as well?'

He sighed. 'Yes. Poor Zena.'

Another ethical problem was buzzing around Pippa's brain now, like a hyperactive bluebottle. This was worse than the Law Society's practice manual. As her therapist, Otto would presumably know more than anyone else in Lucca about Zena's life and, quite possibly, the causes of her death. But would he, like a priest, be bound by the secrets of the confessional? And even if he wasn't, was she the right person to be asking questions? She hadn't any *locus standi* in the case; was only involved at all, so far as she could see, to help Pietro out with his idioms. On the other hand, she was here and Pietro wasn't, and if Otto volunteered information, there couldn't possibly be any harm in remembering it.

'Poor Zena.' she echoed, setting the bait.

'You have heard, perhaps, that she was not a happy person?'

'We - I - did get that impression, yes.'

'Yes.' He looked at her seriously for a few moments. 'Can I ask you - do you know anything about the sources of her unhappiness?'

'Not really. Only that there might have been something political.' That should be vague enough, she thought, to provoke a confidence or two without revealing any official secrets.

His face cleared. 'I am very glad that you have told me that. I think, indeed, that this was the root of her difficulties. Perhaps even the cause of her death.'

'You think someone killed her for...'

'Ideological reasons? I think it is more than probable. You are shocked, my dear. These things do not happen in England. Nor in Austria, at least not for very many years.'

'You're Austrian, are you?'

He smiled nostalgically. 'From Wien. Vienna, you call it. Home of Sigmund, adopted home of Carl. Freud and Jung, that is, the founders of my profession. My first clinic was there, within a few streets of Sigmund's birthplace.'

'Have you been in Italy for long?'

'Several years, yes. I don't have a lot of Italian clients; for them it is still a little disgrace. But there are many Americans. My clinic is in Milan, so I am there most of the time. This week, for example, I was in Lucca only on Wednesday evening, to welcome you, and again since I was called by Elisa yesterday. The rest of the time always in the north. But my real home is in Lucca, I feel, with my dear friends here. I hope you will be one of them.'

'I hope so too.' There wasn't anything else she could have said, but she meant it, especially now he'd been so definite about the political angle. The significance of Gray's photocopying was fading by the hour. By the time she met Pietro, she might have forgotten it entirely.

Agostino Lenzuoli thanked the girl at Ryanair, put down the phone and smiled. Ten years ago at the seminary there had been a lecturer from Galway who had spoken with just that lilting accent.

And it was all right; the English girl had been on Wednesday's last flight, as she had told them. It would have been embarrassing for the Commissario otherwise. He crossed the first item off his list, reached for the telephone again and dialled a short number. Then, before it could ring, he replaced the receiver. The civilian staff at the Stranieri office were undoubtedly conscientious but it was easy to overlook a telephone message, to be distracted by something else. His physical presence would be less forgettable.

From inside, the office was even busier than the queues in the street had suggested. Here there were no lines, only a swarm of humanity, squirming between the four open counters. It was a sunny morning, and the heat and smell were gathering intensity. Agostino watched from behind the counter, reluctant to obstruct the slow process even further. But after a couple of minutes the woman at the nearest desk, sensing his presence, swivelled round on her high stool. She was in her late twenties, though the old-fashioned, rather fussy nylon dress she wore made her look older, sharp and lively as a sparrow.

'Padre!'

'No, Serafina, not that. Sergeant, if you must use a title.'

'*O Dio!*' She struck herself on the forehead, so violently that the stool wobbled and he had to reach out to steady her. 'Why do I keep saying that? You've been in the force for years.'

'Mamma's influence, I expect. After all, she did spend your entire catechism classes telling you about my sacred destiny.'

'He is a priest?' asked the man on the other side of the glass, a tall African with a toddler in his arms and a second perched astride his shoulders. It was Etienne, guiltily grateful for a morning away from the supermarket to renew his *permesso*. He turned to a little girl of six or seven who was clutching the sleeve of his jacket. 'This gentleman's a priest, Angela. Best behaviour, now.'

'Priest, there's a priest here.' The word passed along the tight ranks, to the furthest corners of the room and out of the door. People abandoned their attempts to reach the other *sportelli* and began to press towards Serafina's, in search of asylum, references, blessings or simply a kindly word. Others thought that Serafina, watched over by a man of God, would be more sympathetic than the other officials, more inclined to listen to the details of their stories, to explain the nature of their missing documentation. They were right, in fact, but Agostino's presence had nothing to do with it.

'I'm not a priest!' he was calling now, but only the nearest few could hear him through the security grilles, and few that could hear would believe.

'I heard her call you Father.' objected Etienne.

Serafina had to think quickly. 'That's because he is my father. Aren't you, *Babbo*?'

'Mmm.' said Agostino, trying to remember the circumstances in which it was ethically permissible to tell a lie. Certainly to save life, he thought, and the press of people heading in his direction was becoming alarmingly concentrated. Etienne looked dubiously from Serafina to Agostino and back again, estimating, rightly, that the sergeant could hardly be over thirty-five. It wasn't for him, however, to judge these Italians and their flexible morality. He turned and called to the crowd, his accent crisp and careful.

'I was wrong! He is not a priest!'

Amidst the grumbles of those who wanted to see a priest, those who were ideologically opposed to the very idea of a priest in the room and those who had simply lost their place in the scramble, the man turned back to the counter.

'I'm sorry.' he said, addressing Agostino. 'I shouldn't have spoken so loudly. I see of course that you're only - that you are a police officer. And now I have caused all this trouble. I wish – I wonder – perhaps you would accept a simple supper with my family tomorrow. With your daughter, of course, and any other... Just to show there are no hard feelings.'

More grumbles came from behind, mainly from those who, though familiar with the lubricating effect of a *busterella*, hadn't yet thought of offering private hospitality to speed the progress of their applications.

'We'd be delighted,' said Serafina. 'and no, there's only the two of us. I'll bring a cake. Now I just have to close this window for a moment. You don't mind at all, do you?'

It was one of the qualities in Serafina that made her so good at her job; the ability to ask such a question, almost but not quite rhetorical. Somehow, while still holding out the possibility of a no, she managed to make sure that the other person not only agreed with her but echoed her own optimism.

'Of course not. We don't mind waiting here, do we, children? Lots of people to look at.'

Serafina propped a piece of cardboard up against the glass screen and turned to Agostino. 'Sorry about that. I know you're not nearly old enough to be my dad; I just couldn't think of anything else to say. As long as Mamma never hears about it. And yours, of course.' She shuddered delicately. 'Was there something you needed?'

'Yes, please. I'd like to see the records of an American woman who came here about a year ago.'

'American? An *extracommunitario*, then. From outside the E.C.' she added, as if the term didn't appear daily in the scaremongering editorials of the right-wing papers. Except that they didn't usually mean Americans, or at least not the white-skinned variety. 'She'd have needed a full *permesso*, the old kind, that it takes months to get hold of. The regulations are pretty strict; lots of hoops to jump through. She'll have had to have a job, first of all, or evidence of enough capital to keep her.'

'She was working, all right. As an English teacher.'

'Was?'

'She died, I'm afraid.'

'Oh God, poor girl. I wonder whether she was one of mine? What was her name?'

'Carson. Zena Carson. You might remember her. She was about forty, small and very thin.'

'Like me in fifteen years time then, if I don't have lots of babies and turn into a *palloncino*.' She puffed her cheeks and flung her arms out, teetering precariously on the high seat. The woman at the next counter looked censorious.

'Oops. Chiara's on a diet and she doesn't think these things are funny. She says no one will ever marry me anyway, I talk too much. What was it again - Zena Carson? No, it doesn't ring any bells. Let's go and look at the files.'

She jumped down from the stool, taking Agostino's offered hand, and led him towards a row of filing cabinets at the back of the room.

Fifty minutes later they admitted defeat.

'If she ever had a *permesso*.' said Serafina, shaking her narrow head solemnly, 'she certainly didn't get it in Lucca. Are you sure she didn't stay anywhere else first?'

'Pretty sure. But I don't think it'll be a great surprise to the Commissario to find that she didn't have one at all. Thanks a lot, anyway, Serafina. You'd better get back to that poor man now.

Look, he's reading stories to the children.'

'*É un angelo*! I'm quite looking forward to this dinner. Shall I ring you later to let you know when and where? We'd better arrive together, don't you think? I mean - you are coming, aren't you? I don't want to push you into anything.'

'Of course I'm coming.' he said, grinning at the thought of her six stone pushing him anywhere. A few days later he would learn his mistake. 'Have you ever known me refuse a meal? Anyway, I can't let my favourite daughter down.'

'Is this your first trip to Lucca?' asked the hotel proprietor in German.

For a moment Pseudo-Helmut thought he had been discovered, that the Gamesmaster had primed the man, baited the trap with his own language.

'I...' he began, trying to launch himself into the memorized excuse; his identity as a post-grad art historian, the painting at the Guinigi Museum, so critical to his thesis, the essential importance of inspecting it at first hand. Then, just in time, he realised that the man was only being polite. He must ask all his guests the same question.

'Yes.' he replied firmly, only a few seconds too late. 'Yes, but I've read a lot about it. I'm looking forward to exploring the city.'

'Wonderful.' The proprietor waved an arm towards a rack of brochures. 'We have many informations, also in German. And we are always at your service, if you need anything more.'

'That's very kind of you. Thanks.'

He moved towards the rack, his face averted from the glass front door. That wasn't a bad idea, actually. He had visited hardly anything during the few months that he had lived in Lucca; here was a chance to make up the deficit. And how better to hide than as a tourist? Thank goodness the weather was fine; he wouldn't look so odd in his mirrored shades.

XIV

There was only one chair in the corridor, and even that had a broken back. Dottore Fosecco clearly didn't expect a rush of patients. After ten or fifteen minutes the consulting room door opened and a woman sidled out. She must have been at least seventy, but her hair was dyed banana yellow, and the loose skin around her eyes was clogged with bright blue make-up. She smirked knowingly at Pietro and passed out into the dingy street.

He counted to ten, knocked on the door and pushed it open.

'*Permesso?*'

'*Sì, sì.*' There was a hasty rustling, the clink of glass, a smell of spilt whisky. Dr. Fosecco righted himself in the black leather chair and swivelled it round to face the detective. He was a skinny man of about forty-five, very pale except for a blotchy redness around the eyes, with greasy blond hair fading to grey. Both his clothes and the room's furnishings looked expensive, but very dirty, and there were tide-marks around his wrists and collar showing the limits of his latest wash.

Pietro showed his identity card and the doctor nodded, unsurprised.

'What can I do for you, Commissario?'

'I'm making enquiries about a former patient of yours. A, er, deceased patient. Johann Schwartz. I understand that you gave the death certificate.'

Fosecco's faded blue eyes flickered for a moment, as though puzzled.

'Schwartz? Yes, I remember. The German boy with AIDS. Very sad. What is it that you need to know?'

'The cause of death,' said Pietro, taking a photocopied certificate out of his shirt pocket, 'is given as ARC. AIDS-related complex, I assume?'

'That's right, yes.'

'Could you be any more specific?'

He pondered for a moment. 'No, I don't think I could. AIDS isn't a tidy sort of condition, Commissario. It doesn't follow textbook rules and timescales. I daresay he had the usual symptoms: weight loss, fever, fatigue, diarrhoea. It was some time ago: I really can't remember the details.'

'But you have some paperwork, I assume?'

Dr. Fosecco sighed, forced himself up from the chair and walked, a little unsteadily, to a meagre shelf of books and files. They were coated with a thick layer of dust, and the textbooks looked long out of date. He took a thin folder from the far end and blew on it ineffectually.

'What does the 'G' stand for?' asked Pietro, looking at the stained cover.

'G? What 'G'? I don't know what you're... Oh, there. I forgot. Er, *giallo*, I think.'

'But the file's black.'

'Exactly. If it was already yellow, there wouldn't be any point in marking it, would there?' He gave a small snort of satisfaction, shuffled a few papers in the file and, with a flourish, drew out a dog-eared card. 'Here we are. Johann Schwartz's record card. Date of consultation, symptoms, diagnosis, treatment.'

Pietro took the card and examined it closely, uncomfortably aware of Fosecco's breath on the side of his face. The entries were surprisingly clear, in concise block capitals, showing consultations two or three times a fortnight over a five month period.

'According to this,' said Pietro, inspecting the card closely, 'Signor Schwartz registered with you in May 2001. I understand that he came to Lucca a few months before that. Was he seeing another doctor during that time?'

'I've no idea. He came to me just after he'd had the test, that's all I know. Maybe his previous doctor didn't like AIDS patients. Or Germans. Some of the older people round here have long memories.'

'Of course. You saw him regularly, in any case?'

'Oh yes. As you'll see, I visited him at home three days before he died. His condition was chronic by then, and I didn't think he ought to be alone. He didn't want to go into hospital, or even a hospice, so I suggested that he went to stay with friends. I'm pleased to say that he took my advice: I was called to a different flat to see the body.'

'How reassuring for you.' said Pietro drily. 'This column shows the drugs prescribed, does it?'

'That's right.' Fosecco's blackened fingernail trembled down the list. 'Standard stuff for AIDS patients. Retrovir, that's AZT to you. A reverse transcriptase inhibitor, of course. A couple of protease inhibitors, nelfinavir and saquinavir - Viracept and Fortovase, you'd call them. He didn't have any of the opportunistic infections; no *Pneumocystis carinii* or Kaposi's sarcoma, so I didn't prescribe co-trimoxazole or therapeutic radiology. I'm not going too fast for you, am I? Any questions?'

After years of Bisbiglian experience, Pietro knew better than to let himself be bludgeoned by science, at least not by an amateur like this.

'Yes.' he said, so firmly that the doctor swayed a little, and had to catch hold of the desk to keep himself from falling. 'I can't see any reference to methohexitone here. Or propofol or etomidate.'

'No? No, well I - didn't feel they were necessary. The particular circumstances of the case. In my clinical judgment... Of course, there can be two opinions about these things: I wouldn't go so far as to rule them out completely.'

'Dottore Fosecco?'

'What?' He looked longingly back to the other side of the desk, to the spreading pool of spilt Johnny Walker.

'Do you actually know I'm talking about?'

'Well, in vague terms... I mean, they're always changing the names of these drugs. A lot of new developments. It's not easy to keep up, not with running a practice single-handedly. I don't have time to sit around all day reading medical journals. I'm not a student any more.'

'I realise that, *dottore*. Let me enlighten you. Methohexitone, propofol and etomidate are all intravenous anaesthetics.'

Fosecco's face, already pale, faded to a bluish white. A row of small globules formed across his clammy forehead. He swallowed two or three times before speaking.

'Thank you. As - as you will appreciate, I am not myself an anaesthetist. But the answer to your question is simple. I didn't prescribe these drugs because there was no reason to do so. Signor Schwartz was not undergoing any surgery. Any requirements for pain relief would be met by ordinary analgesics. Taken orally, unless his predilections suggested otherwise.' He sniggered, drawing his lips back to reveal small yellowing teeth.

The guttering candle of Pietro's sympathy flickered and died.

'You would be surprised to learn, then, that on Johann Schwartz's body, an empty hypodermic syringe was found containing traces of methohexitone and another with traces of morphine?'

'What?' His blue eyes were hot and staring. 'But I didn't find anything!'

'No. I understand they had been removed before your arrival. Some friends of the deceased, concerned at the impression that might be given....'

'Impression? Oh, I see. You think he might have committed suicide?' A little greyish colour was creeping across his cheeks. 'Yes, I'm afraid that would be more than likely. Perhaps I was remiss in giving the certificate. But with the syringes removed, and my knowledge of his chronic condition... I'm sure you can understand, Commissario, that the obvious explanation appeared to be the correct one. And after all, as his friends no doubt realized, perhaps this way was better for all concerned. Suicide is still a nasty word, even nastier than AIDS.'

'I'm not really interested in the social hierarchies of medical disgrace.' said Pietro coldly. 'What I want to know is where the anaesthetics came from. From you?'

'Me? Good God, no! I mean, you saw yourself; I don't even know what they're called. You'd have to go to a specialist for that sort of thing.'

'A specialist?'

'Or a hospital pharmacy.' He was speaking more quickly now, almost gabbling. 'Yes, a hospital pharmacy, that would be it. I'm sure there must be people in those places who do that kind of thing. Sell drugs, I mean, for poor sods like Johann who want a quick way out. It's disgusting, isn't it? Corruption. You ought to institute an enquiry.'

'Yes, *dottore*. An excellent suggestion. We will certainly,' he hesitated just long enough for the mildest menace, 'be enquiring further. Meanwhile I'll leave you in peace. No doubt you have many patients waiting.'

'No doubt.' Fosecco was too relieved to notice the irony.

'Oh, and you'll want this back, I daresay.' Pietro held out the record card between finger and thumb. 'You'll keep it safe, won't you? Just in case we need to take another look.'

'Absolutely.' Fosecco made a grab for the card at the same moment as Pietro let it go. It fell, Fosecco grabbed the air again, and the contents of his file spilled onto the floor. Pietro crouched down to help collect them, but he picked up only one sheet of paper, a torn piece of A4 containing a handwritten name and address.

'Zena Carson. How interesting. One of your patients?'

'Yes, she is. Why?' The doctor's face was averted, bent low over the scattered papers.

'Was.'

'What?'

'She was one of your patients. She died on Monday night. Didn't you know?'

Fosecco sat up on his heels, looked directly at Pietro, almost challenging him.

'No, I didn't. Strange that no-one told me.'

'But you don't sound surprised that she's dead.'

'I'm not. She had a very serious heart condition which could have killed her at absolutely any moment. I did what I could for her, of course, continued the treatment she'd been getting in the States, but there was really nothing any of us medicos could do. Shame, really. She was still a comparatively young woman.'

He gathered up the rest of the papers and put them away in the file. 'If there's nothing else, Commissario...'

'She wasn't registered with you, was she? With USL, I mean.'

'No, she was a private patient. There's nothing illegal in that, is there?'

'I've no idea.' said Pietro frankly. 'It isn't my field. But it would have been expensive, wouldn't it, the kind of treatment she needed? Why didn't she register under the state scheme? Her employers would have paid the contributions. Or didn't she have a *permesso*?'

'Don't ask me. It wasn't any of my business. I'm a doctor, not a policeman. I'm here to save lives, not to put bureaucratic hurdles in people's way.'

'Very noble. It's a pity, isn't it, that you weren't able to save lives on these two occasions. A strange coincidence isn't it, that both should have died so young?'

'Not really, Commissario. They both suffered from fatal conditions. As you'll remember from the Gospels, it isn't the healthy who need a doctor, but the sick. I simply try to meet that need.'

'Again, most laudable. I really mustn't keep you from the exercise of your Hippocratic vocation.' Pietro let his eyes flicker, just for a moment, towards the whisky bottle. 'Just one more thing to tidy up. A matter of routine only: I already know what your answer will be. There would be no reason, would there, for you to prescribe intravenous anaesthetics to Signora Carson? Methohexitone, say?' He took a photograph from his pocket and quietly turned it over.

Fosecco looked down at the picture, at the hypodermic placed next to the body.

'Another case of pharmacy-assisted suicide, would you say, doctor?'

'It must have been, mustn't it? If this syringe had the same stuff inside. I really think you need to speak to someone at the hospital, Commissario.'

'Certainly, *dottore*. If you really think it was someone at the hospital who suffocated her, mutilated her body and hid it in the classroom where she taught. Do you think that's likely, Signor Fosecco?'

'I ... don't feel well.'

'No, you look a little pale. Perhaps something to fortify you... did I catch a glimpse of a bottle?'

'Please.'

Pietro fetched the whisky, what was left of it, and the very dirty glass. He poured a generous measure and Fosecco nodded to him to continue. When the tumbler was almost full, the doctor took it and swallowed, almost without pausing for breath.

'Now then,' said Pietro in his kindly neighbourhood voice. 'What have you got to tell me?'

'So what was it?' urged Pippa, swerving violently to avoid an old man on roller blades. They were up on the walls again, having hired their bikes in a more orthodox manner this time. They had even, after a long argument with Lorenzo, managed to pay for them.

'*Niente*. He wouldn't say a thing, not even when I offered to run out for a second bottle. All he did was recite lists of medicines he'd prescribed and repeat how much he'd done for the pair of them and how hopeless their cases were. Any anomalies I pointed out, any mention of the hypodermics, and we were straight back to the hospital pharmacy story.'

'Could there be anything in that?'

'I don't think so. Sergeant Lenzuoli's had a good deal to do with the local hospitals and he's satisfied they're all clean. I don't mean that there isn't the odd packet of aspirin that goes astray, but nothing on the scale Fosecco suggests. No, it's a red herring, that one.' He beamed at the metaphor, terrifying a small nun on an electric scooter. 'Why do you say that, anyway?'

'The 'red' means smoked, I think. Like a kipper.' Pietro opened his mouth to ask about kippers then thought better of it. 'If you dragged one across the trail of a fox then the hounds would lose the scent. An ancient technique of the hunt saboteurs.'

'Ah, yes, I remember. The only surviving English terrorists. If only all this had happened in England...' He drifted into a reverie of deerstalkers and debutantes, collided with a tree, apologised to it and returned to the subject.

'Fosecco was scared, you know. Really scared. Unfortunately not of me.'

'Of who, then?'

'Of whom, I think you mean, Signorina English teacher.'

'Signor Pedant. Of whom was he manifesting symptoms of trepidation?'

'You'll make an Italian yet, with that kind of pomposity. I don't know. Almost any organization is scarier than the polizia. The Mafia, the Red Brigade, Opus Dei - oops. Don't tell Mamma I said that.'

'I'm not likely to, am I?'

'You might. I forgot to tell you; you're invited to our house for Sunday lunch. She can't bear the idea of a poor little English girl a thousand miles away from her mother's home cooking.'

Pippa thought of Sunday lunch at home, the queue of pajama-clad family in front of the microwave, each bearing a pierced plastic box. *Three minutes on full power, tear back film and stir.* 'It's very kind of her. I'm not exactly little, though.'

He turned to scrutinize her, wobbling a little, his eyes finally resting just above the saddle. 'No, not exactly.' he said cheerfully. 'But I wouldn't worry about it. You'll be even fatter after one of Mamma's lunches.'

Pippa, who had meant age, not size, considered for a full two and half seconds the possibility of launching a serious sulk. Unfortunately, Pietro was quite likely not to notice, and an unacknowledged sulk is a lonely business. What was more, she rather liked the idea of this lunch. It would be interesting to see whether the rest of the family shared his random eating habits. She contented herself instead with pedalling faster, in the rather forlorn hope of using up a few extra calories before Sunday.

'You'll come then?' he called, effortlessly overtaking her. 'Do you mind going to Mass, first?'

'In for a penny.' she said, deliberately obscure, so that he would have to slow down and ask her about it, and make a note on the back of the copy death certificate. That reminded him of what they were supposed to be talking about.

'If Fosecco's working for someone else, and I think he must be; he's too drunk to figure out any kind of scam for himself, he'll be a lot more worried about what they'll do if he tells me anything than what I'll do if he doesn't.' He paused for breath. 'I think that's the longest English sentence I've ever managed. Did it make sense?'

'Just about. By the way, Otto thinks it's political.'

'Otto? That nice German who was looking after the old ladies?'

'Austrian, actually. Yes, he had a lesson with me this morning. He was Zena's therapist, apparently.'

'*Gli americani.*' Pietro shook his head in indulgent despair. 'But yes, I think he could be right. Sergeant Lenzuoli's been looking into Schwartz' background for any political stuff.'

'And?'

'Not much so far. A flirtation with the Greens when he was a student in Germany, but that's more or less compulsory, I gather. Nothing here, at least nothing public. He didn't go to any of Luciano's meetings and his name doesn't ring any bells with the *neofascisti* either. Meanwhile I've been trying to find out what happened to his body. It's a bit late for a post-mortem...' Pippa shuddered. '...but there might be some useful indications. The trouble is, I can't find out where in Germany it went. I've talked to the undertakers here, a scruffy little outfit on the outskirts of Prato. I can't understand why Schwartz's friend didn't use a proper Lucchese firm. They showed me the documents, but something's obviously been copied down wrongly. Neither the firm of German undertakers nor the town where they're supposed to be based seem to exist at all. German burial and cremation records are very efficient, as you'd expect and they've done a nationwide search for us but nothing helpful has come up so far.'

'No Johann Schwartzes?'

'Dozens of Johann Schwartzes, but none of them the right one. These were all solid respectable Johann Schwartzes, elderly, or at least middle-aged, with churches full of mourners to vouch for them. Ours doesn't seem to have had any family, grew up in careand didn't stay in contact with anyone. And we can't trace this boyfriend, either, Thomas Schmidt, the one who travelled with the body. We've no record of him in Lucca at all. Of course there are thousands of Thomas Schmidts in Germany but I can't expect the *Polizei* to interview each one on the off-chance.'

'Maybe Johann was buried somewhere unofficially, especially with him having been a Green. You know, a biodegradable cardboard coffin, or none at all. Under the trees, returning to the earth. I've always liked the idea myself.'

'How very morbid of you. Not to mention inconsiderate. Where would your family go on All Souls Day to weep over your bones and polish your photograph? I see what you mean, though. It might have saved Schmidt a lot of paperwork too, particularly with the HIV complication. Plenty of scope for bureaucratic madness there. You're probably right; I don't think we'll get much further with that side of things. What I really need now is to speak to the Americans, the security services, preferably. We've informed the embassy of the death, of course as a matter of protocol, but I'd like to see if they'll tell us anything on the political angle. All hush-hush, of course, but I'll try to get you in with me, if you like the idea.'

'Sounds great.' said Pippa, trying to sound as though she meant it. The idea of a tête-à-tête with the CIA was about as enticing as a date with Mike Tyson, while the mere word 'debriefing' had always given her a shivery feeling about the nether regions. This was no time, however, to be wet and girly.

Pietro looked at her thoughtfully.

'Conference over.' he announced. 'Race you to the *baluardo*.'

Charles sat in the window seat and counted the dangers on his stubby fingers. He never wrote anything down, anything incriminating, that was, and he'd instructed the others to do the same. A capital G was enough to alert anyone who needed to know. What La Carson thought she was doing, putting the full name ... Didn't trust the Seppi, he supposed. But now he had the nagging feeling that he'd forgotten something. Someone, more likely. He looked down into the street, hoping that the passers-by would short-circuit his memory.

One. The *polizotto*, Guinizelli. Cocky bastard with his English idioms and his dinner down his shirt. If people couldn't behave in a civilized manner they didn't deserve to live in a place like this. And those weren't the only rules he didn't play by. Charles had asked around and everyone had the same story: Guinizelli wasn't interested. Power, money, women; he was determined to get them by his own efforts or not at all; had never come near taking a *regalo* in exchange for a blind eye. No, there was nothing they could do with Guinizelli, short of wiping him out altogether. And Charles didn't kill people. That was what this was all about.

There was Bisbigli, though. It was one of the few chinks of light in this whole mess, the fact that Guinizelli reported to Umberto. Oh yes, they were on first name terms; minor but undeniable members of the Tuscan Great and Good. He could be virtually sure of bumping into Umberto at the next gastronomic pomposity-fest and steering the conversation in the right direction. Come to think of it, there was a grappa tasting in Siena on Saturday that the Vice-Questore couldn't possibly bring himself to miss. That was the police dealt with, then. The sleepy sergeant - what was he called, Cushions? - he wouldn't pose any problems. An unfrocked priest, or something like that. Another failure.

Two. The English girl. You had to be a bit careful with the English. Secretive and sly. This one wasn't causing too much trouble at the moment, though. Nicely naive and malleable, pointing in the right direction now. He'd have to keep an eye out, all the same.

Three. The Canadian idiot. The text message had scared him all right, to put it mildly. Repeat as necessary: that was the prescription there. Charles had already wasted too much time on that particular loser.

Four. The girls. They didn't suspect anything, and never would, as long as he went on being careful. He wanted to keep them out of this; enjoyed seeing himself through their adoring eyes. No more about the girls in this company.

Five. The gentlemen from the South. They were angry, of course, at the fiasco on Tuesday morning, trebly so at losing the merchandise. It was only business, though. He'd done the job efficiently before, and he would again. The mistake was using Americans, but they wouldn't hold that against him. At least, he hoped not.

His attention wandered for a moment, along the street below to the church on the corner. A German tourist was going in; his bouncing gait like young Johann's had been. After all, that one had gone smoothly enough to satisfy the most demanding client. He would remind them of that if they started getting nasty.

Six. The Seppi. Never any problems there. Consummate professionals. Well, consummate crooks, anyway. There wasn't any undertaking scam, dirty business or just plain villainy that they weren't mired in up to the black rosettes. You wouldn't catch them losing their nerve, not with twenty-five years each hanging over them. But now he remembered.

Seven. The sodding medico. Dottore just-one-more Fosecco. If only he could have found a bent doctor in Lucca who wasn't an alcoholic. He didn't like doing business with drunks; you might as well fire a rifle in a squash court. But he needed a GP, that's what it came down to; the whole scheme would crumble without one. He should have contacted Fosecco days ago, though, as soon as he knew it had all gone pear-shaped. If Charles had believed in God, he would have prayed to be in time. As it was, he got up and turned towards the telephone, just as the German tourist came out of the church below.

XV

The wooden face of the Volto Santo gazed past the watchers, resigned to horrors beyond their imagination. Its large brown eyes bulged beneath their heavy lids, as if from a thyroid overload. Or maybe it was only the nails rammed into his palms. Around the figure rose an ornate octagonal chapel, domed like an English folly, a gilded Tardis on the wide cathedral floor. The gaunt, blackened Christ within, scarcely visible through the golden mesh, looked like a giant crow trapped in a filigree cage. Pseudo-Helmut shuddered and blamed his Lutheran prejudices. He chose a pew beyond the fringes of the light, where he could see the doors, and bowed his head to wait. Now that he was here, back in Lucca, zig-zagging stealthily from one church to another, he felt unexpectedly calm. The impulse that had brought him here, through a thousand kilometres of menace, couldn't fail to fetch Gray to join him.

And it didn't. Barely half an hour had passed: time for two giggling school parties, half a dozen English couples, didactic and faded, three lunatics, four lovers, and eight or nine elderly Lucchese, bidding good morning to their patron saints while their little dogs waited outside. Watching them, he must have taken his eyes from the door for a moment, for it was Gray's voice that he heard first, that long civilised drawl with the smile inside.

'You haven't read up on the sights then, I guess? Sure, I'd love to show you. Mom says I've been lecturing since I was in diapers and I've never objected to an audience. Just scream when you can't take any more. This is the Volto Santo. The Holy Face, you know?'

There was someone with him. In all his dreams, waking and sleeping, of this moment, in all his calculations, he had never considered this. A woman, too; a young woman, scarcely older than Gray himself. Jealousy rose in his throat like heartburn, mingled with the sickly taste of shame. Had he expected Gray to embrace life-long celibacy in his memory? And if he'd discovered girls, good luck to him; it would make his life simpler in the future. He'd make a good dad.

They were standing in front of the Volto Santo now, shielded from his view by the ridiculous gold columns.

'It's supposed to have been carved by Nicodemus,' Gray was saying, 'You know, the old guy who came to see Jesus at night when the Pharisees weren't watching? The story is that he was carving it from life, in front of the Cross - gruesome, huh? - but he fell asleep so an angel scooted down to finish it off.'

'Hmm.' said Pippa, squinting at the lifesize figure. She wasn't sure what criteria one was supposed to use in judging an angelic creation. The face looked disconcertingly familiar until she realised where she had seen it before; on the lugubrious grocer opposite the Piccola Casa, the one who sold seventeen types of salami but only UHT milk. 'But how did the Volto Santo get from Calvary to Lucca? Did the angel deliver it as well?'

'Near enough. They put it in an unmanned boat and sent it forth on the ocean. Sea, I guess you'd call it. The boat made its way round the *stivale* and found its way to Luni - that's "u.n.i.", before you ask - up in Liguria. The townspeople there managed to rescue it from the marauding Genoese and brought it to their cathedral.'

'So why isn't it still at Luni?'

'Because the Bishop of Lucca, Giovanni the Glorious, had a dream. You must have known there'd be a dream in it somewhere. And in the dream an angel told Giovanni to go to Luni and find a gift waiting for him.'

'Of course. Simple when you think about it. So the Lunatics gave it to him?'

'Not without a bit more miraculous biz, no. They didn't want to hand it over, so Giovanni suggested that they put it in a wagon with a couple of unbroken oxen and wait to see what happened.'

'As you do. And instead of tearing off in opposite directions like any self-respecting unbroken oxen, they meekly trotted ahead and took it straight to Lucca?'

'Exactly, right to the front door of the cathedral. Far more efficient than the *Poste Italiane*.'

They stood in silence for a few moments, looking into the wooden face. There was something about it that grew on you, thought Pippa. Already the resemblance to the corner shop man was fading.

On the other side of the chapel, Pseudo-Helmut eased himself up from the pew, his jaw set in decision. He would slip around quietly and hover next to Gray, whisper something reassuring, quietly enough for the girl not to hear. It hadn't sounded like a lovers' conversation in any case. He was a few feet away, still shielded, when a sliver of gold appeared around the edge of the nearest door. It widened, and a figure padded inside; a smallish, plump figure, blinking in the moment's darkness.

That moment was all that Pseudo-Helmut had. He took a hasty step backwards into the shadows, his heart like a cannonball. *Il Maestro*. He had known, of course, that he might see him, but he hadn't expected it to be here. There was something about the man's domination of his world that left no room for another God. Could he have seen him, followed him here? Pseudo-Helmut had been rash, he knew, striding about the town with only his sunglasses and new beard to protect him. But it wouldn't end like this. He had no intention of being cornered here in this dark cathedral like some tiresome rodent, scrabbling mindlessly among sacred things. Not that. If he died, really died, it would at least be outside. Maybe there was a side exit somewhere. He edged his way along the dark pew, towards the towering nave.

Pseudo-Helmut had been right. Charles hated churches, all of them. The only question was which churches he hated most: the ones he had been brought up to respect, all bare polished wood and bare hopeless Calvinism, or the ones he had been taught to despise, like this one, filthy juxtapositions of birth and feasting and blood-boltered martyrdoms. There was only one way of conquering death, Charles reminded himself, and he had found it.

He blinked in the gloom, bright patches from the sun outside still clogging his vision, and peered about the church. He had only given them two or three minutes' start; they could hardly have exhausted the cultural inspection already. The corner of a blue dress caught his eye, but it was only a dressed-up statue. He shuddered. It must have been a place like this that Elisabeth had come to, on those secretive early mornings, when she would slip out of bed, half-waking him, and return half an hour later, with cold fingers and warm sweet breath. He wasn't going to think about that; of the statues' twofold trick, granting the impossible, then condemning him for not believing it.

He moved away from the walls, to the safety of the open spaces. Saint Elizabeth was always in the shadows, marginal at best, her miracle a mere counterpoint to the important one. What was an old woman's pregnancy, anyway, now that any Italian quack could do it? It had been different two thousand years ago, but still nothing in comparison to a virgin birth. What did he mean, two thousand? It had been different ten years before.

Yes, there they were, skulking around the overgrown birdcage, creeping in timid deference to the man-god inside. They couldn't believe in it, nothing but superstition or sheepish conformity could keep their voices so low. Ridiculously low: Charles had to stand right behind them to hear their conversation.

'I've got to ask you something, Graham.'

'Graham, is it? Sounds heavy. You don't want to know the history of Ilaria's tomb, then?'

'Not right now, no. Graham - Gray - were you at the school on Monday evening?'

The humour trickled out of his face like water onto hot sand. 'Christ, Philippa, you really are a lawyer, aren't you? I already told your pal Pietro, didn't you notice?'

'Yes but - are you sure? I'm sorry, Gray, but...'

'Something lost in the translation, you think? The Tower of Babel effect. It's always happening here. I don't mind going through it again, if it helps. I was over at the john paper factories all afternoon, phrasal verbs and baby-soft asses. At six on the dot, I was about to clear out when this management guy came in with a draft email in English. Apparently it was a really urgent message and he needed it checking before it went. Needless to say, 'checking' was a massive understatement. The text was a load of bull, meaningless where it wasn't outright offensive, and I had to rewrite the whole thing from scratch. By the time I'd got that finished, and negotiated the deathtrap they call the Lucca ring road, I was ready to flop. I went back to my flat and crashed out for an hour or so, then went downtown for something to eat. Like I told Guinizelli, I don't remember where.'

'I know all that.' Actually she didn't, not about the email, but it sounded authentic enough. 'The point is that you went to the Piccola Casa as well.'

'No way.'

'Yes. You left a worksheet in the photocopier. In your handwriting.'

There was a strange hiss, a rapid intake of breath, from one of the tourists behind them. Pippa realized she must have been talking too loudly.

'There's no doubt about it.' she whispered. 'You must have been there.'

'Photocopier. Worksheet.' Gray counted the items on his fingers, trying to look as if he were doing something other than stalling. 'You're right.' He sounded mildly surprised, as though a particularly dull-witted student had answered a question correctly. 'Funny, I thought that was last week sometime. Seems like longer ago than the email fiasco. I just called by to copy a worksheet for my intermediate class - poetry and the pluperfect.   I forgot all about the original. Have Elsa and Elisa still got it? I gave out all my copies and I might want to use it again.'

'I expect so, yes. But...' Was Gray really this obtuse or was it another play for time? 'You do realise that was Zena's last evening at the school? I mean - what time were you there - did you see her - was there anyone else? I'm not trying to do the police's dirty work, Gray, but you must see...'

'Oh yes, I see all right.   Twenty-twenty vision with the specs on. Now then, what do you need? Time - about a quarter after seven. Zena - no. No sign of her either, nor of anyone else.'

His voice was brisk, almost flippant, but his finger rubbed a perpetual circle on a patch of gold mesh. A nearby guide, beginning the story of the Volto Santo in German, stared reproving at him.

'But she must have been in her classroom, mustn't she, teaching Francesca? Could you hear their voices or did she keep the door closed?'

'I told you.' said Gray simply. 'She wasn't there.'

Pippa swallowed hard and tried to concentrate. She could hear the breathing of the tourists behind them, wondered how many of them were listening to the German guide and how many to their conversation.

'How do you know?' she asked slowly, trying to keep her voice even.

'Because I went into the classroom. I needed to check something with Zee so I knocked and...'

'What?   What did you need to check?'

'The...' He waved his fingers in the air, only too obviously casting around for inspiration. 'The past participle of 'to chide'. One of my students wanted it and I couldn't remember how it went. Chide, chided....'

As straws go, it was a flimsy one. In India, perhaps, or one of the more Imperially-influenced African states, it was remotely possible that a student could need the verb 'to chide'. But here in Italy, where the concepts of bedtime, discipline and the nine o'clock watershed were all equally alien...The thought scuttled into a dusty corner. She already knew that Gray had been lying; what mattered now were the crumbs of truth she might be able to hoover up.

'So you knocked at the door? And?'

'And nothing. Zilch. No answer. So I opened the door and took a look inside. Still nothing. No Zena, no student. I assumed the lesson had been cancelled and she'd gone home.'

'But you didn't check her flat?'

'No.' His bonhomie was overlaid with something defensive. 'No, why should I? I wasn't that desperate to brush up on my irregular verbs. I told you, I was bushed.'

'But Francesca says they had the lesson as usual.'

Gray shrugged. 'Maybe she's confusing it with another day. Or perhaps they went out for a peripatetic lesson. It's been known before now. A little *passeggiata* round the walls, maybe finish in a bar somewhere. All I know is, there definitely wasn't anyone in the classroom, not at a quarter after seven. I can tell you that as a fact.'

It sounded genuine, unlike his crazily clumsy inventions. Unless he was really clever, and knew how to lie both convincingly and otherwise, to put her off the scent. Pippa was floundering out of her depth.

'You know I've got to tell Pietro Guinizelli?'

'Sure, of course. I'm only sorry that it slipped my mind earlier. But you know how it is. You see nothing, you remember nothing. End of story.'

'Hmm.' No one, not even a Canadian, could really be that breezy. Certainly not a Canadian with Gray's capacity for panic. 'You're sure there isn't anything else you ought to be telling me? Telling the police, I mean.'

'Dangerous category error, that, Phil. No, there's nothing else.'

Pippa gave him one of her long looks. During her short years as a matrimonial solicitor, she had perfected her long looks, and there were few, either petitioners or respondents, who could face them without squirming. 'Nothing?'

He made a subtle amendment. 'Nothing that could lead you to Zena Carson's murderer. I can promise you that.'

And that, Pippa knew from experience, was probably the best she could hope for.

Agostino paced up and down outside the shabby tower block, wondering whether he looked more like an off-duty policeman or an on-duty priest; priests being, in the nature of things, permanently on-duty. He didn't want to look like either, just like an ordinary, anonymous man, calling round for dinner with friends and bearing a bottle of wine. But judging from the curtains twitching at each floor and the lounging youths who had vanished at his approach, the air of authority wasn't as easy to shed as the uniform. Not that the uniform came off these days without a good bit of tugging. No will power, that was his problem. Next time...

Next time proved not to be far off. Round the corner, like temptation personified, came Serafina, decked out in pink polyester hydrangeas and swinging a large white carton tied up with brown ribbon. Agostino groaned. He knew those cartons well, could recognize the signature of each individual *patisseria* at twenty yards and could make a fair guess at the combination of chocolate, custard, cream and chopped nuts inside. *Next* next time, he amended hastily.

'Ciao Ago!'

'Ciao. What happened to the 'Father'?'

'Father as in priest or father as in Dad? I think we'd better abandon both, don't you? Confess at the beginning and get it over with. Anyway...'

'Anyway what?'

'I'd rather not be that closely related to you. Not yet, in any case.' She glanced mischievously up at him, but he hadn't understood, just kept standing there like a big dumb ox, desperate to please, if only someone could explain what he was supposed to do. Probably he'd never been flirted with in his life, thought Serafina. She wasn't exactly a world expert herself, her amorous conquests being limited to a spotty boy in Criminal Records and an old man who waited at the same bus stop, but at least she hadn't been terminally repressed by a mother like Agostino's. She would have to take things very slowly.

'So we're both Greeks, then.' she said chirpily.

'Sorry, what?'

'Bearing gifts.' She pointed to the bottle under his arm, the tissue paper by now crumpled and damp.

'Oh, that. Well, a bottle of wine's always...' His voice tailed off into a lugubrious flatness. 'Oh no. They'll be Muslims, won't they? It's going to be some dreadful kind of insult, bringing alcohol into their home. Is there a litter-bin around here somewhere? Shame, it was a rather nice prosecco. Maybe if we stick it far enough down we can come back for it later.'

'Hold your horses, Long John Silver. You don't need to bury the treasure this time. Yes, you're right, most immigrants from Senegal are Muslims, but not this family. They're as Catholic as you are, Signor Seminarian, and I'm sure they'll appreciate a good drop of fizz. If not, I certainly will. Now come on in and stop panicking.'

And he had to admit, sitting ten minutes later, around the improvised dining table (a large sheet of cardboard and four empty tomato boxes) that Serafina had managed the explanations rather well. Without actually saying anything specific, she had given the impression that she and Agostino had been conducting a highly romantic but entirely proper courtship which, for complex bureaucratic reasons, would be frowned upon by their respective superiors and so needed to be kept strictly secret. Agostino did his best to keep up with this charade by casting what he hoped were tender glances at Serafina over the *thebouidienne*. That was, whenever he could spare a moment from concentrating on the bowl in front of him. He had felt perplexed at first when, before the meal, Etienne had invited him to hold out his hands and had poured water over them. It felt like being a small boy again, scrubbed up for the aunties. But when the fragrant fish and rice were ladled into each enamel bowl and Juliette, Etienne's wife, had indicated that he should begin, without any more cutlery on the table, he began to understand. The children, Angela and the two year old twins, Thomas and Thierry, had demonstrated enthusiastically, dipping the first three fingers of their right hands into their bowls and scooping the food into their mouths. They were neat and accurate, dropping scarcely a grain and politely suppressing their giggles when Agostino's broad fingers slipped and slid. He didn't mind being the evening's laughing-stock; he was used to that, but it was his only good shirt, and his mother would never let him forget it if he came home looking like Commissario Guinizelli. Serafina didn't seem to be having any difficulty, although with that dress she could get away with spilling a whole bowlful before the hydrangeas looked any odder. She was more devious than she let on, that girl.

It was not until they had finished the *thebouidienne*, the prosecco and the cakes, which proved to be quite as sticky and calorific as Agostino had anticipated, that he became aware of the tautening atmosphere. Angela had taken the little boys away for bedtime stories while the adults sat around the cardboard table, befogged in a sudden silence.

Julie looked straight at her husband.

'We should tell them.'

Etienne rubbed his eyes with long delicate fingers.

'I don't know, Juliette. It was only the one time. Just a stupid joke, I'm sure.'

'When people threaten my children, it is never a joke.' She had seemed such a soft woman when they had first arrived, docile and selfless to the point of negation, but now there was something hard in her pretty plump face. 'We have the opportunity, now, to tell someone. Someone who knows about these things.'

'They warned us not to tell the police.'

'And we won't be. Agostino is here as our guest, as Serafina's friend, isn't that right? He isn't on duty. He doesn't even have to listen if he doesn't want to. I'll tell my new friend Serafina an interesting story, that's all. You men needn't have anything to do with it.'

'They told us not to speak to anyone.'

'Bah! It would take stronger men than those to stop women from gossiping. Isn't that right, Agostino?'

'Quite right.' He had been a policeman for long enough to recognize when the best course was to fade into the background. He wasn't exactly built for fading, but he would do his best. 'Whatever it is, Serafina is the person to tell. Just pretend I'm not here.'

'Easier said than done,' commented Serafina, her eyes following an arc from one side of his stomach to the other, 'but we can try. What's it all about then, Jules?'

Julie took a deep breath, unsure, now, of how to begin.

'Men from Senegal,' she plunged in at last, 'usually come to Italy alone. Without their families, I mean. Generally the women and children stay behind, at least for the first few years. But Etienne and I didn't want to do it like that. We didn't want the family to be separated while the children were so small. And being a Catholic, he didn't have a Muslim brotherhood to help him. He needed us with him.'

'I certainly did.' interrupted Etienne with a dry smile. 'The question is, did you need me?'

'Of course we did. How many times must I tell you? What he means is,' She turned back to Serafina, 'that it was hard for him to find work here. Most Senegalese work as traders, selling goods in the streets, on the beaches, in the supermarket car parks. Etienne keeps trying that kind of work, but it isn't any good for him. He's too shy, too timid. He can't go up to strangers and beg them to buy things, watches, umbrellas, cigarette lighters, things that they neither want nor need. Maybe he's too honest. Yes, yes, I know, Etienne. I'm not saying that our Muslim cousins are crooks, only that they're salesmen. And you aren't, not even to save your life.'

'Or yours. Or the children's.'

'There's no need to be so melodramatic about it. There was never any question of our starving, whatever that stupid message said. All that happened was a bit of role-reversal. Very modern, very Western. I go out cleaning to make some money, while Etienne does a little selling and looks after the children.'

'It's not enough. It's not the answer.'

'Not in the long term maybe. But for now we can survive. And something will come along for you; I know it will. Not like the message, though. I don't want you involved in anything like that.'

'The message?' Serafina was anxious to get the gist of the story before the last bus left Lucca. It was a long dark walk home and she'd never wasted money on taxi fares in her life.

'I have a mobile phone.' Julie explained. 'I know, it seems like a terrible luxury for people like us, but Angela's at school and her teacher might have to contact me. Also, it means that the people I clean for can phone me if they want me to do some extra hours, or if they don't want me to come on a particular day. They have to keep quiet about employing *extracomunitari*, you know. Nothing gets declared.'

Etienne looked nervously at Agostino, who had rested his head on his arms and closed his eyes. He opened one.

'Like the ladies said, I'm not listening.'

'Then I got a text message on the phone one day. It was a particularly bad time for us, about six months ago. Angela had just started school and she needed lots of things: exercise books, pens, a rucksack. It seems like nothing to Italian parents but for us it was almost impossible. And I didn't have much work, only two people to clean for and both of them single men who didn't make a lot of mess. We were wondering how on earth we could survive. Then the message came.'

Agostino opened both eyes this time and they were dark and still.

'What did it say?'

'I copied it out. Yes,' she turned to her husband, 'I know what you said, but I had to. It was a kind of exorcism, I suppose. Once it was on the paper, it wasn't in my head any more. Here.' She reached into a cardboard box neatly stacked with paper and took out a small brown envelope. 'Who should I give it to?'

'Sergeant Lenzuoli.' said Serafina quickly.

He took the envelope, opened it, and laid the slip of paper out on the table before him. The letters, formed in Julie's schoolgirl French script, wobbled only a little.

> THERE IS A WAY ETIENNE CAN SAVE HIS FAMILY. A NEW IDENTITY IN FRANCE AND NO MORE WORRIES ABOUT MONEY. THERE ARE RISKS, BUT MOST DEATHS ARE KINDER THAN STARVATION. REPLY TO THIS MESSAGE IF YOU ARE ENOUGH OF A MAN TO TAKE THIS PATH. TELL NO ONE, PARTICULARLY NOT THE POLICE. I KNOW WHERE ANGELA GOES TO SCHOOL AND THOMAS AND THIERRY'S FAVOURITE SEE-SAW. ACCIDENTS ARE ALWAYS HAPPENING. G.

There was a silence while Agostino smoothed the edges of the paper with his broad white fingertips. When he spoke, his voice was as low as a mourner's. 'Have you any idea who sent this?'

'None at all. I made a note of the number it came from; it's on the back, but it wasn't anyone who'd ever called me.'

'How many people know your number?'

'I don't really know. The people I work for sometimes give it to a friend or relative, anyone they know who wants a bit of cleaning doing. Then Angela's friends all have mobiles of their own, so she has to have a number to give them. Then there's the school, and the twins' *asilo*, and your department, I suppose?'

She looked at Serafina, who nodded.

'But they'd need to know more than the number, wouldn't they?' Julie continued. 'They'd need to know the children's names and that Etienne wasn't working and that we were having trouble making ends meet. And we always tried to keep that from Angela so I don't think she'd have told her friends. Mind you, Italy isn't exactly bursting with rich Senegalese; I suppose they could have worked that one out. But - oh God, the see-saw. Someone must have been watching us.'

'Try not to worry.' said Agostino, replacing the paper in the little envelope. 'We'll be watching you from now on. And not on behalf of the *Fiscale* boys, either. Mind if I take this with me?'

'I'll leap for joy once it's out of the house.' said Julie. Already she had relaxed again, the tense lines across her forehead fading into the warm brown flesh.

Etienne stood up, a little stiffly, and shook Agostino's hand.

'We're very grateful to you both. I hope you will forgive our bringing you here on false pretences.'

'Nothing false about that risotto-thing.' said Serafina cheerfully. 'Anyway, now Agostino can put it down as overtime.' She looked at her lilac plastic watch and tucked her scrawny little arm into the crook of his huge elbow. 'Plus the time it takes to drive me home. I've just missed the last bus.'

XVI

The church was very cool after the rising heat outside, where it was already too hot for comfort at only ten in the morning. Pippa had worn a cardigan over her sundress for modesty's sake, but now she was grateful for its warmth. She shifted a little on the pew, trying to extricate the folds of her skirt from under the ample thigh of Pietro's grandmother. But the old woman was evidently settled for the duration, and nothing short of an earthquake, fork-lift truck or final benediction was going to move her. On Pippa's other side crouched one of Pietro's uncles, tall and spare, his long body bent into a Z shape that could equally represent a sitting, standing or kneeling posture. Why, with half the church still empty, the entire Guinizelli clan had to cram itself into only two pews, Pippa hadn't yet worked out. It was very kind of them to absorb her into their midst like this, but she could not help yearning for a lonely isolation somewhere behind the confessional.

Outside the church she had hardly had time to exchange a couple of words with Pietro before his mother, four and a half feet of indefatigable energy, had launched herself at Pippa's neck and hauled her into something between a maternal embrace and a scrum half's high tackle. How clearly, she wondered, had Pietro explained the nature of their relationship; that she was, at best, only a quasi-colleague, really nothing more than a glorified witness? This degree of family welcome, back in England, would be rather over the top for a fully fledged fiancée.

A little brown priest came down the aisle, preceded by a lanky youth whose off-white robes ended a good eighteen inches above his Juventus socks and large black trainers. Pietro's grandmother - Nonna, she was supposed to call her - dug Pippa sharply in the ribs and mimed to her to stand up. Neither Nonna herself nor the uncle did so, although he straightened his elbows, as though performing a kind of vertical press-up, took a pair of spectacles from his shirt pocket and rested them on his beaky nose. By that nose alone, Pippa could have recognized his relationship to Pietro.

After a few preliminaries, the congregation launched into a ragged recital of a prayer, a few dominant female voices racing ahead of the general drone. Pippa, surprising herself, recognized it as a close cousin to the Anglican General Confession. As a Girl Guide, she had made occasional forays into the Church of England, the effects of which had apparently lasted longer than those of her Needlework badge. *We have left undone those things which we ought to have done*.

She realised, with a little twitch of guilt, that she had still not told Pietro about Gray and the photocopier. It couldn't be put off any longer, not after such a direct divine hint; even if it was supposed to be a day of rest. The ironic thing was that after all that agonizing about betraying Gray, the actual story did at least as much to incriminate Francesca. Pippa didn't know which was worse. She had liked Francesca and still squirmed when she thought of her - how was it Pietro had put it? -'certain doubts'. And the bond of loyalty she felt towards Gray as a fellow English-speaker - well, almost-English-speaker - what was that compared to the imperatives of sisterhood? But it was no good thinking like that, it simply messed up the whole thing. You either had to be in, really in, only interested in finding out the truth or you had to stay out completely. There weren't any half-measures available.

And it seemed, as the *Kyrie* shifted into the *Gloria* and she recognized Pietro's voice, off-key, competing with his cousin as to who could get to the end first, as though her mind had already been made up for her.

The Italian readings meant little, and the sermon even less, but there was a corner of the big sanctuary window that had somehow escaped decoration, and through it she could see the rows of silver-green olive trees climbing up the hillside, the distant clumps of poplars and the cornflower sky.

Then they were on their feet again, reciting what must have been the Lord's Prayer, with cupped palms raised before them, like Evangelicals at home. A pause, another brief exchange with the priest, and then everyone was shaking hands with everyone else. She remembered this from England, too, but there it had been a restrained, embarrassed affair, fingertips just touching and the word 'Peace' muttered as though it were faintly obscene. Here they used two hands at least, and sometimes kissed each other as well, with

Pace shortened to a friendly 'Patch'. The Nonna, still sitting, yanked her down, with surprising strength, and brushed her cheek with a bristling chin before letting her go so suddenly that she almost fell against the gangling uncle. He, with his long prehensile arms, was effortlessly shaking hands with the people three rows behind, but as soon as he saw that Pippa had been released, he turned back and pumped her wrist until it ached. Finally, Pietro vaulted over the pew in front to come round to her, giving his formal little bow and a dry, almost ironic handshake.

She realised then, that there had been no misunderstanding. It wasn't that the Guinizelli had been misled into believing that she was about to join the clan; she was a part of it already, at least on a temporary basis. Families, to the Italians, were simply of such elemental importance that, should anyone be unfortunate enough to arrive in the country without one in tow, they would automatically become assimilated into the nearest to hand. All she had to do was smile, try not to say anything accidentally obscene, and eat as much as possible.

The house was both larger and more simply furnished than she had expected, with plain whitewashed walls and treacle-dark hunks of nineteenth-century furniture. They sat, all sixteen or seventeen of them, out on the shaded terrace for lunch, along an improvised trestle table on an assortment of mismatched chairs, obviously culled from distant corners of the attics and outbuildings. Some of these, lacking half a leg or the critical portion of the seat, were distinctly rickety, but after a jug or two of the dark red wine, no one could be quite sure whether it was his chair or his own equilibrium that had lost its centre of gravity.

The wine was made by the Guinizelli themselves, from the squares of tidy vineyard which, alternating with the olive groves, made a chessboard pattern of greens and greys against the red-brown of the hillside earth. So it would obviously be churlish to refuse it, whatever Jonathan used to say about women who drank at lunchtime. The olives, of course, were theirs as well, as were the sweetish purple globes, barely recognizable at first, which made English pickled onions taste like marinated marbles in comparison. Even the piquant slices of cold meat: *prosciutto, salame* and *porcetta*, came from their own, recently deceased pig.

'His name was Orsetto.' Pietro called helpfully from his place diagonally across the table. 'He was a very dear friend of mine.'

Pippa surreptitiously replaced the third slice of salami she had been about to eat, but Signora Guinizelli, sitting directly opposite, was too quick for her. She spoke almost no English, but she knew when her only son was misbehaving. In a display of co-ordination that would have done credit to a professional organist, she reached her plump right arm around her sister to clout Pietro on the back of the neck while with her left hand she replaced the salami on Pippa's plate, adding two or three more slices for good measure.

'Mamma says I've got to apologize.' said Pietro, as soon as his mother paused for breath in her breakneck tirade. 'All of our pigs since 1952 have been called Orsetto and I've always been the first to volunteer on assassination day. Please eat it, otherwise I won't be allowed any *torta*.'

Pippa did, but Signora Guinizelli had already got up from the table, accompanied by her three daughters, to bring out the next course.

'*Primo*.' explained Pietro's small nephew sitting next to her, who was in his third year of English at school. 'First dish of the healthful meal.'

'First? What was all this then?' She pointed towards the disappearing plates, still loaded with bread, sliced meats and *pecorino* cheese. 'Oh, only *antipasti*.' the boy explained airily. 'The real dinner commences now. *Tortelli al ragu*.'

As the guest of honour, Pippa was served first, so she had a few seconds to survey the shallow bowl in front of her, before the surrounding Guinizelli urged her, with dramatic gestures, not to wait for the others. The pasta squares held some superficial resemblance to the tinned British mess called ravioli, except that they were larger, firmer, more savoury and immersed in a proper sauce instead of watered down ketchup. There was also the minor distinction of their being edible.

She waited for a few seconds longer to see whether a clean knife and fork would turn up, by which time the others had been served, and were beginning to eat, using the same cutlery as for the antipasti. Very sensible, thought Pippa, remembering her mother's frantic rummaging down the back of the sofa and through her father's toolbox in search of enough forks for Christmas dinner. It was only later that she discovered that the Lucchesi always reused their knives and forks, even when alone in a well-stocked restaurant. Curiously, they still shuddered, with as much horror as any fastidious northerner, at the French habit of using the same plate for successive courses.

The pasta sauce was a rich terracotta, red as the farmhouse roof tiles, and Pippa couldn't help glancing, over her laden fork, at Pietro's white shirt front. His mother must have made him wear it; he couldn't not know... How long would it last, the expanse of scrubbed snowdrift? Three, four .... nine and a half seconds. A tortelli speared, a jocular insult from a cousin at the end of the table, an instinctive gesture, and a blob of chopped tomato trickled down his chest like a raindrop down a window.

'*Pietraccio!*' roared his mother and bounced out of her chair, wetted napkin in hand, to mop him up again. She grabbed his shoulder, not much lower than her own, even though she was standing, and forcibly swivelled him away from the table. Then she bent over the poor shirt, scrubbing vigorously, accompanying herself with a litany of muttered exasperation.

'*Mi dispiace, Mamma.*' soothed Pietro, patting her on the back, and wrapping an auburn tendril back behind her ear. He looked out over the greying roots, and smiled towards Pippa.

That was when the floor fell away.

At first she thought that it really had; that the structure of the terrace had given up under the strain, that the tiles were shifting and cracking beneath her feet. She glanced surreptitiously at her neighbours, scanning their faces for signs of panic. Nothing. Even the descendants of Nero couldn't be this phlegmatic, faced with a fifteen-foot plunge to the courtyard below, accompanied by their closest relatives, large chunks of masonry and seventeen refilled bowls of tortelli. The wine, then? Unlikely, unless there was something very strange about Chateau Guinizelli. The usual effect of alcohol on Pippa's constitution was a gradual accumulation of well-being, followed by a rapid decline into sleep. She had never known anything like this sudden brilliance, as though a light switch had been flicked in her brain.

When you have eliminated the impossible... No. No, that couldn't be it. She dared a sideways glimpse, just to eradicate the suggestion. Pietro's left ear floated into sight, and the bottom part of her stomach cannoned three quarters of the way to New Zealand. Oh hell. And he was still smiling at her. She returned to inspecting the cotto tiles and reviewed the situation. On the whole, she could probably cope with the smiling. Yes, she thought, risking another glance, he could definitely stay there, with his mother still nagging at him and his tortelli half-eaten, and a piece of basil stuck between his teeth. And Pippa could happily keep still too, her fork still in mid-air, something suspiciously buglike crawling up her leg, and its second cousin doing the doggy-paddle across her wine. None of it would make the slightest difference, as long as he kept smiling at her. It was only later that things would start to get tricky.

Sure enough, after a few minutes of fatuous smiling, during which the signora gave up her peripatetic laundering and returned to her own pasta, and the small nephew asked a stream of questions about English football to which Pippa replied 'Aston Villa', 'Gary Lineker' and '2:1' in random sequence, her brain reasserted control and demanded to be told what was going on. What, it insisted, about her post-Jonathan vow of celibacy, the infamous unreliability of Italian men, the indisputable eccentricities of this Italian man in particular, and her professional duty, as witness and crypto-investigator, to retain a certain aloof detachment with regard to the cohorts of the Polizia?

Perhaps, she thought hopefully, it was only lust. She could probably deal with lust. She tried it out, imagining herself sprawled with Pietro across his no doubt deep and feather-quilted bed. It wasn't any good. That is, it would no doubt be wonderful, but the chief ingredient of its wonderfulness was nothing to do with which bit of whom went where, but the simple fact that it would give her even more opportunities of looking at him and seeing him smile.

Damn. There had never been anything like this with Jonathan, nothing so unseemly; only a gradual realization of the broad spectrum of his virtues combined with gratified surprise when he condescended to bestow them upon her. Temporarily, of course, she reminded herself . He had soon realized his mistake. But for the first time it didn't hurt to remember that. Not even a twinge.

'She jests at scars that never felt a wound.'

'Shakespeare.' commented the small nephew, as he passed the enormous slabs of lamb that began the *secondo*.

Pippa speared a couple with enthusiasm. Somehow the happiness that was swilling around inside her even encompassed her digestion, and, as the meal progressed, she nodded and echoed '*Ancora*' often enough to satisfy even Pietro's mother. For now it didn't matter how he felt; his mere existence at the same table, on the same planet, was enough. No doubt it would matter soon enough, probably in the early hours of tomorrow morning at about the same time as the tiramisu would have its revenge, but they could both wait until then. Sufficient unto the day, as she almost said aloud, stopped in time by the beady jet eyes of the precocious nephew.

After lunch came the coffee; black and bone-jarringly strong, served in tiny glasses like shots of medicine. Pippa tried to drink hers without sugar, took a sip and thought that someone had scraped the lining off her tongue.

'*Schifoso*?' smiled Signora Guinizelli, and pushed the sugar bowl towards her.

'Disgusting.' translated the small nephew. 'Mega-gross.'

Pippa hung around the table afterwards, desultorily piling plates and coffee cups. Somehow, nothing quite seemed to fit inside anything else. A cascade of spoons clattered down to the floor and she crawled under the table to retrieve them.

'Hi.'

It almost seemed as though he had been waiting for her there. The light, filtered through the cream tablecloth, was soft and golden on his badly-shaven cheek. Before she could think she leaned forward and kissed it.

He raised his eyebrows. 'Thanks. *Touché.*'

On the opposite cheek, just the same, no more and no less.

'We could,' he went on, 'stay here and kiss each other all afternoon.'

There was a scintilla's pause, long enough for Pippa to contemplate the possibility. Yes, she thought, heaven probably would be much like this, maybe with a bit more headroom and fewer squashed olives,

'But I think it might be a little hazardous.'

Above them a faintly tipsy aunt shied from the talking table and grabbed a random brother-in-law for support. Unfortunately she overlooked the fact that she was carrying a pile of pudding dishes.

'I see what you mean.' said Pippa, cringing from the shards of pottery shrapnel. 'Actually, I thought I ought to help with the washing-up.'

'No, you mustn't do that. Don't you realise that they all want to talk about you?'

'They could do that anyway. I wouldn't know what they were saying.'

'Ah, but haven't you noticed yet? No Italian really believes that foreigners can't understand him. We think they're just bluffing. That's why we always speak faster when someone tells us that they're English. Better come for a walk with me instead.'

They took a small path up the hillside, bare and sandy under the sun's relentless glare. Pippa's head and stomach felt ominously heavy. For the first time since the mass, she remembered Gray and the bloody photocopier. She really had to tell Pietro now, but he was striding ahead of her, almost at the top of the hill. The path became steeper, and her sandals slipped uselessly. She felt the sweat thick in her hair and trickling down her spine. If she went back, would he actually notice?

Suddenly he turned, at the edge of a little thicket.

'Sorry.' he called. 'I forgot about your stupid shoes. Here.'

He ran back, squatted down and reached out a hand towards her.

'Hold on tight and I'll haul you up.'

It wasn't the most romantic invitation, and the reality was even worse, both of them with moist slipping hands, faces red with exertion and grunting with the effort, but finally he pulled her on to the tussocky grass.

'*Sei bene?*'

Had he used *tu* before? She couldn't remember, but she wanted to go on hearing it. English was so cold by comparison.

'*Molto bene, grazie.*' Her 'r's were rolling better now, she thought, and remembered the joke about the American and the Scottish waitress. She laughed aloud.

'What is it? What's funny?' He was still holding her hand.

She told him, and so of course he had to look at her from behind, seeing as her sandals had moderately high heels, and that meant letting her hand go, but then he did watch for so long, and so appreciatively that on balance it was probably worth it.

They walked companionably towards the patch of green shade, not holding hands now, but close, so that their elbows brushed from time to time. Under the trees he stopped and turned to her.

'Well?'

Her heart was beating fast. If she didn't say it now then she never would.

'I've got something to tell you. I'm sorry; I should have done it before. I wanted to know what he would say about it first, but I couldn't really see him until yesterday, and...'

'Gray?'

At least he was still smiling.

'Yes, Gray. He...'

'He was at the Piccola Casa on Monday evening?'

'You see, he was at the Piccola Casa on Mon... Oh. You know. How?'

'The same way as you, I expect. Elsa, Elisa and the photocopier.'

'They told you about it, then? Gray's worksheet?'

'Not me, no. I don't seem to be the kind of person who receives these confidences.'

She flushed and stared down at the dry twigs beneath her feet. He touched the end of her nose for a moment.

'Don't look so serious. I'm only teasing you. They didn't tell me, but they told Agostino when he saw them yesterday for the formal statement. I'll need to see Gray myself, of course - another job for tomorrow. How I do love Monday mornings. Unless you've already spoken to him?'

'Well, I have actually, yes.'

Suddenly it didn't seem to have been that good an idea after all. Probably she had dealt some fatefully compromising blow to his interview, jeopardized the admissibility of something-or-other and basically bungled the whole investigation. As a former lawyer, she ought to have known better.

But he didn't seem to mind. On the contrary.

'Wonderful. Much better than letting me rub him up the wrong way again.' He paused for a moment, as though listening to an echo of his own voice. 'Can that really be right; to rub him up? It sounds a bit ...' He waved an arm vaguely in the direction of the denser woods, towards the soft beds of pine needles where unnameable depravities might occur.

'I think it's something like stroking a cat.' said Pippa demurely. 'You know, if you stroke its fur from back to front then it gets annoyed. Anyway, do you want to know what he said?'

For a long time he didn't answer at all; just stood there looking at her, from her eyes to her mouth and back again. She grinned.

'What are you laughing at?'

'That old trick. We used to do it when we were sixteen and we wanted a boy to kiss us. Eyes, mouth, eyes. It never failed.'

He moved half a step closer. 'Didn't it?'

'Never. But you see, it had to be the girl who did it. It doesn't work the other way round. We're too devious, you see. You can't expect us to be defeated by our own tactics.'

'Napoleon was.'

'Was he? When?'

'I don't know. I was just trying to be impressive. Anyway, he wasn't a woman.'

'Reputedly not. And he was French. That must make a difference too.'

'Not French, no. Corsican. It's quite different. When we go to Corsica, you'll see.' That sounded promising. 'Practically Italian, really. But I'm confused now. Do I want to be like Napoleon or not?'

'On the whole not, I think. Although I wouldn't have to go on tiptoe.'

'You won't anyway if I bend down. Like this.'

'Shall I tell you about Gray?' It came out as a series of squeaks, the last yelps of conscience.

He shook his head slowly, smiling, put the backs of his fingers under her chin and tilted it upwards.

Dee-dee, dee-dee, di-de dee dee dee,
Di-de dee dee-dee, di-di dee dee deeee

The electronic notes of an ersatz *Greensleeves* plinked out from tree to tree. Pietro said something brief, Italian and utterly obscene and answered his mobile phone.

'*Pronto? Si.*' His face changed, he took two steps backwards and continued in English. 'Yes, sir, thank you. This afternoon? Yes, certainly. Half an hour. We'll be there, sir. And thank you again.'

He replaced the phone in his pocket and looked over the top of Pippa's head. She might have been a shrub or Sergeant Lenzuoli.

'The Americans will see us now.'

XVII

Since the Second World War, American military bases have been popping up in Italy like pimples on an adolescent nose, the rash spreading down from the Alps to Sicily, with a particular predilection for areas of otherwise unspoilt beauty. One such is Camp Darby; U.S. Mediterranean seaport command, equipment mega-depot and beachfront playground for American service personnel, Defense Department employees and British prime ministers taking advantage of the special relationship. Needless to say, the advantages of Camp Darby's seaside facilities are denied to the hapless locals who instead have to queue and pay through the *naso* for their ten square centimetres of sand on the Viareggio seafront. However, judging from the rumours about the types of ammunition kept there during the closing years of the Cold War, most Tuscans wouldn't go near the place in a state-of-the-art radiation suit, never mind a micro-bikini. Not so deficient in hap after all.

It was not, in fact, Camp Darby itself to which Pietro had been summoned, but a much smaller and less glamorous establishment further inland amidst the scrubby marshes. The unnamed base appeared on no road signs, but Pietro had been there before and the route was securely embedded in his slightly sozzled braincells. He was expected by the soldiers guarding the entrance, but Pippa was not, and it took a good half hour of crackling radio conversation, form-filling and an intimate search by a crew-cut female officer before she was grudgingly admitted. They were directed to an anonymous grey office in an anonymous grey block and their presence announced by a gangling blond Texan who read their names laboriously from a chewing-gum wrapper.

'Commissioner Goo-in-Zelly and,' He took a deep breath, preparing to tackle another collection of random consonants, looked at the wrapper again, and broke into a wide grin. 'Miss Laud, sir!' he yelled in triumph, adding, in a confidential undertone that could probably be heard on the beach at Forte dei Marmi. 'As it happens, ma'am, I'm a Lord myself. Lord E. Loftinghouse the Third.'

'Yeah?' came a voice from inside the room, and Lord nudged them over the threshold. Inside, behind a broad reddish desk sat a broad and even redder man. Despite the four desk fans directed towards it, his face resembled nothing so much as a rapidly ripening beefsteak tomato, and he mopped his brow every few moments with a copy of the *Herald Tribune*.

'He's from Maine,' murmured Lord at the decibel level of a medium-sized jet fighter. 'Accidentally volunteered for Italy when his secretary lost her reading glasses and read out the temperatures for Rejkavik instead of Rome.'

'Wassat?' bellowed the man behind the desk, deafened by the roar of the ventilators. Reluctantly he reached out and switched them to a lower setting.

'Aha! Glad you could make it, Commissario, And - Lord, Lord! A chair for the lady. Can't have her thinking we Americans are all uncivilized brutes. Eh, Commissario? You'll explain to her, will you, that we weren't expecting...'

'That's all right.' said Pippa.

The American stared at her open-mouthed, as though the wastepaper basket had just sprung into life.

'She speaks English?'

'I am.' explained Pippa. 'English.'

'All the same.' He sat almost still for a few moments, shaking his head gently.

Lord, stationed just outside the door, processed through it with a third chair held aloft and the beginnings of an interesting story about the Loftinghouse ancestral rocker.

'Save it for your next psychiatric assessment, would you Lord? Yes, yes, sit down honey. So, Commissario, you're investigating Zena Carson's death.'

'That's right, sir.'

'Just a moment.' interrupted Pippa. The absence of a 'sir' hung in the air like a dead pig outside a wholefood bar. 'You haven't told us your name yet.'

'Oh. Well, my dear... Would that be an official request, Commissario?'

'I...er...' It was seldom that you saw an Italian lost for words.

Pippa looked at him coolly. She might be ready to lay down her heart and soul before his unravelling shoelaces but this was business. 'Never deal with a client who won't give you his name,' the senior partner had told her on her first day and it still sounded like good advice. Pietro swivelled his neck from one to the other, like a puppy caught between an illicit sausage and a pat on the head. The sausage won. 'It would be helpful, sir.'

'If we must, then.' A laminated rectangle skimmed across the desk on to the floor. 'Oops.'

Pippa stooped to pick it up.

'Lieutenant George Washington. George F. Washington. Remarkable. What does the...?'

'That'll do nicely,' said Pietro, grabbing the card and cutting his finger on one of its corners. 'Thank you very much. Yes sir, we - I'm dealing with the Carson case.'

'Hmm.' Washington leaned back in his chair, lifting its front legs off the floor. For one blissful moment it looked as though he might topple over backwards into the open filing cabinet behind. He wobbled, blanched, clutched the desk and the moment was over. 'Information-wise, perhaps I oughtta clarify my position. I have no connection whatsoever with the military establishment stationed in Iddally. In hosting this pre-debriefing encounter, I represent an autonomous agency pursuing the legitimate interests of the U.S Government, European-wise, in a non-accountable, non-negotiable roaming remit.'

'I understand, sir.'

'Wish I did, Commissario. Tell me, buddy, is there something I can call you that's less of a mouthful?'

Pietro grinned with the side of his mouth nearer to Pippa.

'Pete?'

'Pete it is. What I propose, then, Pete, is that we pool our information on the Carson case and then, subject to my agency's security clearance, we proceed on a joint and several, mutually co-operative, dually independent investigative basis. Can you run with that?'

Pietro nodded, not quite trusting himself to speak.

'Fire away, then.'

Washington reached under his chair and fished out a gigantic cardboard bucket of popcorn which he inspected carefully, picking out foreign bodies; small change, cigar ash and dying insects.

Finally he held the bucket out to them.

'Want some?'

They shook their heads in nauseated fascination.

His face fell, sagging like last week's party balloon.

'Gum? Soda? Peanut butter and jelly?'

'We've just eaten, thanks.' said Pippa hastily, seeing that Pietro was about to ask about peanut butter and jelly and remembering the suet pudding débâcle. There were more dignified issues for Nato to fall apart over. Pietro reluctantly cleared his throat and began.

'Zena Margaret Carson was born on the third of January 1959 and arrived in Lucca about a year ago.'

Washington grunted, leaning back at another precarious angle. He dug into the popcorn bucket and surveyed Pietro with the pessimistic tolerance of a man who has read every bad review but is determined to sit through the movie anyway.

'We think she came direct from the United States, though it doesn't look as though she got a *permesso di soggiorno* in Lucca, or registered her address with the Questura. We understand that she came from the state of Nebraska, but we don't have any more information about her background.'

'Fortunately I can help you there, Pete. Ms Carson was an enlisted soldier in the US Army from 1977 until 1998. After her discharge she was employed in the Eldorado program, teaching English to Hispanic kids in California. I guess that's what gave her the idea of coming here, seeing as she'd already picked up the lingo.'

'This is Italy, not Spain.' pointed out Pippa. She hadn't meant to speak again but her tongue was growing sore with the number of times she'd had to bite it.

Pietro gave her a pained glance. 'Sir.' she added.

'I know the difference between Iddaly and Spain, hon. Even Lord's worked that one out.'

'Yessir?' The voice from the empty doorway was quick and keen.

'Go back to sleep, Lord. I'm just telling these good people what a whizz you are at geography.'

'That's right, sir. Straight Bs right through junior high. Anytime you folks need to know the principal exports of Lithuania you just holler out, okay? Yessir. Back to sleep on the double, sir.'

Washington gazed towards the doorway, shaking his head. 'Too much protein, that's what does it. All that red meat. Another memo to the Catering Corps, I guess.' He scribbled something on a block of paper before delving back into the popcorn bucket. 'Where were we? Oh yeah, Spain and Italy. Same thing, as far as we're concerned. Yurrup is Yurrup after all, though the Frogs are worse than the rest. Do go on, Pete.'

'Thank you. And we're very grateful for the further information.' Pietro caught Pippa's eye and she knew what he was thinking. If Luciano Bianchi had known that Zena was a former American soldier, then his vague suspicions of her might have been solidified very quickly. Had he known? Could she have told him, in the first heady days of her Committee membership, before September 11th gave a jolt to her loyalties? But if he had known then why hadn't he said so? She broke out of her musings to listen to Pietro.

'....worked at the Piccola Casa d'Inglese, teaching English to individuals and small groups. For the first few weeks she stayed in a small flat - apartment - in the school itself, before moving out to a place on the Via San Giorgio. She became involved with a group known as the Committee for Radical Re-engagement...'

The American snorted, spraying half chewed popcorn across the desk.

'I do beg your pardon, ma'am. But I'd be right in thinking, would I, Pete, that these are some kinda Communists? Those guys really get my goat. The amount of cash the States has poured into this crackpot country, you wouldn't believe, and still they keep on popping up. Who was in charge of this particular infestation?'

'As I understand it,' said Pietro a little stiffly, 'the organization had no formal chain of command.'

'Come off it, buddy; you don't have to be coy with me. It was Luciano Bianchi, right? Thought so. He's behind most of the anti-American activity round here. I don't know the guy personally; no doubt he's kind to his mother and mows the yard every week, but so far as my superiors are concerned, he's a little piece of Stalinist crud who can go right up there on the Pentagon hit-list alongside his pals Saddam and Bin Laden.'

'Can we quote you on that?' asked Pippa.

He stared at her for a few seconds, his small red eyes rounding into half-sucked M&Ms. Then he laid the popcorn bucket carefully on the desk and leaned forward.

'Listen to me, missie, and listen good. I don't know where you've come from or what you're doing here. I figured that seeing as how it's the Lord's day and your boyfriend brought you along, I'd be happy to extend a particle of U.S. hospitality. I've got a little girl myself back home and I wouldn't like to think of her waiting in an automobile on a sizzling afternoon like this. But it seems like we need a few ground rules. You don't quote anything from me, ever. Not a word, not a cough, not even a goddam fart. Excuse my Frongsay. As far as the rest of the world is concerned, you've never been here, you've never met me and we're certainly not having this conversation. *Capeesh*?'

She nodded, furious to find herself blushing.

'Good. Because if you didn't, we might be compelled to remind you. And I don't like to see that kinda stuff.' He retrieved the popcorn. 'Do continue, Pete, as long as you can keep your little lady under control. How long did Ms Carson hang around with these jerks?'

'We think she was actively involved until September the eleventh. After that, as you might expect, she seems to have, ah, lost her enthusiasm for the cause. She still went to meetings and stayed a part of the group, but there were suspicions, by the other members, that she might be passing information to ... outside sources.'

'Meaning us?'

'I believe so, sir.'

'Hmm. You'll understand, of course, that I can't comment on any matter that might have national security implications. But go on. Assuming, for the purposes of argument, that 9/11 did indeed bring her to her senses, that henceforward she carried out her patriotic duty as an American citizen by informing the relevant agencies about subversive activity - do you think the Commies put the hit on her?'

'A political motive,' said Pietro carefully, 'does seem, at this stage, to be the most fruitful avenue for exploration.'

'Quite the British diplomat, aren't you? Do you have any other fruitful avenues, or are they all dirt tracks?'

'Not quite. Several people have told us that she seemed unhappy during the past few months. That may have been connected with her position within the Committee or it may have had another cause. We haven't traced any, er, emotional attachments so far, but it remains a possibility.'

'Done to death by her Latin lover, you mean? Well, she was in the right place for it. But you haven't found any boyfriends. Or girlfriends, come to that.'

'No. In fact, she doesn't seem to have been particularly close to anyone. Another teacher, Graham Garrett, arrived from Canada about six months later. They seem to have got on reasonably well together, but she didn't confide in him.'

'And no nookie?'

'*Amore*? No, nothing like that. He was considerably younger than her and in fact he ...'

'Fairy, is he? Might have known. Namby-pamby job for a man.'

'There is one other potential motive. It seems that Miss Carson was accepting paid commissions for translation work and then deceiving her pupils into carrying out the work for her. We know of only one instance, but there may have been more.'

The American shrugged. 'Free enterprise. It might have been a tad shady, but if they were dumb enough to fall for it... We didn't build a great nation by losing sleep over business ethics. Look at the Indians. Well, I reckon we've heard enough about motives. What about the mechanics of the thing? Dates, times, evidence, alibis.'

'Of course. The death occurred between Monday evening and Tuesday morning. The body was found at the Piccola Casa D'Inglese although it may have been moved from another location. The last person we know to have seen Miss Carson alive was Francesca Columbini, who had a lesson with her from seven until eight p.m. Miss Columbini, a medical student at the University of Pisa, has given us a full account of the lesson. Apparently it ended at the usual time, and Miss Carson was still in the classroom when Miss Columbini left.'

'That right? And this Columbini - she's not a member of your Commie Committee by any chance?'

'No-o.'

Washington looked up sharply. 'Sounds like there ought to be a "but" in there somewhere.'

'She's a friend of Luciano Bianchi. But she isn't involved in politics at all. I understand that she's a very devout Catholic.'

'No guarantee of nothing, that. South America's full of commie priests, or it was until Ollie North fixed 'em. I'm an Episcopalian myself. Don't hold with too much religion. Anyone else there at the school that night? Administrators, cleaners, nightwatchmen?'

'The cleaner only comes twice a week, on Tuesday and Friday evenings. There's no nightwatchman; it's only a tiny place and the owners carry out all the administration themselves. They are two elderly ladies who live in a flat on the floor below. They left the premises at half-past six that day and didn't go back until the morning.'

'Hear anything?'

'No, sir. They had the television on in the evening and I think they may be slightly deaf. There was, we understand, one other person at the school on Monday evening; Mr Garrett, who called in to do some photocopying.'

'Garrett?' He looked down at his scrawled notes. 'Graham, right? The Canadian faggot. He see anything?'

Pietro glanced at Pippa before answering. 'I haven't in fact had the opportunity to interview Mr Garrett personally...'

The American raised his pale eyebrows and Pietro continued hastily,

'... but my colleague Miss Laud has, I believe, done so.'

'Oh yeah?' The seat tipped back another two or three inches. With any luck he would topple over backwards, as his mother must long ago have warned him. 'And what did you find out, then, honey? What colour necktie he was wearing?'

'I'm afraid not.' Pippa had the nasty feeling that she was dropping Pietro into something sticky, but it was too late now. She had offered to tell him earlier; it wasn't her fault that his mind had been on other things. She pulled herself hastily together. 'All I know is that he went into the classroom at about quarter past seven and no one was there. Neither Zena nor Francesca.'

'What?' For a moment Pietro forgot where he was. 'Neither of them? There wasn't a lesson at all? Why on earth didn't you tell me before?'

'I tried to, remember? But maybe I should have insisted.'

A reminiscent smile passed across his face.

'No, it wouldn't have done any good. Not in that dress.'

Pippa pulled the edges of her cardigan closer together while Washington coughed up a piece of recaltritant corn.

'Tender as this scene is, perhaps we could proceed?'

'Certainly.' Pietro wrested his gaze away from Pippa's neck. 'The body was found on Thursday morning, concealed in a cupboard in the classroom.'

'By?'

'By Miss Laud.'

'You don't say?' Another scrawl in the notebook. You had to suspect whoever discovered the body; he knew that much from *Columbo*.

'The post-mortem showed that death was by suffocation, and there were large quantities of methohexitone - that's a clinical anaesthetic - and morphine in the body. An empty hypodermic syringe, containing traces of these drugs, was found in Miss Carson's pocket. Oh, and there were words written on her wrists in ballpoint pen. *Girotondo* and *No-Global*.'

The pen slithered excitedly between Washington's greasy fingers.

'More Commie cells, huh?' Well, Pete, it seems that your case is pretty much sewn up. I assume that arrests are imminent?'

'Not as yet, no.' Pietro spoke drily. 'There are one or two loose ends. Why, for example, if the killing was intended as a political demonstration, was the body hidden in the cupboard?'

The sweeping gesture knocked a good third of the remaining popcorn across the desk. 'I wouldn't fret about that. These guys just want to create the maximum possible disruption.'

'There's also the question of Miss Carson's passport. It was found, together with her driving licence, money and other documents, in the school's own apartment. The one Miss Carson had moved out of ten months before.'

'Who found those, then?'

Pippa coughed. 'Actually that was me as well.'

'Re-ally?' His eyebrows were now so high on his forehead that they could have doubled as a light toupee.

'It seems to me, sweetheart, that you're mighty convenient on the spot whenever anything suspicious turns up. Got any terrorist connections yourself, have you?'

Pippa thought for a moment. Would a lapsed membership of Friends of the Earth count? Judging from his expression, it probably would.

'Don't bother, we'll find out anyway. Meanwhile...'

Meanwhile, the telephone rang.

'Yeah? Yeah. Oh yeah? Yeah. Yeah. Yeah.'

He replaced the receiver.

'A fisherman, are you, Mr Gooney-Zelley?'

Pietro smiled, but cautiously. 'From time to time, yes. My uncle and I used to go a lot when I was a boy. On the Serchio, mainly, or up in the lakes of the Garfagnana. I can take you along next weekend if you like. Or if you prefer saltwater we could go to Livorno.'

'That's real good of you Pete, but I reckon I'll have other plans. What about fishing in other folks' waters without a permit?'

'Sir?'

'That was my superior on the line. Seems he's been having a little chat with your boss. A Vice Quester Big Billy, is that right?'

Pietro nodded, his face set.

'Good. At least we've got one thing straight. Mind you, Big Billy wasn't too pleased at being disturbed on a Sunday afternoon. Seems he was at some festival. Opyra, would it be? Not that we kept him long, you'll understand. Just long enough for him to confirm his instructions. The instructions he gave to you, Pete, a couple of days ago. Now, what were they, again? Oh yeah, that was it. *Take no further action on the Carson case.* It doesn't sound too difficult to me, but then maybe you've spent so much time learning English, you've forgotten your own language Eh?'

'Yes sir. I mean, no sir.'

'No *sir*. Perhaps if you Italianos concentrated on listening to your superior officers instead of messing about with English dames, you wouldn't need us to defend your country for you. Big Billy also advised us, quite categorically, that he gave you no authority to contact any US organization. Particularly no organization even remotely connected with the one I represent. That clear, is it Pete?'

'Yes sir.' It wasn't a lack of imagination. Pietro could think of a wide range of responses, but none of the rest would keep his pension intact.

'I should hope so. We're waging a war against terror, remember, on behalf of all of you tadpole countries; Italy, Britain, Luxembourg. This case is a part of it, just as much as the Taliban and the towelheads. When a US citizen is murdered, martyred, I should say, in the cause of freedom, that's a matter for our people to deal with. We don't need any wishy-washy Yurrupean input.'

He stood up, showering popcorn on the desk and shook his head sadly.

'A pity. You'd be a nice pair of youngsters if your heads weren't stuffed with liberal horse feathers. Forget the politics and take her to the movies. Lord!'

'Yessir!'

'Kindly escort these two lovebirds off the premises.'

XVIII

'I see what he meant about the Indians.'
'What?' Pietro was struggling with a small piece of white plastic. 'Why can't Mamma buy a car with air conditioning? Or at least windows that open. You could cook a pizza in here. Sorry, what about an Indian?'

'Not *an* Indian. The whole nation of native Americans. They gave up their entire territories in return for measles, smallpox and a few missionaries. Like us today. We told Fat George everything we know and in return all we found out is that Zena used to be a soldier. Doesn't sound like a fair bargain to me.'

'I suppose not. But it doesn't matter now, does it?'

'Doesn't it? Why, was something else going on between the lines? Was all Lord's stuff about Lithuanian exports really a coded security leak?'

He glanced up from his demolition operations. 'It doesn't matter because we're off the case. You heard what the man said.'

'Yes, but...'

'But nothing. That's it.' He gave up on the window, started the engine and switched the fan on to maximum. Outside the camp he quickly, too quickly, changed up to fifth gear to leave his right hand free. It found hers and squeezed it affectionately. 'Don't worry.'

'What?' It was impossible to hear anything at less than a costermonger's bawl.

'We can still see each other.' He grinned. 'I wasn't only interested in your linguistico-legal abilities.'

Pippa snatched her hand away and snapped off the fan. Literally. She added the piece of black plastic to the white one on the dashboard.

'We'll have a chess set soon.'

'Sorry.' she said automatically. 'I mean sorry for breaking it, not sorry for being angry. How dare you?'

'How dare I what?'

'Pretend that you wanted my help with this case, just to get me into the woods with you then drop the whole thing as soon as some poxy little American,'

'He was rather a large American.'

'As soon as any dimension of poxy American tells you to. You're not answerable to him. Why couldn't you just tell him to get stuffed?'

'Get stuffed? I've always wondered about that one. Is it a reference to taxidermy or public school sodomy?'

'I don't know and I don't care. There are more important things in the world than idioms, you know.'

'I know.' His tone suddenly deepened. 'Like the precarious nature of America's crusade against terrorism. Like the fragile relationship between Italian society and the U.S. military. Like the existence of a chain of command, however flaky one or two of the links might be. Like the minor detail that I'd rather like to keep my job. It's quite true what the so-called Washington said. Bisbigli did tell me not to take the case any further.'

'But you didn't take any notice then.'

'No I didn't. Generally he's got no idea of what he said five minutes ago, never mind three days. But once he remembers, I have to start taking notice.'

'I don't see why. It's obvious he was only saying what the Americans wanted hear. I expect he'd change his mind again if you caught him at the right moment. And as for bloody Abraham Lincoln, if these people won't even give their proper names, or tell us who they're working for, I don't see why we should take any notice of them. What about democratic accountability?'

'What about it? What about flying pigs, Cloudcuckooland and the island of Atlantis? Get real, Pippa. We don't upset the U.S, especially not now. And as for you, of course I wanted your help. And I found you attractive.' Pippa tried not to notice the past tense. 'The two aren't mutually incompatible, you know. At least not in Italy. But if the whole thing was just a plot to get you, what did you say, "into the woods" it wasn't very successful was it? It wasn't exactly an afternoon of torrid passion.'

'Perhaps George Washington saved me just in time.'

'Perhaps he did. Perhaps you ought to be grateful to him. Anyway, like I said, there's nothing more we can do about Zena Carson.'

'So you're abandoning the case?'

'*Madonna*, you are obstinate, aren't you? Don't you understand, I've got no choice? As it is I'm going to get a formal reprimand from Bisbligli as soon as he can drag himself away from the Puccini and cocktails.'

'But a woman's been murdered. We can't just forget about it. Something's got to be done.'

'Possibly. But I can't be the one to do it. No doubt the Americans will need you as a witness if they decide to proceed. Personally, I hope they don't. I'd rather see no-one convicted than the wrong person. Two people.'

'Luciano and Francesca?'

'Looks like that, doesn't it?'

'But you're not going to lift a finger to help?'

They were back in the outskirts of Lucca by now. Pietro jammed his foot on the brake and skidded into a dusty forecourt. He turned to her, his face white. 'Which particular bit of this don't you understand, Miss Laud? An American citizen has died. The Americans have the right to investigate the death. They believe there may be a terrorist connection. Several thousand Americans died, seven months ago, as a result of terrorist activity. Italy has a history of political violence. Italy joined the losing side in the last two world wars. Consequently, we are blessed with ten thousand U.S. soldiers, together with enough weapons to keep us all under military rule for the next half century, should we fail to be appropriately co-operative. *Ha capito*?'

'I understand enough, thank you. Enough to recognize a pension hanging in the balance.'

She was struggling with the door handle and Pietro, with automatic courtesy, reached across and opened it for her. She clambered out, with about three tons less poise than she would have liked, but by now she was too angry to care.

'Don't worry; I won't interfere with your promotion prospects. After all, what's a dead teacher more or less compared with a Vice-Questore? I can walk back from here.' The door slammed, a few flakes of paint pirouetting to the dusty ground.

The grandeur of the gesture lasted for about seven seconds, until she heard the driver's door close, rather more gently than hers had, and running footsteps behind her.

'You're going the wrong way.'

'I'm taking the scenic route.' she shouted back over her shoulder, and strode on more determinedly than before.

'It'll be a long walk in this heat. Let me give you a lift. Please.'

She didn't slow down, much less turned her head, and a couple of minutes later she heard the car shudder away. That was that then. It wasn't quite the shortest romance in Pippa's history; there had been a dreadful mistake at a youth club disco when the lights had unexpectedly fused, but it came pretty close. Needless to say, she didn't care.

Most of the first five kilometres were taken up with not caring, analysing the precise reasons why she didn't care, and planning the variety of ways in which not caring would manifest itself; principally in her single-handed solution of the Carson case, bringing simultaneous outpourings of gratitude from Messrs Bush, Blair and Berlusconi. Well, maybe not the last bit. She would make do with being appointed honorary Professor of Criminology at Pisa University, decorated with the highest honours of the Republic and assigned Commissario Guinizelli as one of her lowly bodyguard.

After that there wasn't really anywhere to go but back into reality, a remarkably hot and empty reality. She felt suddenly shrivelled under the sun, dehydration clawing at her throat and patches of darkness scudding across her vision. It was open countryside again now, with only an occasional roadside tree and twenty minutes since she'd passed a bar. She should have stopped then, but her last two euro piece had clinked into the offertory bag and *Italian Without Tears* didn't include many begging conjugations. A few cars whistled past, wing mirrors skimming her elbows, but the only sentient beings she met were a herd of skinny sheep, dark brown and very smelly, coaxed along the road by an old man in a straw hat and a face like a cherished conker. He raised his staff courteously, but, like a teacher on a school outing, had to concentrate on saving his straggling charges from becoming roadkill, and didn't have a lot of time to stop and chat.

Two or three kilometres further, when the persistent rubbing of her sandal straps had turned into agonizing puddles of damp pink flesh, she saw the tap. At first she thought it was a mirage, the kind of thing that Great-Aunt Agatha might have conjured up from a desert-maddened mind. If so, it was very detailed mirage, complete with abandoned beer cans, a regular drip and a persistent smell of marshy vegetation. Even the most crazed psyche couldn't invent that smell. Not a mirage, then, but some sort of emergency standpipe, conveniently located in the middle of nowhere, perhaps for the rapid sluicing down of the wandering sheep. That meant that it was riddled with disease, probably cholera. Was cholera quick, better than a slow death by dehydration and the lingering amputation of both feet? If only she had re-read *The Secret Garden* at school, instead of wallowing in *Jackie* and *Seventeen*. 'Ten Tips for Sensational Snogging' wouldn't be nearly so much help, not unless the shepherd returned in an amorous mood.

Cholera it would have to be, or maybe typhoid. As she tottered towards the tap, composing her deathbed address, full of bittersweet forgiveness, and wondering whether anyone would be around to hear it, a battered Land Rover cut in front of her and rasped to a dusty halt. A stocky woman with short grey hair climbed out, followed by three red setters. She opened the back of the Land Rover and flung out a collection of empty plastic bottles, demijohns and five-gallon water containers, all of which she proceeded to fill from the tap. The dogs chased one another around, stopping from time to time to lap up the splashing water and to lie, panting, in the narrow fringes of shade.

Pippa approached the woman and spoke carefully, having practised five or six times before.

'Er, *scusi. Dove siamo, per favore?*'

'Good question.' said the woman, without looking up from the bottle she was filling. 'Where are we indeed? Where are we going? Have we got a map? No, you silly girl, I said "map", not 'snack'. You can have something when we get home.'

After a few moments, Pippa decided that the silly girl was probably one of the dogs, though she scarcely minded either way, such was her relief at hearing an English voice. A very English voice, as well, straight from Cheltenham Ladies' College, via Crufts and the Great Yorkshire Show.

'Is the water safe to drink, then?'

'Safe? It's the best bloody water this side of the Appenines.' She tightened the last cap and straightened up. 'Going for a walk, are you? You're not exactly dressed for it.'

'I know. There was a bit of a - misunderstanding.'

'Huh. Always is, in this damn country. One giant misunderstanding, the whole place. No one knows what's going on, no one. I tell you, I'd be straight back to Blighty in a flash if it wasn't for those barbaric quarantine laws. And house prices, of course.' She stuck out a square hand. 'Muriel Stanhope.'

'Pippa Laud.'

'Hmm. Had a spaniel called Pippa once. Picky eater but randy as hell. Had to lock her in the coal cellar whenever she was on heat. Little whore. Which way you headed, then?'

Pippa pointed forward to where the road gently curved and climbed. A cluster of grey houses clung to the hillside around a delicate campanile.

'And where are you planning to get to?'

'Lucca.'

Muriel snorted through her nose like a superior horse. 'You won't get to Lucca that way, girl. Not without a spot of circumnavigation. I'd better give you a lift. You can't walk any further, not in those ridiculous shoes. I suppose you know you're tearing your feet to shreds.'

'Perhaps there's a bus.'

Another snort. 'Not till Wednesday week or the feast of Saint Felicitoso. They put a special one on then to carry the mushrooms. No, get yourself a drink and then get in. You don't mind dogs?'

'Of course not.'

'That's the first sensible thing I've heard you say. You won't object to Penny on your lap, then? She had an op. last week and she needs something soft under her. One or two of the stitches are a bit dodgy - Italian vets, you know - but there's a towel somewhere if you're worried about blood on your dress.'

'I'm not.' said Pippa stoutly, clambering up into the passenger seat and patting her thigh for Penny to follow her.

'Good girl. Where are you staying, anyway?'

'At the Piccola Casa d'Inglese. Do you know it? I've got a job there.' I hope, she added silently.

'Not a tourist, then? Yes, I know the Piccola Casa. How are old Elsa and Elisa? I haven't seen them for a month or two. Had to tear them off a strip for riding those bikes of theirs through my sunflowers. Hooligans, the pair of them, but jolly good chaps.'

They were passing the shepherd and his unruly flock, precariously close, but without actually hitting any. Muriel wound down her window and called out something cheerful.

'He's a jolly good chap, too. So, what made the Hell's Angels give you a job?'

'The last teacher was murdered.'

There didn't seem any point in beating about the bush with Muriel. She gave a little hum of approval.

'That sounds final enough. Going to make it official, or not?'

'What do you mean?'

'The bureaucracy. *Permesso di soggiorno, codice fiscale*, all that jazz. Some do and some don't, same as the Italian themselves. Some jump through the hoops, pay their taxes, fill in all the compulsory bumf, some don't bother. Doesn't seem to make much difference in the long run.'

'Oh, I think I'd better do it by the book. I was a solicitor in England, you see.'

Muriel snorted again. 'Suit yourself. Have you been down to the Questura yet? The central police station.'

'No, I haven't. I only got here on Wednesday.'

'All the same, I think I'd get started if I were you, if you really want to put yourself through it. It could be a long process. And by the way.'

'What?'

'Don't think for a moment that there's really a book you can do it by. More like the entire British Library. Loose-leaf.'

XIX

Agostino had mixed feelings about Monday mornings. On the one hand he liked his job and his colleagues' brisk indifference after a weekend of Mamma's plaintive regrets. He could never sit through Mass and forget her mourning presence beside him, gazing at the priest before the altar and telling herself that it could have been him. Although yesterday the atmosphere had been lightened by Serafina on his other side, giving little chirps of agreement with the Gospel and fluttering her hand within his during the Peace, like a tiny captured bird. He had no idea why she had moved across the aisle from her usual place beside her own mother and aunts, but he couldn't think of a way to ask without making it sound as though he didn't like her being there. Which he did, rather more than he would have thought possible.

On the other hand, Mondays always seemed to bring the dullest, most tedious kinds of police work, all the things that had been postponed from the weekend, routine enquiries that had to be done within office hours, paperwork from Saturday night's hoard of traffic accidents and Sunday's post-prandial drivers, the ones who couldn't keep their feet on the accelerator and drifted gently into roadside ditches. And this Monday was going to be particularly dismal. Pietro had phoned him the night before, sounding formal and deflated.

'I'm sorry to bother you at home, Ago. The thing is, the Carson case is off.' He had explained briefly. With Agostino, you could be as brief as you liked. 'So I'd better call into the Firenze station in the morning, and see what's going on there. And you?'

'Back to credit card fraud, I expect. I'm sure it's good for me in some completely incomprehensible way. Meanwhile, would you like me to keep an eye.?'

'I would, yes.' For the first time, Pietro's voice had a hint of animation. 'I really would.'

But there was no need to plunge straight back into the esoteric ennui of PIN numbers and magnetic strips, not while Juliette's text messenger was hanging around undetected. The answer came more quickly than he had expected; evidently the IT staff hadn't yet turned up to mess about with the system, but it was less than conclusive. The phone, or at least the SIM card inside it, had been bought in Milan about nine months ago, but the identity card and *codice fiscale* given by the purchaser had been false. The only ray of hope was a little flag by the entry indicating that a previous police check had been made on the same number. The enquiry had been made only six days before, by the Pisa force. Agostino smiled. A few months earlier, a complex five car pile up had taken place exactly on the border between the two provinces. Agostino had agreed to deal with it in Lucca and so had a favour to call in. Sergeant Castiglione, that had been the chap. Carlo.

'Ciao Agostino. *Com'e stai*? You wanted to know about that mobile check on Tuesday morning?'

'If you've got anything, yes. The same number's come up here in connection with something rather odd.'

'Rather odd is what we've got as well. Two scruffy blokes in a white van, driving aimlessly around near the airport at four o'clock in the morning. In the back of the truck, along with last week's sandwiches and porno mags, we found two paintings rolled up in pieces of sacking. The driver and his mate obviously knew very little about them, except that they were valuable, stolen of course, and that they were supposed to deliver them to a man in a hearse. He hadn't turned up at the lay-by rendezvous, so they were rather half-heartedly looking for him.

'A man in a *hearse*?'

'That's what they said. Whether the hearse would be empty or full, they didn't know and, so far as I could judge, hadn't liked to speculate. They'd collected the paintings from an Autogrill on the A1 and were under the impression that they'd been stolen to order, probably for an American. The first contact they'd had with the operation was a text message offering them the job. They're petty villains, used to a bit of illegal couriering and get-away work so they leapt at the chance to do this one. They were paid above the odds as well, I understand, or would have been, if they hadn't been picked up first.'

'Did you find out anything about the paintings?'

'Yes, a good deal more than we did about the phone. They're

valuable enough, fifteenth century, pinched from one of the smaller museums in Rome, less security-conscious than the big guys. We're holding on to the paintings for the time being, but we've let the van men out on bail.'

'With a guardian angel?'

'Something like that, yes, so far as manpower allows. We're hoping that someone might want a word with them about what went wrong. Seems our best bet now we've reached a dead end with the phone. So, what's your angle on it?'

Agostino explained about Etienne and Juliette.

'Senegalese, eh? Wouldn't have thought there'd be a big market for Renaissance art over there.'

'There was a mention of France in the message.'

'True, but the French aren't generally any more keen on acquiring Italian art than we are on trying out French cuisine. Could be just a stop-over point, mind you.'

'Or something completely different. It sounds a bit over the top for a normal couriering job - change of identity, new country of residence, a fat enough wage-packet to keep a family of five…'

'A Senegalese family of five. I don't suppose they go in for conspicuous consumption.'

'That's true. And identity papers don't cost much if you know where to get them.'

'The mystery is why your man was approached at all. Has he got any special expertise or connections?'

'All I know is that he's a Catholic and a rotten salesman. I can't see either being much help to anyone. I'll find out, though, if I get the chance.'

'Please. If you can shed any light on this one you'll be the Roman Art Squad's blue-eyed boy as well as ours.'

'I'll see what I can do. It's all unofficial, though; I'm supposed to be on twenty-four hour credit card fraud.'

'Yeah, that sounds like a good Lucchese crime. Broccoli still flourishing, is it?'

'If you mean our historic and elevated oak trees, yes, they're doing fine. Nice clean air we get in Lucca.'

'Plenty of compost, more like.'

'Well, whatever it is, at least our towers stay upright without having to call in an Englishman to prop them up.'

Having exchanged the traditional insults, obligatory whenever a Lucchese and Pisan have met during the past thousand years or so, they agreed to keep in touch and said goodbye. But Agostino, as he put down the phone, was thinking neither of the Torre Pendante nor of the Torre Guinigi, topped by the famous holm oaks.

'Why a hearse?' he said aloud, so that a couple of passing secretaries remarked to one another that even Sergeant Sanctitá was getting the Monday morning blues these days. 'It's black, I suppose, but hardly inconspicuous. And it's not as though they needed the space, not for two rolled up pictures. So why a hearse?'

Never mind the British Library, thought Pippa, squeezing herself into the crowd; this place was more like the Tower of Babel, the UN General Assembly and the Black Hole of Calcutta all rolled into one. She edged her way towards the least disorderly clump of people, the one that most nearly resembled the English concept of a queue. Not very nearly, even then, the likeness was only that of an Old English sheepdog to a dachshund or a dismantled marquee to a tailored suit. She took the dog-eared copy of *Italian Without Tears* out of her bag and turned again to indirect personal pronouns.

Serafina never minded Monday mornings. To be honest, Serafina very rarely knew which day of the week it was, although she always had to know the date, for the eighty or ninety documents she was obliged to sign and stamp daily. But today she knew both the day and the date, and both were ringed in red on her Sacred Heart desk calendar. Today she was having lunch with Agostino. She still wasn't sure how she had fixed it, in the nanoseconds of his mother's inattention, but fixed it she had, and it wasn't going to get unfixed. She took a puce lipstick from her bag and reapplied it, for the fourteenth time that morning. The *eau di nil* eye shadow could do with replenishment as well, but she'd better not push her luck, not with Chiara glaring at her from the next cubicle.

'Next!' called Serafina, and a dark-haired girl with resolute elbows struggled forward. Excuse me.' she panted, dumping a pile of documents on the counter, topped by a battered paperback. *Italian Without Tears*, Serafina read upside-down, and her chirpy spirits fell by a twig or two.

'I wish to make the permit.' The grammar was marginally better than the pronunciation; that was the best you could say. At least she was making the effort.

'Yes, of course. Are you American?'

'English.'

Serafina beamed. 'England. How lovely.' She would have been hard-pressed, if challenged, to name a single point of English loveliness, except perhaps that old Queen with the gin and racehorses, but she was in the mood for beaming. And the paperwork was marginally less Byzantine for an EC citizen. She took a few sheets of paper and pushed them across the counter.

'You need to fill this form in, sign it here, and return it with these documents. Originals and copies please. And we need four passport sized photographs. Okay?'

No, it obviously wasn't. The girl was looking at her apologetically, brows knitted and head on one side, like someone acting the word 'owl' in a charade. Serafina tried again, pointing at the papers. 'Complete. Sign. Bring. With copies. Photographs. Four. You understand?'

'Yes. Very much thank you.'

'A pleasure. Next!'

As the girl struggled away from the counter, through the inexorable crowd, something slipped from her armful of papers. A man reached down and picked up the burgundy bound passport. 'Hey, signora!' No response. Quickly he leafed through the pages until he came to the end. 'P- heelippa Laud! Signorina Lord!'

'Isn't she the teacher at the Piccola Casa?' Serafina asked half an hour later, over her Nasto Azzuro and clams. 'The one who's helping on your Carson case?'

'Mmm.' agreed Agostino, through a mouthful of farro. It was described as salad on the menu, so the hundred calories per mouthful didn't count, nor the olive oil he'd drenched it in. 'But it isn't our Carson case any more. Pietro's been warned off by the forces of democracy.'

'The what?'

'Americans. Backed up by Bisbigli Apparently the boss got called away from one of his operatic dos to sort it out, so Pietro's heading the Least Likely to be Promoted list. He's been sent to

Grosseto to interview an English teenager who came onto the Elba ferry with a matchbox full of cannabis.'

'Is that serious, then?' Serafina's experience of drugs was limited to the mail-order slimming pills in which Chiara placed such constant and disappointed faith.

'Is it, *palle*?' Signora Lenzuoli, in her cocoon of piety, had never discovered the secondary meaning of the word 'balls', and so Agostino let himself use it on special occasions. 'The kids just share it around at their beach parties, no harm done to anyone. It's the same the world over. This lad was just unfortunate that the box fell out of his pocket on the quayside, right under the nose of a Guarda di Finanzia Alsatian. Even they couldn't ignore anything quite so blatant. But there wasn't any need for our lot to get involved; Pietro's just been sent there as an exercise in humiliation. He said he'd call in here on his way, but I don't suppose I'll be able to cheer him up.'

'Grosseto's not so bad these days. At least you can get through the Maremma without being struck down by malaria.'

'I wouldn't be so sure. It's not really that, though, it's more about being taken off the Carson case. Pietro doesn't show it, but he takes his responsibilities seriously, especially with a murder. If he can't get it cleared up himself, then it seems to hang around at the back of his mind, nagging at him.'

And if there was one thing Agostino would know about, thought Serafina, it was things that hung around nagging.

'I think he's a bit concerned about that English girl, as well. Did she get her passport back, by the way?'

She had, adding it to the teetering pile and steering a patient course through the crowd and out into the street. Once outside she found an unoccupied doorstep and, feeling oddly shaken, sat down to sort the papers out. The girl in the *Stranieri* office had been pleasant enough, more than pleasant, helpful and sympathetic, but it was the helpfulness of a nursery nurse rather than an equal. Until she had at least mastered *Italian Without Tears* - *without* tears, she reminded herself fiercely - it would all be like this, experiencing every conversation like the youngest toddler, understanding little and expressing even less, forced to trust that the grown-ups knew what they were doing and would look after you. Even in their English lessons, the Italians were on home soil, back in charge as soon as the clock struck the hour and the real world resumed. The only one she could talk to on roughly equal terms was Pietro, and she wasn't going to think any more about him.

Her resolution was genuine, but she'd chosen the wrong spot to carry it out. On the other side of the street a figure was loping towards the Questura's main doors, each long stride echoing through her stomach. She stood up, the half-sorted papers falling into the gutter along with all her good intentions.

'Pi...'

'...etro!' Another voice finished the word. A scooter had drawn up by the kerb, on the double white lines, and its rider was gesticulating wildly, impeded only a little by the helmet slung over his elbow. Her elbow, Pippa realised, catching a glimpse of the rather tight and well-filled black T-shirt. Pietro still hadn't noticed her, his hands thrust deep in his pockets, and head bent as though searching for evidence on the gum splattered pavement.

'Pietrino!' the girl called again, kicking the scooter on to its stand and running to catch him. He turned, smiled, was crushed against the T-shirt, and Pippa could watch no longer. She gathered up her papers and trudged in the opposite direction, kicking a stone in front of her like a small boy whose team has lost again.

'So you're working on that bank robbery thing again, are you?'

Serafina spoke in an exaggerated whisper. They were the only customers sitting at the tables, but you couldn't be too careful where police work was concerned. Any of those old men at the bar, drinking *caffè corretto* and leafing through *La Gazzetta dello Sport* could be a secret underworld spy, his hearing aid set to supersonic levels to pick up every syllable of their conversation.

'Credit card fraud.' corrected Agostino, in his usual boom. 'No sane criminal would try robbing a bank in Lucca these days, not with these Star Trek entrance capsules they've all installed. Ten minutes I was stuck in one last week, with more video footage than Mel Gibson at a premiere, never mind the armed guards. To be honest, though, I haven't actually got back to the file yet. I've spent most of the morning looking into that phone number.'

'For Etienne and Julie? I knew they could count on you.' Two narrow pink fingers snaked across the table to his gigantic palm.

'You found out who it was?'

'I'm afraid not.' He explained how far he had got. 'And the mobile phone company say they can't give us any more information.'

'Nonsense!' In her indignation Serafina forgot the likelihood of Mafia infiltration. 'They know everything; where the phone's been, what numbers it's called, who those numbers belong to. Why don't you get them to give you a list of other people who've received calls from that number? That way you and the Pisa people would both have something to work on.'

'It's not as simple as that, Seraf.' For a moment he faltered, his mind reeling with angelic hierarchies. *Gloria in excelsis*. 'Giving out that kind of information is a massive infringement of personal privacy; they'd need all sorts of high-level authorization. I'm not officially investigating this thing at all, and even if I was, I'd need to go right to the top to get an order like that.'

'What about your friend in Pisa?'

'Carlo? He's only a sergeant, like me. Anyway, it won't be a priority as far as they're concerned. The paintings have been recovered, no one's been injured and they've got a couple of stooges to charge for the handling. There'd be lots of kudos if they cracked an international conspiracy, but it's not likely to happen. That kind of thing's really the business of the Art Squad, anyway. The Pisa force has got enough on its own plate without trying out fancy stuff that belongs to Rome.'

'Let Rome do it, then. These swanky Art Squad people - would they take it on?'

Agostino shrugged, his huge shoulders rolling like a tidal wave. 'No idea. I don't move in such exalted circles. They wouldn't do anything on my say-so, in any case. And if they did want to look into it, off their own bat, it would only be from an art theft point of view. They wouldn't be interested in Etienne's problems. It could even make things worse for him in the short-term.'

'The Commissario, then. Dottore Guinizelli?'

'No chance. I mean, he'd help if he could, but he's tied up in Grossetto now, and after yesterday...'

'He can't risk another black mark. I see what you mean. There's nothing else for it, then.'

'Yes, it's a shame. I'll keep an ear out, though, and if anything else happens…'

'I didn't mean we should give up!'

'No?' Something about her use of the first person plural made Agostino nervous. 'What then?'

'I'll do it myself.'

'Eh?' It was Agostino's turn to lower his voice. 'Hack into the phone company's computer?'

'Don't be silly. I don't know a megabyte from a margherita. I know where all the Questura's stationery is, though, and the official stamps. I can easily forge the authorities we need.'

'No, Serafina.'

She looked up at him, her face very still and her bird-like eyes gleaming. 'Is that an official 'no', Sergeant Lenzuoli?

'It is, yes.'

'I'll make a note of it. I suppose I'm being reprimanded as well?'

'You certainly should be.' he said, not completely in control of the corners of his mouth. She wriggled with pleasure.

'That's all right then. There's no question of your involvement.'

'Serafina…'

'After all,' she added pensively, 'I wouldn't really mind getting sacked. It's a pretty lousy job. And I have to think about the future. I'm not really sure I approve of working mothers. Do you, Agostino?'

If Pippa had hung around for long enough to finish sorting her papers, and perhaps discover the identity of the pneumatic *motociclista*, instead of stomping off in an entirely random direction and getting lost for the rest of the morning, both she and Pietro might have cheered up a little. As it was, she wandered in bad-tempered circles among Lucca's lesser glories, discovering a couple of *carozzerie*, piled high with wrecked cars, innumerable pharmacies and an English pub, which, even closed, carried around it a miasma of authentic drizzle and depression. Pietro, meanwhile, needed no warm bitter to fuel his melancholy.

'Thanks, Ali,' he muttered, as the scooter zoomed away down a one-way street, 'but I really didn't need to know that.' What did it matter to him now that the hypodermic syringes found on both bodies were of an old design, withdrawn ten years ago and replaced with a new latex-free model? Maybe the

deaths had been engineered by a pharmaceutical wholesaler, trying to get rid of his surplus stock. Less frivolously, they could have come from abroad, from somewhere that couldn't afford to replace its medical supplies so quickly. Russia, perhaps? George F. Washington would like that one. He would have to tell Pippa…
Merda.

XX

The noise of barking crackled along the wall like fire. Pippa, skirting her eighth baluardo, took a savage consolation from the sound. Since she had left the Questura an hour before, she had come across six or seven dogs, but all of them solitary, disciplined and silent. Even thrust together, with half a kilo of *salsiccia to* quarrel over, it was hard to imagine them creating this joyous fracas. So, she hadn't passed this way before; that was something. It had taken forty minutes in the backstreet wilderness before she had even found her way up to the walls, and she wondered how many circuits it would take before she found something familiar to guide her down. Her feet, loosely sheathed in a pair of tacky flip-flops, had collapsed back into yesterday's state of raw pulp, and it was only by keeping her mind resolutely on other things that she was able to keep walking at all.

Unfortunately, the other things weren't appreciably less painful. Commissario Guinizelli, for example. The brief hope of a reconciliation fluttering on the Questura steps had been firmly crushed, together with Pietro's breakfast, against that 38D Lycra chest. There was no hope of peeling it off there. Even now, at her most hard-nosed (if soft-footed), she had a nasty suspicion that Pietro might have been The Real Thing, but it was too late to brood. She had a job to get on with; two jobs, if you counted the teaching one. That reminded her; she had another lesson with Otto at two o'clock, with perhaps a bit of mild therapy on the side. 'Canst thou minister to a mind diseas'd?' she mused, startling a couple of sparrows and a little old lady on a skateboard. Feet diseas'd would be more to the point: weren't there any Lucchese chiropodists who needed to brush up on their language skills?

Approaching the next curve, she suddenly realised that the barking had stopped. That was, if it had ever existed at all. 'A compulsive fantasist', Jonathan had called her, in his valedictory email, and perhaps he had been right. Maybe the barking had only been an auditory hallucination, a projection of her internal turmoil.

But around the corner a banner stretched across the path:

LUNA PARK PER I CANI - THINK PINC!!!

Pippa sighed. If she was going crazy, then at least she would take most of Italy with her. She fished in her bag for the dictionary, without much hope. Some sort of environmental awareness campaign, she supposed. 'Moon park for cans'. Very eco-spiritual. Presumably whoever wrote it had got his colours mixed up, and meant to say 'Think Green'. But the dictionary decided to break the habit of a lifetime and be helpful, coming up with '*luna park*: fun fair or carnival', while a brief flurry of renewed yapping ahead reminded her that *cani* didn't mean 'cans' at all, but dogs. *Pinc* remained a mystery, though, and the best the dictionary could offer was *pinco*: twit or fool. Back to Pietro.

'*Ciao.*' said a cheerful voice at her elbow. It was Francesca. 'You want a *depliant*?' She held out a yellow flyer.

PINC - Protezione Integrale Nel campo dei Cani.

'I see - I think. And the luna park?'

Francesca pointed over the outside edge of the wall, towards the wide green spaces which separate it from the ring road. Thirty or forty dogs, mainly mongrels in varying proportions of Alsatian, Boxer and West Highland White Terrier, lay prone and silent upon the grass. None was asleep, though, or even dozing, for each ear was cocked alert and each nose raised to the almost imperceptible breeze. In the centre of the group stood a straw-hatted figure in front of a large plastic barrel. From time to time she - it was certainly a woman this time - would reach into a canvas bag slung over her shoulder and call out a number, followed, in a lower voice, by the name of a dog.

'*Numero ventotto* - Tonio.'

There was no mistaking those patrician tones.

'It's Muriel.'

'*Sì.*' agreed Francesca. '*La conosci? Guarda.*'

Pippa obediently watched while a small terrier picked its way delicately through the crowd. Muriel stepped aside to reveal a toy archery target, the kind made of Velcro, propped eighteen inches above the ground. She held out a small ball to Tonio who took it in his jaws, leapt at the target and left the ball stuck decisively on to the central disc. Muriel reached into the barrel and brought out a goldfish-shaped dog biscuit.

'*Bravo*!' cheered Francesca, as the little dog trotted back to its place. '*Complimenti*, Tonio!'

'Well done!' called Pippa. 'Bullseye!'

It seemed a perfectly appropriate comment to make. As Francesca pointed out later, after less than five days in the country Pippa couldn't have been expected to know how often Italian dogs are given English names, and certainly not that the hugest and hairiest participant in the game, a lumbering Great Dane - St. Bernard cross had been christened Bullseye. At the sound of his name he was instantly alert, or as alert as he ever was, before breaking something and being told to go back to sleep. Bullseye wasn't stupid, or at least, not very stupid. He had noticed what was going on around him. Dogs' names were called; they went to the caller and two minutes later they returned with a biscuit. What happened in between was a bit hazy, but the biscuit shone with the clarity of divine illumination. Now it was his turn. He creaked to his feet and turned towards the source of the sound. Then he ran.

But Bullseye was not the only dog to have recognized something about Pippa's call. At the edge of the group, her stitches resting on the softest patch of clover, lay Penny, the red setter. She wasn't very interested in the game, and her mind was wandering, to the ache in her belly, a hare sighted that morning, the young men playing football on the other side of the stream. Then she heard the voice and her thoughts moved again; back to the day before, to the bumpy jarring ride and the comfort of a yielding lap and gentle hands. She stretched, a little painfully, and raised herself up to stand. Yes, there she was, the owner of the lap, at the top of the steps which led up to the wall. Penny took a few hobbling paces forward. The steps wouldn't be easy, but she could make it. Even from here she could smell that her friend's feet were still bad, in need of a good lick. She could do that, at least.

She had almost reached the bottom step when Bullseye blundered into her path. 'Crumph.' he rumbled, which could have been an apology but was probably only his noise for 'biscuit'. He thundered ahead, and Penny, her stitches forgotten, tore after him, barking in sharp warning. She would protect her friend from this monster.

Convalescent as she was, Penny was still fitter than Bullseye, and she caught him up on the last step, so that they launched themselves together at their unsuspecting quarry. They hit her simultaneously, one on each shoulder, with the ebullient efficiency of bowling balls out for a strike. Pippa toppled straight backwards, not even pausing to crumple, into a pair of waiting arms. Oh no, not Francesca. She was a skinny little thing, especially without the rabbit padding, and entirely unequal to the combined weight of a large dog, gargantuan dog and less than sylph-like *Inglese*. The outcome was inevitable; they would fall together and plunge to a sticky end under the next trundling Ape.

The reality was less gory. Muriel, surprisingly nippy for her genetic code, was already halfway up the steps. 'Heel!'

Penny froze mid-lick, turned and slunk, an abject courtier, down to her mistress's side. You know how it is, said a rueful kink in her tail, this Divine Right business. No hard feelings.

Bullseye, less well acquainted with English commands, hesitated for a few seconds longer before recognizing the mingled scents of biscuit and power. With the grinding rumble of a malfunctioning vacuum cleaner he heaved himself up and shambled towards them. Francesca, meanwhile, peeped out from the compost skip behind which she had taken refuge.

Pippa was left, as a heroine should be, to gaze around distractedly and wonder who might be embracing her. It was a fairly sturdy clinch, featuring a pair of brown and muscled forearms covered with fine blond hairs. For a moment … Then a low voice in her ear scattered the gathering dreams.

'*Entschuldigung Sie bitte.*'

It had a certain ironic symmetry. Four days ago she had mistaken Pietro for a German and now she had mistaken a German for Pietro. She struggled upright, and turned to face her rescuer, reflecting how badly cast she was in the swooning damsel role. Francesca, who was sashaying out from behind the compost, would have pulled it off with much more conviction.

For a moment they stared at one another, he at the top of her head, she at his beard. Then, 'Oh.' they said together, and smiled.

'But I think you are the airport girl, with the very heavy bag. I am most delighted to meet you again. You are not injured by the dogs, I hope?'

'Thanks to you I'm not. Thanks to you a second time. Are you in the habit of acting as knight errant, or is it a personal service?'

'I'm sorry?'

'It doesn't matter. Just thanks again. My name's Pippa, by the way.' She wondered whether she ought to suggest a coffee, a sort of *Handgelt*, but didn't want to make it look as though she were trying to pick him up. Which she wasn't. After the Jonathan and Pietro fiascos – or should it be *fiaschi* here? - she was definitely off men this time. In any case, no average British female was ever going to pick up more than a dropped lollipop stick with Francesca standing beside her.

'Pleased to meet you.' He held out his hand. 'I am - Helmut.'

He didn't seem all that sure, thought Pippa, but perhaps if she was called Helmut, she would be hesitant too. She shook his hand and introduced him to Francesca, before whom, oddly, he managed to avoid falling on his knees. Muriel arrived, slightly out of breath.

'Guilia's here now so I can take a break. Hello again, Pippa. What's all this then, spreading insubordination in the ranks?'

'I'm sorry. I didn't realise...'

'No harm done. Bloody silly name for a dog, anyway. Good to see that Penny recognized you. Are you going to join us?'

'What, for lunch? I've got a lesson at two, but...'

'Lunch? Good God, you're as bad as the dogs. Don't you think about anything but your stomach? Pink. PINC. Hasn't Francesca given you a handout?'

'Oh, yes.' She glanced at the piece of yellow paper still in her hand. Bullseye had eaten half of it before realising his mistake and the rest was rather blurred with mud and slobber. 'A sort of rescue organization, is it?'

'That's right. We're here every morning this week, organizing activities, spreading the word... Tomorrow's going to be a bit special. *Who Wants To Sniff A Million Trouserlegs?* Multiple choice scent recognition. We need all the help we can get.' She turned to Helmut. 'How about you? Are you a dog-lover?'

Helmut scanned the horizon, from the rattiest Yorkshire terrier to Bullseye's lumbering haunches. He shook his head regretfully. 'I still prefer men.'

XXI

Muriel was the first to recover.

'Had a setter bitch like that once. A washout on heat, but she tackled brambles like a bloody rotovator. I'm Muriel Stanhope, by the way. You've met Fran? And the murderous Pippa?'

'Murderous?'

'Well, someone polished off her predecessor, so she's the prime suspect. *Qui bono*, isn't it? No, Roly, bon*o*. Greedy swine.'

Francesca looked up from the dog turd she was burying, her face clouded with something more than ordinary nausea. 'But Zena dies in the Monday night, when Pippa is in England.'

'Zena?' The German's face paled under the tan, faint freckles showing through. 'Who is Zena?'

'Was Zena.' corrected Muriel. 'An American teacher at La Piccola Casa, the dottiest of Lucca's language schools. She got herself bumped off last week, for no discernable reason, and Pippa's got her job. I daresay the police are baffled.'

'The Polizia,' said Pippa carefully, 'have been instructed to withdraw from the case. I think the Americans are dealing with it now.'

'Oh Lord, not that shower. World War Three here we come. But how do you know about it, Fran?'

'Zena has been my teacher. And my lesson is the last before the death.'

'Really?' Muriel looked at the girl intently, as though assessing her breeding potential. 'Doesn't that make you the chief suspect then? Even dodgier than old Pippa. You didn't do it, I suppose?'

'No.' Francesca's voice was confident, but her eyes shifted sideways, back over the wall to the safety of the dogs.

'Didn't think so. I can generally judge a temperament. But it's time to relieve poor Guilia, I think. She'll never get the hang of a choke chain, not if a Crufts medal depends on it. So I can't persuade you two to stay?'

'Perhaps tomorrow.' said Helmut

'Fair enough. We'll still be here. Come!'

After Muriel had stridden away, Francesca trotting at her heels like a well-trained spaniel, Pippa set off for the school. She had her bearings now, and the mention of lunch - her mention of lunch - reminded her that she had eaten hardly anything since the Guinizelli's party. If she really scooted, she might make the corner shop before the shutters clanged down at one o'clock. Pecorino, tomatoes and focaccia, with one of those big knobbly apples that looked sour but tasted as though it had been seeped in cinnamon syrup.

'Excuss me please.' So Helmut was still here. For such a large and vigorous youth, he was surprisingly inconspicuous. 'I think - do you know another English teacher? A Graham Garrett, please?' Something must have flickered in her face because he went on more confidently. 'He is - a frient of a frient. This frient gave me a dress.'

'What? Oh, I see. *An* address.'

'An, of course. Thank you. But there is no one. Graham is moved, I think. Please, you know to where?'

'I, ...' Pippa's experience of male gay relationships was confined to one slightly nauseatingly monogamous couple at university, and she had no idea of the proper etiquette. If she was Gray, she thought, she would probably be delighted to have a large blond hunk like Helmut turn up on her doorstep, beard and all. The only real drawback seemed to be his name, and you could probably get around that by calling him Cuddles or Boris. On the other hand she wasn't Gray, and had no idea of the sadistic storms which might rage beneath Helmut's Teutonic calm.

'I don't know his address myself,' she said, then realised, with some surprise, that she was speaking the truth. On their way back from visiting the Volto Santo, down one of the cool narrow side streets, Gray had waved an arm in the vague direction of a tall yellow-fronted building and declaimed, 'I live up there', but since most of Lucca's streets were cool and narrow, and most of the buildings tall and yellow-fronted, she was really very little the wiser. 'I could give him a message, though.' she added, as the fine Nordic features fell into a doleful defeat.

'You can? *Wunderbar*. Here.' He took a small sensible notebook from his pocket and Pippa winced at a momentary flutter of bus ticket. 'This is my name and my mobile phone number.'

'And your friend? Do you want to put down his name as well?'

'Of course.' He seemed to hesitate for a moment before writing. 'It is done.' He tore off the sheet and handed it to her. *Helmut Lebens*, then a phone number, and then the other name. *Johann Schwartz*.

'But this, isn't this the one who died?' Full marks for tact, Philippa. Probably he didn't even know. Judging from the reappearance of the blanched freckles he certainly didn't know. And bearing in mind what Johann died from, and the physical nature of at least one side of the triangle, Helmut might have more to worry about than not having sent a wreath. But if so, she, like so many Britons before her, had underestimated the Germanic capacity for recovery. He gave himself a little shake and smiled sadly.

'Yes indeed. It is a great tragedy. I am missing him very much.'

'But...' Pippa would have liked time to work this out in peace, but there was no guarantee of seeing Helmut again. '...have you been to Lucca before, then?'

'Oh no. This is my first trip.' He sounded unnecessarily adamant.

'But then how did Johann tell you about Gray? He died here, didn't he? Unless he wrote to you?'

'Yes, that's right.' Was there a touch of relief in his quick reply? 'He - Johann - knew that he did not have long to live, and also he knew that I wished to come to Italy. He wanted to make it possible for his two closest frients to meet one another. It was one of his characteristics; a great generosity.' A fleeting smile rippled across his broad face.

'And Thomas?'

'Thomas?'

'Didn't someone called Thomas take Johann's body back to Germany? Gray seemed to think that Thomas was Johann's,' what was the phrase? '- long-term partner?'

Helmut snorted. 'Oh, *that* Thomas. He was liking to believe so. Or maybe he was thinking that Johann would have money to leave, which was not the truth. In any way, he is gone now. We have no contact there.'

'Right.' The conversation seemed to have run out of steam, exhausted by Helmut's anti-Thomas vehemence. 'I'd better be off then. I'll give Gray the message as soon as I can.'

Helmut inclined his head formally. 'It will be very kind.'

She was too late for the corner shop after all; the heavy metal blinds were already rolled down and the streets were empty except for a few northern tourists, not yet syncopated into Mediterranean biorhythms. There were plenty of bars open, but she felt in need of a quiet ponder, and it wasn't easy to ponder, surrounded by the previous night's football replayed on Eurosport, a graphic description of the bartender's weekend and the ubiquitous cluster of old men in shapeless black berets, like a French extras' convention. No, pondering was best achieved in the dingy solitude of the flat, over the remains of last Wednesday's English lunch; three soggy cream crackers, half a packet of Fruit Pastilles and an individual pork pie. After some thought she rejected the pork pie, which was turning a little blue around the edges. She threw it in the wastepaper basket and almost immediately retrieved it. No doubt there were strict regulations prohibiting the importation of pork pies from disease-ridden Britain, and it would be just her luck to have a cleaning lady who moonlighted for *la Dogana*.

Having wrapped the pork pie in layers of Saturday's *La Repubblica* and hidden it in a corner of her suitcase, she shoved the last soggy cracker in her mouth and set out to meet Otto. Gray was staggering away from the photocopier, weighed down by a small eminence of A4. Wearing camouflage trousers and a khaki gilet festooned with various sized pockets, he looked like an intellectual Action Man.

'Hi. Fancy a third of a text book?'

'What?'

'One of my students got hold of a real English textbook and I twisted his arm', Gray flexed his small mud-coloured pectorals, 'until he agreed to lend it to me. I figured that if I only photocopied every third page, I wouldn't be so far up the creek with the copyright brigade. I've made a copy for you, too.'

'Great. Does that make me an accessory in a third of a crime?'

'Guess so. Still, it has to be better than the Little Brown Brethren, and we can use our imagination to fill in the gaps.'

'Mmm.' said Pippa, leafing through her stack. One page finished halfway through an account of George Best's career, demonstrating the third conditional: 'If he had been a teetotaller, he might have become the England manager,' while the next began with dramatic dialogues featuring the Exchange Rate Mechanism. It would take a fair chunk of imagination to bridge that gap.

'I've got something for you as well.' She took out the torn notebook page. 'Only a phone number, I'm afraid. I met him this morning - well, fell into his arms, actually, and we got talking.'

'As one does.' Gray unfolded the note. His soft, beardless cheeks, flushed with the success of his copyright piracy, faded to pale green and reddened again, like a malfunctioning traffic light. 'What's he like?'

'Helmut? Just German. You know: blond, polite, cautiously enthusiastic about greater European integration... I've met him before, actually.'

But Gray wasn't listening. He was folding the note into tiny concertina pleats before stowing it in one of his smaller pockets.

'I don't know if I can face him, Phil. All this harping back to Johann isn't doing my emotional health a whole bunch of good. I thought I'd reached some kind of closure before this stuff with Zena brought it all back. Otto was really pleased at how I'd moved on.'

Pippa's tonsils gave a sympathetic hum. 'Talking of Otto, I'd better get moving myself . Thanks for this.' She brandished the truncated textbook and winced as the pages cascaded to the floor.

'Mooseshit. It'll take you hours to get them back in order.'

'I don't think I'll bother. They might be more effective taken at random. A more genuine simulation of authentic linguistic experience.'

'Wow, you're right.' Carried away by the possibilities of the haphazard method, he began to shuffle his own meticulously paginated bundle. 'Maybe you've invented a whole new pedagogical technique.'

'Could be. By the way, while we're being scientific, did you know anything about Zena's heart condition?'

'Er...' He had obviously changed his mind about the benefits of randomization, for he found himself quite unable to reply until all his pages had been restored to their proper order. 'Er, heart condition? I'm not quite sure. I don't think I remember anything, but then I didn't always listen that closely. The call of the muse, you know. What do Elsa and Elisa say about it?'

'I haven't asked them yet.' Pippa sighed. Surely even a poet ought to remember something like that without having to call in third party witnesses? Especially witnesses as flaky as Elsa and Elisa.

'I do remember something else, though.'

'Yes?' Hope sprang back, like good knicker elastic.

'She was allergic to kiwi fruit.'

XXII

'Kiwi fruit, kiwi fruit.' Pippa was still muttering the mantra as she closed the door behind her.

'Dear me.' said Otto from the window. 'You have not been dreaming of kiwi fruit, I hope? Deeply disturbing, if you are a disciple of the Freudian school; only slightly less so for the Jungians.'

'But you're neither, are you, Otto?'

'Oh no. My interpretation is much more simple. If you dream of kiwi fruit then either you wish for kiwi fruit, or you are afraid of kiwi fruit. Which is it in your case?'

'Neither, I'm afraid. It was Zena. According to Gray she was allergic to them.'

Otto frowned, his pale eyebrows knitted in a single caterpillar of concern, but his blue eyes were sparkling. 'Could this be a clue?'

Pippa laughed. 'Hardly. What I really wanted to know was about her heart. Apparently her doctor told the police that she had a serious heart condition, although the post-mortem didn't show any evidence of it.'

'Ah.' His grave expression seemed suddenly genuine.

'I suppose you can't tell...'

'I would really rather not.' His lunar face was troubled. 'It is safer in my experience never to betray a confidence. In this way all know that someone can be trusted. You, for example, if you wanted to tell me anything...'

Pippa felt suddenly crestfallen, like the only child at a party not to have brought a present. Otto chuckled.

'Don't worry; it is not compulsory. And I think, perhaps, that I can, after all, tell you something more about poor Zena. Certainly she told me about this condition of the heart, certainly she also told her doctor. Whether she herself believed it, I do not know. She was a little - my more ruthless colleagues would say a fantasist. To me -' he shrugged, 'a small overflow of imagination.'

'But wouldn't the doctor check up?'

'Most doctors, yes. But - how can I put this? - in life sometimes the laws of magnetism are reversed, and it is the weak who attract one another. In any case I cannot believe that Zena died from a weak heart any more than from one of your hairy little kiwis. Except, of course, that they could both have been symptoms of a certain - exhibitionism, the kind of attention-seeking behaviour that led her to get mixed up with that rabble of anarchy.'

'You still think the murder was political then?'

'Oh, no doubt about it, in my amateur opinion. But what does your policeman friend think?'

'He's not on the case any more. It's been transferred to the Americans. And...' Stop there, she told herself, but there was something about Otto's nod that led her over the edge of English reticence. 'He isn't exactly my friend any more, either.'

'Oh my dear girl!' His round benevolent face seemed to get even rounder and more benevolent. 'I am so sorry. Elsa and Elisa told me that you had been together a great deal. I thought that perhaps...'

'Yes, I thought that perhaps as well. Never mind.'

'Plenty more fishes in the pond. But if you aren't asking these questions on behalf of the police...' The corners of his eyes crinkled into tiny concertinas. 'Oh Pippa! Have you been playing detectives?'

'And that's when I started to snivel.' she confessed, telling the story to Pierrotino on the tiny roof terrace that evening. 'Pathetic, isn't it?' The cat rubbed himself sympathetically against her legs. 'Yes, I know. If I had to turn myself into a blubbering mess, it would have been much better to have waited until I got back to you. But Otto is a bit like a fat old cat himself, don't you think? The kind you can mistake for a cushion without its being mortally offended.'

Pierrotino made a smart pirouette at the end of the wall and a reverse rub on the way back as if to say that, yes, he knew exactly, and he intended to become that sort of cat himself in a century or two.

'So, once I'd started I told him everything; all about Pietro and the tortelli and George F. Washington and the row.'

Pierrotino nodded sagely, or perhaps he was only flicking at a passing fly.

'And then, of course, he pointed out the obvious. Very nicely, but quite categorically. And I suppose it was obvious really, wasn't it, even to you?'

The cat reserved judgment; he wasn't getting trapped by that one.

'Like he said, it's not as though I can even interview anyone unless they speak English. I haven't got past Chapter Three in *Italian Without Tears*. And if the Americans found out I was trying a bit of freelance investigation, they wouldn't be too happy. Not that I'm scared of the Americans.'

Of course not, Pierrotino's ear scratch agreed.

'Nor of the Red Brigade or whoever Otto thinks is behind it. But, like he says, if I really want to see justice done, I'd be better going back to England and joining a criminal legal aid practice. Jonathan owes me a reference, at least. And Otto says he'll keep an eye out here and liaise with embassies and lawyers and stuff. He seems to know what he's talking about.'

Pierrotino paused enquiringly, one paw in the air.

'I know it's not very glamorous but he's probably right. I'm not going to find anything out here, blundering around getting under people's feet. And to be quite frank,' She paused, feeling it safer to be tactful, even when addressing a cat, 'the whole Italian thing doesn't seem quite as alluring as it did a couple of days ago. I know I've got you, and the sky and the pasta, but somehow it doesn't turn out to be quite enough. So, I'm off tomorrow morning, *amico. A casa.*'

Charles rubbed a stubby hand over his eyes and blinked back at the computer screen. It still said the same, in its discreet, modest font, nothing fancy, letting the figures speak for themselves. A proven correlation between the two allergies, sufficient cases of simultaneous occurrence to convince even the most sceptical anti-statistician. So that was it. Or, to be precise, part of it; it didn't explain the cupboard or the no-global slogan but those were, as he'd always suspected, peripheral. It was the primary cause that mattered, just as it had with Elisabeth. The stupid Yank, why hadn't she told him? But even as he asked himself, he couldn't be sure that she hadn't said something, and that he hadn't dismissed it as menopausal hysteria. Just like Elisabeth.

He could hear his friends on the stairs, laughing, calling out that they were waiting; he must have checked his email by now, the weather was perfect for sitting outside. He turned off the computer the brutal way, jabbing at the buttons until the accusing figures faded from the screen. Then he went down for afternoon tea.

XXIII

The mobile phone company had promised, on pain of dismemberment, death and judicial enquiry into the acquisition of their franchise, to fax the list of names and telephone numbers to Serafina by nine o'clock on Tuesday morning. To be more precise, they had promised to send the fax to Marshal S.E. Rafina, a wholly fictitious Carabiniere liaison officer, but since Serafina's desk was nearest to the fax machine, she considered herself fairly safe, provided she didn't have to leave the room for any reason.

After three and a half hours of waiting, her bony knees clamped together like the jaws of a rabid terrier, she finally heard the machine whirr into action. She didn't dare get up, having only managed to halve her usual two litre morning Coke habit, but shuffled her chair in the direction of the spewing paper.

'Another of those junk faxes, I expect. I'll grab it quickly and send it straight back. That should give them the message.'

'But it's a computer, Serafina.' explained Rita, the office's newest recruit. 'It sends them out automatically. You can't teach it anything.'

'Wanna bet?' But Rita's education would have to wait. Serafina was leafing through the falling sheets.

Seven Hundred New Ring Tones for your Telefonino
Eat every scrap of Mamma's Pasta and Still Lose Weight!
Exotic Girls in Anatomically Impossible Poses

'*Porco misere*!' she swore, and Chiara, in the next cubicle, flinched as though despoiled by spittle. She had just become *affidanziata* to a scion of one of Lucca's oldest families, and was trying to gain in aristocratic manners what she hoped to lose in kilos.

Amaze the Lads; Delight the Lasses - 7 centimetres more! read Serafina, regardless. *Wave Goodbye to those Embarrassing Noises. For the exclusive attention of Marshal S E Rafina. This fax contains confidential and sensitive material. If you are not the intended recipient...*

Relief flooded her. Literally. She grabbed the sheaf of faxes and fled to the loo. Behind her, Chiara sniffed.

'Serafina's behaving very oddly these days, don't you think?'

Rita, who had recently moved to Tuscany from Bolzano, where they spoke German and indulged in a semblance of organization, nodded enthusiastically. Everything in Lucca was odd, so far as she was concerned, but it was a relief to find a focus for her uncertainties. She was a loyal girl, though, and Serafina had been kind to her.

'I think she's just in love.'

Pseudo-Helmut was sitting on a piece of ruined wall, swinging his legs and shaking his mobile phone. The little symbols claimed that the battery was fully charged, that the ring volume was on maximum and that the phone had a signal. But then they would, wouldn't they? Nineteen hours and twenty-seven minutes since he had given the number to the English girl. What if he'd got it wrong, transposed two of the digits or confused the code? Being German didn't really guarantee perpetual efficiency, whatever the old ladies had thought. Or perhaps the girl had simply forgotten. She had looked a bit dippy, now he came to think of it, not to mention shell-shocked from the seventy kilos of raw dog. All the same, he thought he could probably rely on her.

That left Graham himself. Maybe he, Pseudo-Helmut, should have said more in the note, added a cryptic hint or two. It would have been easy enough, with all the jokes they had shared. But then, of course, this silence would have been even worse. He whirled the phone around his head a couple of times, to the delight of a Norwegian toddler, who proceeded to do the same with his cup of carrot juice. Perhaps German phones didn't work on Tuscan airwaves, some sort of post-partisan embargo. Yes, that would be it.

As usual, Pisa was a few degrees hotter than Lucca, and Pippa, in her university duffle coat, was sweating in offensive abundance. She had stuffed it in at the last moment, a pledge that she would stay in Lucca at least until the clear cold nights of winter. Either that, or as a security blanket. But now its allotted half of the suitcase was filled with presents: buccellato, olive oil, parmigiano and a ridiculously expensive bottle of Brunello di Montalcini for

Uncle Eric, who hallucinated himself as a connoisseur. However overheated, her homecoming would at least be convivial. She sighed and joined the long snaking queue that led to the check-in. A small blond boy, immaculate in linen shirt and shorts, turned around and stared at her.

'Daddy, that girl's wearing a winter school coat!'

His father grunted from behind the *Financial Times*, purchased from the airport newsstand at a breathtaking mark-up. He didn't actually want to read the bloody thing, but one had to indicate one's status. International monetary catastrophe, his frown suggested, would inevitably ensue if he waited to pay the sterling price at Stansted. When one travelled by Ryanair, as an exercise, obviously, in cross-cultural irony, these things were especially important.

'Be quiet, Nathaniel. She's probably a student.'

'Oh.' The child sounded disappointed. 'Not a bloody 'Talian, then?'

'Not this time.'

With a sudden lunge of the guts, Pippa realised who the father was: the unsuccessful haggler in Lorenzo's bike shop. She pushed her trolley tight against theirs, defying the English canons of personal space. Partly she wanted to hear more but it was mainly just to irritate them. There was nothing like a bit of gratuitous crowding to quell the queasy feeling under her ribs. The queue creaked forward until they were within sight of the check-in notices.

'Why's there a picture of a gun, Mummy?' asked Nathaniel, recognizing that the holiday, and the paternal quality time that went with it, had been left behind with Teddy in the hired Audi.

'They're things you mustn't take on the plane with you.'

'Oh I see.' He read through the list with relish. '*Guns, knives, scissors, snooker cues, razors,...* What's a hippo-dermic syringe?'

'Hypodermic, darling. A kind of needle people use to put medicine into themselves.'

'What kind of people?'

'Student kind of people.' interjected his father, casting a venomous glower at Pippa's encroaching trolley. 'Then they get their stomachs pumped at the taxpayer's expense. Personally, I'd leave them to it. If some inadequate wants to do us a favour and detonate herself with that muck, she ought to be allowed to get on with the job. All the State need do is tidy the body away afterwards.'

'I think the airlines are more concerned that they might be used as weapons.' said his wife nervously. 'They aren't really worried about potential suicides.'

'Well they jolly well ought to be; some of the long-haul flights I have to sit through. Bloody dreadful films and the Scotch is nothing to write home about Business class, too. You don't know you're born, just popping across to Italy every couple of months. Not that Ryanair doesn't have its own drawbacks.'

He turned slightly and raised his voice for Pippa's benefit. 'The class of fellow passenger, for one thing.'

But Pippa had gone.

Agostino's enormous forefinger ran down the column of names, like a snowplough through the post-toboggan slush. Occasionally it paused and a veil of perplexity clouded his open face.

'I know some of these names.'

'Habitual criminals? Murky underworld characters? Suspected *mafiosi*?' Serafina gripped her fork tightly, jabbing the air with each question mark.

'No, none of those. Although there are a couple of Sicilian gentlemen we could do with checking out.'

'What, then? Come on, Ago, you can't drag a girl all this way and then leave her dangling in tantalizing suspense.'

'Me drag you?' As far as Agostino could remember, he had simply suggested that Serafina should bring the list up to his office. It had been entirely her idea that, to ensure a safe and comprehensive investigatios, they really ought to take it out to lunch. 'No, don't explain again. The thing is that a lot of the people on this list cropped up last week in the Carson case.'

'The dead *Americana*? The one the CIA forbade you to investigate? Wow. It's a good thing we came out here then, isn't it? This could be a really heavy security risk. Do you think we're being bugged?'

'I shouldn't think so, no. Mind you, perhaps you ought to speak just a little louder. There's one deaf old man in the *bagno* who didn't quite catch all of that.'

'Oops.' She lowered her voice to a conspiratorial croak. 'Who was it that Signor X rang, then?'

'Zena Carson herself, look here, several times in these few days before she died. Then here's her doctor and that other teacher, Graham Garrett, the Canadian poet. Looks as though he – what are we calling him - Signor X? - called Mr. Garrett... Uhh?' Either one of the stuffed olives had gone the wrong way or something had occurred to the sergeant. 'This final column - that's the time of the call, right?'

'Looks like it. What *is* it, Ago?'

He made no answer but plunged his hand into his capacious jacket pocket and fumbled about, in the nearest he had ever got to impatience. Finally, after several false starts involving crumpled handkerchiefs, holy medals and empty packets of pine nuts ('I'm trying to give up chocolate') he drew out a narrow black diary and plumbed its depths.

'Thought so.'

'Ago!' It sounded like a diminutive of 'agony'. 'When are you going to tell me what's going on?'

'On our way to the language school. How's your English, by the way?'

She thought for a moment. 'Minimal, I think is the word. Am I going to have to use it?'

'It's quite possible. Mine got stuck at the *Johnny likes fish and chips* stage. Come on, Marshal, that's your third Coke, isn't it? Wouldn't you be better leaving it here?'

'I had a bit of catching up to do.' Serafina gulped the last half glass, her narrow throat bulging like a baby gannet. 'Anyway, we Carabinieri have guts of reinforced concrete.'

For a man with such short legs, and a such a substantial torso balanced on top, Agostino's walking pace was breathtaking. Literally, in Serafina's case, as she skipped and hopped to keep up with him. But gradually the inexorable forces of gravity began to operate, even on his size 49 brogues, and he slowed enough to speak.

'It was last Thursday afternoon, when I was at the school. Pietro was out interviewing another witness, so I was holding the fort. And Elsa and Elisa's hands. The body had only been found that morning, and they were both a little fragile. Anyway, Graham Garrett arrived, in a sort of dynamic desperation, saying that he'd got some vital information and he needed to speak to Pietro.'

'Why not you?' asked Serafina defensively.

'Calm down, comrade, it wasn't anything rankist. I think he'd have been happy to be interviewed by one of the Drugs' Squad's sniffer dogs, if only he could get it off his chest. No, the problem was that his Italian was nearly as bad as my English. The old dears, charming as they are, especially when they get pulled over for riding those death-machines without helmets, wouldn't really do as official interpreters. So I had to sit with the lad for an hour or so while we waited for the boss. Longest hour of my life, except that last interview with the bishop. I felt like a real lemon.'

'Nah.' said Serafina, cheered by the discovery that she could jog and speak at the same time. She would bet a Lycra wedding dress that Chiara couldn't. 'Watermelon, maybe.'

'You watch your tongue, young Marshal, or we'll send you to the Carabinieri for good. Might suit you, all that hair.'

Since the recent admission of women to the Carabinieri , those officers too young and feminine to grow the traditional moustache had adopted an alternative badge of identity: a cascade of frizzy ringlets, as nearly black as possible, preferably almost waist length, and rippling out from under the natty peaked cap.

'Anyway, it was Pietro the lad needed, so we just had to wait. He rolled up in the end, with the English girl in tow, and they were about to begin, when Graham's phone gave one of those hiccups.'

'*Un text?*'

'That's what you youngsters call them, is it? A message, like the one sent to Etienne's wife. Graham didn't even want to look at his at first, but we, being kind, civilised, completely brain-dead police officers, insisted that he should. We thought it was going to be the ice hockey results.'

'And was it?'

'Not unless he's the most obsessed fan in the history of organized sport. Whatever was in that message terrified him worse than Juve going down 4-0 to Chievo. He clammed up faster than a nun's *corsetto* and we never got any more out of him. Nothing useful, that is. Just platitudes and vague biographical speculation.'

'And the message came from Signor X, right?'

'It looks like it; it was sent at the right time. And I was sitting next to Graham for a full two hours that afternoon. I'd have heard if he had any other messages.'

'So we're going to see this poet now, are we, to clear up the whole thing? You could solve Etienne's mystery and the Carson case in one fell swoop. That shouldn't do your promotion prospects any harm. Commissario Lenzuoli. It's got a solid ring about it. The sort of name you could settle down with, buy a nice semi-detached *villetta*, start a cadet force of your own...'

'Hang onto those horses, Serafina. I don't think she'll let me go that easily. And, more to the point, I'm not touching the Carson case with an extendable fibreglass vaulting-pole. I'm far too conspicuous to risk the attentions of US military intelligence.'

'Isn't that what the literature profs call an oxymoron?'

'All the more reason. What could be easier for the propaganda boys - set up the snares and what should lumber in but a great hippopotamus of a dago sergeant? Gotcha.'

'I don't believe you're afraid of them.'

'No? Living in our house gives you a healthy respect for the irrational foe. But if you're determined to put me in a more flattering light I suppose you could argue that Zena Carson is already dead - God rest her soul -' He made a brief sign of the cross. '- and finding out how won't be of any help to her now. Etienne and Julie, on the other hand, and the children, of course, are very much alive, and very frightened by this text joker. If we can nail him for this one, that's good enough for me. I'm not the right shape for big-game hunting. So, you can take your pick from the motives. If you choose the right one, you'll know more than I do myself.'

But Serafina, from the moment she had first glimpsed Agostino across the playground, plump, solitary, but oddly peaceful, had been quite sure that she saw further than anyone else, with the dubious exception of God, into the Lenzuoli psyche. She grinned lopsidedly, showing a couple of missing teeth and gave a double left-footed skip to keep up with him. There were definite advantages in being a Marshal.

Gray, as usual, was keeping vigil over the photocopier. He turned at Agostino's tread and nodded. 'You again.' His Italian was basic and heavily accented, but clear enough. Perhaps they could have got beyond the weather after all. 'I thought it was finished. Philippa said...'

'It isn't the Carson case this time. Or not directly. You received a text message on Thursday afternoon..? '

Gray's face closed like the stroke of one o'clock, steel shutters rolled down over his eyes.

'We only want the name.' said Serafina. 'The man who sent the message. Or woman.'

'I don't know.' It was the ubiquitous *stranieri* answer. '*Non lo so*', easy to learn and endlessly useful, whenever you weren't quite sure of the question, but didn't want to sound openly obstinate. Serafina heard it thirty or forty times a day.

'Just the name.' she repeated more gently. 'Only the name. Please.'

He shook his head. 'That's what I don't know. His name.'

'Description, then. What did he look like?'

'I don't know.' The dreadful starkness of a new language, no synonyms to mitigate the repetition. 'I never saw him.'

'Signor Garrett.' Agostino took over again, forgetting the pre-school vocabulary, though his voice was as slow as ever. 'You already know that we're not investigating Zena Carson's death. Neither are we interested in any organizations you may or may not have been involved in. We're happy to leave all that to your North American neighbours. But the person who sent you that message used the same tactics to terrify a young immigrant family. I'm sure you wouldn't like to think of them going through all that.'

Gray had turned away slightly, fiddling with the enlargement buttons, but his rigid brow had softened into hesitancy. Agostino waited. One Mississippi, two Miss... The silence was broken.

'What's more,' chirruped Serafina, 'we suspect him of being involved in a serious art theft. A minor museum in Rome...'

'Art theft!' Gray exploded into English. 'What does a fucking *art theft* matter when someone's been murdered? You guys better start thinking about your priorities while you've still got a damn heritage to whinge about. Like I've told you three times, I've never met the guy who sent that message and I haven't the remotest idea of who he might be. One thing I do know, and a damn sight better than you, is that he's fucking dangerous. So if I had any information, which I haven't, who do you think I'd be telling? The security forces of the strongest nation in the world, as you say, our next-door neighbours, investigating the death of my friend and colleague, or a couple of Laurel and Hardy characters chasing after Julius Caesar's chamberpot. Come on, *passaparola*, or will you try an answer?'

'Can I help at all?' said a soft voice from the doorway.

'*Dottore..?*' It had been one of the worst things about parish work, Agostino's memory for names.

'Otto, please.' He held his hand out to Serafina. '*Piacere*. A translation, perhaps?'

'I'm really sorry.' said Serafina for the eighth time, as they reached the final flight of steps.

'I told you, it doesn't matter. He probably wasn't going to tell us anything anyway. Come and have an ice-cream. We missed *dolce* at lunchtime, having to race over here. Mamma doesn't like me to go without a pudding.'

The entrance hall, which had been empty when they arrived, was now fortified by a mop, bucket and spreading lake of floor polish. They skirted its edge, murmuring apologies to the woman wielding the mop.

'That's all right, Sergeant.'

He stopped, stricken. 'Julie, I...'

'Don't worry about it. I daresay I'd be the same if it were the other way around. White people coming to Senegal to clean our floors.' She laughed with only the faintest wisp of bitterness. 'They'd all seem the same to us; it wouldn't be worth looking at their faces.'

'We didn't know you worked here.' said Serafina, deliberately missing the point. She had to get that dreadful blundering look off Agostino's face.

'I don't, usually. Apparently someone died here last week and their usual cleaning lady has refused to come in since. I do some work for a friend of the owners and he asked me to help out.'

She walked out with them as far as the outside step, stretching her back in the sun.

'I'm getting paid, but it's as though I'm doing them a favour as well. It feels good. Everyone likes to give a little, sometimes.' She smiled vaguely and went back inside.

'Do you give a little, Agostino?' asked Serafina, restored to cheerfulness.

'More than a little, when I'm unexpectedly crushed.'

'I'll remember to warn you first.'

Charles looked down at them from the usual window. Another mistake; the African couple. He had misjudged them, assumed that desperation would overcome all the rest. Not that it mattered now, as long as the fat policeman didn't start asking the right questions. He would have a word with Umberto, make sure the walrus was put in its place. He might be going out, but at least he could do it in style.

XXIV

'Hippo-permic syringes,' repeated Pippa, tracing huge figures of eight with her luggage trolley across the open spaces of the airport. 'If people want to detonate themselves...' Could that have been just what Zena had done? But, unlike the brontosaurus in the queue, someone hadn't wanted to let her get on with it. Or, at least, they hadn't wanted her to be seen to have got on with it. She stopped the trolley mid-pirouette, quite Torville and Dean, only to be rammed from the side by a young man on a vehicular floor-polisher. Roadhog. Why couldn't he stick to a 750 Harley like a normal speed-crazed teenager?

Someone, or a pair of someones, still autonomous entities despite the decades of shared cashmere. Elsa and Elisa. There was even a precedent; the syringe they had taken from Johann's body to dispel the suspicion of suicide. This time they must have missed the narrow T-shirt pocket, and with no convenient medical condition to blame (a pity they hadn't heard the heart disease story) they had simply bundled her into the cupboard with the intention of doing something respectable with the body later. Had they known where it was all along, then, even when they directed her to the cupboard in search of textbooks? Surely not. Perhaps they had been struck by some kind of collective amnesia. Post-traumatic stress. It had filled out plenty of skeletal witness statements in the past; there was no reason why it couldn't be wheeled out again.

So, what are the flaws in the theory? Pippa asked herself, wishing that her inner voice could speak without Pietro's accent. The fact that Zena died of suffocation? Nasty, that one, unless it was some weird side-effect of the drug. The only other explanation was that she hadn't actually been dead when Elsa and Elisa found her; that it was the lack of air inside the cupboard that finally killed her. It didn't look like the kind of cupboard that could ever run out of air, great chilly draughts of it, but she supposed it was all a question of angles. Pippa had always been a bit hazy about angles, apart from the ones that came along with Saxons. She would leave that bit for the medics to work out.

What about the inscriptions on Zena's wrists? No, no real problem there. She could easily have done them herself, before the injection, or while she waited for it to take effect. Thinking of them now, Pippa remembered that the letters had been shakier on one side than on the other; just what you would expect of anyone but the perfectly ambidextrous. And she had done it, Pippa supposed, as some sort of valediction, an explanation, perhaps, or apology. At least by writing your suicide note on your own body, you could be sure that it would be found.

The documents and money in the bedside table? Zena could easily have brought them to the classroom with her, ambivalent about her plan perhaps, giving herself the illusion of an alternative, the fantasy escape to Greece. Elsa and Elisa, in their confused state, might have argued that the cupboard, while safe enough for a corpse, was not the place for valuables. They wouldn't have put them in their own cash box; not for fear of discovery but in case they might accidentally spend the money that was not theirs. They probably didn't even notice that half was in dollars.

But now, did she need to do anything about it? She thought of Elsa and Elisa, their absent-minded kindness, tried to imagine them in the dock. It couldn't be murder, of course, but any competent prosecution could make out a pretty watertight manslaughter case. It was hardly reasonable or responsible conduct, upon finding a warm body, however dead it appeared, to shut it in a closet and forget about for the next three days. It would break their hearts, of course, and poor Otto's, and what for? It wasn't as though anyone else would be falsely accused; it was obvious that the Americans simply planned to sit heavily on the whole story. She would be much better going back to England and forgetting about the whole thing.

She heaved her trolley round again, in the direction of the Ryanair queue, and prepared to join the end along with the other motley stragglers, the ones who didn't fret about check-in times or the convention that you waited until lunchtime to start your serious drinking. Her perambulating speculations had cost her twenty or thirty places in the line, but never mind. It was worth it to be among the rest of the human flotsam, away from the brontosaurus brood. She was edging into place, behind the end of a torrid holiday romance, when she heard her name being called.

'Miss Laud? Miss Philippa Laud?'

She must have dropped her passport again. But no, there it was in her pocket, the narrow burgundy spine that would conduct her back to cottage pie and common sense. What then?

'Remember me, Miss Laud? Your namesake?'

'Of course I do. Mr - or is it Corporal? - Loftinghouse.'

'I'd prefer plain Lord, ma'am.'

'I'm Pippa, then.'

He seemed taller here, stooped in his faded uniform like a heron among a crowd of chattering budgies.

'Heading home, are you, Pippa?'

'That's right. And you, Lord?' It sounded like the chorus to an old-fashioned spiritual. Any moment now she would be raising her hands to heaven.

'You bet. Alitalia to Milan,' he pronounced it *Mee*-lan, like the football team, 'then good old Pan-Am back to Houston. I'll be munching on Mom's blueberry shortcake by suppertime tomorrow. I'm being replaced.'

'Oh, I....' Pippa would have offered commiserations, if he hadn't been beaming quite so broadly.

'Yeah. Like Lootenant Washington said, I've got many military qualities, but spin-doctoring ain't among 'em. And that's what he needs, sez he, once Guiseppe Public hears about these arrests. So Lord's headed back West while some medical dude gets his butt kicked in the opposite direction. Begging your pardon, ma'am for the terminology. But it's a mighty peculiar world, the army.'

'It must be,' said Pippa, hoping that her duty towards her fellow Lord didn't include explaining what a spin-doctor did. What do you mean, arrests?'

'Oh, didn't you know? It's that Carson case of yours. The Loot figured it out faster'n a coupling coyote. Seems there were two of them in it. Frannie and Luke, would it be? Ring any bells?'

'A whole carillion. But they didn't do it, you know.'

'No? That's not how GFW sees it. According to him this Luke's a dangerous Red terrorist who planned to take out Miz Carson in revenge for her passing info to US Intelligence. The spooks confirmed that she'd been on their books since nine-eleven.'

'And Francesca?'

'Frannie, right? Seems she's a med student who had an English class with the deceased on the critical night. Hey, you told us that, didn't you? Smart work. You and that Italian cop. He's not taking the trip to Ingerland with you?'

'Not this time.'

'Pity. You made a fine couple. And talking of couples, it seems that these two, Frannie and Luke, they had a thing going too. Classic criminal pair. Bonnie and Clyde, Starsky and Hutch, Calamity and Jane. And between them, they've got the three aces: motive, means, opportunity. A real no-brainer, sez the Loot. Even I could have got there in the end.'

'Yes but look, Lord, it's all very neat but it's wrong.'

'How so?'

'Nobody killed her, not deliberately, anyway. She gave herself the injection, then someone else found her and put her in the cupboard.'

'Why would they do that?'

'You have small towns in America, don't you? And people who are shocked at the thought of suicide, and act in a panic to cover it up?'

Lord nodded slowly. 'Yeah, we got all of those a cactus throw from Mom's backyard. That's what you reckon happened, is it?'

'I'm sure of it. Can't you go back and tell Lieutenant Washington?'

'Left-tenant? Ain't nothing left about that old soldier. Made Ronnie Reagan look like a fellow-traveller. But no, Pippa, I can't go back. I'm under military orders, see? Court-martialling offence to miss the plane.' As he spoke he looked up at the departures' screen where the Alitalia flight for Milano was flashing ominously. 'Gallopin' groundhogs! I gotta go, Pippa. Give my regards to all those British Lords.' He vaulted a couple of ropes and loped towards the departure gates.

Meanwhile Pippa had reached the front of the queue.

'Stansted?' asked the woman behind the desk. Judging from her expression, it wasn't the first time of asking. 'Are you planning to fly to Stansted?'

Pippa looked down at the crumpled printout in her hand, the blessed confirmation number that had been her escape.

'Sorry.' she said. 'No, I'm planning to do something entirely different.'

Driving back from Grossetto to Empoli, it was natural to take the autostrada. The fact that the petrol gauge hit zero and Pietro's stomach hit empty simultaneously, just after Massarosa, was entirely coincidental. It wasn't his fault that the next junction was Lucca. Nor was it his fault that, when he came to sign the credit card slip at the service station, he found that his favourite pen was missing. When had he seen it last? Certainly at the Piccola Casa, noting vocabulary on the back of his bus tickets. But after that; had he taken it to the Agora or left it in the classroom? He had an irritatingly clear mental picture of the pen glimpsed only that morning on his bedside table, but as an experienced detective, he knew better than to trust mental images. The only safe course was to call in at the language school. If Pippa happened to be there, they would just have to act like rational adults...

..Pippa wasn't there, of course, nor the pen, though he had almost forgotten to ask for it. She, apparently, would be somewhere over the English Channel by now; the pen could be at the bottom of it for all he cared. Meanwhile it was too early to brave the Empoli one-way system; he would leave that until mid-siesta. He turned north towards the Questura, towards Agostino, the station bar, and some quasi-priestly sympathy.

Agostino's door was pushed almost shut, which wasn't like him, so Pietro paused outside, which wasn't like him either. It didn't sound as though the sergeant was there, not even surreptitiously changing his shirt.

'Anything but clerical black,' he had explained the last time he'd been discovered semi-naked, 'does tend to bring on Mamma's hysterics. And since I'd really rather not appear to the general public as a fully paid up member of the Il Duce Fan Club, it's easier all round if I change at the office.'

But there were none of the usual elephant-escaping-from-a-paper-bag sound effects, so Pietro felt pretty sure that his colleague, if inside, would be fully clothed. If the Commissario had spent more time during the past few days at the Lucca Questura, or had been sufficiently disentangled from his own troubles to listen to a bit of police gossip, he might have been less confident of that. But he hadn't, so he wasn't.

He pushed open the door just as the telephone rang inside. Agostino had arranged the room so that, in order to answer the heavy desk phone, you had to be looking out of the window. He had admitted once, after a longer lunch than usual, that the layout was designed to maximize divine assistance during his mother's two or three daily calls. Pietro supposed that it would be her now, the twelve-thirty check-up, calculated to find out whether he had gone out for lunch and, if possible, to prevent him from doing so. The ringing stopped and a mellifluous voice answered.

'*Allô?*'

The liquid parts of Pietro coagulated in the doorway. There was only one member of the Tuscan polizia pretentious enough to answer the phone in French, and that member was not Agostino Lenzuoli.

'*Mon cher ami.*' purred Vice-Questore Bisbigli. '*Comment allez-vous?*'

A pause. 'To America?' He had reverted to Italian. 'Are we not crazy enough for you in Lucca? Ah, I see. No, as yet I haven't had the honour, I'm afraid. I just have to keep limping on here, doing my civic duty...'

Snout in the civic trough, more like, thought Pietro, wondering whether to retreat. It was Bisbigli's own fault, of course, with his kleptomaniac tendencies towards subordinates' rooms. On the other hand, Pietro was in the Vice-Questore's bad books already, it wouldn't be wise to have his name illuminated there.

He was about to inch back when Bisbigli spoke again. 'The Carson case? Yes, quite out of his grubby little hands. I had a word with our transatlantic friends, as you suggested, and, putting the thing in the right light, they quite saw that it ought to be their pigeon. Got quite tetchy with the *giovanotto*, so I hear. No, no problem. He needs taking down a notch or two, that young man. Just because he's read a few English novels... What? Again? Even Guinizelli...'

Another pause, during which Bisbigli resumed breathing. 'Oh, the pet hippo. No, you've nothing to worry about on that score. Brain submerged six feet under. He couldn't add two and two without expressing the answer in doughnuts and eating them on the way home. But he wasn't really trying to re-open the case, was he? Related matter? Well of course it would be, everything's related, isn't it? Especially in Lucca. Even I, without Guinizelli's educational advantages, know that much English literature. Only connect. Or, in this case, only disconnect. Yes, don't worry, I'll disconnect Sergeant Lenzuoli. What's that?'

A longer pause, with faint screechings audible through the receiver which Bisbigli held an inch or two from his ear. Did he have a new hairstyle to maintain, Pietro wondered, or was he afraid that obesity might be contagious? Eventually he resumed. 'Link *you* with the death?' The hollowest of laughs. 'Even a devout Forsterian such as myself wouldn't make so *outre* a connection. No, I completely appreciate your concerns. Your clients and your friends, quite. And naturally we wouldn't want any suggestion of police harassment....' His voice died away in amused incredulity.

Pietro, sensing that the end of the conversation was imminent, melted out of the doorway and down the corridor. If he could intercept Ago before the knell of Bisbigli's summons, they might still have a chance. Lunchtime, for the Vice-Questore, held some of the powers of Lethe: he could never be relied upon to remember anything that had gone before.

Pseudo-Helmut shook his mobile phone, switched it off and on again, and called the automated number to find out how much credit he had left. The same amount as last time, and the time before, and the fifty-seven times before that in the past twenty-four hours. Then it occurred to him that Gray might have tried to call during the two seconds that the phone was switched off, or the seven seconds it had taken to check the credit, and he resolved not to touch it again for at least half an hour. Maybe it had been a mistake to call himself a friend of Johann's, maybe Gray was jealous or angry. Or simply indifferent. He thrust the phone back in his rucksack between *Siddartha* and the camping stove, where it would be hardest to reach, and resumed his seventeenth circuit of the wall.

XXV

Pippa's first thought, on parting with Lord, was to make her way to the base and explain her theory to the Lieutenant in person. Unfortunately, although the airport foyer was plastered with leaflets offering car hire, tours of Siena and express buses to Florence, the American military had been unaccountably forgotten. By the time she had worked her way to the front of the information queue, only to be rewarded by a blank stare and photocopied list of campsites, all the taxis had gone. She lugged her suitcase back inside and bivouacked in front of the car hire desks. Easycar, Hertz, Europcar: the choice was dazzling - for anyone who could drive. Plonking herself down on the case (probably the First Cause of the Montalcino flood) she felt her inner voice shift out of Pietro's accent and into Jonathan's Estuary drawl.

'Nobody, Philippa, can fail their driving test six times.'

'There was that woman...'

'Nobody, I should have said, who has ambitions beyond the freak shows of the docu-soaps. Can you imagine a partner catching the bus?'

None of the ink-blooded androids at Quine & Co, no, but by then Pippa had given up imagining herself in their silver-tongued ranks. Soon afterwards she had abandoned driving lessons altogether, concluding that there was a category of human creation that wasn't intended to drive, and that she was indubitably a part of it. Most of Italy, she now thought, belonged to the same group, although the fact never deterred them.

A smartly-dressed woman approached with a coin in her hand. Pippa, cheered by a sudden vision of Jonathan's face on seeing her as a mendicant, got up hastily and caught the next bus back to Lucca.

On the walls once more, Muriel was uncharacteristically flustered. It was bad enough having to manage without Giulia, whose first wisdom tooth had appeared the night before, but now Francesca hadn't turned up either. She shouldn't have been surprised, she supposed, but somehow, with all the time they had spent together over the past few days, she had almost come to think of the girl as an honorary Englishwoman.

'Own fault.' she berated herself brusquely, removing a troublesome dew-claw with one hand while the other checked a skittish Schnauzer bitch for signs of coming into season. 'Should have remembered that breeding will out. Can't expect to make a Gloucester Old Spot out of a *cinghiale*.'

As if Fate were rewarding her for returning to the fold of orthodoxy (she had once been a reserve judge at Crufts) Muriel lifted her head from the Schnauzer's hindquarters to glimpse a perfect specimen lumbering towards her. It was the classic Modern Briton, female of the breed, a mongrel mixture of the Celtic, Saxon and slumming Roman. It was wearing a heavy duffle coat and trailing a large wheeled suitcase which teetered drunkenly on the tussocky grass, emitting gurgling noises and the unmistakeable smell of escaping Brunello di Montalcino. Bullseye and Penny recognized her immediately, unless it was only the wine, and broke free from the ranks to launch themselves at her toggles. Muriel followed, only slightly less enthusiastic.

'Glad to see you've changed your mind. Welcome aboard.' She sniffed in the direction of the coat. Expecting snow, are you? Haven't had any in central Lucca during my fifteen years, but there's always a first, even in April. Be prepared, as Brown Owl no doubt told you. Jolly good show. You'll have noticed that Fran hasn't turned up this morning. Typical Italian. Probably gone to the beach.'

'I don't think so.' said Pippa in the first pause available. 'Actually I've got some bad news.' She gave it with as stiff an upper lip as she could manage, but even Muriel's was looking wobbly by the end.

'Rubbish.' she snapped, but the tone was unsustainable. 'W-why?'

'Well, from their point of view, Luciano had a motive – rabid anti-American fever, while Francesca had the means, being a medical student, and the opportunity. After all, she was the last person to see Zena alive.'

'The last *identified* person.' The centuries of patrician blood were reasserting themselves. 'Beware of sloppy thinking, Philippa.

When exactly is she supposed to have died, anyway?'

'Last Monday night, they think. Francesca had a lesson on Monday evening from seven till eight.'

'Balderdash!'

'What?'

'Twaddle. Baloney. Claptrap.'

'But she did; I've seen it on the calendar.' The calendar was documentary evidence, and Pippa's remaining legal synapses were determined to hang on to it.

'Bugger the calendar. She might have had a lesson every other Monday evening, but she certainly didn't last week. She was up at my house in the Garfagnana for a PINC planning meeting. Half seven they arrived, for an early English supper, and they left around midnight.'

'They?' But Muriel was still talking.

'Come to think of it, she did say something about a lesson. He asked her about it as she came in - had she remembered to cancel as otherwise she'd have to pay? She told him it was all sorted out.'

'But who's him?'

'"Who's him?" What do you teach, grammar or bricklaying? If you mean 'who is he', he's Luciano, of course, that moonstruck young lecturer. You don't think he'd let her out of his sight for a whole five hours, do you?'

'You think he's really keen on her, then? He seemed a bit lukewarm when we spoke to him.'

'Good Lord, what do they feed the young on these days? Was Troilus really keen on Cressida, Anthony on Cleopatra, Richard Burton on Elizabeth Taylor? Has true romance really faded so far in the British soul? He might not carry on like some emaciated urchin out of *Eastenders*, but, yes, I think you can take it that Luciano's "really keen". He wouldn't have dreamed of coming to the meeting otherwise. It's not exactly his thing, as a hard-bitten radical politician, to start worrying about poodles and heartworm jabs. I'm not at all sure that in Luc's Utopia, pet dogs wouldn't be put against the wall as traitors to their species. Or at least re-educated.'

The dogs, tired of waiting, and with laudable impulses that even Luciano couldn't fault, had launched into an egalitarian game of Blind Man's Buff in which no participant was blind, apart from a fat old bulldog with glaucoma, and every tail was a legitimate Buff.

Muriel bawled out an old hockey war cry and ran down the bank with a ferocity that made the Assyrian look positively lackadaisical. Pippa followed her, rather less impressively, as she was still wearing flip-flops, and sailed the last five metres on her bottom.

'But why,' she panted, resolving, as she had already abjured men, sex and romance, to go the whole hog and buy herself a pair of Muriel-style galvanised Birkenstocks, 'did Francesca pretend to have been at the lesson? She went into minute detail about it, as well; even gave us a copy of the article they'd discussed. Except the end. She was a bit hazy about the end...'

Muriel, engaged in disentangling the three terriers and a beagle, was unenlightening.

'You're the one who started playing detectives, Pippa. Since you and your policeman friend helped to get Fran into this mess, perhaps you'd better do some thinking about how to get her out again. But for goodness sake don't mope about it. Try looking on the bright side. *No*, Barbarella, *drop it*!'

At the Piccola Casa, Pippa abandoned her suitcase at the bottom of the stairs. The Montalcino, no longer content to announce its presence by bouquet alone, had seeped through the layers of clothing to ooze out of the canvas in a satisfyingly sinister splodge. Perhaps, she thought, trying to find a bright side to look on, a passing poliziotto would notice it and hand her over to Lieutenant Washington. As a plan, it was about as watertight as the suitcase, but she was starting to get desperate. Luciano's political *amour propre* might get a bit dented if was discovered that he'd squandered his talents on a glorified dog show, but it would hardly be worse than a murder charge. Perhaps Francesca had just confused one Monday with the one before. If so, her memory should have clarified by now, under the force of a Washingtonian interrogation. But would the Lieutenant believe the new story, even with Muriel as an alibi?

The first person Pippa saw at the top of the stairs, head bent towards his drumming heels, was Nicola. He didn't look up, even when Elsa bustled out of the office.

'Philippa! *Hai dimenticato qualcosa*?'

'Forgotten...no. I just wanted to ask you something.'

'That sounds exciting. *Cos'è*?'

'I wanted to ask...' Whether by any chance you had come across Zena's comatose body on Monday evening, assumed she was dead, stashed her in the nearest cupboard, thereby actually killing her yourself, and suffered a convenient brainstorm allowing you to forget the whole thing? '...if I could stay on for a few days?'

'Of course, *cara*, as long as you like. And you'll give Nic a lesson now you're here? He's been waiting since eleven; dotty old Lisa forgot to tell him you'd left. Onset of dementia, I'm afraid, poor thing. But Nic's got exams next week, haven't you treasure? and he's frightfully worried.'

He looked it, too, head still bent, lower lip bitten into a crimson arch and long-lashed eyelids blinking furiously.

'*Certissimo*.'

Fortunately for them both, Nicola had brought several pages of grammar exercises with him and wanted nothing more than to write the answers on the board for Pippa to correct. She tried to talk to him about his forthcoming exams, but every enquiry was met with a monosyllable. The poor boy was obviously happier enmeshed in the vagaries of the past continuous than contemplating his academic future. Pippa drifted into classroom autopilot, manhandling verbs with the surface of her mind while the submerged depths wrestled with the Washington Problem. After half an hour she had got precisely nowhere. Wrestling with George F. in person could hardly be less futile.

'Is this one right?'

'Sorry Nic, which..?'

'Number twenty-four.'

She looked up at the board. *George read the newspaper when the phone was ringing.*

'No, I'm wrong. *George was reading when the phone rang.* It's better?'

But Pippa hadn't got beyond the first word. To be precise, she hadn't got beyond the first letter of the first word. She was staring, in graphic illustration of the continuous tense, at Nicola's elaborate capital G, looped at top and bottom, almost a treble clef.

'Do you always write your Gs like that?'

He flushed. 'I think yes. It's wrong? I am taught this way in the *prima*. I think most Italians write so.'

'That's what I meant. And no, it's not wrong and you're quite right about the sentence, too. The reading is past continuous, in the background, then the phone rang, sudden event - past simple. Number twenty-five?'

Conscientiously, she managed to fix her attention on the grammar until the end of the lesson, and to wait until Nicola had left before going up to the blackboard and examining the letter in detail. Even without the photographs there could be no doubt about it. This had been the distinction, not merely the contrast between the right and left hands. The G in *No Global* had been of this looped Italian variety, that of *Girotondo* the English style, a simple curve topped by a short bar.

Where was her suicide theory now? According to that, Zena had written both slogans herself, before lapsing into unconsciousness. Was it likely that she would have used a different calligraphy for each? Unless Elsa and Elisa had written the words, one taking each wrist. Over the years they had each picked up the other's spoken language, but they would still write as they had been taught as tiny girls, seventy years ago and seven hundred miles apart. But what possible reason could Elsa and Elisa have for writing political graffiti on their employees? It made no sense, unless perhaps they themselves were secret guerrillas, keeping the flame alive from the old partisan days.

Then there was the persistent problem of the medical evidence. The pathologist had been positive that the actual death had been caused by suffocation. Could the anaesthetic have caused that, or was it solely the fault of the cupboard – a *novus actus interveniens*, as they'd said at law school? Pippa wished that her own medical knowledge hadn't been confined to the Brownie First Aid badge. If only she had an expert on hand...

Through the open classroom door she could glimpse the foyer, a couple of chairs, a stack of magazines and the edge of the computer Gray had talked them into installing. That was it. If not an expert, she at least had a few million others to call upon. She flexed her mouse-clicking finger and prepared for action.

XXVI

It had been a few months since Pippa had used the Internet for anything but frenzied job-hunting, and she had forgotten how frustrating it could be. After a couple of hours of searching under 'methohexitone', she had managed to do little but rediscover what the pathologist had already told Pietro, along with a jumbo portion of indigestible Latin. There were some bright points, though, especially for a former litigator. Methohexitone, it turned out, had a wealth of exciting side-effects, from hiccups to erotic hallucinations, although not many of these had led to full-scale malpractice suits. There were a few tragedies, however; the terrible tale of the nervous patient given methohexitone in place of diazepam, and, saddest of all, the Swiss anaesthetist who had killed his own wife.

'Charles D.' he was called in the web report, perhaps because the case was still technically *sub judice*. Proceedings had been brought against him in Geneva, but he had fled the country and apparently changed his name. So long as he was no longer practising as an anaesthetist, no one seemed much inclined to pursue it further, not even his wife's family, who had added a dignified message of forgiveness to the dossier.

He had been fifty-eight when the death had happened, an accomplished but arrogant practitioner, well-known for his cavalier bearing towards patients and their idiosyncrasies, particularly their claims to allergies, intolerances and hypersensitive reactions. His wife, Elisabeth, fourteen years younger, had been suffering from some minor complaint - the report was gallantly silent upon the details, from which Pippa guessed piles – and Charles decided to operate personally. He wasn't, of course, a surgeon, but thought that thirty-five years of watching lesser men more than qualified him to take up the scalpel. A local anaesthetic would have been enough, but for some reason, his wife's nervousness or simply his own love of the craft, he chose to put her completely under, using a normal dose of methohexitone. The site of the operation was well away from the mouth and throat and so he decided that there was no need for bracheal intubation; that is a tube into the throat that artificially 'breathes' for the patient.

Unfortunately, what Charles did not know, or, to be more precise, did not believe, was that Elisabeth was nearly five months pregnant. They had been childless throughout their long marriage and when she had announced that the miracle had finally occurred he had dismissed it, and her subsequent weight gain, as menopausal hysteria.

The report veered into some technical details about the effects of pregnancy upon the digestive organs. Pippa skimmed through it quickly, vowed neither to eat nor have sex for the remainder of her life, told herself not to be such wimp, reconsidered the eating part, and read it through again. Basically, she gathered, the combined effects of new and exciting hormones and the presence of a third party in the womb were to relax the oesophagus, make the gastric contents more acid ('there is no such thing, 'quoted the report, 'as a pregnant woman with an empty stomach', and Pippa, remembering her sister-in-law's perpetual Wotsit-munching could see what it meant) and to increase the pressure on the whole area. In a healthy conscious woman, these factors only lead to the irritating regurgitations rather romantically called heartburn. But if she was unconscious she might, simply by breathing in, bring the acid up into her trachea, causing the chemical pnemonitis known as Mendelson's syndrome. There was a consensus, therefore, that a breathing tube was essential for an anaesthetised patient who was more than sixteen weeks pregnant. Without it, the consequences could be fatal.

And so they were for Elisabeth D. While her husband watched, helpless, she had breathed in the poisonous sludge of her own stomach and choked to death, together with their unborn son. Charles, *in absentia*, had been charged on five counts...

'The Hinternet!' cried Elisa, bursting through the door laden with patisserie boxes. 'Wicked. Try w.w.w.' - she pronounced it the Italian way; 'voovoovoo' - 'harleydavisonpuntocom. Vroom!'

Pippa typed the address quickly, glad of the light relief.

'You are very skilful.' said Otto over her shoulder. 'Your generation, I suppose. For us oldies, the kinkdom of the computer is still a great mystery. Oh, and speaking of mysteries...' He took a folded sheet of paper from his shirt pocket, 'I have been asked, for I don't know which reason, to give a little talk to the Oklahoma Freudian Association. I think they must have me confused with someone else, but no matter. I have never been to America, it will be a merry trip.'

'With you on board I'm sure it will be.'

He made a little bow. 'Thank you kindly. I am only sorry that I cannot persuade you ladies to join me. But I fly the evening after tomorrow; there is too little time. I am, how would you say it? - a last minute chosen one. A stopping-gap. Some more worthy Freudian has pulled away and I am all that they can find. But it's bully for me. I will have a small holiday and, as you know, I like to talk. There is just one problem...'

He unfolded the sheet of paper to reveal four or five dense paragraphs, meticulously typed on an old manual machine.

'The English?'

He bowed again. 'The English, exactly. If you could have a look...'

'Of course.' It wasn't bad, a bit stilted, with the odd dodgy idiom and some bizarre sentence formation.

'This word, *repeat-constriction*, here. I don't think it's quite right, but I'm not sure of the English equivalent.'

'We have dictionaries in the office.' said Elisa. '*Prego.*'

Pippa settled herself behind the desk and stacked the books in front of her. They made her feel oddly secure, like being back at Quine & Co, hiding from the scariest clients behind fifteen volumes of *Halsbury's Laws*. She wasn't quite sure, though, that an English-Italian dictionary was what she needed. The word sounded Freudian in the most technical of senses and so she might be better starting with the man himself. The biographical dictionary, then. Although it was a sunny afternoon, the little room was dark, and she had to switch on the desk lamp to read the fine print.

FREUD, Sigmund, born 6 May 1856 in Freiburg, Moravia...

Odd. She'd had the definite impression that he was born in Vienna, only she couldn't remember for the moment what had made her so sure. Never mind.

Publications: Studies on Hysteria, The Interpretation of Dreams.....

She had been working for five minutes or so when the light went out and she heard, from the foyer, the dying whine of the computer. Otto put his head round the door.

'There is a storm coming, I think. The Italian electricity systems are not so robust. Fortunately we don't need power to finish eating the cake.'

'You up for a walk, Pierrotino? Midnight stroll?'

The cat yawned and turned pointedly towards the Torre dell'Ore.

'All right, a two o'clock in the morning stroll then. I thought your species was keen on nightlife.'

The imminent storm had still not arrived and the night was humid. Pippa had slept for barely half an hour, dreaming fitfully, before she woke with the certain knowledge that sleep would be impossible until dawn.

She should have gone walking earlier in the evening, the proper time for a *passeggiata*, instead of struggling to get back online. The power cut had only lasted a few minutes, giving her plenty of time to tidy up Otto's speech, but it had done something drastic to the computer, which refused to do more than emit a low hum of insolent boredom.

'Not that I'd found anything,' she explained to Pierrotino when they met again in the silent street, he having spurned the stairs and made his way down by a series of apparently death-defying leaps from one window-sill to another. In fact the jumps had been perfectly planned and held no danger at all. Italian cats have only seven lives, and Pierrotino had no intention of wasting any. 'But I might have been about to. There are a billion pages on the Internet; one of them must have something relevant.'

Pierrotino, the angle of his jaw suggested, thought not.

'Suit yourself then.' She turned right at random down an alleyway, then another, and again, like a squared off spiral, until she reached a tiny courtyard, cool and damp. A tap in the centre was dripping, and she crouched on the ledge around it, holding her fingers under the heavy drops.

'What should I do, Pierrotino? Try to get to the U.S. base and talk to George Washington? Or should I see Muriel again, find out whether there was anyone else at that meeting?' This had been the worst part of being a solicitor, the three a.m. agonies over affidavits and interlocutory applications. At least Pierrotino was marginally better company than the *County Court Practice*.

The cat's opinion, succinctly stated, was that she should go back to bed and forget it all until the morning.

'I suppose you're right.' She wound herself out of the courtyard; left every time ought to take her back, while Pierrotino sloped away on some shortcut of his own.

The blow came from behind, on to her left ear. All she felt was surprise; at the thing's happening at all, at the absence of pain, at her own detachment. With a distant benevolence she contemplated the sequence of increasingly implausible facts: the existence of life on earth, the uncanny symmetry of Pierrotino's ears, her escape from Quine & Co and the irony of her arrival here in Lucca, where street violence was almost unheard of, only to become the victim of a thoroughly Anglo-Saxon mugging. She heard herself giggling and wondered, with academic interest, whether she was to be robbed or raped or both, and, if the latter, the exact legal charges available to the prosecution. Aggravated something, no doubt. She'd never been hot on the criminal side.

Then the fingers came around her neck, and a hissing behind the other ear, and a familiar smell, too sweet, and then the fear and the pain at last. The final thing was a kind of screech, but whether she heard it or felt it, she couldn't tell, although she supposed it was her own. Something red rose up, a stage curtain with the film running backwards. That was all.

XXVII

There was something wrong with Pippa's head. Not a headache, exactly, and not what she supposed to be a migraine, but something was definitely askew. The nearest she could come to it was that her brain seemed to be the wrong shape to fit inside her skull. She shifted experimentally and a ramrod of pain barged through her inner ear. There was nothing to lose by opening her eyes.

They sat there solemnly, staring at the bed like children awaiting the beginning of the Punch and Judy. Sergeant Lenzuoli was in the middle, grey flannel overlapping the flimsy plastic seat. On either side of him, perched on the front of their chairs, as though in counterbalance, were two young women. The one on the left, skinny and sandy, looked startlingly like the girl behind the Stranieri desk at the Questura while the one on the right, if not the pneumatic brunette on the scooter, was a pretty accurate Doppelganger. Pippa decided she must be hallucinating. Definitely a Wizard of Oz moment.

'Where's Toto?' she croaked. On second thoughts, her head and ear didn't hurt at all, not in comparison with this.

'It's better not to speak.' said the dark-haired girl. 'He is only bringing some coffee. All the other times he is here to see you.'

Pippa tried to mime absolute perplexity without moving any of the more sensitive facial muscles. Raising her eyebrows was just about possible.

'I'm sorry.' said the girl again. 'We're not presented yet. Alessandra Binni - Ali. I'm a pathologist.'

A little premature, perhaps. Pippa resolved never again to complain about Italian procrastination.

'And you remember me?' said the other girl, sounding more like the Scarecrow than even Lord at his most homespun. And then here he was, loping down the ward, bearing a cardboard tray of specimen-sized *espressi*. Not Toto. Pietro.

She had to close her eyes again for a moment, just for the pleasure of opening them again and finding him still there. The mysterious thud against the bedside table and the four new brown ovals across his chest only confirmed that this was reality. At some point she would have to consider the implications of Ali-the-well-endowed- pathologist's being here with him, but not yet. She was about to try the eye-closing routine again, to see whether it was still as good the third time, when he spoke, almost angrily.

'Who was it?'

'Pietro!' warned Ali, her hand over her throat. Pippa managed a little squeak of bewilderment. Who was what? The last thing she could remember was going for a walk with Pierrotino.

'I'm sorry.' He passed the tray of empty beakers to Serafina and sat down on the edge of the bed. 'I'm really sorry, Pippa.' Unlike her face, her hands were able to move without difficulty, except that they seemed to have declared unilateral independence from her brain, for one had already, with no cerebral instruction, found its way out from under the tight sheet and across to his fraying cuff. 'Someone attacked you last night. Fortunately Agostino was keeping an eye out, and he scared the bastard off.'

Sergeant Lenzuoli, grasping the gist, interrupted in a flow of vehement Lucchese.

'*Va bene*, Ago. He says he didn't, actually; it was the cat. He was too slow, he says. Personally, I don't believe a word of it. We had nearly as many cats as pigs when I was growing up, and I learned a few things about them. Cats only look out for number one.'

Maybe number two, once every seven lives.

'Anyway we didn't get him. Or her. Ali reckons it was someone about your height or only a little taller; that's why the grip wasn't better.'

Pippa's other hand fingered her bruised neck. She wasn't actually dead; that must be what he meant.

'It seems that he was scared off quickly, maybe by the cat after all, and by the time Agostino got there he'd scampered off down one of those little streets. *Vicoli*, we call them. What is it in English?'

'An alley.' she whispered hoarsely, and the pathologist started and grinned. Pippa watched them both for a few seconds, but there were no exchanged glances, either of tenderness or complicity. The number of signals she misread, she could have got a job on the privatized railways.

'So you haven't any idea who it was?' asked Pietro. 'No, don't speak or shake your head, I can tell from your face. Nothing? Don't worry, we can work from the other end. Up to last Sunday afternoon,' he touched her fingers briefly, 'you knew everything I did about the Carson case. And vice versa, I think. No, don't raise your eyebrows like that. I'm not investigating the murder of Zena Carson; I'm investigating the attempted murder of Philippa Laud. Quite different. It just so happens that - What? What is it, Pippa, what's the matter?'

It was nothing, she signalled, only the shock of finding herself an attempted murderee. There was something not quite respectable about it. Jonathan certainly wouldn't have approved.

'Sorry, that was a bit blunt. It does look, though, as if someone wanted you out of the way, or at least a bit quieter. And the most likely reason is that you know more than you ought to about Zena's death. You may not even know that you know, which makes it trickier. Unless you've managed to make some completely unconnected mortal enemies during the week you've been in Lucca? No? I thought not. We know it can't have been Francesca or Luciano because they're under arrest by the forces of democracy. But other than that, it could have been anyone. What we need to know, if you don't mind, is everything you've found out since - since we spoke last. Perhaps…' He dug in his jeans pocket as usual - was it Pippa's imagination or were they looser than before - but came out with nothing but a screwed up tissue. 'Damn, I haven't been on the bus this week.'

Agostino came to the rescue with a sensible police-issue notebook and a stubby little pencil. Writing without using her neck muscles proved surprisingly difficult but a few cryptic key words were enough for Pietro to fill in the gaps. She had no idea of Muriel's surname or address, other than its being mountainous, but Serafina assured them that *English-dogs-Cheltenham Ladies College* would be sufficient to track her down. Similarly, she managed to convey, by a combination of charades and cartoon sketches, her insight that it needn't have been the same person who administered the injection and stashed the body in the cupboard (although she didn't mention her suspicions of Elsa and Elisa), the discrepancy between the initial Gs of Girotondo and Global and her futile attempts to discover more about methohexitone from the Internet. What had she found? asked Ali, and she filled a whole page of the notebook with drawings of mice, hamsters and unfortunate eccentrics undergoing ECT treatment. Ali had nodded encouragingly but there was clearly nothing new there.

'You didn't come across anything else?' asked Pietro, and she showed him a blank page. There was no point in airing her nasty PI lawyer's habits; the trawl through the malpractice suits had simply been voyeurism of the most regressive kind and she felt rather ashamed of herself. 'Nothing else at all?' Oh yes, Gray hadn't heard about any heart condition. The only thing the matter with Zena, so far as he knew, was that she was allergic to kiwi fruit.

'*Il kiwi*?' Alessandra, who had been examining the chart at the end of Pippa's bed, looked up, startled. 'There is something – no, it's gone.' She shook her head fractiously, as though trying to shake sixpence out of a piggy bank. 'I have a *lapsus*.'

There was an awkward pause, into which Pietro plunged.

'As you'd imagine, from my craven intransigence on Sunday,' He'd practised this speech, thought Pippa, trying not to smile. There was something encouraging about the thought of it, of his rehearsals in front of the coffee machine while she slept. 'I've got nothing at all to offer to the discussion.' This was not strictly true, but he suspected that the Vice-Questore's overheard conversation was a card he would need in his final hand, best kept hidden even from his partner.

'Agostino and Serafina, however, have gone far beyond the bounds of duty, not to mention the bounds of legality, to come up with some rather interesting phone records.'

He took out a copy of the annotated list and shuffled up the bed to show it to Pippa. 'Here, you see, is a call to Gray Garrett last Thursday - you remember that? The Sergeant has asked him about it again, by the way, but he's declined to tell us any more. These are calls to Dr. Fosecco, and these to the brothers Seppi - the undertakers who took Johann Schwartz's body back to Germany. It could be coincidence but I don't think so. Ali and I thought we'd take a trip to see them all this afternoon.'

Alessandra looked up from her musing - kiwi fruit still? - with a wide smile and Pippa realized, completely and decisively, that she had nothing whatsoever to fear from her.

'It would be better if you could come as well,' continued Pietro, 'but there's a distinctly reptilian nurse at the other end of the ward, slithering in our direction, and I think she's about to banish the rest of us and handcuff you to the bed.'

A quick thought scampered into Pippa's mind at that, but it wasn't the sort of sentiment that ought to go into a police-issue notebook, so she made do with raising her eyebrows.

'I'll come back later and hunt for the key.' he promised in a lower voice. 'Was there anything else? Oh yes, something about the syringes. What was it again, Ali?'

'*Cosa*?' She was deep in thought. 'Oh, *si. Erano vecchi.* Old. *Aspetta...*'

But there was no time to wait, not with the ward sister, even more terrifying at closer quarters, now within fire-breathing distance. It took only seconds for the bedside to be cleared - a scorched earth policy in action - and for Pippa to be dosed with enough painkiller to keep her comatose at least until Ferragosto, if not Armageddon itself.

Charles stood in his usual place by the window, with the view six floors down to the quiet street. Only this morning the shutters were still closed, so that all he saw was his own reflection, hazy on the faded brown paint. He concentrated hard on the image, moulding it to fit the one in his mind.

He had never set out to hurt anyone before, not even in play. He remembered the drunken tussles of the other students, launched as much for the pleasure of touching one another's bodies as for the niggling ostensible cause. But Charles had held himself back, watching them with bittersweet contempt, conscious of his vocation. 'Hippo', they had called him, but he had only been a little overweight, nothing, if he had been a few inches taller. No, it had been the Oath that had brought him the name and he bore it with pride, even in its humiliating diminutive.

I swear by Apollo Physician and Asclepius and Hygieia and Panaceia and all the gods and goddesses....

They had always made more sense than Elisabeth's plaster saints.

If I fulfil this oath and do not violate it, may it be granted to me to enjoy life and art, being honoured with fame among all men for all time to come; if I transgress it and swear falsely, may the opposite of this be my lot.

A straight bargain, then, and they got him on a technicality, tricky, like the gods have always been.

I will not use the knife, not even on sufferers from stone, but will withdraw in favour of such men as are engaged in this work.

Such men! Barbers then, butchers now, he would never have entrusted Elisabeth's flesh to their arrogant knives.

He didn't blame the gods. They'd nailed him, unfair and square, with the oldest trick in the pantheon, the one Cronus himself had fallen for, the hidden child. It wasn't for revenge that he'd begun the Game, chosen the players, administered their own oath.

I, Girotondiste, He still liked that, the Revolutionary overtones. They had the right idea, those Communards, *swear by Autolycus, master of deception, by Thalia, muse of comedy and by the great Nemesis herself, that I will play the Game...*

Every one had been willing, more than willing. Money, travel, a new identity, there were plenty who would undergo far more pain and danger than the Game had required. And he hadn't lost one, not until Zena. Kiwi fruit; another Olympian joke. Nemesis had not, despite the flattery, quite been placated. All the same, he wished it hadn't ended this way; the hands that had held Hippocrates' vow wrapped around the girl's neck. And it hadn't even done any good, thanks to the damned cat.

He opened the desk drawer and checked the tickets again. Twenty-seven hours until his third life could begin.

Pseudo-Helmut was growing restless. He hadn't come back from the dead for this; a perpetual motion of cultured tourism, from villa to chiesa to palazzo. If he saw another Romanesque facade he would have to do something drastic. He was beginning to understand why his ancestors felt impelled to sack Rome with such tiresome regularity. He would give it one more day, he decided, long enough to catch a bus to Segromigno and look at the Villa Mansi. It was haunted, reputedly, by the lady Lucida, one of its less virtuous chatelaines. She had sold her soul to the Devil, like Dorian Gray, in exchange for unwithering beauty. With any luck, some of her ruthlessness would rub off on him. Then, if Gray hadn't called by tomorrow morning, he would take matters into his own hands. He wasn't yet sure what he was going to do, but some of these cumbersome Teutonic inhibitions were going to end up in the garbage. And along with them would go this ridiculous name. *Auf Wiedersehen*, Helmut.

XXVIII

'Gone west, I reckoned.'
'I beg your pardon?'
Dr. Fosecco repeated himself, the spaghetti western accent less confident this time. 'The Carson case. Been kicked across the Atlantic, I'd heard. Or at least as far as Camp Darby.'
'So?'
'So what are you doing bothering me again? Routine police harassment or is there something special?' He turned an appraising eye towards Ali; only one, the other was having difficulty in focussing on anything past the fresh whisky bottle. Jim Beam this time, noticed Pietro. Hence the accent, perhaps.
'Unless this is a private visit. Lady undergoing some difficulties, is she?'
'Certainly not.' Ali introduced herself sharply.
'A colleague, then. Charmed. And what can I do for a pathologist? Are you in search of specimens to practice on? I'm terribly sorry, but I seem to be out of fresh corpses this afternoon. Perhaps if you called back tomorrow?'
'We're investigating...' began Pietro.
'Not the Carson case.'
'No. A related matter.'
'A murder?'
'An attempted murder.'
'Fascinating. And you retained Miss Binni on the off-chance that it might turn into the real thing? What a dreadful temptation for you, my dear, just to nudge matters on and shift it into your own territory. Tell me, was the victim one of my patients?'
'No.'
'In that case, I hardly see how I can be of any assistance.'
Pietro decided to shift up a gear or two. He had meant to go softly with the doctor, but softness had its limits, and being treated like the archetypal dumb cop, with Ali as his bit of accompanying

skirt, went well beyond them. If nothing else, there was a real chance that, if Fosecco called her 'dear' again, she might decide on a bit of freelance homicide on her own account. Pietro had seen her with a monkey wrench in her hand, and it wasn't a tender sight.

'Whose is this number?'

Fosecco slid the paper towards him with a weary benevolence, like an uncle on Boxing Day. 'I've no idea, I'm afraid. It's one of those cellular ones, isn't it? They don't mean anything to me. It could be my own for all I know.'

'No, it isn't yours, doctor. Not unless you have a second one you bought in Milan under a false name. But the owner of this number calls you regularly on your own mobile. Take a look at this printout. There you are, you see, that's your number, with your name beside it, just to make it nice and easy. And let me see - ah, yes, that's the last one. Last Friday at a quarter to four. Funny, that must have been just after we had our little discussion. Ring any bells now?'

'I'm a very busy man, Commissario. People call me all the time. I really can't be expected...'

'This person phoned Zena Carson as well, pretty regularly, until the day she died.'

Fosecco shrugged. 'Lucca. It's a small town. Everyone knows everyone else. I, for example, am well-acquainted with Vice-Questore Bisbigli.'

Pietro ignored the threat. 'And this number is implicated in a serious art theft.'

'Art theft!' The doctor snorted contemptuously. 'It's very flattering, but I think you're pushing the boat out a bit there. Do I look like someone who knows anything about art? What do you think I am, some sort of Renaissance Man? Leonardo da Vinci: a morning's anatomy, sonnets for lunch, then polish off a fresco or two?'

Ali took over. 'Would you be surprised to know that Zena Carson received no treatment for her supposed heart condition?'

Another shrug, combined with the refilling of his glass. He held the bottle out to them in a parody of invitation. 'I referred her; that's all I know. I don't go around spying on my patients to see whether they follow my recommendations. I leave that sort of thing to the more authoritarian professions. If you want to succeed as an independent medical practitioner, rather than a police stooge,

I'd advise you to do the same.'

'Thank you, *dottore*. I should also mention that, according to my independent medical examinations, there is no evidence that Miss Carson ever suffered from any abnormality of the heart.'

'So she was a fantasist? She wouldn't be the first. You'd be astonished at how many people, especially middle-aged women, invent a romantic illness to make themselves more glamorous. I had to take her word for it; all her records were back in the States. I'm grateful to you for telling me all this, though. Next time I have a round of golf with the cardiac consultant I'll apologise for wasting his time. Bisbigli will be able to tell us whether it's a serious criminal offence. We generally catch up with him and the senior magistrate round on about the seventeenth hole. Now, do you have any more fascinating observations to make regarding Miss Carson's medical history, or can I get back to work. My surgery opens in ten minutes.'

'There was just one thing.'

Pietro's heart plummeted into his size forty-seven plimsolls. She was going to say it. Ever since the morning she'd been obsessed with that last, most trivial piece of Pippa's information. They had even had to stop at a greengrocer's on the way so she could buy one of her own, to prod and shake and nuzzle. Most girls adopted a small dog when they started getting broody, but then Ali had never been much like most girls. He could see it now, a furry green curve rising up from the depths of her shoulderbag. And she said it.

Fosecco stared at her, his watery eyes freezing into chips of blue ice.

'No, *dottoressa*.' He flicked her title from the tip of his tongue, like an insult. 'I didn't know that. Neither did I know her favourite flavour of ice-cream, how many sugars she took in her coffee or whether she was forced to eat broccoli as a small child. Those of us with living patients to care for have rather more important matters on our minds.'

Pietro intervened. 'That's rather the point of our visit, *dottore*. Just how many live patients do you have left? 'We' - actually Serafina, who knew how to coax the mainframe into revelation - 'have been carrying out an interesting piece of research. The results are in this table. The first row shows the number of deaths in Lucca over the past two years, excluding road accidents, deaths in hospital, *bona fide* tourists and persons aged over 65. The columns subdivide them by age, sex, race etc. The second row shows how many of these deaths were of non-Toscani, people born and brought up outside the region. So that includes resident foreigners, immigrants, Southern Italians...'

'I think I'm getting the idea, Commissario. And the third row?'

'The third row is the number of second-row deceased persons who had you as their doctor. I'm no statistician, but the proportions do look a little higher than average, wouldn't you say?'

Fosecco, judging by his blanched cheekbones and the speed with which his hand shot out towards the whisky bottle, would have preferred to say nothing. Pietro, however, was looking like a man who wanted answers and Ali was looking like a woman who wasn't going to let him leave until he got them.

'I didn't *cause* their deaths, if that's what you're trying to get at. I just certified them when they'd already happened. That's my job, when I'm allowed to get on with it.'

'An interesting angle.' commented Ali. 'In my experience, most GPs see their primary role as preventing death, not tying up the paperwork afterwards.'

'In *your* experience, *dottoressa*?'

She changed tack quickly. 'Johann Schwartz, he was one of yours, wasn't he? One of your - certifications. 'AIDS-related complex'. Odd, don't you think, that none of the AIDS clinics or support groups have any record of him?'

'He probably attended anonymously. If at all. There's still a stigma about it, you know. Plenty of people avoid advertising their condition.'

'Not Herr Schwartz. All his friends knew, plus his colleagues and employers. The only people in the province of Lucca who didn't know were the medical authorities. Except you, of course. And then Massimo Bindi, he was a similar case, wasn't he? You remember that one?'

'Of course. Tragic.'

'Tragic's the word, isn't it, when a nineteen year old boy dies of leukaemia without so much as an outpatient's appointment at any hospital in Tuscany. It's a good thing his family were so far away, isn't it? You can't be asked so many questions all the way from Calabria.'

'I referred him in the proper manner. It isn't my fault that they'd riddled with superstition down there. "If my number comes up, that's it", they say, as though modern medicine was just a variation on *Fotocalcio*. Fatalism. It's the curse of the Mezzogiorno, worse than the Mafia, by far.'

'Hmm.' It was Pietro's turn again. 'What happened to Massimo's body?'

'How should I know? Once I've given the certificate, I'm not involved any more. I daresay it was sent down South to be buried near his family.'

'You daresay right, according to the records. The body was transported by the Fratelli Seppi, funeral directors. Come across them at all?'

'I might have done. Can't say I take much notice of undertakers' names. Local, are they?'

'Not really no. That's what makes it so interesting. There are plenty of decent funeral directors in Lucca and yet, what? over eighty percent of your dead patients get sent out to the Seppi, tucked away in a scruffy industrial estate on the other side of Prato. Mind you, their registered office is in Milan. Do you find anything odd about that, *dottore*?'

'Word of mouth, I suppose. When one customer receives a good service, he naturally tells his friends. That's how society works, when it isn't being brow-beaten by so-called public servants.'

'I see. And who exactly, in this instance, would be passing the word? The grieving relatives? The deceased themselves, in ghostly murmurings? Or the owner of that mysterious mobile phone, the one you know nothing about, who the day before every one of your mysterious patients' deaths, telephoned you, telephoned the Seppi brothers and telephoned the future corpse? If I had friends like that, I think I'd want to be talking to someone else. Wouldn't you, Dr Fosecco?'

'He'll have warned them, of course.' said Pietro, clambering off the back of Ali's scooter. The air was dusty and hot but fresher than inside the helmet. He wouldn't have worn it at all, disciplinary tribunal or no, if Ali hadn't made him. These authoritarian women could be a little wearing by late afternoon. A sudden memory flashed into his mind of Pippa's bruised neck above her hospital nightshirt.

'Too right. He'd already picked up the phone when I went back in.'

'What did you go back for, anyway?'

'Take a dekko at his syringes.'

'And?'

'Nothing doing. His were new ones, hypo-allergenic and latex-free. Of course, he might have others stashed away somewhere.'

He noticed with some alarm that she had taken the kiwi fruit out of her bag again and was caressing it roughly, like a housewife testing a tomato. He hoped that this wasn't going to turn into a serious fixation.

They were right, the Seppi had been warned, and had taken comprehensively evasive action. The helpful young receptionist who had met Pietro's previous enquiry had disappeared, replaced by a human bulldog whose limited conversational style, 'Got a warrant? Fuck off then.' was made up for by the variety of menacing faces he was able to make without blinking his bulging red-veined eyes. Pietro, watched by Ali from the doorway, managed to restrain himself from actually apologising, but the tone of his promise to return was more that of a hostess replying to a cocktail invitation than of a law enforcement officer issuing a serious threat. Not that he had any idea where he was going to get a warrant from, except that he wouldn't even try Bisbigli. Maybe Agostino's Pisan contact could do something...

Pippa was asleep when Pietro got back to the ward and he had to swear by half a dozen obscure saints not to wake her before the fire-breathing sister would let him through. But she opened her eyes as soon as he came in, and even the dragon could see that he was blameless.

'Sleep well?'

'Like a cataleptic log. And my throat's a lot better. How was Dr. Fosecco?'

'Quite illuminating, actually. Unintentionally, of course.'

'So, he did it, did he? Injected Zena and Johann and all those other bodies Serafina dredged up for you.'

'What charming metaphors you use. Must be the company you keep.' He waved boyishly at the sister. 'No, I don't think he did.'

'Bother. That was my new favourite theory. I was working it out all the time that Nurse Drago was shoving painkillers down my throat. Actually I thought she might be in on it as well, Dr. Fosecco's *amante*, called in to finish off the job. I'm sure she'd do a better job than last night's bully-boy. So I didn't swallow anything after that, just kept them under my tongue until she wasn't looking. Here.' She lifted a corner of the pillow to reveal a whitish sludge. 'You can take a bit for analysis if you like.'

'I'd rather not, if it's all the same to you. You're lucky that she only put them in your mouth. Usually we get suppositories.'

'Respect for the British bottom, obviously. I knew there was some point in keeping the monarchy. But if Fosecco's innocent, what did he do to enlighten you? Socratic dialogues or magic mushrooms?'

'I didn't say he was innocent. Far from it. I just don't think he injected the stuff. No, his job was to make out the death certificates. He practically told me so. They were all his patients, so that part was easy, and he'd diagnosed them with conveniently fatal conditions which might carry them off at any time. Then the bodies were quietly disposed of by the Seppi brothers.'

'Except Zena's.'

'Except Zena's. Something obviously went badly wrong there, since she didn't get her death certificate either. I think you were right about the cupboard. Somebody else put her in there, someone who wasn't in on the usual arrangements.'

'But what was it all for? Just a bout of collective mania - serial killing by committee?'

He shrugged. 'You tell me.'

'Okay, I will.' The adrenalin of recovery surged high through her veins. There was definitely something sexy about logic. 'These victims,'

'Alleged victims. We haven't any real evidence for any of this.'

'Alleged victims, then. I didn't realise we were in court.' On second thoughts, though, Sister Drago did bear a startling resemblance to one of the more irascible District Judges back home.

'What did they have in common, apart from being Dr. Fosecco's patients?'

'Not much, except that they were young - Zena was one of the oldest - unusually healthy before the onset of their mysterious diseases, and none of them originally came from Lucca. Or anywhere else in central or northern Italy, come to that. The only Italians on the list were from south of Napoli.'

'So they had no family nearby to ask awkward questions?'

'Exactly.'

'Hmm.' Pippa pondered for nine or ten seconds, her braincells racing and colliding like a Saturday night *tangenziale*. 'Sweeney Todd.'

'Who? Oh, the demon barber. I told you, Italians don't like meat pies.'

'Do you have to be so literal? Update it a little. How about organ transplants?'

'Kidneys and things? It's possible, I suppose, though with the stock from desperate living donors I'm not sure it would be worth the risk. And would the higher-level stuff - hearts and so on - be technically feasible? I think they have to be pretty fresh.' He suddenly wished that he had gone further from the Seppi's premises before buying that roadside burger. It wasn't as though his MacDonald's boycott was really going to collapse the global military-industrial complex.

'What about medical research, then? According to the British press, Italy's full of power-crazed rogue scientists bent on impregnating every woman over eighty and cloning anything that moves. Would a supply of warm corpses be any good to them?'

That burger had definitely been dodgy. He would phone the public health people tomorrow, if he survived that long.

'I've no idea. The real problem with any of these theories is the uncertainty of the method. Ali says it wouldn't easy to be sure of killing someone with methohexitone, not without using an enormous dose. Certainly the amount given to Zena Carson didn't kill her, even with the little bit of added morphine.'

'That could have been the mistake, though, giving too low a dose. We know that Zena's case went wrong somewhere, maybe that was the beginning of it. She was so very small and thin, perhaps their normal calculations didn't work properly.'

'True. We shouldn't use the exception to work out the rule. But the problem remains; why use methohexitone at all? The murderer obviously had access to morphine as well, why not simply use that? It's easy to kill someone with a good slug of morphine.'

Sister Drago, who was hovering about doing technical things with bedpans, caught the last few words and glanced across sharply.

'See what I mean?' said Pietro without lowering his voice. 'They're all at it, despatching the old dears to Saint Peter to clear the wards for Easter. Don't worry, she doesn't understand English.

That generation all did French at school. Much more refined.'

'No!' cried Pippa, so vehemently that the nurse dropped her bedpans with a clatter and clacked across the tiles towards them.

The nice young man had showed her his warrant card and pleaded to be allowed to interview this vital witness for an urgent, high-level investigation. But high-level or not, she wouldn't have her patients harassed, not even rapidly recovering ones like this, who would no doubt insist on being packed off home in the morning. There was something of the *brutta figura* in quite such rude health; no Italian girl would let herself be cured with such haste. A good fortnight of convalescence, with proprietary pills, flower-strewn foothills of *cioccolatini,* and the constant attendance of female relatives... She recalled herself. After all, the policeman didn't appear to be doing anything too unspeakable; the girl was sitting straight up in bed, gesticulating with an almost native exuberance.

'They weren't supposed to die at all! That was the point of Dr. Fosecco. He had to give quick certificates, not because they died of something else but because they weren't actually dead. And that's what the text message to Etienne meant. Remember, it talked about a new life in France?'

'Whoa, slow down a little. You're giving the Sister vertigo. Let's take it step by step. Someone injects the - do we still call them victims?'

'No, horrible word.'

'Fair enough. Someone injects the - protagonists - with methohexitone. Or they could do it themselves, I suppose, being willing participants. The dose isn't enough to kill them, but effective enough for the untrained observer to think they might be dead. Right so far?'

'Right. Oh, but what about the morphine?'

'Morphine's no problem. Ali told me about that. You give it along with the methohexitone to reduce the pain of the injection. I think it might cut down on the involuntary movements as well. Nobody likes a twitching corpse.'

'Good. So the body looks nice and dead. What happens next? Oh yes, Dr. Fosecco turns up to do his certifying stuff. How does he explain that, though? It would be a bit of a giveaway if he simply hung about in the wings.'

'True. It must happen sometimes that a doctor finds his own

patient's dead body, but the statistical probability can't be that high. He couldn't get away with it too often.'

'There must be an accomplice then; some friend or colleague who might quite naturally be the first to discover the death. They could call Fosecco and meanwhile keep inquisitive eyes from examining the body too closely. They'd want some independent witnesses, but kept at a safe distance. The effects must start to wear off pretty soon, so the whole thing would have to be well-organized.'

'It's hard to imagine anything involving Fosecco being well-organized, but I suppose he only had to follow orders. It's the mastermind in the middle that we need. What happens next?'

'The corpse - pseudo-corpse - gets picked up *subito* - really *subito*, not Italian time-scales - by the Seppi brothers. Then they - oh, I don't know. I'm getting sleepy.'

'I ought to leave you in peace.'

'Don't.' She yawned, like Pierrotino after a night on the *cotto*. 'Just tell me how the story ends.'

'I'm not sure about how, but I can make a guess about where. The back streets around Pisa airport.'

'Sergeant Lenzuoli's mate?'

'Exactly. The men in the van where he found the paintings said they were waiting for a hearse.'

'With an empty coffin?'

'You're not that sleepy, are you? With an empty coffin. Or maybe not empty; that might be too much of a risk. The Seppi do real funerals as well; cut price cremations with no discernable mourners. They must have the odd spare body knocking around. Just pop that in the coffin, tuck a bit of contraband around it - it needn't always be art: could be drugs, jewels, guns.... add the grieving friend to accompany it and what customs officer, however hard-nosed, is going to pry too deeply? Even if they did, the friend doesn't know anything about it, someone has desecrated her beloved's caskets, blah blah blah.... No one's going to prove anything.'

'Are we?'

'Going to prove anything? That's the tricky one, isn't it? He's clever, this man in the middle. But it's all too complicated... In Italian we say *vuole fare il furbo*.'

'Too clever by half?'

'That's it.' In the absence of a bus ticket he scribbled the phrase across Pippa's temperature chart, to the bemused fury of Sister Drago. 'He's started to make mistakes. First Zena dying, then his attempt to...'

But her eyes were closed, already at the edge of a dream, a plump efficient spider in the centre of its web, unItalian in its precision, weaving and weaving with fingers that smelled of lavender. Freud wasn't born in Vienna.

Pietro tiptoed away under the Sister's glare. He hesitated by the bed for a moment, but investigating officers didn't kiss their witnesses. Not even on the tips of their noses.

XXIX

Julie was polishing the rosewood mirror when the phone began to ring. He had some beautiful things, Monsieur, ancient and delicate. Touching them, she felt more like a curator than a twice-weekly cleaning woman. He wasn't really French, of course, but he spoke the language well enough to make her ache with nostalgia for the plains of home and the tongue of her schooldays. She liked to take her time here and wait for him to come back from his morning trip to the baker and the newsagent, maybe share a cappuccino and a Gallic analysis of *La Repubblica*'s lead stories. But today she had to hurry, she was due to meet Etienne at half-past eleven for a meeting at the boys' nursery. The ring grew louder.

She set down the bottle - no cheap aerosols for Monsieur - and reached into her apron pocket. It couldn't be anything but bad news, Angela's school probably. The child had complained of another stomach ache that morning, and Etienne had wanted to keep her at home, but Julie had insisted that she go. Angela was already too nervous, shy, oversensitive, just like her father. These morning colics could easily become a habit, but the girl needed her education. She wouldn't have any other advantages.

The pocket was deep, and stuffed at the top with all her cleaning materials: the fine duster, the glass cloth, the damp one for sticky marks. If Julie had to do this kind of work, she could at least bring to it all her intelligence and precision, for the glory of God, as the nuns used to say. She sent up a quick prayer for Angela. Only then, with the relaxation of faith, came the memory, a cold current through her cheekbones and knuckles. 'Accidents are always happening.'

She scrabbled at the top cloths and had thrown down the first two before she realized that the ringing was coming from the other room. The phone must have fallen out of her pocket while she was bending down. The tune was unmistakeable - the *Marseillaise* - growing louder and more insistent with each repetition. She followed it into the eau-di-nil sitting room, to the walnut desk, the small middle drawer open by three or four centimetres. Even as she eased it out, imagining the screams, appendicitis or worse, there was a part of her mind still calculating how it could have got there, how the handle must have caught on a button as she reached across to wipe the window. There was a patch that was always clouded, as though a child breathed on it to make patterns on the glass. The phone must have slipped into the drawer as she stepped back to check for smears. Monsieur would never have left it open but neither would she ever pry.

"Allo?' she said, forgetting to use Italian.

'*Maes-* 'came a voice, a male voice, and then the line went dead.

'*Pronto, pronto?*' she repeated into the silence, then took the phone away from her ear to ring the caller back. '*Maes…*' what had he been trying to say? *Maestra*? What was the matter with Angela's teacher that she couldn't call herself?

It was then that Julie realized something else. This wasn't her phone. She stared at it, unseeing, engulfed by relief. It was similar, very similar, the same make, size and colour, but this was a much more expensive model. It must be Monsieur's own, hence the Francophile ring tone. Not really such a coincidence once you came to think of it. She glanced at it again, before replacing it in the drawer, wondering what so many buttons could possibly be used for. Like hers, it had its own number across the top of the display: sensible, it was difficult to remember all those digits. Sometimes there was a date you could pick out, or a little piece of childish arithmetic. Here, for example, was 1848, the year of the revolutions, and then six take away four was two and…

The chain broke, her heart thumping harder than ever. It couldn't be the same number, not exactly the same. Two of the digits must have been transposed in her memory. It was an excellent memory, all the nuns had said so, but it couldn't be infallible.

She put the phone down on the desk and picked up the slim cardboard wallet that had lain underneath it. Monsieur's plane tickets for tonight. She opened it, only half-conscious of what she was doing, searching for the official words that would confirm his genial solidity: his name, his flight, his onward connection, his appointment at - *Rio de Janeiro*.

For a moment she didn't even recognize it as a place, assumed it was the name of the airline clerk who had taken the booking. An

American company; they would employ hundreds of Hispanics. Then the door opened and she understood.

The message must have arrived in the night. Breakfast at the hotel was hardly formal, but there was a sign in four languages, asking guests to turn off their mobile phones, and Pseudo-Helmut, who usually did as he was told, complied. Or almost complied, that morning. His finger was on the 'off' button when he noticed the tiny envelope icon in the corner of the display. Some advertising message from the phone company, he supposed, but he would get it out of the way before his brioche. Today was not a day for any kind of procrastination.

ok meet 12 noon piccola casa. gg

It had never occurred to him that Gray might send a text. In retrospect, though, how like him it was; careful, cautious, testing the waters. The arrangement to meet might have been reckless, if it hadn't been made on neutral ground with plenty of potential chaperones, the English girl herself, Elsa and Elisa ... Elsa and Elisa. He would have to be careful there, the last thing he wanted was to waltz in and give them both heart attacks.

Four cappuccinos, seven croissants and a bowl of muesli later, he had formulated his plan. The flat above the Piccola Casa was empty; at least, it had been twelve months ago, and above it was a forgotten roof garden, withered and ghostly. Gray would remember it; they had spent a tender evening there towards the end. He would wait in the garden, on the wooden bench with a view of the stairs, and try to catch Gray alone.

Déjà vu never happens when it ought to. The scene at the Piccola Casa, when Pippa, having discharged herself from Sister Drago's appalled attentions, arrived on Thursday morning, was exactly the same as when she had returned from Pisa airport two days before, right down to Nicola's kicking his rubber heels on the foyer floor. But it felt like a different planet.

'Oh good.' said Elsa, coming out of the office. 'No *rabbia* then?'

'*Rabbia*? You don't mean rabies, do you?'

'Isn't that what you get from being attacked by a cat? I've told Lisa before about that Pierrotino of hers. He'll really have to be put down this time.'

'Pierrotino didn't attack me, Elsa. It was a m..' She mustn't jump to sexist conclusions. '.. a human. The cat defended me. He probably saved my life.'

'*Davvero?* I might have known Lisa would get the story all wrong. Lisa! *Non c'era il gatto.*'

'*Cosa?*' Elisa appeared at the door, apparently covered in icing sugar. 'Oh, *ciao cara. Come stai?*' In her hand she carried three or four thin cardboard folders that once might have been green.

'*Bene grazie.* But look, it wasn't Pierrotino who did it.'

'*Ma naturalemente*! Don't tell me. Helsa has the wrong stick again. No matter. Here is Nicola once more, waiting for a lesson. Such a keen student. Or it is the natural magnetism of the teacher. You're well enough, Flipper?'

'I think so. Just - '

Elsa interrupted. 'Lisa, you look like a snow-woman. Whatever have you been doing? *Brutta figura.*'

'Same to you with nops on. I have found the registers, *finalmente*. They were ready for Flipper when she first came, but you put the box of millefeuille on top of them.'

'Nonsense, I didn't even know we had any millefeuille. You're always hiding things in strange places, Lisa. Like an old squirrel. And fancy not giving Philippa the registers before now. You know it's a legal requirement to keep them up to date.'

'Legal collywobbles. It is only for the accounts, so we don't forget to send the bills. But please, if you can make them correct, Flipper.'

'Of course.' She took the thin sheaf of cardboard. 'There aren't many, are there? Otto, Nicola, Francesca...'

At the sound of his name, Nicola sat down and stood up again, his face flushing crimson then fading to a greenish white.

'Sorry, Pippa.' he blurted and muttered something in Italian before making a dash for the door. They listened to the slopping sounds of his trainers on the stairs.

'My natural magnetism must have been put in the wrong way round. What did he say?'

'That he had to go, he was sorry, he had just remembered an appointment to see a tree, a *leccio*. How do you say that in English, Helsa? *Leccio?*'

'Oh Lisa, you know I've no idea at all. I got kicked out of the Girl Guides for taking twenty-seven lipsticks to camp. I can't tell an oak tree from a gorsebush. You'll have to ask one of those hearty types.'

'I don't suppose it matters anyway.' said Pippa.

In a week of getting things wrong, that was quite possibly her biggest mistake so far.

'I am so disappointed.' said Monsieur, hovering in the doorway to maximum effect. 'If you need more money, you have only to ask.'

'I wouldn't steal from *you*.' The careful layers of subservience stripped harshly from her voice. She was the superior now and she knew it, flaunted her contempt like a hen bird in grotesque display. As long as he was here with her, he couldn't get to the children. She held out the phone, tempting him nearer.

'It was you who sent that message. How could you? When they've been here with me and you played with them. Angela wrote you a story and the little ones did pictures. You've still got them on your kitchen wall.'

'I know.' He took the phone from her hand, steered her down on to the chair. 'I know, Julie. And I'd never have hurt them. You must believe that. But the - the offer we made to Etienne, it had to be completely confidential. That was the only way I could be sure you would not go to the police.'

Something must have shifted in her face, for his hand on her shoulder tightened imperceptibly. 'You haven't been to the police, have you, Julie?'

'Of course not.'

'Good. You know, it is a pity Etienne did not accept our offer. You could all have been miles away by now.'

'Not as far as you'll be tomorrow, though. Rio di Janeiro? Someone catching up with you, are they?'

'I have to be careful.' His right hand pressed a little more firmly, as the left opened a second drawer behind her line of sight. 'Extremely careful.'

'You - ow!'

He was in front of her, left hand in his jacket pocket, right reaching out to steady her. 'Julie, what is it?'

'My arm - a wasp, I think. It's nothing, leave it.'

'Are you sure? The sting - I have tweezers.'

'No-o.' Her resolution was fading but still she fought. 'No.'

'Okay. Now - this phone number you were speaking of. What

is it again?'

'One. One. I can't ....one.'

Her head flopped forward on to his supporting arm. He nodded. The calculations were right again.

Pippa spread the registers out on the classroom table. There wasn't much to do, just fill in the date and time of the lesson and summarize what they had done. She completed Otto's, putting ditto marks under Zena's minimal entry, *Conversation*. Francesca, poor Francesca, had received no lessons since that last one with Zena. It wasn't any consolation to think that she was now surrounded by English speakers. That left Nicola. She ran her eye along the dates. He usually had two lessons a week, Tuesday and Thursday, presumably on the way home from school. She reached the last entry, prepared to write the next, and stopped. Again she looked back, then at the calendar, and then at Francesca's register. Idiot she'd been. Taking out her phone, she called the first saved number.

'Pietro?'

The classroom door swung open with a bang and Muriel marched in.

'I'm on the phone.' mouthed Pippa.

'Not blind. Never mind all that. Any news about Fran?'

'No, but I'm - Pietro? Look, I've found something out.'

'I should damn well hope someone has.' said Muriel.

'Listen. It's Nicola. Nic Columbini. He's Francesca's brother.'

'Hallelujah and bugger the bishop. Is that the extent of your sleuthing? Anyone in the province could have told you that.'

'Muriel, will you shut up?' Twenty years of frustration went into the cry, twenty years of carrying round the cakes at W.I. committee meetings and being told how she'd grown, and not to touch the French Fancies and shouldn't she try a panty-girdle? Twenty years and now she hadn't even time to relish the moment. 'They switched classes last Monday night. It was Nic who... What? No, he's not here at the moment. He went - Muriel?'

A well bred Englishwoman of Muriel's pedigree does not take umbrage easily, but when she takes it, it gets a good hearty run to the next market town and back.

'Muriel, I'm sorry. Look - what's a *leccio*?'

'Holm oak.' she answered, with the lightning reaction of a pub quiz veteran. 'There's a good specimen on the top of the Torre Gunigi.'

Torre? Oh God. 'Hear that, Pietro? We'll meet you at the bottom.'

Gray had been wandering the streets all morning, in search of a subtle internal rhyme and waiting until it was time to meet Helmut. Forty-seven minutes to go. J*eopardy* and *leopard, he*. Not exactly Auden, but it would do. Now, if he could find a nice inversion for the penultimate line... He turned the corner and nearly collided with Philippa and a leathery middle-aged woman. They appeared to have been running, most unsuitable for the *centro storico*. One ran around the walls, at dawn or dusk, suitably attired in co-ordinated sportswear, not through the piazzas in Laura Ashley and sandals. He was about to murmur some apology and sidle past when Philippa grabbed his arm. This must be serious; in Gray's experience the English never volunteered bodily contact unless impelled by ungovernable passion or medical emergency

'It's Nic, on the Torre Guinigi. Come on, quickly.'

'Oh dear.' The inverted epigram, perfectly formed and thematically faultless, appeared for a moment in Gray's brain, paused and passed on, leaving no shadow. 'I'm not very good at crises. And the thing is - '

'Are you Gray Garrett?' said the older woman abruptly.

'Yes ma'am.'

'I saw one of your poems in the local paper. About mistreated donkeys in the Algarve. Rather fine. And it rhymed properly, not like this T.S. Eliot nonsense.'

It had been a satire, Gray remembered, and not a very successful one, a parody of the sort of sentimental doggerel beloved of the philistine *hoi polloi*, its irony intended to highlight the unregarded plight of human tourist-fodder. And Tom Eliot was the nearest Gray had to a personal god; he would cheerfully lay down his life to save the Master's reputation. All the same, no aspiring poet could afford to look a fan, the first fan not also a blood relative, in her rather horsy mouth.

'Thank you.' he said with rehearsed modesty. 'What....?'

'The Torre Guinigi!' urged Pippa. 'Now!'

Julie's inert body was heavier than it looked, and Charles was seriously out of breath by the time he had moved it into the tiny guestroom. He could have done with a couple of the Seppi boys, but there was no time to summon them now. He arranged her in the classic recovery position, with only one or two minor variations to make the posture more natural. She ought to be safe like that, however long it took her to come round. He didn't want any more deaths.

In the bathroom cabinet he found what he was looking for, an almost empty bottle of a hundred aspirin. You couldn't buy it like that any more, thanks to the universal nanny state. He took the bottle through and laid it on its side next to her hand. The cap could go on the floor, as if cast aside in haste. The scenario was depressingly plausible. What could be more likely but that a woman in Julie's position, poor, black, in a strange country, should take impulsive advantage of the contents of her employer's medicine chest? Everyone knew that he never used the spare room, and with the door closed as usual, he couldn't be blamed for not discovering her earlier. Of course, when she recovered she might tell a different story, as hysterical women often did, especially those whose religion looked so critically on the noble traditions of self-slaughter. Even if anyone believed her, he would be well on his way by then, safely in Brazil long before they could think of drawing up an extradition warrant.

He closed the door gently and went into the bedroom to pack his suitcase. There wasn't much to take, a few lightweight clothes, the notes of his successes, to be published posthumously, the phone and the plane tickets. In the tiny hallway he paused. There had been a lot of noise on the stairs a few minutes ago, and he didn't want to meet anyone, especially not the old women. They would want to say goodbye, even for the three days they thought he would be gone, and he couldn't trust himself not to make an occasion of it. He was genuinely fond of them; in a different life he could have been as they imagined him. No, from the roof garden there was a fire escape down the back of the building. He would go that way and never say goodbye.

XXX

Apart from the walls themselves, the Torre Gunigi is the most potent symbol of Lucca's eccentric prestige. Dating from the fifteenth century, it is the tallest building in the city, red-brick, with fearsome battlements. But above the battlements, incongruously pastoral, grows an ancient holm oak, an object of veneration to the Lucchese and derision to their Pisan neighbours. After all, their own tower, if not precisely perpendicular, is at least not topped by what appears to them like nothing so much as a bunch of sprouting broccoli.

Pietro was waiting beside the ticket booth with Ali.

'I paid for us all.' he said, waving a fistful of tickets and starting on the first flight of steps. 'Easier than explaining. A lad went up five minutes ago, sounds like Nicola. There's no one else here. Come on.'

Pippa kicked her useless flip-flops off and followed him, barefoot, with the others behind her. On the first landing lay a piece of paper, folded in half, soft and fuzzy from repeated re-reading. It was a handwritten note in Italian.

'Very bad Italian.' said Pietro. 'It was either written by a foreigner, or our school system's worse than I thought.'

'Never mind the stylistic analysis, what does it say?'

He began on the next flight, reading as he went and stumbling a little over the less even steps. 'Tries to say. *It was you on Monday evening, wasn't it, not Francesca? Don't worry, I won't give you away, so long as you keep quiet. After all, it was you who actually killed her. She was only unconscious, you know, until you shut her in the cupboard. You suffocated her, deliberately. That's murder. I suppose you did it because you were angry. She'd sold your pathetic little committee to the Americans. All those doomed rainforests. Do you know what they do to terrorist murderers in prison? G.*'

'Poor Nic.' They increased their pace, especially Gray, who had been at the back with Muriel, but now ran up to join Pietro. 'Could I look at that?'

'I suppose so. There won't be much left by way of fingerprints. Here.'

'And here.' Gray reached into his neat money belt and brought out another note, on the same thick cream paper. This one was in English, or almost.

As in the telefonmessage, you will not speak. It is your fault she died, for you were too late. If you tell, you will be accessory to fraud and also, at the least, Manslaughter. You will be sent to Amerika where there remains the Deathpenalty. Think of it. G.

'What does he mean, 'too late'?'

'I was supposed to arrive just after Francesca, so that she'd have discovered the body – what she would have thought was a body – and I could call the doctor. Zena wasn't really supposed to die.'

'Yes, we'd worked that out.'

'Had you? Cool work. But I was fifteen minutes late - that jerk asking me about his email - and no one was there. All that was true, just the way I told you before. I did the photocopying as well so I'd have an excuse for being there. I didn't realise I'd left the original in the machine. Anyway, when I couldn't find anyone, I assumed that Zena had chickened out. She'd been pretty ambivalent about the whole thing from the beginning. And when I went to her apartment and found her passport gone, I thought she must just have scarpered, got the train east and the ferry to Greece like she was always saying she would.'

'The passport was in my flat,' said Pippa, 'with her driving licence and some money.'

'I guess that was her fallback position, then, her second string. She was supposed to leave everything behind, of course. She'd have got a new passport with the new identity. And the cash, of course.'

'How much?'

'I've no idea. She only told me the minimum, what I needed to know and which doctor to call.'

'Fosecco?'

'That's right. He wasn't the guy behind it all, though, she told me that much. Fosecco was just an old soak who's do anything for a regular booze supply. No, there was someone else, the Gamesmaster, they called him, some high-up medic. I guess that's what the G. stands for in the letters. Either that or Girotondo.'

'Girotondo?'

'Yeah, didn't I say? That's what they called the whole operation, Girotondo. It was like a game, Zena said, except you didn't know who else was playing. The music stopped and it was someone's turn to go in the middle. This Gamesmaster was pretty proud of the idea, according to Zee. Said it was a present for his own kid. I don't know what he meant by that. Anyway, he was majorly pissed off when the Nanni Moretti crowd used the name for their political protests.'

'I can imagine. But the - the game. Zena had to anaesthetise herself, did she?'

'That's right, yeah. It was all worked out: the exact dose, time, everything. She wasn't allowed to eat for hours before and she had to write a G on her wrist so the funeral directors would know who she was and keep an eye on her in the hearse. I guess she wrote the full word just to be sure. Zena never trusted Italians. After that the Gamesmaster himself would be waiting at the funeral parlour to check she was okay as she came round. Then she'd get the false papers and she could go wherever she wanted, so long as she never came back to Italy. Whoever this guy is, he has a sharp brain. Warped, but sharp.'

They were on the last flight of steps now, and could see the holm oak's branches above them, crazily clear against the bright blue sky. Nicola was sitting on the ledge, writing furiously in a school exercise book. The others froze in the opening. Now they were here, no one knew what to do. I should have gone on that counselling course, thought Pietro, or at least called in a trained negotiator. If he jumps, or even falls backwards, it'll be my fault. All I've done is brought a pathologist to look over the edge and certify the body.

Nicola looked up calmly. 'I killed her.' he said. 'I've got a letter here somewhere here telling me so.' He began searching in the backback beside him.

'You dropped it on the way up.'

'Did I? You know all about it, then. I'm writing my confession now, before I jump. It'll make the thing easier, I think. I'm sorry I wasn't brave enough to do it before. They will let Franca go, when they read it, won't they? And Luca? It wasn't anything to do with them. Luca said it didn't matter about her being a traitor, but I knew better. I wasn't just us she was betraying, it was the whole planet. The fucking trees.'

He wiped his eyes with the back of his hand. 'That's what I was going to say to her that night, when Franca forgot to cancel the lesson and I said I'd go instead. I wasn't going to hurt her, just explain. Lots of people don't understand, you see, what's going to happen to the world. I was going to tell her that we're all, like, really sorry about the Twin Towers thing, but that doesn't mean it's America against the world. I was going to say - I don't know. I never got the chance. I thought someone else had got there before me, and not just to talk to her, either. There she was, dead. I mean, I thought she was dead, with 'Girotondo' written on her arm. That was kinda weird. I mean, the Girotondo lot are usually peaceful, middle-aged liberals, boring really, but I guess anyone can get pushed too far. So I thought I'd just add our message on the other side. She wasn't cold or anything, so it wasn't too creepy.'

He was silent for a moment. 'I suppose I should have known she wasn't really dead. Funny I didn't feel her pulse, writing on her wrist, like that. Or maybe I did, and just thought it was mine. Then I got in a panic, thinking about fingerprints and handwariting analysis and all that. They'd be bound to think I was the one who murdered her. I wondered about rubbing the writing off, but I thought that might make it worse.

'I don't really know why I put her in the cupboard. I just thought; no one ever looks in there, and maybe by the time anyone does, she'll just be a skeleton. Skeleton in the cupboard, yeah? Then it'd just be a kind of creepy joke. I don't really know what I was thinking, except that my head was all messed up. Doesn't really matter now, I suppose. I killed her, that's all that counts.'

'No you didn't.' said Ali gently. 'You didn't feel a pulse because she didn't have one. Zena died of suffocation, but not the kind you get from being shut in a cupboard.'

'Anyway, I've seen the cupboard.' put in Pietro. 'It's got three airbricks and gaps round the door wide enough to drive an Ape through. No one could suffocate in there.'

Ali continued. 'Zena was allergic to kiwi fruit, Nicola. It's an interesting allergy. It's often connected to one or two others: bananas, avocados - and latex.'

'Latex? What - like rubber?'

'A type of rubber, yes. The type that was used in the syringe she injected herself with. But the anaesthetic never got the chance to work. She died immediately, from a massive anaphylatic shock.

Her throat must have swelled up straightaway, her blood pressure plummeted, and she wouldn't have been able to breathe. Suffocation, yes, but not the kind you imagined. If anyone had been with her at the time, anyone medically qualified and properly equipped, they could have given her adrenalin, got her oxygen, probably saved her life. But this Gamesmaster, whoever he is, however skilled at anaesthetic calculations, didn't bother to take those elementary precautions. No decent doctor uses latex syringes these days, and no decent doctor would ever dream of leaving an anaesthetised patient alone. Apart from everything else, it's just sheer bloody-minded arrogance. I bet he didn't even ask her about allergies, or didn't bother to listen to the reply.'

There was a pause, during which Muriel translated as much as she could of Ali's speech for Pippa and Gray. Nicola, meanwhile, had been helped down from the ledge by Pietro and was wandering, dazed, around the holm oak repeating, 'I didn't kill her' and patting the trunk as if to reassure himself that he was still in the world.

'...listen to the reply.' finished Muriel, and an echo rang in the dusty recesses of Pippa's brain.

'Like the man in Switzerland,' she said aloud, 'who didn't believe his wife was pregnant.' Then she remembered when she'd read about him, and who had come in, and why she'd thought that Freud was born in Vienna.

From the Torre dell'Ore, a few yards away as the pigeon flies, the great bell rang twelve o'clock. Pseudo-Helmut heard it from the roof garden, could hardly fail to hear it. The difficulty was how not to be deafened by it. He was disappointed, but not really surprised. Gray wasn't the type to keep his rasher assignations. He peered down the stairwell in case and almost missed the tiny bleep from his pocket. Another miniature envelope.

sorry held up torre guinigi

'Held up'? Pseudo-Helmut's English was excellent, but he had trouble with the more ambiguous modal verbs. A 'hold up' was a hijacking, wasn't it, or a robbery? From the other end of the garden, by the fire escape, he would be able to see the top of the Torre Guinigi. He moved there quickly, typing his reply as he walked.

r u ok? take care - j.

It was only when he had pressed the final 'send' button that he realised what he had said.

'I - do - not - understand.' said Elisa in English and then in Italian, speaking slowly and clearly for the poor benighted African. 'Why do you think your wife is here?'

'Not *here*.' repeated Etienne for the fourth time, keeping his temper with difficulty. 'At the doctor's flat upstairs. I have knocked but there is no reply. Please. I think something must be wrong. She would not miss this appointment without sending a message. Also, I have telephoned her with no reply. I thought, perhaps, you have a key?'

'He means Otto!' cried Elsa with sudden enlightenment. 'When you said 'doctor' poor Lisa didn't understand. It's Otto he wants, Lisa. His wife must be Otto's little cleaning lady.'

'*La donna delle pulizie*! *Che bella*! Such a nice lady, nearly not African at all. And you think perhaps she is fallen, a fallen woman?'

Otto bit his lower lip before he dared speak. 'I think there may have been an accident, yes. If we could hurry.... You have a key?'

'Otto's key, Otto's key... Lisa, where in heaven's name have you put it?'

'I don't know, *cara*. Under his *zerbino*?'

'Doormat? Lisa, you are so irresponsible! We'd better have a look.' She craned her plump neck up towards the stairwell. 'Oh! Oh! There he is, Otto himself. Otto! Ottino! No, he hasn't heard me, but he's gone up to the roof, so we can follow him there. Maybe he knows where the little black lady's gone.'

'*Ven-ga*.' said Elisa. 'Come - with - us.'

'J?' said Gray aloud. No one was listening to him. Pippa was recounting as much of Charles D's story as she could remember, while Pietro and Muriel disagreed about the subtleties of translation for Ali's benefit. Pippa hadn't mentioned her suspicion about Charles' identity yet. She was still vaguely hoping that by the time she got to the end of the story it would sound too ridiculous to be spoken aloud.

'I suppose his surname might begin with a J.' said Gray to himself, wandering over to the other side of the tower to compose his reply. 'Unless.....' The thought came to him, complete, flawless, and too perfect to be possible.

girotondo?

He sent it before he could change his mind. If Helmut was really only Helmut, he would merely think that Gray was mad, and stop bothering him. He could see the Piccola Casa building from here, the little roof garden with a figure at its edge. The figure was bent over something held in his hands; he straightened up, waved...

ja

Gray raised his hand to wave back. It froze in mid-air. There was another figure on the roof, walking towards the fire escape carrying two bags, a suitcase and a briefcase, the rectangular, reinforced kind. He put down the larger case, took the other in both hands and slowed his pace to a furtive tiptoe.

Johann was singing now, at the top of his brawny voice, something German and joyful, about beer and oompah bands and mountain goats and compliant *Mädchen*. The sound was unmistakable, even from here. Gray tried shouting, but the wind was gusting in the wrong direction and his words drifted uselessly back to him. He waved with both arms but Johann just waved back, determined to outdo him in exuberance.

Gray took the phone again, tried to write another message, but his fingers were slippery on the keys. There were three more figures now, a tall one, dark against the sky, flanked by two short, plump... Suddenly Gray knew them, all of them except the dark figure in the middle who was running forward to tap Otto on the shoulder. He, the dark man, hesitated, almost in time to miss the spinning blow and fell backwards onto the paved floor, skidding into the terracotta urns and planters. He picked himself up, streaming blood and rushed forward again, but not before Elsa and Elisa had taken an arm each, those reassuring arms that had comforted them so often, had kicked the briefcase skittering across the tiles and said in triumphant unison, loudly enough to break into Johann's song,

'*Arresto cittadino.*'

'I'm surprised you didn't guess.' said Pietro. 'That English forensic brain we read so much about. And then it takes an American poet to point out the culprit.'

'He did have a slight advantage,' she protested, 'watching the next murder about to happen. Or do I mean the first murder? Zena's was only manslaughter, I suppose.'

'I don't think we'll be short of charges, anyway. Agostino had a look inside that briefcase as they took him away. It'll just be a question of who gets him first, us, the Yanks or the Swiss. Not to mention the Germans, Senegalese, English....'

His phone rang and he listened in silence for maybe a minute or two. *Bene. A più tardi.* Julie's fine. She won't be properly with it for a few hours but she's well on her way back.'

'And Etienne?'

'Nothing but the bloody nose and a graze or two. Elsa and Elisa are squabbling over which of them suspected Otto from the beginning and which of them knew all along that Johann wasn't really dead. Oh, and Gray and Johann are gazing into each other's eyes, horrifying the entire Questura waiting room. Homophobia's still an entry requirement for most of the polizia.'

'They won't be charged, will they?'

'I doubt it, not if they keep on being this co-operative. Johann might have a struggle getting his old identity back, though; he could have to resign himself to being a perpetual Helmut. He looked at her quizzically. 'But you had guessed about Otto, hadn't you?'

'Only right at the end when I remembered about Vienna.'

'Vienna?'

'Long story.'

'You're right. We've had enough long stories now.'

The Torre dell'Ore tolled one o'clock as, on its tree-topped neighbour, a young man in a misbuttoned shirt put his fingertip under the chin of a barefoot girl. He tilted her face towards his as his *telefonino* rang.

'Maybe next time.'